PRAISE FOR DANA HAYNES

Ice Cold Kill

"[A] strong, complicated plot as believable as any real-life terrorist threat. Daria is destined to become a favorite in the growing arsenal of female thriller leads. She combines brains and experience to craft unbeatable strategy, and she has the requisite combat skills to quash any agent in her path as well as a witty, moderately well-adjusted (under the circumstances) perspective that's sure to charm."

—*Booklist* (starred review)

"Enough intelligence agencies, bad guys, and gruesome viruses for a month of nonstop massacres. When Haynes runs out of guns and knives to put in the hands of superheroine Daria, he turns oxygen tanks into missiles for her to launch." —*Kirkus Reviews*

"*Ice Cold Kill* is exciting, inventive, and chillingly plausible. I thoroughly enjoyed it—this book is a blast!" —Meg Gardiner, author of *Ransom River*

"A superb thriller. Dana Haynes has crafted a brilliant tale, brimming with well-drawn characters, clever action set pieces, and shocking twists. You won't want to put this story down until you've turned the last page."

—Boyd Morrison, international bestselling author of *The Midas Code* and *The Roswell Conspiracy*

MORE . . .

"Dana Haynes's *Ice Cold Kill* is a twisting, complex thriller featuring a former Israeli intelligence officer who learned her trade from the worst and does it the best. A terrific, compelling book!" —Jamie Freveletti, *New York Times* bestselling author of *Dead Asleep* and *Robert Ludlum's The Janus Reprisal*

Breaking Point

"The large cast of compelling characters, nonstop action, and realistic feel of the investigation make this novel a standout . . . A thrill ride." —Associated Press

"A top-notch, tension-packed techno-thriller."
—*Booklist* (starred review)

"Spine-tingling . . . a page-turner." —*BookPage*

"A well-written . . . white-knuckle thriller."
—*Library Journal*

"Jaw-dropping . . . There is mystery, action, suspense, death, and romance from beginning to end."
—Bookreporter.com

"[A]drenaline-filled . . . edge-of-your-seat thrills."
—*Shelf-Awareness*

Crashers

"Outstanding! *Crashers* combines the ferocious action you usually see on a movie screen with a fascinating look at the way a major airline crash is investigated."

—Phillip Margolin, *New York Times* bestselling author of *Supreme Justice*

"You absolutely must read *Crashers*. I literally couldn't put this book down. Dana Haynes is a gifted writer who grabs you on page one and doesn't let you go until the final page."

—Nelson DeMille, *New York Times* bestselling author of *The Lion*

"Strong characters, gruesome crash details, and the ticking countdown to another attack make this novel an explosive mix of *24* and *CSI*."   —*USA Today*

"Dana Haynes delivers big-time with *Crashers*, a spectacular, timely, un-put-downable, near-perfect thriller whose every page sizzles with action, intrigue, information, and intelligence. If you're a thriller fan, or even just a lover of fine writing and terrific story-telling, do yourself a big favor and buy this book."

—John Lescroart, *New York Times* bestselling author of *Damage*

"This is a thriller that lands a rare and satisfying hat trick: The action sequences hit hard, the characters are idiosyncratic while still feeling like real people, and the 'snappy' dialogue actually snaps." —*Kirkus Reviews*

"Filled with excitement and knowledge of NTSB procedures and problems. Highly recommended."
—*Library Journal* (starred review)

"Haynes's compelling first thriller takes familiar elements—a mysterious airplane crash, a bent FBI agent, a deadly female spy—and mixes them with the world of National Transportation Safety Board aviation disaster investigations . . . The forensic details fascinate. Haynes nicely integrates several subplots involving terrorism. The slam-bang crash landing of a conclusion will leave readers anxiously awaiting the promised sequel." —*Publishers Weekly*

"Lively and fast-moving . . . generates plenty of tension. A solid debut." —*Booklist*

"A supersonic jet of a thriller, loaded with compelling detail and page-turning suspense and action!"
—Jeff Abbott, *New York Times* bestselling author of *Trust Me*

"Imagine an entire season of *24* crammed into a single book. That's what you get with *Crashers*, a fast-paced, twisty thriller that's just begging to be made into a movie." —April Henry, *New York Times* bestselling co-author of *Face of Betrayal* and *Hand of Fate*

Also by Dana Haynes

Crashers
Breaking Point

ICE
COLD
KILL

DANA HAYNES

St. Martin's Paperbacks

This is a work of fiction. All of the characters, organizations, and events portrayed in this novel are either products of the author's imagination or are used fictitiously.

ICE COLD KILL

Copyright © 2013 by Dana Haynes.
Excerpt from *Gunmetal Heart* copyright © 2014 by Dana Haynes.

All rights reserved.

For information address St. Martin's Press, 175 Fifth Avenue, New York, NY 10010.

Library of Congress Catalog Card Number: 2012040101

ISBN: 978-1-250-03693-3

Printed in the United States of America

St. Martin's Press hardcover edition / March 2013
St. Martin's Paperbacks edition / December 2013

St. Martin's Paperbacks are published by St. Martin's Press, 175 Fifth Avenue, New York, NY 10010.

10 9 8 7 6 5 4 3 2 1

To Katy King.
I love you.

Acknowledgments

I am forever thankful for the tremendous help of the following Oregon Health Authority officials: Dr. Grant Higginson, M.D., MPH, former state health officer and deputy administrator, Public Health Division; Dr. Michael Skeels, Ph.D., MPH, director of the Oregon State Public Health laboratory; and Dr. Katrina Hedberg, M.D., MPH, state epidemiologist and chief science officer, Public Health Division.

Also, my gratitude goes to everybody at St. Martin's Press for their faith in this project. To my editor, Keith Kahla, for his unparalleled understanding of how to make a story better. And for my agent, Janet Reid of FinePrint Lit, for blazing the trail.

Prologue

Ray Calabrese looked up from his BlackBerry to see Daria Gibron stride into the Rodeo Drive wine bar in Lycra exercise togs and sneakers, her hair slicked back, sans makeup.

It wasn't the part of Los Angeles where that many people tried to carry off the I'm-just-back-from-kickboxing look. She used her fingertips to brush still-damp black hair behind her ears. Her togs were two-piece, skintight, abdomen-baring, and black with red piping. She either had been working out or had joined the Justice League of America; Ray couldn't tell at a glance.

She poured herself into the opposite chair. "Hallo, Ray."

Ray smiled across the table at her. "I thought we were meeting after your appointment with that Portuguese importer."

Daria took a sip of Ray's wine and held it on her tongue before swallowing. "Not bad."

"Montepulciano. The business guy was a no-show?"

"He had to cut and run."

Ray had been digging into the investor's background from his headquarters, the L.A. Field Office of the Federal Bureau of Investigation. "I'm a little glad. If I were you, I wouldn't reschedule that meeting. That guy? I think he's trouble."

Daria Gibron said, "Me, too."

Four hours earlier . . .

The commission came out of the blue. A fledgling Portuguese import firm needed a translator who spoke Arabic and German. It was a relatively uncommon combination of languages for Los Angeles.

The Portuguese importer, João Patricio, had left a message on Daria's smartphone in musical English. He offered three times her daily commission for two hours of work, provided she could come today. She thought about the other offers currently on the table. Two banks had her on standby for talks involving euro-zone debt (boring). One Hollywood production house needed her help to lure the latest young hunk from the French cinema (she'd seen his movies; they were both *terribly important* and terrible). There was some petroleum deal that sounded far worse than dull but the negotiations would take place on a yacht off an exclusive resort in Costa Rica (that one at least showed merit).

The Portuguese deal, though, was one afternoon. And while the work itself might be awful, the new winter lineup of Christian Louboutin's had arrived, and the importer's timing couldn't be faulted.

From her condo in West Hollywood, Daria booted

up her computer and checked out Senhor Patricio's bona fides. He owned Iberian Exportações of Lisbon. She checked its history, its holdings, and found very little of interest. She called her FBI handler, Ray Calabrese. He agreed to check out the firm and to meet her at a favorite Tuscan wine bar later that evening.

She went online and checked in with one of her contacts at the Drug Enforcement Administration. The woman was famous for her uncanny ability to track down European sources on both sides of the law. Daria e-flirted with her a bit, then logged off and contacted some of her favorite European thieves, a man called Diego, with whom she had conducted business over the years. She flirted with them a bit, too.

Nobody had any hard information for her. Which, in and of itself, was okay. As far as it goes.

The Portuguese commission was a stroke of good fortune. Daria was wary of good fortune. Always.

Senhor Patricio was working out of a second-story office in a run-down, three-story building near LAX. It would be optimistic to say the neighborhood had seen better days; it probably hadn't.

Daria's used beige Honda Civic, which she had bought for cash, fit in nicely in the near-empty parking lot. When it came to cars, Daria usually opted for bland over speed. And she had never owned a car that kept its Vehicle Identification Number for longer than an hour.

Daria herself stood out quite a bit more than her car. She was a compact, athletic woman, five-six, with a heart-shaped face. She was dressed a bit risqué for a

late-afternoon business meeting: black skirt just a tad
too short, stilettos a tad too tall, crimson blouse showing a hint of her midnight blue bra, over which she wore
a light, fitted jacket. It might be November, but it was
still seventy in Los Angeles.

She checked her phone and found a text from her
friend at the DEA. It read, simply: *POI JUAREZ.*

She tried calling back and got voice mail.

She tossed the strap of her leather handbag over her
shoulder and took the stairs up to the second floor. João
Patricio was waiting for her in the hallway. He was a
small, spare man with slicked-back gray hair and a
tightly trimmed goatee. She subconsciously clocked his
suit as off-the-rack, something of the genus buy-one-
get-one-free. He shook Daria's right hand, his left hand
cradling her right elbow.

"You found us all right, Miss Gibron? I didn't know
from where you were coming. Everything in California
is farther away than I imagine."

The building was one of Los Angeles's small-business
incubators, renting office space for small- to medium-
sized start-ups, rates by the month or year. They stood
in the corridor, the maroon carpet freshly cleaned and
smelling of ammonia. One door had been propped open
a few inches to the right of the stairwell, she noted, but
another hung almost fully open to the left of the stairs.
A temporary, peel-off sign on the door read *IBERIAN
EXPORTACOES.* Apparently, the maintenance company's
printer hadn't been able to navigate the ç or the õ.

Patricio stood close to her, still holding her hand and

elbow. His eyes darted quickly around the hall, as if worried about business competitors. Or a wife.

"Your English is quite good," Daria noted. "So my lack of Portuguese won't be a problem?"

"No. My lack of Arabic and French is the problem." He shrugged disparagingly and gently nudged her in the direction of the fully open door. "May I discuss the details with you?"

Daria smiled and pivoted gracefully on her tall heels.

As she turned, Daria caught a fleeting glimpse of motion from the second, slightly ajar door on the far side of the stairwell. She also noted three important details.

First, the rented office had been retrofitted with a Leveque Works magnetic card reader that articulated three thick steel bolts built into the door frame. The fresh wood shavings on the carpet meant the card reader was newly installed. It was not your standard security setup for a rental building near the airport.

Second, she discerned the telltale tightness, horizontally, beneath João Patricio's cotton shirt and striped tie. He wore a bulletproof vest.

Third, she noted that Iberian Exportações occupied a one-room office, not a suite. The door was wedged between the west-facing window and the stairwell.

Combine those three facts with the text from the DEA that labeled Patricio as a POI—Person of Interest—in the Juarez drug cartel, and the elements started to coalesce. Daria had had a run-in with the Baja cartel three months earlier, which had resulted in the most unfortunate death of a pillar of the drug-running community.

Still, *Person of Interest* isn't a conclusive statement, Daria thought to herself. She had been a person of interest in several crimes on three continents. Some of which hadn't been her fault at all.

What finally made Daria casually reach for the blade in her purse was Patricio's self-deprecating joke about his poor Arabic and French.

The contract was for a translator fluent in Arabic and German.

Patricio wasn't a businessman. He was an actor who had muffed his lines.

As soon as the Portuguese asshole led the curvy, black-haired Jewess into the office, Guerrón and Banguera emerged from the slightly open door to the right of the stairs. The *narcotraficantes* sprinted silently into position.

Guerrón, the whip-thin Ecuadorian, wore his trademark, checked keffiyeh headscarf, which hung to the middle of his back. The only thing the Americans feared more than the narco cartels was al Qaida, and Guerrón had taken to wearing the Yasser Arafat–style headdress just to head-fuck the DEA.

He checked the stairwell while Banguera, a steroid-enhanced Sinaloan in a wifebeater, checked the second-story window overlooking the parking lot. Both carried waterproof canvas satchels.

There was a one-in-four chance that this was the *puta* who tracked down and killed Carlos "the War Dog"

Ramos in a bordello in Amsterdam. Gibron was one of four female contractors known to be working with Western, antinarcotics agencies at the time. The other three were being interrogated by teams in Miami, London, and Stockholm.

The soldiers checked the stairs and the parking lot. There was no sign of anyone else. The woman was alone.

They could do with her as they pleased.

Daria's small knife was old and well used. It had been a gift from the only person in the world she truly called family. It had been given to her before she was a translator. Before she was an FBI asset and an expatriated immigrant marooned in America. Even before her time in Israeli intelligence.

He'd given it to her on the very day she had been adopted into the battle for the Middle East. Daria was probably nine years old at the time.

The sheath was leather, caramel brown and shaped like the playing card, a spade, but with the upper portion rounded. The leather had grown shiny and supple from years of being touched in alleys and bars and battlefields, in boardrooms and bedrooms. The sheath was approximately the size of Daria's palm—and Daria's hands were not large.

The blade, once steel, had been replaced many times and now was a hardened plastic with a serrated edge. It was tough enough to slice through cowhide, if used properly.

Daria could use it properly.

* * *

Think of it as a waltz.

Daria, her right hand and elbow held by the small Portuguese businessman. Her left hand sliding into the unseen pocket slit in the bottom of her shoulder bag (like all of her bags).

João Patricio steps to his left, smiling nervously behind his silvery goatee.

Daria steps to her right and, her weight on one foot, deftly kicks the door closed with the other.

Patricio blinks in surprise when the door shuts and he hears the *ca-clack* of the steel bolts deploying into the door. That wasn't part of the plan.

In the corridor, Guerrón and Banguera moved to the door of the rental office. As they stepped toward the door, it swung shut.

Ca-clack.

The new magnetic card reader and attached steel bolt security system had been installed to ensure privacy when they interrogated the *Judía* bitch. But the door had shut and the lock deployed too early.

The men exchanged perplexed glances.

Daria and Patricio were still moving, face-to-face, and turning. Patricio looked a bit surprised. Daria smiled languidly.

She gripped his right hand fiercely and stepped farther to his right, twisting his arm as she moved. Before he was aware of it, she slid behind him, pulled up his arm, and twisted painfully. His shoulder popped out of its socket and lights flashed before his eyes.

Daria raised her left forearm and drove it into the base of his skull, slamming his forehead into the door.

His vision blurred and his knees buckled. Daria held him aloft against the door and raised his dislocated right arm higher.

Her thumb flicked the plastic blade from its sheath. She slid the serrated edge the length of Patricio's right arm, from the heel of his hand as far up the inside of his arm as his suit coat allowed.

The skin split easily. Warm blood roiled from the long, surgically clean wound.

Daria held the gushing right wrist over Patricio's left shoulder, and directly over the card reader.

A Leveque system can be short-circuited easily enough. Water worked fine, as would wine, but really, any liquid would suffice.

João Patricio moaned as his blood gushed into the magnetic card reader. Daria smelled smoke rising from the short-circuited locking mechanism.

Time to see what would happen next. The one-room office, between the stairwell and the outside wall, was too small for an ambush from within. That left her free to ignore any potential threats within the room.

Daria used her strength, weight, and training to pin the half-conscious importer between herself and the door.

Guerrón and Banguera waited a handful of seconds for the Portuguese businessman to unbolt the door

from the inside. Doing this favor for the cartel was eras-
ing a very large debt Patricio owed.

Nothing happened. The soldiers thought they heard
a *thump* from inside the room.

Banguera, his absurdly muscle-bound upper body
gleaming in sweat, reached into his shirt pocket and
pulled out a magnetic card. He swiped the card through
the lock and awaited the *ca-clank*.

Nothing.

The LED light on the card reader flickered red. There
was a strange hiss from the locking mechanism.

The Sinaloan soldier swiped the card again.

Another hiss. This time, they didn't even get the red
LED. Nothing.

Guerrón brushed his checkered keffiyeh behind
his back, set down his waterproof satchel, pulled out a
Heckler & Koch MP-5 machine pistol. He slapped home
a banana clip. He waved his friend out of the way, and
thumbed off the safety.

He stepped in front of the cheap wooden door and
kept the sound-suppressed MP-5 on single fire. He
tossed seven .9-mm. slugs into the door.

The bullets cut a perfect half circle in the door, surrounding the steel bars in the locking mechanism.

The gunmen heard a grunt through the perforated
door.

Wearing a Kevlar vest is good but Daria knew, from
painful experience, that standing behind the person
wearing one is better.

The door took the first impact. The front of the vest

took much of the rest. Patricio's body absorbed the hydrostatic shock. The back of his vest dampened the remainder of the impact.

Daria took very little.

She felt around his waist for a gun and found nothing. She found a puny, five-shot, chrome .22 with an ivory handle strapped to one ankle. It was, as her old gunnery sergeant would have said, a complete piece of drek. She imagined firing such a weapon at plastic ducks to win a stuffed animal. *But beggars and choosers*, she thought. She pulled the little gun and shot Patricio in the left knee.

Patricio cried out in agony. He dropped to his knees and Daria dropped with him, still pinning him against the door.

"How many?"

Patricio began chanting in Portuguese.

Daria cocked the little .22 and placed it against his left elbow. She whispered in his ear, as a lover might. "Senhor. . . . my fee . . . is going . . . up."

"Two! Two! Please, God, please."

"Two total?"

"Two in the hall! Two in the hall! There's a van in the alley, a fat man! Waiting! Please, by all that's holy!"

He had lost quite a bit of blood by now. But that didn't mean he couldn't be of use.

João Patricio's head lolled to one side, revealing two of the seven splintered holes evenly spaced in a half circle in the wooden door. Daria stuck the barrel of the pip-squeak .22 into one of the larger holes and fired once.

* * *

Guerrón smiled at the perfect half circle of bullet holes in the wood. He considered himself an artist with a gun. He stepped back, ready to kick it in, when they heard a second shot from within the room.

Guerrón took another step back. And another.

He looked down. Blood began seeping from his iliac artery, halfway between his left hip and his testicles.

Daria squinted through one of the other holes in the door. She saw a man's legs stumble backward, saw a bloodstain blossom on his jeans.

One down.

Still on her knees behind the convulsing, bleeding-out importer, Daria took a moment to scan the office. One generic desk, three generic chairs on rollers with cheap but durable cloth seats and backrests. A window that looked out on gnarled, dyspeptic trunks, which is what passed for trees in L.A.

She rummaged through the dying man's trouser pockets, leaning him up against the smashed door like the legion of cadavers at Fort Zinderneuf. She found a lighter—old, burnished, and brass—and a fat calfskin wallet. She opened it and found what she wanted: a thick wad of dollars and euros.

Perfect. Money can't buy happiness. But it can buy time.

Banguera drew his own matching machine pistol, leather strap over his sloped shoulder. His eyes bulged as his partner stumbled back and fell on his ass against the far wall of the corridor. The ruptured artery in his groin was dampening his jeans with a fast-growing red stain. Guerrón began to twitch as his body went into shock. His H & K fell to the carpet by his side.

Daria left Patricio on his knees propped up against the door. She kicked off her stilettos and hitched up her already-short skirt to a decidedly unladylike level. She leaped up onto the cheap desk and used the lighter to ignite João Patricio's stash of money. She held the burning end under the mandatory smoke detector that she had found in every room of every public building she had entered since defecting. *I do so love American paranoia,* she thought.

An earsplitting alarm sounded and the tiny, tin windmill beneath the ceiling-mounted spigot began to rotate, splashing water everywhere.

Daria dropped to the far side of the desk. Soaked to her skin, hair matted with water from the sprinkler, she stripped off her jacket—it was last season's anyway.

It was her own damn fault. She shouldn't have come to the meeting without a gun. Oh, well. Kill and learn.

She remembered a drill instructor from her Shin Bet days. *Whatever can't be used defensively, use offensively.* The IKEA desk wouldn't repel bullets but the cheaply made furniture was light enough to maneuver, and it rested on coasters so the office could be easily reconfigured for each new renter. She shoved the chairs out of the way and spun the desk anticlockwise so the short end faced the door.

She started shoving. Her bare feet struggled to find

purchase in the soaked carpet, but the light, cheap desk on its concave coasters picked up speed.

João Patricio—kneeling against the door, barely conscious, right arm hanging limp and spooling out blood—half-turned to see the narrow edge of the desk only a meter from his face and moving fast. He screamed.

The alarm blared in the hall. Banguera felt the wheels fall off their well-crafted plan. He knelt to hoist up his friend as the busted door exploded off its hinges. He scrambled away as the door toppled like a felled tree, trapping Guerrón's legs and drawing a howl of pain from the Ecuadorian. The Portuguese importer tumbled out into the hall, skull staved in, blood arcing in every direction. The fire alarm continued to shrill. *Madre de Dios,* Banguera thought, landing on his stomach, *lo que el Diablo?*

He shook his head to clear his thoughts. He felt his machine pistol dig into his side, the strap still around his shoulder.

He rolled over to free the gun but his eyes caught on a pair of bare feet standing on the felled door, which pressed down on Guerrón's badly bleeding leg. Banguera's eyes traveled upward from long, tapered legs, a short skirt, a soaked and translucent blouse, to a heart-shaped face.

Only then did he realize the figure was holding Guerrón's sound-suppressed machine pistol.

There were only a handful of offices in the incubator building and the fire alarm was sufficient to drive the few employees out into the parking lot on an otherwise dull Monday afternoon. No one noticed the bedraggled, barefoot woman, soaked to the skin, carrying stilettos and a limp, wet jacket, who padded out through the fire door and climbed into a nondescript car. She put the car in reverse, maneuvered it around the building, and into the back alley lined with Dumpsters.

Doctor Hector Avila was no doctor. They just called him that because he enjoyed using surgical tools during interrogations.

He preferred to let dumb foot soldiers like Guerrón and Banguera subdue the subject before he got involved. That's why he sat in the van, in the alley, smoking a hefty joint with the passenger-side window open, smoke billowing out. He wanted to be relaxed before beginning his bit. Breaking a person is not an amateur's business. It took a calm, steady hand.

Hector Avila was lost in his thoughts about how to begin: fear first, then pain? Pain, then fear? Different *patients* required different *remedies,* the doctor knew.

An unremarkable beige compact backed into the alley and had come to rest a foot from the front bumper of the van. Avila squinted through blue smoke, as the driver's door opened and someone climbed out.

Wonderful, he thought. A civilian. Just what he needed.

It was a girl, young, barefoot. Avila tried to wave away the smoke haze to get a better look at her. She circled around and padded up to his passenger-side window, a sodden jacket draped over her left forearm.

Avila leaned out to tell the *puta* to get the hell gone.
She probably was a junkie seeking a handout. Or maybe
one of his few remaining spliffs. Before he could growl
at the girl, she let the sodden jacket flutter to the concrete, revealing a Heckler & Koch with a silencer. She
pointed it at his face.

"Good afternoon, sir." Her Spanish was flawless with
the flair of a Catalan accent. "Do you represent the
Juarez cartel?"

Dr. Avila froze, eyes bulging.

"Sir?" The woman seemed ever so calm.

"I . . ." The fat man felt his asthma kick in.

"I thought so." The girl looked both ways down the
alley, then back at him. "Could you step out of the van,
please?"

"W-wait . . ." He heard his voice crack. "I just follow
orders. I do as—shit!"

The joint singed his finger and thumb. He dropped
it. It hit the knit shirt stretched over his obese belly. His
hands flapped, slapping it to the van floor.

The girl tapped his cheek with the sound-suppressing
barrel to regain his attention.

Avila whimpered.

In his storied career as a torturer, Avila had heard
many men whimper. He knew the sound and considered it a sure sign that a man was breaking. Now he
heard himself and blushed.

"Tsk. You mustn't feel embarrassed." The girl sounded
genuinely sensitive. And absolutely insane. "That's how
I reacted the first time I was shot. I was eleven years

old. The second time . . . well, I suppose I was still eleven." She shrugged. "It's a difficult age."

She opened the passenger door. She waited a beat.

Avila hefted his bulk out of the van.

She slid open the rear door of the van. In the back she spotted rope, handcuffs, a small culinary blowtorch, a car battery with two cables that ended in alligator clips, and his doctor's bag.

"Get in, please. Facedown."

The girl spoke as one does to a distraught child: soothingly. "I would like you to send a message to the Juarez cartel for me. Will you do that, sir?"

"Yes!" Avila's heart skipped. This might not end with a bullet to his brain. "Yes. Of course. Yes. Anything."

"Thank you, sir."

She slid the door closed.

Once it was closed, Daria looked to her left and right again. No witnesses. She opened the gas cap of the van. She took Guerrón's long, al-Qaida–style keffiyeh and stuffed the cotton scarf into the gas tank as far as it would fit. She waited a few seconds for it to absorb petrol, then used Patricio's lighter on the tail end.

She moved back to the passenger window. "Thank you, sir."

Lying on his belly, Doctor Avila gulped. "Miss? What . . . what is the message?"

Daria said, "You'll see."

She walked to her car, opened the trunk, and pulled

out her gym bag. She climbed into the compact and pulled away.

About twenty minutes later, in an elegant Rodeo Drive wine bar, a waiter brought Daria Gibron a goblet of Montepulciano and professionally ignored her spandex attire and just-showered hair.

She sipped. "That's lovely."

"Nice." To Ray Calabrese, all red wines tasted more or less alike. He played with his glass a moment, avoiding eye contact. "Look, I'm sorry to dump this on you but . . . I'm no longer your handler."

Daria let a few beats of silence pass. "No?"

He looked up and approximated a smile. "The bureau decided. You're a citizen. Your work for us, for the DEA, for ATF has . . . um . . . this seems crass, sorry. It's *bought* you citizenship. You'll ace the test. Then you'll be an American. One of us. Congratulations."

Daria sipped her wine. Ray seemed really proud. But also sad. In his own Ray Calabrese way, he seemed to be saying "hello" and "good-bye" at the same time.

Daria thought an appropriate response from a normal person might be something along the lines of, *This is marvelous news!* So she went with that.

"Okay! Well . . ." Ray lifted his glass.

Daria did, too. They toasted.

"All right then. Welcome to America, citizen. What's next for you?"

Daria thought about the bled-out importer in the rundown office building, the bullet-riddled bodies of the narco soldiers, and the burnt husk of the fat man in the van. And she thought about the message she had just sent the Juarez cartel. Would they heed the warning?

No way to tell.

She mulled the offers for translation work that were on the table. She considered the job awaiting her in Costa Rica. "A vacation, I think."

"Good for you," Ray said. "You deserve a break."

Daria thought long and hard about taking Ray to bed that night but, in the end, decided it was a bad idea. He was genuinely one of the good guys.

And she genuinely wasn't.

One

The prisoners lay in their cots. It was one cot per cell. The cells were slightly larger than a bad room at a youth hostel or a kibbutz. Each had its own heater, a little partition between the cell doors, and a toilet. Really, as cells go, these weren't bad.

Asher Sahar lay on his back, ankles crossed, hands steepled on his chest. He wore a ratty sweater and ratty jeans and slippers. He spoke with a soft, sibilant whisper. " 'I'll Be Seeing You.' "

In the next cell, a grizzly bear of a man lay in the same posture, ankles crossed, hands steepled. His feet hung off the end of his cot. His name was Eli Schullman. He replied, "Irving Kahal."

"No." The other man reached up to adjust his round, wireless glasses, forgetting that he had taken them off for the night. He'd worn glasses since the age of fifteen. "Irving Berlin. But, to your eternal credit, you were incredibly close. I mean, close in a wrong sort of way.

Both, simultaneously, wrong and close to right but mostly just very wrong. It was—"

The lights in the cells and in the corridor and in the guard station blinked on. They were aging, low-efficiency lights, phosphorescents, and they blinked on intermittently: this one first, then off, then that one, then the first one again. Harsh, unforgiving. They buzzed. Both men shielded their eyes. Schullman, the bear of a man, said, "What the fuck?"

It was night. In the nearly four years they had been prisoners, they had rarely seen the lights come on at night.

"Asher?"

Asher Sahar lay still.

When the big man realized Asher hadn't risen, he didn't either. But they could hear other prisoners up and down the row of cells gathering at their bars.

The ticktock clang of the outer iron doors reverberated. Someone from the World was walking into the cells. At night.

This, too, happened only rarely. Except when someone was about to be executed.

The outer iron doors had never opened for a priest or a rabbi. Or for an envoy from the governor's office waving a reprieve. Or for a crusading detective with exonerating evidence. Or a cook with a last meal. It wasn't that sort of prison.

Asher Sahar whispered, "This might be interesting."

He fumbled for his glasses, which lay on the knee-high stack of hardback books, two books deep, two wide, that served as his bed stand.

The main door rumbled sideways under the power of an ill-greased motor. They couldn't see the door, only hear it. The next sound was the absolutely unexpected clack of women's heels. Round, sensible, solid heels.

Asher sprang out of the bed as if ejected. He ran both hands through his thinning hair. He straightened his sweater. "Eli," he said.

The bear rose quickly, knowing an order when he heard one. Even a whispered one.

The heels clacked closer. Asher folded his hands behind his back.

An armed guard came into view, then another and a third. None wore any rank or insignia or any identifying marks.

And in walked an elderly woman, very thin and tall, with birdlike shoulders, her bones seemingly visible even under a trench coat. Her hair was stark white. Her outfit was immaculate and tasteful.

She smiled warmly.

Asher Sahar said, "Hannah," the same way you'd greet a neighbor who regularly drops by for coffee.

"Oh my God. Asher. Look at you."

They spoke in Hebrew.

"You look well," he whispered. He cleared his throat, conscious of the soft rasp in his voice. "How are things in the world?"

The three guards looked far less than happy to be conducting this reunion. Two of the three touched their holstered sidearms. The elderly woman said, "Not good. A situation has arisen. And we have need of your talents."

Asher nodded solemnly. "You needed my talents four years ago."

The woman said, "And today." She offered no explanation about the situation four years ago. She offered no explanation about the years in between.

Asher said, "Something has arisen?"

"Unfortunately."

He said, "War?"

"Democracy."

A smile spread across Asher's still-youthful, bearded face. The harsh lights glinted off his round glasses. "Who could have foreseen that?"

The woman shook her head. "As it turns out, you did, dear. You'd laid out this contingency years ago. Now, you've been proven prescient. Our friends have moved heaven and earth to free you. So that you can do what you must."

Asher was aware that the giant, Eli Schullman, was standing at attention in his own cell, even though Asher couldn't see him. "And my men."

The woman said, "Of course."

"I'll need financing."

"Which you shall have."

"And independence."

She laughed. "As if anyone could grant you that! Of course, independence. You never followed orders, anyway."

He smiled. "Well, *never* is a little harsh. Get us out of here. Tell us the situation. Give us time to formulate a plan."

The woman said. "Out of here, you shall be. The

situation shall be made clear. You have seventy-two hours to formulate a plan."

Asher said, "I've been in this prison for almost four years."

Hannah laughed again. "Only your body, love. Only your body."

She made a quarter turn to the nearest guard, gave him the gentlest of nods. The guards glowered at one another, expressing how unhappy they were to be doing this. But they nodded back to an unseen someone in the control room and, a second later, the doors to the cells holding Asher Sahar and Eli Schullman clanked open.

The other prisoners kept mum, watching, wondering.

The elderly woman said, "We have transport outside. Plus clothes and hot food."

Schullman's voice was a gravelly rumble. "Give me a smartphone. Or a laptop. Anything with a wireless connection."

The guards flinched when he spoke. Schullman seemed to absorb more than his share of the harsh light of the corridor. Hannah looked up at him, then she made the same quarter turn to the nearest guard. She did not speak.

The guard grumbled to himself, reached into a tunic pocket, and produced a smartphone. He handed it over, reaching as far as his arm could stretch, keeping clear of Schullman the best he could. The phone almost disappeared in Schullman's palm.

Hannah turned to Asher. "There is a preliminary plan. It's rudimentary. Just a sketch. Many of us think

it's unworkable and foolish. Quite possibly suicidal. Definitely horrific. But possible. With you to guide it . . . ?"
She shrugged.

Schullman stabbed at phone buttons with the pad of his beefy thumb.

Asher said, "Where?"

"It begins in the United States."

Asher smiled. It was a sad, knowing smile, and Hannah interpreted it correctly. "Yes, dear. Daria lives in the United States these days."

Asher laughed, and shook his head. He removed his glasses and began to clean the lenses on the hem of his sweater. "Of course. God being the ultimate jester."

Hannah nodded to the lead guard. The man jerked his head toward the exit.

The other prisoners in their cells still did not speak. Most didn't understand Hebrew, but even those who did watched silently.

Eli Schullman glared down at the tiny phone screen, then rudely bashed Asher's shoulder with the back of his hand. He thrust the phone over. Asher studied it a moment, then nodded.

Everyone began moving toward the exit. Outside, more guards stood with M-16s.

Schullman growled lowly. "'I'll Be Seeing You.' Irving Kahal."

Asher studied the smartphone. He shook his head. "Damn it. I could have sworn Irving Berlin wrote that."

Two

It was the first Monday of November, and the five friends—three Secret Service agents and two spouses—met as they did one Monday per month for Denver's Greatest Federal Law Enforcement Book Club and Pizza Fest.

The pizzas this month were thin crust—one all cheese, one with sausage and pepperoni. The book was *Moby-Dick*. The drinks were beer. Except for Stacy Knight-Mendoza, wife of agent Phil Mendoza. She was seven months pregnant and drank San Pellegrino water with wedges of lime.

The friends always picked the same booth at a Denver pub within walking distance of them all. The booth was curved and sat all five easily, with a table wide enough for two pizzas and the books.

The night's debate started well—two of them thought the novel was excellent, two thought it contained more blubber than an actual whale, and Will Halliday hadn't read it yet. He was the only unmarried member of the book club. Halfway through the evening, Halliday agreed to get refills for everyone's drinks.

He went to the bar and got two Bud Lights, a Heineken, a Dos Equis, and the sparkling water with lime for Stacy. He tipped the cute bartender in the Broncos jersey top and white shorts. As soon as she turned away, he slipped a two-inch-by-two-inch envelope out of his wallet, opened the flap, and let a pale pink pill spill into Stacy's drink.

The pill dissolved, the effervescent water masking the chemical reaction.

When the last residue disintegrated, Will Halliday pulled out a cell phone—prepaid, not his own—and hit speed dial 1.

"It's done."

He listened a moment, then hung up and slipped the phone into the trash can near the restrooms. He carried the tray of drinks back to his buddies.

Brooklyn, New York

Asher Sahar heard Will Halliday of the Secret Service say, "It's done."

"Understood. Thank you."

Asher spoke softly into the phone. He wasn't being covert; he was by nature and by injury a soft-spoken man. Almost fifteen years earlier, a tiny fragment of a plastic clasp, the remnant of a cheap, vinyl suicide vest, had clipped his neck and damaged his vocal cord. Asher Sahar could no more shout than he could sing an aria.

Will Halliday hung up before Asher could confirm the next stage of the operation. But that was okay. Halliday was not an X factor. Asher was sure Halliday would carry out his end of things.

Just like the rest of Asher's team. Everyone would do his job. Admirably. Asher Sahar had many skills but chief among them was the ability to pick the best people and to inspire them to greatness. One of his secrets was demanding near perfection and total dedication from his people, then praising them when they achieved it. The combination tended to inspire true loyalty.

Asher adjusted his round, wire-rimmed eyeglasses, then hit his own speed dial on the disposable, prepaid phone. The message was being routed eastward like a rock skipped across a pond: from Denver to Brooklyn, Brooklyn to Tel Aviv.

The line was picked up after one ring, despite the time difference. He spoke in Hebrew. "It's time to alert the CIA. Set it up."

The man who answered responded in English. "You are sure about the names?"

"Yes." Asher spoke only slightly louder than a whisper. "Belhadj is—hold on."

His other cell phone, his regular one, danced a little jig on the cheap bedside table in the motel room. Asher noted the readout, turned his attention back to the burner phone. "Sorry. Belhadj knows more than he should. We need to distract him."

"And the Gibron woman?"

Asher paused. "We have our orders. Her as well."

"Very good."

The line went dead.

Asher set down the burner and picked up his regular phone. He punched in a nine-digit security code and a text popped up on the screen.

YOUR PARENTS HEADING TO LONDON.

Asher smiled at the text and deleted it. Good for them, he thought.

He stood up from the saggy bed and walked to the cheap bathroom with its peeling tile floor and mottled gray-black shower grout. He peed, carefully washing his hands with the pump bottle of antibacterial soap he had picked up at the store. He stood a moment, his knuckles resting on the bathroom counter to either side of the sink, staring at his own reflection in the mirror.

I look tired, he observed with a clinical neutrality. It wasn't a complaint, it was an observation. *I look forty.* When the hell had he started looking forty? He remembered his adopted parents at forty—*they were my age!*—hosting barbecues and laughing about kosher dogs and his adopted mom joking, "Should I serve dessert or wait for the barrage?" and his adopted siblings snickering and elbowing one another.

He remembered the siblings' funerals. He remembered the barrages.

Asher turned his head twenty degrees to the left, twenty degrees to the right. Hair beginning to gray over each ear. Face thin, his cheeks hollow. The old, comma-shaped red scar on his throat—a decade and a half old—was still the first thing that caught his eye. *You'd think I'd be used to it by now.*

He wondered if getting Daria Gibron involved in the

next stage of things was downright brilliant or downright stupid. Or a little of both. It didn't matter much.
The woman who had issued the order had been specific. She wasn't just his superior. She was among the
most noble, heroic, and brilliant people Asher had ever
known. And it was an honor to follow her.

Even where Daria was concerned.

Costa Rica

Daria Gibron rose out of the Pacific Ocean off the coast
of the Nicoya Peninsula. The water was deliciously
warm and azure blue, the sun sparkling on the waves.
She shoved her goggles and snorkel up into her slicked-
back hair and reached for the lower rungs of the *Belle
Australis*'s ladder.

She stripped off her flippers and quickly climbed
the ladder to the burnished wooden aft deck of the
seventy-meter megayacht, salt water cascading down
her long, nut-brown legs. She wore a black, front-zip
wet suit vest and bikini bottom. She was aware that two
of the Jamaican crew were watching her and smiling.
She didn't mind in the slightest.

Daria didn't enjoy much about her work as a translator, but every now and then an assignment surpassed
her expectations. This was one of those jobs. Daria had
been asked to be an interpreter for a set of negotiations
taking place on board the yacht of an oil magnate, off
the shore of Costa Rica.

Nice work if you can get it, and a change of setting
was definitely called for. Especially since she'd left four
bodies in her wake back in Los Angeles.

A Jamaican steward had left a fresh terry cloth towel on her chaise longue and Daria toweled herself dry. He'd left a Grey Goose martini with olives, too. She slipped on the knockoff designer sunglasses she'd picked up at the Tango Mar resort and took a half hour to absorb both the sun and the martini, reveling in both.

The job had started the day before. *Job* being a relative term, when compared to, say, spying or soldiering. She spent much of the previous day in a sundress and gladiator sandals, translating between the oil magnate, a Saudi petroleum wholesaler, and the Salvadoran buyers. The work was untaxing and diverting. She spent part of the afternoon in the cabin and the bed of the magnate. Again: untaxing and diverting.

The Jamaican steward—all knowing smiles—brought her a second drink. "Is there anything else, madam?"

Daria beamed from behind her shades. "No, thank you."

"Madam was up very early. It is important to get your rest, yes?"

Very early. The steward must have passed by Daria's room around four in the morning and heard her moaning, or the scream she stifled into her pillow. Daria didn't mind the Jamaican's smirk or the innuendo. She lowered the sunglasses down her nose and batted her eyelashes at him.

"Early to bed, early to rise . . . ?"

The Jamaican laughed. "Yes, ma'am. Very good ma'am." He hurried away, shaking his head in amusement.

* * *

After sunbathing and the martinis, Daria returned to her cabin and booted up her laptop. She checked her e-mail, deleting everything unopened and unread. She checked the Web sites for the BBC, al-Jazeera, Haartz .com, *The Wall Street Journal*, the *International Herald-Tribune*, *The New York Times*, and the *Los Angeles Times*. She lingered over the *LA Times*, which had a story about four bodies discovered in and around a Los Angeles commercial building. The killings were described as "gang related."

Satisfied, she logged on to her private, password-protected Web site, which she did once per day, every day. Only friends had access to Daria's Web site and its encryption security. She found one pending message. At first, she assumed it was a message from Ray Calabrese.

Then she remembered: Ray no longer was her handler. He was simply . . .

. . . her friend?

Daria had been a bit unsettled at first but, as days passed, she became more comfortable with the FBI's decision. Ray Calabrese was a truly great man and an inspired criminal investigator. He was dogged, determined, patriotic, and loyal. The problem, of course, was that he saw Daria as being very similar.

Daria smiled at the notion. She had once assisted the FBI in stopping a plot by Northern Irish terrorists. Another time, she had saved the lives of two of Ray's friends. Ray, ever willing to see the best in others, had written up official reports in both instances that painted Daria as some sort of heroine.

Heroism hadn't played much of a role in either incident. But try telling Ray Calabrese that.

No, Daria thought. *I'm an adventurer. At worst, an adrenaline junkie. Best to sever official ties with the FBI before Ray discovers the truth.*

Turns out, the online message wasn't from Ray after all.

> *Chatoulah. Must meet with you soonest.*
> *Flying to NYC.*
> *Life and Death. CBS.*

The message went on to list a day, time, and venue: uptown Manhattan.

CBS was Colin Bennett-Smith. An old friend, a crazed Brit, and ex-spy, Colin had been one of the few people on Earth to still call her Chatoulah: Hebrew for *cat.*

Bennett-Smith was often drunk but rarely melodramatic. *Life and Death?*

Brooklyn, New York

In a hotel room, Asher Sahar touched the shoulder of his team's hacker. "She has opened the message?"

The hacker gave him a "did you ever doubt me?" shrug. "Moments ago. The bitch just responded. She thinks I'm this Bennett-Smith. That was a nice touch, by the way. Chatoulah. How did you know what he called her?"

Asher slid on bifocals with curved earpieces. They made him look academic, he knew, and he was self-conscious about it. The cardigan and the neatly trimmed beard didn't help. "I used to call her that, as well. I think Colin heard it from me first."

"What if the bitch—"

"Could you do me the kindness not to refer to her as that?"

The hacker looked up. Seated as the hacker was, the overhead lights glinted off Asher's round glasses, obscuring his eyes.

"Yes, sir. I was going to ask, what if she tries to contact Bennett-Smith, to confirm their appointment in New York?"

"Another team killed him, two hours ago."

"Ah. Good." The hacker liked that the boss saw all the angles, accounted for everything. "Can we trust this American Secret Service agent?"

"Halliday? Yes. He is motivated by a perfect cocktail of hatred and greed. That makes him predictable."

"Then the only question is: will Gibron go to New York on Wednesday?"

Asher wondered the same thing. "Absolutely," he replied.

They were interrupted by a pounding on the door. The hacker almost toppled out of his chair in shock.

"Asher!" A baritone voice boomed in Hebrew. "Get your ass out here!"

Only one man on earth ever talked to Asher Sahar like that. Eli Schullman. The men had been fellow fighters and friends for years. They had started out in the Air Force then joined the Mossad. Then four years in a prison that didn't officially exist. They had emptied many bottles together and each had saved the other's life frequently but neither knew who had saved whom the most.

Asher tapped his hacker on the shoulder and adjusted his bifocals. "Keep me posted on her moves."

Asher grabbed a plastic bottle of water—the water coming from the bathroom sink smelled of rust—and stepped out on the long railed breezeway that linked the motel rooms. The rooms were cheap and shabby but perfectly fine as a staging area.

Eli Schullman had the next room over, and he had left his door ajar. It was identical to Asher's room down to the cigarette burns on the furniture and odd stains in the aging, industrial carpet. Schullman sat on his bed watching CNN.

Asher sat next to him on the bed and cracked open the seal on his water. "What is it?"

CNN was covering a bombing. The setting was urban and definitely Middle Eastern. Smoke billowed from a storefront and the cars in front had their windows blown out. A ticker on the bottom of the screen read, AMMAN JORDAN.

Schullman's voice was a deep rumble. "It's started."

Schullman was a giant of a man, the apparent size of a bison. Since his release from the prison, he'd gone back to shaving his skull daily. Asher was slim with pianist's hands. He favored cardigans. Almost no one had ever heard him raise his voice. Schullman was loud and gruff. They made an odd combination.

"They targeted a Jordanian hard-liner." Schullman

grumbled. "He had just sat down with two of his lieutenants. A small, shaped charge, likely under their very
table, went off. Semtex, I imagine."

That was a lot more information than CNN currently
had, but Schullman was an expert with explosives. He
eyed the blast radius on the TV screen and derived the
rest.

Asher sighed. "Israel."

"Who else? When it's confirmed, the Americans
and Europe will go insane."

Asher looked around to see if Schullman's room had
a coffeemaker. It did not. "In two weeks, the Palestinians go to the General Assembly to petition for statehood. If they can prove this was an Israeli raid, the
Palestinians will get a much warmer reception."

Schullman grimaced. "Our traditional allies are going to become very quiet. All because some *vantz* in
Tel Aviv got a hard-on for a Jordanian."

"Yes." Asher shoved his round, wire-frame glasses
up onto his forehead and rubbed his bloodshot eyes.
"Our intelligence services have been taken over by
fools. So. It is up to us to give our allies something to
get behind. We go with the plan as it is."

He stood and crossed to the door. "I need coffee.
Are you coming?"

Schullman rose and the bed groaned in relief. "And
food. I need food."

"Of course you do. Come."

They stepped out on the walkway. Schullman threw
on a military-style jacket. "Does Hannah Herself still
want to implicate Daria?"

Asher smiled. Schullman always used the full nickname: "Hannah Herself." He used it reverentially.

"She does. The Group does. Daria and the Syrian, both."

"Daria is living in California. Did it ever dawn on the Group that if we leave her alone, maybe she'll leave us alone?"

Asher smiled up at his old friend. "The Group knows what it's doing."

Schullman said, "And the genie?"

"The *genie,* as you say, will be ours to command."

The big soldier grimaced. "Sure, sure. Because fairy tales that begin like that never end badly, do they?"

Asher laughed. "We will control this particular genie."

"Which will kill thousands."

Asher said, "Yes." The sun glinted off his flat round lenses.

"Indiscriminately."

"No. Very, very discriminately. More's the pity."

Langley, Virginia

The CIA breaks down into roughly two camps: operations and analysis.

John Broom was an analyst.

A thin man with narrow hips, standing five-ten, he looked slighter than he was. He had a bachelor's degree from Columbia in political science, a master's from the Kennedy School of Government, and a law degree from Harvard. He had joined the agency two weeks after passing the New York bar and had proven adept at reading foreign crises. In a little less than ten years, he had become one of the agency's premier crystal ball gazers in the arenas of foreign military endeavors and weapon development.

Now, however, John was ready for a change. In a week, he was leaving to join the staff of the long-standing chairman of the Congressional Joint Committee on Intelligence. Such was John's reputation as a guy who could deliver reliable intelligence that the director of Central Intelligence himself had dropped by his cubicle to try to talk him out of leaving.

It was going on 9:00 P.M. Eastern, on a Monday, his last Monday at the agency, as John hauled his fatigued body out to the underground parking lot and the tunnel that led to the metro. He'd spent hours holed up in a cubicle, peering at computer monitors. He longed for a good jog.

A Lexus pulled in, half a row ahead of John. Stanley Cohen, assistant director for antiterrorism, or ADAT, struggled out of the car and set his attaché case down on the hood.

John approached him. "Mr. Assistant Director."

"Mr. Broom."

John loosened his Italian silk tie. He looked around the underground garage. Without moving his feet, he could see no fewer than seven CC cameras.

"So. You're moving to Congress, huh?"

"Better cafeterias."

"Can't argue that." Stanley Cohen was a waspish man who squinted and held himself in tight check, shoulders always slightly forward, his head moving only when necessary. It made him look volatile or vigilant when, in fact, it was the result of a lifetime of back pain.

Cohen said, "You have a certain flair, John." He pulled a pack of wintergreen gum out of his pocket, pulled out a stick. He waved it toward John, who shook his head. Cohen slid the gum into his mouth in lieu of the cigarette he so wanted. "You should hang around. You don't completely suck at this."

"Thank you. But I resigned."

"You could unresign."

"Yes, but—"

"Bullshit. You're a natural. You are hell on a pogo stick. You are exactly the guy we need doing exactly what you've been doing."

A couple of cars exited the underground lot, their tires screeching despite their low speed.

"Senior Adviser for Foreign Affairs and Intelligence," John Broom spoke the words reverentially. "Senator Singer Cavanaugh. Chairman of the Joint Committee on Intelligence, ranking member of the Senate Foreign Relations Committee. First elected to Congress about the time King James was having the Bible rewritten. War hero. Former FBI director. The guy's a legend. How could I turn down that job?"

Stanley Cohen said, "Cavanaugh's, what? A hundred and thirty years old?"

"He turns seventy this year and have you met the guy? God willing, I should be so healthy. My job will be to consult and advise. That's it. Consult and advise. Period. No more . . ."

John let the sentence peter out.

They were silent for a while. Stanley Cohen checked his watch. "That thing in Switzerland . . ."

John said, "Yeah."

"It's the CIA, John. Most days, we get three trage-dies before lunch. That one went south but it wasn't your fault for—"

"Yeah," John exhaled. "It was. I should have pulled her out. She asked to be pulled out. I made the call to ignore her gut instincts. It was my fault."

Stanley Cohen chewed his gum and shoved his hands into his pants pockets. He seemed to be studying an oil stain on the floor. "The work sometimes takes lives."

"Advising a senior senator and a lion of Congress doesn't. I don't think it will, anyway." John stepped away from the director's Lexus and held out his hand. Stan-ley Cohen paused for a moment, then shook it.

"John? That gift card going around for you? I didn't contribute a goddamn dime."

After saying good-bye to John Broom, Stanley Cohen retrieved his attaché case and took the secure elevator up to his office. Inside, he popped open the case and began deciding which highest-priority files he needed to read that night, which he wanted to read, and which he would leave for morning. He was still sorting when his telephone buzzed.

It was the night-duty watch desk. By answering his phone, Stanley Cohen became the first brass at Lang-ley to hear about the top-secret communiqué from

Israeli intelligence. He scrounged a pen and jotted down several names.

One was Daria Gibron.

Another was the President of the United States of America.

Three

Tuesday's emergency briefing at CIA headquarters started at 6:00 A.M. sharp. Special Agent Owen Cain Thorson had the podium. Associate Director Stanley Cohen was there, along with four senior administrators from his shop. Five top leaders from Operations were present, as well as three senior chiefs from Analysis. The Secret Service had been invited to sit in, and four senior officials joined the meeting.

Among the crowd was John Broom. Since tendering his resignation, John assumed he'd be sidelined with softball assignments. Looking at all the brass in the room, that appeared not to be the case.

The presence of Owen Thorson, the fair-haired boy of the Ops Division, meant this operation had political legs. Thorson's father had served as U.S. Secretary of State and his mother was a former vice president at the World Bank. His uncle had been L.B.J.'s closest civilian adviser, first in his kitchen cabinet and later as director of Central Intelligence. Thorson had worked hard to overcome the stigma of being the Crown Prince of the CIA, becoming known for his work ethic and the hours that he put in. He could have opted for analysis and a clear shot at administration, but instead he chose not only ops, but fieldwork. Thorson tried like hell to look like one of the guys; black suits and generic ties, white shirts. And yet his blue blood was immediately obvious to everyone he met.

The lights dimmed and a screen flashed white. Thorson held the clicker for the ceiling-mounted projector.

"Thank you everyone," Thorson began. "As some of you have heard by now, Tel Aviv has alerted us to a possible attempt on the life of the president of the United States of America."

An image flashed onto the screen. It was a tough-looking man, early to mid-forties perhaps, with Mediterranean looks, hard eyes, a tight-lipped scowl, longish black hair cut badly, and a rough, thin beard that looked like a few missed chances to shave rather than a fashion statement.

"Major Khalid Belhadj. Fifteen-year veteran of the Mukhabarat, or Syrian Military Intelligence Directorate."

Someone snorted derisively. "Which Syria."

"All of them."

In the past decade, Syrian intelligence adventures had fallen into three categories: Operations that were loyal to Assad, the senior; operations that were loyal to Assad, the junior; and a random and almost unpredictable array of operations that had followed the Arab

Spring and the breakup of any identifiable lines of authority in Damascus.

"Belhadj was part of the old guard," Thorson said. "But he served Kid Assad just like the old man. He's Tehran's guy, too."

John Broom almost spoke up to disagree. It would be difficult to overstate the importance of Iranian influence on Syrian operations, but certain sectors of the Mukhabarat, some of the older, more experienced Syrian solders, were the ones least likely to take orders from Tehran.

"Belhadj is black ops," Thorson continued, "an assassin as much as a spy. Our Israeli friends informed us last night that Belhadj flew into Frankfurt under the ID of an Egyptian doctor. From there, he flew to Shannon, Ireland. He is feet-wet over the North Atlantic, right now, heading for Montreal."

Stanley Cohen said, "Final stop?"

"It appears he's coming to New York to meet a gunrunner."

Another member of the brass said, "Is this info good?"

"The intelligence is considered pristine, and only a couple of hours old."

Someone said, "The gunrunner?"

"According to the Israelis, Belhadj is coming to New York to meet *this* person."

Another image flashed onto the screen. It was a woman, dark-skinned, black-haired, prominent cheekbones, and almond eyes. Lovely and athletic. The photo showed her browsing the outdoor bin of a bookstore, left hand brushing straight hair away from her eyes. From her clothes, it appeared to be spring or early fall.

John Broom recognized her but Thorson beat him to it. "Daria Gibron. Adopted by a Lebanese father and an Israeli mother. Raised in Tel Aviv. Did her required service in the Israeli Army but reupped, did two tours before being recruited by Shin Bet."

One of the senior analysts squinted up. "Sorry?"

John spoke up. "It's Hebrew. The Unseen Shield."

Thorson nodded, not surprised. "Yes. Israeli intelligence. They're usually domestic only but Gibron's unit was an exception. She served for almost three years as an undercover agent in Beirut, Jordan, Syria, infiltrating Fatah and, later, Hamas."

Thorson hit the remote control and a new image appeared. It was an Israeli street, the photo taken from a newspaper clipping, distorted by being blown up so large. The street was filled with police cars, ambulances, and fire trucks. Some of the blobby figures wore blue windbreakers with block letters scrawled across their backs: FBI.

"Four years ago, Gibron caught rumors of a project by a Mossad splinter cell to kill a liberal member of the Israeli parliament, or Knesset. The plan was to blame it on Lebanese extremists, and use it as an excuse for an all-out attack on Fatah forces. Operatives of both Shin Bet and the Mossad were involved. Gibron didn't know who to trust. An FBI resource team was in Tel Aviv at the time, doing advisory work. She turned to them, told them the story. They intervened and stopped the assassination. During the melee, Gibron got herself gut-shot. The lead FBI adviser, a . . . ah . . ."

Thorson checked his notes.

"Ray Calabrese, took the initiative to have her airlifted to Ramstein Air Base. According to Calabrese's file, there were two attempts on her life while she was at the base. Both failed. Gibron asked for and was given safe haven in the States. Calabrese was officially posted in the L.A. field office, so Gibron was set up there."

"That," said the assistant director for antiterrorism, unwrapping an antacid tablet, "would be one hell of a good cover if you wanted to get into the U.S. to do Bad Things."

The others could almost hear the capital letters. *Bad Things* was a CIA colloquialism for terrorism.

"Yes, sir," Thorson said. "She gets seriously high marks from the FBI. They say she was influential in two separate investigations regarding airline crashes: one involving international espionage, one involving domestic, corporate malfeasance. The first was the Vermeer crash in Oregon two years ago. I imagine everyone remembers that one."

Heads nodded.

"However, her record isn't unblemished. Calabrese himself—and by the way, he's a Boy Scout; record beyond reproach—Calabrese refers to her as an 'adrenaline junkie' and 'addictive personality.' She runs marathons. She kickboxes at an international competitive level. She's an archer and fencer. She's"—Thorson cleared his throat, suddenly uncomfortable—"ah, sexually active. Sorry. That's probably apropos of nothing. It's just in the file."

Cohen hid his smile at Thorson's blush. "Gender of partners?" Cohen didn't really care; he was just pushing Thorson's buttons.

"Ah, both, sir. Although primarily men. After her surgery at Ramstein, Gibron developed an unhealthy need for Vicodin. I'm not sure we can call it an addiction, in that she beat it pretty quickly. But again: it goes to the notion of an addictive personality. For the last two years, she was working for ATF. First, setting up criminals in the L.A. area. Later, actually doing undercover work in Mexico. She was hooked up with an ATF unit that came close to being indicted for gross violations of both U.S. laws and international treaties. After the unit was broken up, Gibron returned to L.A. She still consults for the FBI and the Drug Enforcement Administration."

John Broom hadn't stopped listening but was using his tablet computer to look up the official CIA report on Daria Gibron.

It wasn't hard to find. John had written the report.

Someone piped up, "What's she doing now?"

"Gibron has a bureau-created business as an international translator. She's a polyglot. It's L.A. There's plenty of work in that line."

John raised his hand. Thorson nodded. "Broom?"

"I did the analysis of Daria Gibron, after the Oregon disaster and again after the incident in Montana. I have to say, flat out, she does not present as a danger to the U.S. This woman is on the side of the angels."

"I know you wrote the report. It's why you're in the room. But I need to point out that Gibron lived under-cover in Beirut, the West Bank, and other Arabic countries for several years while she was in her twenties. Who did she have contact with during that time? Who knows whether she was radicalized there? She wouldn't be the first."

John didn't look inclined to back down. "Daria Gibron saved lives in both of the reported incidents. That includes civilians and federal personnel. I've inter-viewed her handler, Calabrese. I'm telling you, this smells wrong."

Thorson hit the back button and the image of Khalid Belhadj, the scowling Syrian intelligence officer, reap-peared.

"I know what your gut says. But a high-ranking official in Israeli intelligence says this intel is one hun-dred percent. And when I say *high ranking*, I mean Cabinet-level or better. What we have here is a Syrian assassin very high up on the terrorist watch list coming to New York City to meet a woman whose *cover* is as a weapons provider. A woman who has successfully woven her way into the inner circles of the Federal Bureau of Investigation, Drug Enforcement Adminis-tration, and the Bureau of Alcohol, Tobacco, Firearms and Explosives."

Someone in the room breathed out, "Goddamn."

"Exactly," Thorson agreed.

Cohen chewed his antacid. "They're meeting in New York?"

"Yes, sir."

Cohen turned to the senior representative of the Secret Service. He didn't have to ask the question. The senior agent said, "The president is speaking tomorrow at Emory University in Atlanta. The topic is a new arms deal with Israel. We just moved the threat rating into the Red category and have tripled-up on his security. We'll stay there until you bring in those two."

He nodded at the flat screens.

Cohen turned back to Thorson. "Okay. You have a full code. But we need to take them together. Questions?"

John's eyebrows rose. *Full code* meant that the security protocols were maxed-out. Lethal response on domestic soil was authorized. For all parties involved.

Owen Thorson nodded. "I want to put a full quarantine on the FBI. Especially the L.A. field office. We—"

"No," Stanley Cohen cut in.

"Sir, this woman has them enthralled. Whatever we tell them, she'll know within minutes."

Cohen winced and stretched his back. "Gibron has been an asset for the FBI, the ATF, and the DEA. You recommend we freeze them all out of a domestic op in midtown Manhattan and just hope they don't notice? Besides, if this manhunt leaves New York, who do we turn to for help? The Rotary Club? Forget it. The political fallout would last months."

Thorson said, "I understand, sir, but—"

"Do we know when the Gibron woman and the Syrian are meeting?" The debate was over.

"Yes, sir."

The assistant director picked up his leather portfolio and moved toward the door. "All right, then. They leave the rendezvous either in your custody or in body bags."

Denver, Colorado

Before dawn on Tuesday, Secret Service Agent Boyd Renfro pulled into the parking lot of the Federal Building. He had to guess where the parking stripes were, due to the snow on the ground. He turned off his engine, listened to the cooling metal click for a few seconds, then stepped out, the snow crunching under his Wolverine boots.

He checked the time on his watch. It was too freaking early for this kind of milk run.

A Ford F-250 with chrome rims pulled into the parking lot, rooster tails of snow arcing behind it, and fishtailing just a bit before pulling into a slot. The dome light popped on, revealing a blond head and a megawatt smile.

Agent Will Halliday hopped down. He wore a quilted, hooded parka and waterproof snow pants tucked into boots.

Boyd Renfro pulled up his coat to draw out his phone. He checked the pdf he'd received, frowning.

"Halliday?"

The big man looked like the all-conference fullback he had been in college. He swaggered over to Renfro.

The senior agent glared. "You're not on this detail."

"You heard about Stacy?"

"Who?"

"Phil Mendoza's wife. Stacy. She's in the hospital."

Boyd Renfro winced. Stacy Knight-Mendoza was something like seven or eight months pregnant. "The hell happened? She's not due."

"Don't know, man. I got the call, hour ago. Said Phil's with his wife in the emergency room. Said she'd miscarried and she's really sick." Will Halliday's white parka bobbed in the harsh parking lot lights as he shrugged.

Renfro slapped his forehead. "Jesus! That's terrible."

Halliday's blue eyes didn't reflect much emotion.

"All right. Guess you *are* up." Renfro turned and began clomping toward the Federal Building. Halliday, a full head taller, fell in beside him.

"What are we transporting?"

Renfro snorted a nonlaugh. "They didn't say and I didn't ask. Supposed to be a cakewalk, though. Let's just hope we get no more surprises."

That hope lasted all of ninety seconds.

Boyd Renfro and Will Halliday stomped snow off their boots at the entry to the rally room, adjacent to the underground parking garage in the Denver Federal Building. Two identical black Escalades, parked perpendicular to the parking stripes, awaited them, along with four other Secret Service agents. The senior-most agent, a wiry veteran with a thick gray mustache, was on his cell phone. His steely eyes found Renfro as he

blindly, eyes slowly scanning the traffic and the hill-sides.

"So," the Goldfish said. It was the first word anyone had spoken in fifteen miles. "That's weird about Mendoza's wife. I saw her at church on Sunday. She was being so careful about her health."

From the backseat, Will Halliday said, "You never know, I guess." He wasn't worried about the pill he'd put in Stacy Knight-Mendoza's San Pellegrino water the night before. By the time she eventually died, the drug would have broken down and wouldn't show up in a standard autopsy.

They drove in silence for a while. The Goldfish said, "Bet you guys wish you'd gotten called up for the president's security detail."

Renfro kept digging into the diminishing bag of pistachios between his legs. "It's not a beauty contest. The presidential detail pulls in who they need. Rest of us do our jobs. Just like yesterday, just like tomorrow."

In the backseat, Will Halliday felt through the pocket of his parka, found a remote control, and slid the mechanism to the on position.

The Goldfish said, "But have you ever gotten the call to—"

Halliday thumbed the firing mechanism. *Pakk!* He felt the vehicle shudder.

"The hell was that?" Boyd Renfro's eyes searched the highway in every direction. The sound had been acoustically wrong for a gunshot. Still, his left hand rested on the Glock in his belt holster.

"Hey," the Goldfish said, and jutted his chin forward. Steam began hissing from the hood of the Escalade.

Renfro glanced at the temperature gauge as it bobbed upward.

"Pull in there," Halliday leaned forward and pointed toward the gravel parking lot of a motel, not thirty feet from the Genevieve River and its levee. The parking lot held three cars but was large enough for thirty. The motel rooms were laid out in a C shape, and each building was designed to look like a log cabin. A snow-capped sign on a tall stand read *ROCKY VISTA MOTEL.*

The Goldfish turned in.

Renfro undid his seat belt and gripped his sidearm. "See anything?"

From the backseat, Halliday said, "Nope." He drew his own Glock.

The black Escalade glided to a halt in the dead center of the near-empty lot. More steam rose from the hood. The temperature gauge spiked into the red zone.

Renfro said, "Check it out."

The Goldfish killed the engine and stepped out and down from the SUV, his boots leaving a perfect waffle-sole print in the frozen snow.

Renfro's eyes moved mechanically, professionally, from trees to the motel's faux log cabins to Interstate 70 and its thin traffic. "You see anything?"

Behind him, Will Halliday deftly screwed a silencer onto his automatic.

A mid-nineties panel truck flashed its turn indicator and vectored toward the parking lot.

"The hell's this?" Renfro asked.

The Goldfish popped the hood, obscuring his view of the SUV cabin.

As soon as the Goldfish's vision was blocked by the raised hood, Halliday placed his silencer against Renfro's ear and pulled the trigger, once.

Renfro died before his head ricocheted off the dashboard.

Will Halliday climbed out and circled the big SUV. A plume of steam roiled from the engine. The newbie glanced at Will, turned his attention back to the engine.

"I think there's something here," the kid said, a gloved finger jabbing at the mechanism that had severed the coolant line. Halliday strolled over to his side. "You did the walk-around before we left the garage. Did you notice—"

Halliday fired once. The Goldfish's body flopped onto the engine, his squall-line jacket and the skin of his face beginning to blister and crack.

The panel truck pulled up next to the Escalade so as to block the SUV from prying eyes on the highway or windows in the motel rooms. Both front doors opened and two of Asher Sahar's mercenaries stepped out. Both Israelis, neither looked all that happy to be in Colorado in November.

Halliday opened the front passenger door of the Escalade and helped Renfro's body fall to the parking lot. He squatted and dug through the senior agent's pockets, finding the key to the steel-reinforced cage that lined the back of the Escalade. He opened the back door, unlocked the cage, and pulled out the canister and its cooling tanks.

Halliday grinned at the two mercenaries. "How we doin', fellas?"

The two men did not answer, but took either end of the canister and moved it into the panel truck.

While they worked, Halliday retrieved a cheap, purple vinyl backpack from the panel truck. It didn't weigh much. Halliday slung it over one shoulder, checked to see there were no eyewitnesses, then trudged away from the highway, across the empty parking lot, through the snow, and clomped into a scrubby expanse of grass. Waxy weeds poked out of the snow. The field ended at the foot of the stone wall that had redirected the Genevieve River away from the highway. A Works Projects Administration wall, it was sturdy and thick, not pretty but competently crafted, and given a chance, it could stand for another two hundred years. Will Halliday tucked the backpack amid the weeds at the base of the river wall.

He jogged back and joined the mercenaries in the panel truck. The silent men pulled back onto Interstate 70. A mile later, Halliday grinned at the Israelis. "Everyone having fun?"

The mercenaries glowered at the inappropriately cheerful American.

"Sweet Jesus. You guys gotta learn to enjoy a job well done! Look: how often do you get to do this?"

He drew the detonator out from beneath his seat and made a show of punching the red button.

A mile behind them, the purple backpack's explosives shrieked and evaporated a quarter ton of stone and mortar.

The Genevieve River roared into the motel and its parking lot, smashing everything to bits.

Four

Khalil Al Korshan met his cousin, Mohammad Al-amour, as he did a few times per week, at a favorite tea-shop in the southern half of Rafah. The tea was good, but the cousins picked the shop because they could watch the new security wall and sentry posts being installed on the Philadelphi Road, which separated the Egyptian side of Rafah—their side—from the half of the city inside the Gaza Strip.

The Bedouin cousins had just come from the tailor shop that their families had operated for decades. Many of their best customers had lived in the denser, northern end of the city. But at the dawn of the 1980s, the year of the Israeli-Egyptian Peace Treaty, everything had changed now that the Jews and their damn wall had split the city in two.

The cousins ordered hot tea. They had just been

down in the basement of the tailor shop, examining their newly excavated tunnel, which led straight north.

"It's too small," Alamour grumbled, keeping his voice low. "There's barely room for the pallets, let alone for a worker to get them through to the other side. I'm telling you, the tunnel needs to be twice as wide."

"And I'm telling you, *ibn 'amm*, that you worry too much. A wider tunnel would get spotted. Either by the police on this side, or the Israeli Defense Forces on that side. Either way: poof." Al Korshan bundled his fingertips together and blew on them, as one might blow on a dandelion.

The larger, more populous sector of Rafah lay north of the checkpoints that split the city itself. All entry points into north Rafah, and the rest of the Gaza Strip, were heavily guarded by Israeli Defense Forces soldiers. The Jews watched all vehicles like hawks and all shipments were inspected. Reports of shortages on the Gaza side—from food to medicine to clothing—were rampant.

Which is why the Bedouin cousins, Khalil Al Korshan and Mohammad Alamour, had excavated their tunnel under the Philadelphi Road. Their family had known for years that shortages just mean profits for those with the will to make it happen.

But Alamour's visual inspection of the tiny tunnel, with its long and frayed cable stringing together weak yellow work lights, had been vastly disappointing. There was no way workers could maneuver pallets of goods through the long, narrow tunnel.

Al Korshan sipped his tea, enjoying the sagelike flavor of the desert herb, habuck. *"Ibn 'amm."* The term meant *cousin.* "I think I have a solution. Look behind you."

Alamour turned in his aluminum chair.

An urchin stood outside the teashop, filthy face pressed up against the glass. He watched as a patron at another table stood and reached for the basket of week-old newspapers from Cairo, printed in Arabic, French, and English. As soon as the patron stood, the street child bolted. He was rail-thin, maybe six or seven years old. He dashed into the shop, grubby hands snatching the remainder of the patron's breakfast roll, and was out the door before the patron turned or the teashop owner, smoking from a tin of Prince of Monaco cigarettes, could react.

The owner shouted a curse but the homeless boy was already out of sight.

"Fast, that one," Alamour observed.

"I see him here most days. Feral, starving. And stronger than he looks. A patron caught him last week. The demon child fought like a Janissary. The Six-Day War would have lasted a lot longer than six days if the Faithful had had a few soldiers like him, let me tell you."

Alamour turned back to their table. "There are plenty of starving orphans on the Gaza side. And there will be plenty more."

His cousin smiled and gestured toward the grubby spot on the window where the urchin had leaned. "That," Al Korshan said, "is our newest employee."

Alamour almost choked on his tea. "That devil?"
His cousin corrected him. "No. That tunnel rat."

The Bedouin cousins caught the homeless boy in an
alley and paid him a single coin. In return for which,
the boy climbed into the cousins' tight, ill-lit, and almost airless tunnel. They had provided him with a
snow sled from England, flat-bottomed, cherry red and
plastic, with a twined rope that the boy tied around his
waist so he could crawl on all fours. The first shipment
for the snow sled was a stack of French cigarettes. Other
cousins on the Gaza side received the boxes of cigarettes and sold them with a 100 percent markup. The
entire shipment sold in a little under an hour.

The orphan pulled the plastic sled back to the Egyptian side. Caked in sweat and dirt, only his eyes shone
beneath the grime. He rose from the tunnel, held out a
dirt-caked hand, and said, "More!"

The boy worked ten-hour days, crawling with his
sled stacked with canned food, spare parts for automo-
biles, cigarettes, and even American dollars, the only
currency that some shops in the Gaza Strip accepted.
The cousins waited two weeks to make sure the system
was working, then added marijuana and heroin, which
proved handsomely profitable.

"More!" the boy would shout, emerging on the Egyptian side of the border. "Canned food. And cigarettes.
And lighters. And hashish, if you can get it."

As the Bedouin sons and nephews scoured South
Rafah for the goods, the homeless boy tore into a bowl

of lentil soup and a wedge of stale bread. They paid him a pittance.

Alamour made more money in those first three weeks than he had in the previous six months. But he still looked askance at the manic tatterdemalion devouring his food.

"How do you even understand the little hellion?" he asked. "What language is that?"

Al Korshan laughed. "A stew. Some of it is Arabic, some is Hebrew. A little French and English, too. Some I don't recognize. Yiddish, I think maybe."

Alamour looked stricken. "Hebrew and Yiddish? Are you saying the child is a Jew?"

Al Korshan shrugged. "I don't know and I doubt the boy himself knows. That is God's business. Ours is commerce. That brat could be the cousin of the Pope in Rome for all I care. So long as he can work the tunnels."

Costa Rica

On board the *Belle Australis*, off the Nicoya Peninsula, a Jamaican porter made strong coffee for two of the guests, weaker green tea for two more, a Coke Zero with a wedge of lime and no ice for the fifth, and the Captain's Blend (two-thirds Nescafé, one-third Glenfiddich). He put all the drinks on a tray, along with tablet computers for each guest, preloaded with their newspapers and magazines of choice and a bowl of fruit. Finally, he added small crystal vases, large enough for one short-stemmed rose for each guest.

He hoisted the tray with the beverages, fruit, computers, and flowers, and began distributing them around the megayacht, which sat so serenely in the Pacific waters they might as well have been in the George V Hotel in Paris.

The sun had not yet risen. The palm trees were black against the indigo horizon, the white beaches empty except for colonies of seabirds standing asleep vertically.

The steward headed for the long, claret-carpeted guest corridor and gingerly knelt before each door to leave a breakfast, a tablet, and a flower. His knees popped each time he knelt. He paused at the door of the long-legged beauty; the translator with the indeterminate accent. The steward smiled.

As with the morning before, he again heard the sounds of moaning coming from her room. The sound was ghostly, throaty, rising in crescendo. The steward smiled and shook his head, leaving the morning treats, as the moaning behind the wooden door gave way to a howl, poorly silenced by a pillow.

"*Jeune fille de bon chance,*" he observed, clucking in appreciation. He was glad someone was having a good time aboard the floating palace.

Daria awoke under the bed, moaning.

As she did so many mornings.

She was bathed in sweat, her eyes alight, flowing from within a Molotov cocktail of pain and betrayal and pure distilled terror. She was a little girl. An orphan. A child war veteran.

No! She forced her brain to scramble through the

morning time travel terrors. *Not a little girl. Not the Gaza Strip. There were no bombs, no blood. No callused adult hands, torn and bloody, reaching for her. No diggers above her, screaming for more help. No fire dying in a woman's eyes. No lips silently breathing apologies.*

She was aboard the *Belle Australis*, off the shore of Costa Rica. The sweat-sodden sheets were rucked around her hips; she had dragged them down off the bed with her. Daria grabbed a fistful and shoved the sheets over her mouth and screamed in panic/hate/pain.

Her morning began much as usual.

Daria made reservations for a Wednesday sortie of flights—two puddle jumper hops and one crossing the Western Hemisphere—culminating in New York City. That left her free to accept the dinner invitation from the yacht's first officer, a Moldovan woman with lush blond hair and the body of a distance runner.

She and the first officer sat in the Tango Mar seaside café with glasses of crisp Italian prosecco. The music turned out to be 1950s jazz. The first officer wore a polka-dot dress—quite a change from her well-pressed white uniform with blue button-down epaulettes and sensible, rubber-soled shoes. She had exceptionally fine calves. Daria registered the thought that one doesn't necessarily expect naval officers to be runners. You expect them to have other skills, like knot tying. Sure enough, a few hours earlier, the first officer had proven most proficient at that, too. But to have exceptional calves? And in flat sandals? Remarkable.

Daria sipped her sparkling wine.

"You seem distracted," the first officer observed in French, which was their common tongue.

"I am. By you." Daria smiled and leaned forward to touch the woman's hand. "Let's order some food."

Actually, Daria was distracted. Within one week, she had been unlinked to the FBI, and she had been contacted for an urgent meet with Colin Bennett-Smith, an old British friend from her predefection days.

Coincidence? Daria hated that word.

Five

The security officer at Aeroport International Pierre Elliott Trudeau de Montreal looked bored. Syrian intelligence officer Khalid Belhadj had counted on boredom. He had timed his flight so he would arrive toward the end of the morning security shift.

"Votre passeport, s'il vous plait."

Belhadj handed over a well-worn Egyptian passport.

"Combien de temps allez-vous rester en Canada?"

He shifted his weight from foot to foot and peered through old, scratched eyeglasses. "Am sorry. I have no French. I speak some American?"

Belhadj knew very well that airport security personnel the world over are trained to watch for foreigners with superior language skills.

"English," the officer corrected. "It is called English. Business or vacation?"

Belhadj pointed to his shabby, faux-leather portfolio. "Business. Ah . . ." He shrugged and opened the portfolio, withdrew a twofold brochure for a medical line of penile catheters. He began to demonstrate how they work.

That was enough for the security guard. He stamped the passport and pushed it through the half-circle opening in his Plexiglas shield.

"Thank you. Welcome to Canada. Next!"

Within the Trudeau terminal, a woman with a baby stroller knelt near the baggage claims carousel, digging through a massive backpack for a clean diaper, baby powder, and wipe-ups. After Khalid Belhadj passed her with his portfolio of catheters, the woman spoke into her sleeve.

"We have Bowler."

New York City

Midmorning on Wednesday, Daria landed at JFK with a white canvas beach tote and a glowing golden tan. She looked anomalous amid the snow shovels, bulbous parkas, and sallow complexions of New York in November.

She didn't know what Colin Bennett-Smith's situation was, but she owed him her life a couple of times over. If he wanted a life and death meeting—his words—she would show. If she could help him, she would. If not, she'd have some time, a few days, to enjoy New York City. Even in November, cold as it was, the city was lovely. The Christmas decorations were in full bloom and, while Daria wasn't the holiday sort, she did love the vivid colors of the season.

She hefted her tote and joined the queue walking or half-jogging toward baggage claim and ground transportation. Her almond eyes swept the crowd methodically, although subconsciously. It was the habit of a lifetime.

She just passed a news kiosk as the airport's P.A. system sounded: *Dee Jean D'Arc. Please return to the Alaska Airlines booth to retrieve your purse. Dee Jean D'Arc. Please return to the Alaska Airlines booth to retrieve your purse.*

She froze.

Dee was Daria.

Jean D'Arc was Joan of Arc.

Translation: *Daria . . . you are burned.*

It was an old code. Far older than her time with Shin-Bet. It was a code from her childhood.

Her first assumption was she was being followed. If so, then the surveillance team was good because she hadn't spotted them yet. Shaking them would be a good idea. Just on principle. Step one: thin the herd.

She gave up on the notion of collecting her luggage from baggage claim. The bag contained nothing she couldn't replace. In fact, if push came to shots-fired, Daria could ghost out of her own life, just like she'd been trained to do since before she'd hit five feet tall.

She stopped in the women's restroom, waited a few minutes in a cubicle, then stepped out and returned to the news kiosk. She spotted a businessman with a carry-on bag eyeing a rack of magazines. Daria had a copy of that week's *Time* magazine in her tote. She pulled it out, caught the man's eye. "Excuse me?"

She gave him her brightest smile. He glanced over, turned away, then did a double take. Beautiful women didn't smile like that at him every day.

Daria proffered her magazine. "I'm done with this one and I hate to just throw them away. Do you want it?"

The guy had been looking for *Field and Stream* or *Golf Digest*, but free is free. "Sure! Thanks."

Daria had noted his wedding ring before she approached him. She winked at him. Predictably, the wink made him glance around, to see who else had noticed.

"Business or pleasure?"

"Excuse me? Oh, my flight. Ah, I'm . . . I've got a business thing. In Atlanta." He shrugged. "Conference."

"Lovely. Well, *bon voyage.*"

He gestured toward the magazine. "Thanks. Um, hey, you know, thanks. Bye."

Daria felt just a little bad that she was so good at flustering married men.

A janitor in a jumpsuit, with a water bucket and mop, touched the comm unit in his ear. "Batsman just made contact. Unknown male. She handed him a magazine. He's glancing around, looking for surveillance? He hasn't made me. He's putting it in his carry-on. Over."

The CIA agent running the surveillance team toggled

back. "Stick with the stranger. See where he goes. If there's a chance to grab the magazine, do so. Over."

"Confirmed."

Two members of the CIA surveillance team peeled away.

Daria left JFK without approaching the baggage carousel. It took her three cabs, a brisk walk, and a short subway ride before she found the perfect place to stop. The convergence of a convenience store, a small restaurant, and a construction project that had closed one of two traffic lanes, and a harried-looking police officer, bundled against the cold and trying to keep the sluggish traffic moving.

She located an ATM machine and dug through her tote for her collection of debit cards, which nestled beneath the removable cardboard bottom of the bag near the spade-shaped knife. She never traveled without them and never trusted them to her checked luggage. Each card featured a different name and different alphanumeric password, and each was linked to a different bank. She pulled a total of twelve hundred dollars out of the three accounts.

She dashed to the convenience store and found a large, cheap pair of sunglasses and a folding map of Manhattan. She headed to the restaurant and ordered French onion soup with warm corn bread and coffee latte. She chose a table where she could watch the irritable traffic cop standing between orange traffic cones, mouthing, "C'mon buddy . . . move it . . . let's go . . ."

She ate without noticing the quality of the food.

She studied the map. Colin Bennett-Smith had asked her to meet him at 2:00 P.M. on Forty-second Street, west of Lexington, at an entrance to Grand Central Terminal that hunkered beneath the Park Avenue overpass. She ran a trimmed, buffed fingernail over the spot, realizing she recognized it. There would be plenty of foot traffic and plenty of automobile traffic. It wasn't a half-bad place for an impromptu meeting.

Except for the warning at the airport.

She glanced up at the traffic from time to time. The block provided virtually no parking and with construction slowing everything to a snail's pace, it became unlikely she was being followed by a car that was circling the block. The irritated traffic cop would have noticed by now. And no customers younger than sixty had entered the restaurant since she arrived.

Adjacent to the Grand Central entrance that Bennett-Smith had indicated stood the H-shaped Grand Hyatt Hotel.

Daria paid cash for her food and carefully refolded her map. Outside the restaurant, she hailed a cab. "Fifty-first and Park, please."

She climbed out at Saint Bart's church and sauntered over to Lexington, pretending to talk on her cell phone, her wrist and forearm, along with the new sunglasses, in the line of sight between passing cars and her face. She took a quick right into the open-air market that led to Grand Central. The tunnel also featured a side entrance into the Hyatt. She paused over the produce bins for three minutes, watching through the smoked lenses for foot surveillance.

Satisfied, she dashed into the hotel lobby. It was packed with visitors and staff. She strode up to the concierge's desk and, in her best midwestern accent, asked, "Hi! Can you tell me where the registration is for the convention?"

Twenty minutes later, Daria wore a stick-on name tag with a generically American name, plus a swag bag from an association of Midwestern insurance companies. As a translator, she had attended a dozen of these events and knew that half of the swag bags get thrown out almost unopened. And extra name tags were kept around for attendees who had not registered in advance.

Daria strode into the hotel's mezzanine-level bar. It offered an extended view of 42nd Street. She scouted out the scene.

It looked cold outside. She hadn't packed a coat for her trip from Los Angeles to Costa Rica—who would?

In her mind, she didn't think *from home to Costa Rica* . . . her kind didn't have a home. Homes are a luxury for noncombatants.

She had two hours to kill before the meet. She ordered white wine that she ignored, sat and watched the street for forty minutes. Whenever someone walked past her, she held her inert mobile phone to her ear and said, "Um-hm . . . yes . . ."

She saw nothing outside in the crowded street that made her nervous. Most of midtown was festooned in red and green, with holly and elves and silver bells and

all the rest of the retail kitsch that annually invades
every city in America like festive kudzu. The sun etched
the sky, white with pollution.

Dee Jean D'Arc . . .

Daria, you are burned.

It seemed someone was watching her. And someone
else was watching *out* for her.

In both cases, she didn't know who.

She unfolded her Manhattan map again, studied it
for a few moments, then left the bar and returned to
the concierge. She pointed to a spot on the map. He
grimaced. "Very bad traffic, ma'am. Avoid it if you
can."

She thanked him kindly and asked if there was a
computer she might use. He pointed her to the hotel's
business center. There, she did a MapQuest search of
the coordinates she had shown the concierge.

Daria found an X, where Broadway intersects
Seventy-second Street on the Upper West Side. There
was a small park and a subway stop. In the vicinity was
a sandwich shop, a chain bookstore that also housed a
coffee shop, a bank, a women's clothing store, and a
photocopy shop.

Perfect. She returned to the second-floor window of
the hotel and activated her cell phone.

Most CIA operations can be run from high-tech, high-
def wired operations rooms burrowed deep in the bow-
els of the headquarters in Langley, Virginia. The ops
rooms are known as Shark Tanks. Each operations

room was as secure as Fort Knox, featuring more high-definition wiring than a Super Bowl game.

But when an operation comes together too quickly for a traditional setup, mobile command centers become the focal point of the operation. There were few enemies of America who could hope to outmaneuver the sheer calculating power and communication technology of a CIA command vehicle.

Such vehicles—long truck-and-trailer rigs—are pre-positioned around the globe. Each serves as a mobile ops room, complete with the latest in wireless surveillance equipment, GPS-fed monitoring stations, real-time data feeds to Langley, and enough weaponry and defensive technology to face off against a small army.

Such command vehicles are rarely used within the borders of the United States because, as any intelligence analyst, lawmaker, or journalist can tell you, the CIA does not operate domestically.

At least, not officially.

Owen Cain Thorson and two tech-savvy agents occupied one of these long, white trucks, marked on the outside with the stylized logo of a Hollywood film crew. They had parked on Forty-second Street, a half block from the meet. Earlier in the day, Thorson's techs had positioned eight cameras, no larger than lipsticks, at strategic locations on every side of the block, both at ground level and on upper floors of the surrounding buildings. Eight small monitors in the truck were being fed live images.

Thorson removed his ear jack and voice wand, and reached for a walkie-talkie. "Goddard? What was Batsman wearing when you lost her? Over."

"Ah, black leather jacket, jeans, flats, red button-down blouse. Oh, and her hair is longer than in the briefing photos. Shoulder-length. Straight. Over."

Thorson acknowledged the transmission. One of the agents in the truck grumbled, "I can't believe Goddard's team lost her at JFK."

"We weren't there." Thorson turned his eyes back to the monitors, which showed strategic intersections and sidewalks within a two-block-by-two-block radius. "Don't second-guess his team. She's a trained spook. Maybe she made them. Maybe she assumes she's always under surveillance and takes countermeasures. Look, study this."

He produced a file folder, about a half-inch thick. "Backgrounders for both the Syrian shooter and this Gibron woman. We put the team together so fast, I didn't have time to brief everyone."

He handed the folder to the nearest agent.

Daria's Manhattan meeting place was under surveillance by the CIA.

Both Daria and the CIA team, in turn, were under surveillance by Asher Sahar and his crew. After all, the whole event had been orchestrated by Asher. He had no intention of missing the show.

His procurement specialists—completely separated from his tactical field specialists—had provided a third-floor storage space above a diamond store. The space was remarkably low-tech despite its content: eight-foot-tall wooden chests of drawers, the drawers all uniformly four inches wide by three inches deep, all filled with velvet-lined boxes of diamonds and other gems. Upon reviewing the space, weeks earlier, Asher and Eli Schullman had come to the conclusion that the only security was a sign on the door that read *NO ADMITTANCE!*

Three wood-framed windows looked out on Forty-second. Schullman had coated the inside of the windows with static-hold sheets, adhered them with blasts from a hair dryer. The sheets reduced lens flare from the cameras and rifles inside the diamond exchange.

Asher's surveillance experts—a cell of good people, well isolated from procurement and tactical—had provided wide-spectrum receivers to monitor the CIA teams. The guys in surveillance had bought the CIA frequencies from the Russian FSB. Strange bedfellows . . .

Asher, Eli Schullman, and two others manned the third floor of the diamond exchange. Two more men waited below them in a Jeep Grand Cherokee with a well-faked handicapped parking permit.

Asher pushed his eyeglasses up into his thinning hair and raised binoculars, adjusted them. "Timing for Belhadj?"

One of his men, an Ethiopian Jew, checked his handheld. "We assumed he'd come into Penn Station but he switched trains. He should reach Grand Central Station inside the hour."

"Terminal," Asher whispered, making minute adjustments to the binoculars. "Grand Central Terminal."

Schullman rubbed his Cro-Magnon jaw. "And Gibron?"

Asher clucked his tongue. "I'm sure she's around."

In the CIA truck-and-trailer, one of the techs, a taciturn Texan, spun from his monitor and deftly doffed his headset. "Got her! She's calling the FBI!"

"Block it!" Thorson rose from his bolted-down seat.

At the Los Angeles Field Office of the FBI, Ray Calabrese glanced down at his cell phone, which sat atop a pile of files. The phone rang once. He reached for it, but it didn't ring again.

Odd.

As he pulled his hand away, Special Agent in Charge Henry Deits knocked on his door. He held his laptop, propped open, cradled like an infant.

"Have you checked the dailies from the CIA yet?"

Ray leaned back in his chair. "No. They got something good?"

Henry looked more pale than usual, which was saying something. "Something, yeah. Not something good."

He stepped into the room and showed Ray his laptop, with the twin photos of Khalid Belhadj and Daria Gibron.

The Texan in the CIA command vehicle redirected Daria's call away from Ray Calabrese's cell phone. Thorson's crew and those back home in the Langley Shark Tank listened to the recorded intro they had pirated from Ray's cell earlier that day. "Hi, it's Ray. I'm on another line. Please leave me a message." *Beep*.

The three men in the long, technology-laden mobile ops center kept quiet, doffing their own headsets. The truck included an interior door that led to the cab but no driver sat up there. Nothing looks more like surveillance than a driver behind the wheel of an unmoving truck.

After a couple of clicks, a voice rang through the speakers inside the truck. Thorson grabbed a pen and a notepad.

"Ray?" The voice was digitally recorded on no fewer than three devices; a backup for the backup, as well as a device back at the Shark Tank beneath Langley. "Hallo. It's Daria. I'm in New York, believe it or not."

The Texan studied his monitors. "She's bouncing off a cell tower within a mile of here."

Daria sounded cheerful. "I wanted you to know, an old friend, Colin Bennett-Smith, is in town. He was MI-6 but washed out. I told you about him . . ."

Another CIA agent quickly jotted down the name. "Bennett-Smith?"

Owen shushed him. He was not surprised a trained spy was using a code name for the Syrian assassin over a cell phone.

"Anyway, he wants to meet me. Don't know why. He set a meeting at two, at Forty-second and Park Avenue, in midtown. He said it was Life and Death. That means he's using his old codes. We're really meeting at four o'clock at some place called Verdi Square. I've never heard of it."

Owen Thorson no longer was seated.

"I wanted you to know, in case this ends up being something the FBI wants in on. So, anyway. Miss you. Take care. Bye."

The line disconnected.

"Shit!" one of the agents barked.

"It's okay," Owen said, catching the attention of everyone: The men in the truck, the cadre of agents on the streets and rooftops, and the people back in the Operations Room at Langley. He adjusted his voice wand. "All teams: The meet isn't happening here. We are mobile. Repeat: we are mobile! Verdi Square: Where is it?"

The third man in the truck rifled through a Thomas Guide. "Ah . . . got it! Seventy-second and Broadway!"

Thorson pointed toward the door to the empty cab. "Drive."

At CIA headquarters in Langley, a dozen agents monitored the communications. Eight large, flat monitors caught the images from the eight CC cameras set up around the rendezvous site. One was Nanette Sylvestri, a tall African American woman a few years past sixty. John Broom stood next to her with his ubiquitous coffee cup, watching the flat-screens.

He had all but begged to be allowed in the field for this one, given his knowledge of Batsman. He'd literally written the book on Daria Gibron. Owen Cain Thorson had declined. "You're Analysis, not Ops. Besides, you'll have a different perspective if you're seeing real-time intelligence from home. You might see something I don't."

Now, John listened to the pirated transmission. He had studied Daria Gibron but had never heard her voice. It was pitched lower than he'd imagined. He tagged her Middle Eastern accent but it was spiced with something else. Not just dulled by her years living in America, the woman's voice had picked up a ragout of dialects from the many languages she spoke. John thought that Daria Gibron sounded like the future. Like a world without countries.

As Thorson galvanized his Manhattan team, John froze with a coffee halfway to his lips.

"The hell . . . ?" he whispered.

Asher Sahar's team in the diamond exchange and the men in the Grand Cherokee overhead Daria's whole message, as well as the site-to-site chatter from the CIA.

Eli Schullman threw off his foam headset. "What the fuck is this about a code? What goddamn code?"

Asher Sahar took a step back from the third-floor window and lowered his binoculars. His eyes darted the length of Forty-second Street. His anxiety level spiked. None of the other men could tell, but Eli Schullman had been his friend for years.

"What?"

Asher continued scanning the street.

"Asher? You didn't expect her to show?"

Asher ignored the big man.

Their radio chirped and one of the men sitting below them in the Jeep Grand Cherokee swore in English. The man was a Bosnian Croat mercenary from the Neretva Canton of Herzegovina. "Base: this is fucked! What are your orders?"

Asher set down the binoculars and turned to their communications man. "We need to redirect the Syrian, please. He's going to the wrong site."

The second man in the Grand Cherokee shouted into his mic. "He'll be suspicious. He won't—"

"Gentlemen?" Asher reached up and lowered his glasses back into the bridge of his nose. "The plan calls for the CIA to intercept Mr. Belhadj. The CIA is no longer going to be on Forty-second. They are going to be at Verdi Square."

He made a gesture to Schullman that the big man correctly interpreted. Schullman began looking up Verdi Square.

The Cypriot said, "If we move the Syrian fucker, he'll know—"

Asher interrupted quietly, "Please do it," and disconnected.

Schullman looked up from his laptop. "Uptown. West Side."

Asher said, "Thank you. Can you lead the mobile team, please?"

Schullman shrugged into his jacket, hiding a shoulder holster and a hand cannon. "And Daria?"

The faint echo of a smile crossed Asher's thin features. "I don't think we need worry. She'll be there."

"But how—"

Asher patted him on the shoulder. "That's Daria. When she dances, she always likes to lead."

Syrian agent Khalid Belhadj's commuter train was just reaching the Hudson River when his cell phone vibrated. He confirmed that the call was being routed through a secure server in Estonia, then accepted the text message.

Belhadj returned his phone to his pocket. He wore a shapeless dun raincoat, brown trousers, shoddy oxfords. He knew he looked and moved like a soldier, so he'd added a brimmed hat, a few sizes too large for his head. The brim hid his granite-hard eyes and watchful stare. The baggy clothes hid his rigid, on-point body language. The coat hid a Springfield .45 handgun that could punch a hole through cinder block.

He pondered the message. It seemed his meeting was being moved to the Upper West Side of Manhattan. The change of venue would have made Belhadj suspicious. Except he'd been suspicious about each and every aspect of the meeting for days now. The change of plan didn't trigger further suspicion; it confirmed his instincts.

Daria remembered one of her trainers in Israeli Intelligence expounding on the subject of countersurveillance: "You don't shoot birds in the bushes, idiot! You spook them, get them to fly. Surveillance can be easy to hide but difficult to transport."

From her second-story perch in the Hyatt bar, Daria

could not tell which unmoving trucks, which idle pedestrians, which slowly cruising taxis had been watching Forty-second Street, waiting for her. Hiding in plain sight.

Until they weren't.

She caught the motion of the long, white truck with the logo of a film company, as well as five pedestrians who, simultaneously, touched their ears or glanced around, then hurried away in the same direction. Individually, they had blended into the scene nicely. Now choreographically mobile, they became a unit, an ensemble.

That wasn't what worried Daria.

No. It was the movement on at least two, possibly three, roofs. Snipers.

This was not a benign surveillance unit. This was a kill squad.

In Langley, John Broom spun around, located Nanette Sylvestri, the Person in Charge. The tall, gangly woman towered over most everyone else in the Shark Tank. She was willow slim, with tightly cropped hair the color of old nickels. She'd been in the agency for nearly thirty years and had run many operations. She was the one you called in to run the Shark Tank for big events like today.

"Nanette?"

Her eyes were glued to the eight flat-screen monitors that reflected real-time intelligence from Forty-second Street. She nodded, acknowledging she had heard him, but keeping her eyes darting from screen to screen.

"Something's wrong here."

She offered a grim smile. "You think? We're out of place."

"No," John said, "It's something else."

Six

The tool Owen Cain Thorson used to regain control of Operation Pegasus—the name selected at random by a computer somewhere at Langley—wasn't some high-tech CIA gizmo. It was Google Maps. He typed in the intersection the Gibron woman had named.

He was pissed about being caught off guard like this, but he refused to let his team see that. Rather, he exuded an easy calm that seemed to indicate: *No worries. We got this.*

"It's a busy intersection," he told the men in the truck as well as those on the streets, the rooftop shooters and the Shark Tank at Langley. "Subway stop, bus stop, tons of foot traffic, retail in every direction."

Translation: tactically, Seventy-second and Broadway was a circus.

Another agent turned in his seat. "I sent Daniels ahead on his motorcycle. We'll need four or five parking spaces for this freaking whale."

Owen said, "Good, thank you," his eyes locked on

the Google map, toggling between satellite images and the gridded map image. "Skyhook: status, please."

The leader of the three-man sniper team had been on the roof of the Grand Hyatt. He hopped down maintenance stairs, three stairs at a time, his rifle in a golf bag on his back. "Copy! We are on the move but you're gonna get there first!"

The man carried a British-made L115A3 long-range rifle, which fires a heavy, 8.6 millimeter bullet that, over greater distances, is less likely to be deflected by wind than the average bullet. His other shooters carried similar weapons.

"Copy that, Skyhook." Thorson peered at the computerized map. "We have a fifteen-story building to the northeast. We have a twelve-story building to the northwest. Both with good line of sight. We are working on getting you access to both. We have a lot of civilians on foot but . . ." he paused, lied, ". . . we're working on a way to clear some of that before you're green-lit."

The sniper team leader burst out of a maintenance door of the Hyatt just as Daria was exiting the hotel on the far side.

In the Shark Tank beneath Langley, John Broom looked up at the tall scarecrow of a woman who ran the room.

Nanette Sylvestri said, "And you are absolutely sure . . . ?"

John nodded.

"Go."

With Nanette's permission to jump into the communications stream, John bent at the waist to put his lips closer to the microphone that stood up on a flexible metal wand from the main communications array. "Pegasus: hold position! You're being faked out!"

The dozen other analysts in the room waited, some rising to their feet. Everyone heard static. Then the Texan's voice sounded from the mobile unit in midtown Manhattan. "Ah, no can do. We are mobile."

John sat and began stabbing keys on the computer console. Nanette Sylvestri touched his shoulder. "John?"

"Hang on."

"Talk to me, John! What are you seeing, the rest of us aren't? Thorson's team has to reacquire the targets. You heard Gibron's call. She's not meeting the Syrian on Forty-second. They're—"

"Bennett-Smith," John said, scanning through CIA archives. "That's the name she used when she called the FBI. Hang on . . . hang on . . . Colin Bennett-Smith."

"We know she's meeting Belhadj. The other thing's just a code name."

But John shook his head. "No, he's real. Bennett-Smith. Former MI-6. Mother was Egyptian. He can pass for Middle Eastern. Resigned in 2009 . . . um, alcoholism. . . . Worked with Shin Bet during the first and second intifada. Worked in Fatah camps. Daria Gibron last worked with him . . . ah, seven years ago."

"So what? Either she's using an ex-spook's name as code for Belhadj, or she and Belhadj are meeting this ex-spook. Right?"

He turned and looked up at the woman who—had he been standing—still would have towered over him.

"I don't know. Something isn't scanning. Whether Bennett-Smith is Belhadj, or whether he's meeting Belhadj and Daria, either way: why tell Ray Calabrese about any of it? He's in Los Angeles."

Nanette thought about the chess pieces. "So what are you thinking?"

"That Daria knew she wasn't leaving the message for Calabrese. She was leaving it for us."

Daria took the subway and emerged near Lincoln Center on Sixty-sixth Street. She meandered, enjoying the cityscape. She wanted to give the surveillance team plenty of time to set up.

Her wardrobe was fine for business or air travel but she planned to venture within plain sight of the watchers. That would call for an upgrade. Or more accurately: a downgrade. On a side street, she spotted a funky clothing store that catered to the clubbing scene and the leather crowd. She stepped in, realizing in a heartbeat that, in her early thirties, she was the oldest customer by a decade.

"Hey. We help you?" The clerk was a hunky lad with a shaved skull, a nose ring, and a leather kilt.

Daria waggled her fingers at him and smiled. "Just shopping." Within ten minutes, she'd found a thin, supple, slate-gray lambskin tank, a short latex skirt in silver, and boots with more zippers, studs, and chains than actual leather. She found a black pleather duster so long it actually scraped her boot heels. She found a small tube of molding paste for her hair. "Is there a changing booth?"

She walked up to the counter a few minutes later, hair slicked back and wearing the new clothes plus the very large, plastic-rimmed sunglasses. She paid with cash.

"Here's your change," the young clerk said.

"Thank you."

As she reached the door, he added, "I'm, ah, off at ten. If you'd like to get, you know, a drink or something?"

He was maybe twenty-four years old. This gladdened Daria greatly. "Maybe another time. Have you a stick of gum?"

The kid was only too happy to provide a stick. She folded it in two and slipped it onto her pink tongue. The kid blushed.

Daria strutted out in leather and latex.

Owen Cain Thorson put his CIA team back together on the West Side, near where Broadway cut a diagonal swath through the rigidly gridded blocks. Not easy, given a massive truck and three roof-bound snipers.

Thorson reported to Langley that Project Pegasus was in position at Seventy-second and Broadway a full thirty minutes before the rescheduled 4:00 P.M. meeting. Things were going right for the white hats.

All told, Thorson's team was eighteen people deep: four in the truck, three snipers on the roofs, five pedestrians, and six in vehicles ranging from a Kawasaki motorcycle to a Land Rover. Everyone was in place when the Texan relayed the news from Nanette Sylvestri and John Broom, back in the Shark Tank: the change-of-venue thing might have been a clever con by the Gibron woman.

* * *

Khalid Belhadj's train pulled into Grand Central Terminal at 3:35 P.M. The Syrian, in his shabby suit and too-large hat, drew nobody's attention as he bought a city map and realized he no longer was within walking distance of the rendezvous. He stepped out onto Lexington and hailed a taxi.

Someone in the command truck had pasted a Post-it note over one of the terminals: *leather jacket, jeans, flats, red blouse, shoulder-length straight black hair.* Next to it was the two-year-old photo of Daria in front of a bookstore, wiping shorter hair away from her forehead.

Eighteen pairs of eyes were on the lookout.

Daria stopped along the way and bought a disposable mobile phone with prepaid minutes.

With her hair slicked back and dressed in punk-vogue, the long coat billowing like a cape, Daria strutted past the newly reparked command vehicle, heading toward the subway stop. She chewed her gum enthusiastically because the act of chewing, plus the shadows cast by oversized sunglasses, can fool face-recognition software.

She approached the plaza from the south, oblivious to the cold.

"Hang on."

One of the watchers in the truck used a joystick to zoom in on a female approaching the zone. She was the right height but the leather-and-latex outfit was wrong. Her long thighs pistoned in and out of the duster, revealing comically hip boots. She seemed fifteen years too young for the printed-out profile he'd just scanned. He squinted at the screen. His eyes darted to the Post-it with the wardrobe Daria had been wearing at JFK.

He was about to speak up when the punk girl turned sharply right and stepped into a bank.

Just then, the comms crackled. One of the snipers, fifteen stories off the pavement, spoke into his epaulette mike. "Look alive. We have Bowler."

The Texan adjusted the camera hidden in the roof air vents of the big rig. He panned the sidewalk and Thorson and his men watched the monitor.

Khalid Belhadj, the Syrian terrorist, stood at the crosswalk, waiting for the light to change. He wore a baggy coat and too-large hat, but there was no mistaking those eyes.

Owen Cain Thorson said, "We got the bastard."

Daria was third in line for a bank teller. She kept the sunglasses on and chewed her gum vigorously, aware she was on closed circuit television. When it was her turn, she deferred to people standing behind her. She was waiting for the eldest of the cashiers, the one with *MANAGER* on her name tag.

The bank manager's name tag read *MARY LU.* "Hi. How can we help you today?"

"You are about to be robbed."

The cashier's cheery smile faltered.

Daria had adopted a bad Central European accent. She sounded like an extra in a *Dracula* movie. "Do you see the big, white truck over my left shoulder?"

The manager's blue eyes flickered over Daria's left shoulder.

"See the two men lounging on the bus bench across the way?"

Blue eyes flicked toward the little triangular park, and back again.

"The first thing you should know is that we are heavily armed." Daria pronounced *we* as *vee*. "We represent the People's Army of Slomeria and we are willing to sacrifice our lives and the lives of capitalist fools for our cause. The second thing to know is that we are happy to use our weapons. Yes? The third thing to know is that we have snipers on roofs, so even if our ground troops are compromised, lives will be lost. The fourth thing to know is that my commander will walk in here in ninety seconds with two duffel bags. You will instruct your clerks to empty their tills. You will not call police. Do you understand?"

The manager nodded.

Daria turned and exited the bank.

Once outside, she pivoted away from the CIA command vehicle. She moved quickly but not so quick as to draw too much attention. She was almost half a block from the bank before her hackles twitched. She spotted a man in a raincoat and hat, cross the street. She didn't recognize him, but she knew she knew him. Or *had* known him from somewhere in the past. Dark-haired, compact, unshaven, shoulders tense under the coat, the brimmed hat failing to hide either his unruly hair or the battle-hardened eyes that raked in the scene.

The man was a player. But who?

Remembering her plan, she stroke confidently out of the zone, toward West End Avenue, turning her back on the stranger. She pulled the new mobile phone from her jacket pocket and dialed 911.

She did not call in her own "bank robbery." The bank manager would take care of that. Daria had bigger fish to fry.

Belhadj steeled himself to avoid reacting violently. His fist clenched and he became aware of the weight of the Springfield in its shoulder holster.

The Syrian was not fooled by the leather, latex, and slicked-back hair. He recognized Daria Gibron. He had studied her for years. He knew how she moved, how she walked, the cant of her long, narrow neck, the way her head subtly swiveled, eyes raking the scene.

The meeting in New York was a trap. There was no other explanation. His communication lines were breached, his team in jeopardy.

But if all that was so, why was the damned Daria Gibron walking *away* from the scene?

He wondered what had just happened.

Asher Sahar, Eli Schullman, and two mercenaries repositioned themselves in the Jeep Grand Cherokee to watch the scene unfold.

The Croatian driver pointed through the windshield. "There. Belhadj."

Schullman spotted a young woman dressed for clubbing. "Is that Daria . . . ?"

Asher squinted in that direction, cleaning his glasses on the tail of his cardigan. He watched the woman in the duster stride away.

"No," he whispered. "Keep your eyes on Mr. Belhadj, please."

Asher slid the rounded earpieces of his glasses back into place. He noted the sound of police sirens drawing closer.

Back at Langley, everyone listened to the audio from Thorson's command vehicle. Nanette Sylvestri caught the attention of a tech and nodded to the room's eight flat-screen monitors. "Turn those off."

They no longer had use for the lipstick cameras and the closed circuit video feeds from the now-pointless Forty-second Street rendezvous site.

Two of the on-foot CIA watchers picked a bus bench as a good place to perch. One pretended to text while the other read the *New York Post*. Within seconds of sitting, five NYPD units, sirens blaring and lights flashing, braked hard at the intersection, arriving from Amsterdam Avenue to the north and from Broadway to the south.

A police SWAT van roared in from the west.

Across the street from them, Major Khalid Belhadj knelt to tie his shoelace, his back to the street. When he stood, he was walking in the opposite direction.

* * *

Normally, heading into a bank robbery in progress, police are not sure about the exact nature of the bad guys, their weapons, or their vehicles. Fortunately, the woman who had called this one in was an experienced bank manager and her information had been invaluable. The caller had described the crew, their vehicles, their stakeout positions, even the fact that they had snipers.

A seven-man SWAT unit in Kevlar and helmets leaped out of the armored vehicle and surrounded the white film production truck. Cops from patrol cars organized on the two men sitting on the bus bench. These officers were clockwork itself.

In the truck, Owen Thorson realized just how badly, and quickly, the scene had deteriorated. His well-trained team and the completely contained meeting site melted like dew at dawn. Behind him, the Texan informed Langley.

Across the street, on a roof and leaning next to a tin cube of HVAC vents, the sniper leader watched the scene unfold through his scope. He caught an image of three NYPD officers with binoculars checking the roofs. That's when he heard the approach of police helicopters.

"We are blown, people! Go, go, go!"

The snipers scrambled to disassemble their weapons and abandon their aeries.

From across the street and a block away, Belhadj watched the pandemonium. He noticed that no one was bothering him.

He thought: *Daria Gibron*.

He had no idea what had just happened but he felt certain, to the depths of his soul, that no living person could foul up the works as quickly and cleanly as that hellspawn.

Seven

Operation Pegasus went to hell in a rocket ship.

The command truck was compromised, the watchers on the ground the same. The snipers were in danger of getting their asses shot off by New York's Finest. One of two targets, the Syrian, had appeared, then evaporated during the melee while the second target, the Israeli ex-pat, never even showed up.

Owen Thorson's crew kept a Ziploc baggie of federal shields in the truck. The CIA, for obvious reasons, doesn't carry badges in the field. These faux IDs led to false identities in the Drug Enforcement Administration, which might—*might*—be good enough to get them out of this jam.

Thorson doffed his suit coat to show that he was unarmed, threw open the back door of the truck and, federal shield in hand, descended to the pavement. His two men followed. No sooner had the last man disembarked than SWAT officers began sweeping on board.

"Hey! Hey!" Thorson bellowed, ID pressed forward. "What the hell is this?"

SWAT officers shouted over one another. *"Down! Now! On your knees! Do it!"*

Thorson surged forward. "We are DEA! You get on *your* goddamn knees! Now!"

The New York cops hesitated in the brunt of his obvious command.

"Who's in charge here! *Who's in charge!*"

A man in Kevlar and helmet, his laser target boring a hole in Thorson's sedately striped tie, said, "I'm senior com—"

"This is a federal investigation! Stand your people down! Now!"

"We are investigating a bank robb—"

Thorson thrust his ID into the face of the leading officer. "I am not asking! Stand down! Now!"

Confusion spread among the police officers. The takedown had seemed to be going like a well-rehearsed dance number. But now . . . ?

Television news crews began arriving in microwave trucks. Someone must have called them in advance, since this was record-breaking time even for them. Owen Thorson began to have a very bad feeling.

Cops and spies shouted at one another, arguing for dominance and situational protocol as the news camera crews set up.

Thorson focused on the SWAT officer who identified himself as commander. "I am a federal investigator. Get those camera crews back. My people cannot be photographed at this scene."

"We are gonna call this in but—"

"I'm telling you there's no time! We're with an intelligence unit. We can't be photographed. Entire careers are at stake here. What's your name, mister?"

"Jacob Willis. We're—"

Thorson spoke into his voice wand. "All units, stand down, stand down. Assist local law enforcement! Do it! Get the civilians out of the plaza now." He turned to the SWAT commander. "Willis? This is a federal investigation. Call this in. Call whoever you gotta call in. But keep the camera crews away from my agents!"

Willis made the decision. He toggled his shoulder-mounted mike. "NYPD. We have friendlies. Repeat: Friendlies. We are red for stop. Create a cordon. Street units, keep the media at bay!"

The scene was chaos. Civilians scrambled for cover or reached for cell phone cameras, to show their loved ones and buddies, *Hey! Did you see that on TV? I was in that shit!*

Police and CIA agents hesitated, both sides giving each other wary glares. Both sides wore ear jacks, and both sides had heard their bosses call a truce. But guns were waving; those things are hard to ignore.

In the Grand Cherokee, Asher Sahar watched the melee and sighed theatrically.

Eli Schullman whistled, high-low. "What in the name of a righteous God just happened here?"

Asher absently ran the pad of his forefinger over his old and jagged throat wound. "Oh, I have a few suspicions. But for now, if one of you could place the satchel, please?"

The Cypriot nodded and stepped down from the Jeep, carrying a leather satchel. The man was unarmed, so as to eliminate any chance of encountering police or the CIA. He quickly melted into the chaos of civilians in the plaza scrum.

Both cops and CIA agents began hearing more sirens approach. Someone called it in to the NYPD unit on scene. "Commander Willis!" a lieutenant shouted. "We got a bomb threat!"

NYPD Commander Jacob Willis and Owen Cain Thorson said, "What?" almost in harmony.

"Bomb threat, sir! Disposal units are en route. It's not the bank! It's the bookstore!"

The commanding police officer and the commander of Operation Pegasus turned together to look at the bookstore.

Commander Willis hesitated. He was still wrapping his head around a federal drug operation broken by a bank robbery. The words *bomb threat* pinged around his brain like a pinball. "It's . . . what?"

Back at Langley, John Broom took advantage of the single most important piece of technology in the room, the coffeepot. He lowered himself down onto the second of three steps in the auditorium-style room, elbows on his knees.

Nanette Sylvestri, all joints and angles, rested her rear on the closest desk. "Hey."

John looked up.

"You were right. You called it. We were being played by this Daria Gibron."

John gave her an obligatory smile. "Cold comfort."

She stood, taking a second to touch John's shoulder with her fingertips, as if to say thanks.

"Why'd she do it?" John asked.

"Hmm?"

But he was staring at his coffee. "Why'd she do it?"

Nanette thought that was obvious. "Gibron? To shake her surveillance."

He slowly shook his head. "No. That was the shtick on Forty-second Street. The Life and Death code to move our carnival uptown. If her goal was to shake her surveillance, all she had to do was move south, away from the scene. What's with the bank job and the bomb scare?"

He looked up at Sylvestri, looming over him, as he sat on the stairs.

"She's not done."

A bomb disposal unit from the New York Police Department was still three blocks away as NYPD Commander Willis oversaw the civilian evacuation.

The bookstore occupied a corner storefront in the building that stretched over the six-way intersection and stood eight stories tall. It housed more than fifty businesses, both small and mid-sized. A police dispatcher began the protocol of contacting building security who, in turn, began calling the businesses. The evacu-

ation had been practiced often enough since September
2001.

The street scene was chaotic. People streamed out of
the building, slamming into one another. Others got
stuck in the revolving doors as hordes tried to jam
through the exits. A subway train had arrived and commuters, unawares, sauntered out into the insanity.

Police began cordoning off Seventy-second Street
(east to west), Amsterdam Avenue (north to south) and
Broadway, which slashed laterally between them. They
didn't have barricades yet, so they used their patrol cars.

Owen Thorson glanced back to see that one of
his team had the foresight to take the wheel of the white
truck and was moving it out of the likely blast radius.

Security officers in the bank directed customers
to the exit, then quickly locked down all the tills and
set the weekend alert for the vault. They were the only
people in a three-block radius still wondering if a bank
heist was under way.

Television news helicopters roared overhead.

Thorson glanced around. His eyes hunted Daria Gibron and Khalid Belhadj. He also kept an eye out for
the heavy cameras and bulky microphones of TV re-
porters. Which is why his vision slid past the handful
of bloggers and correspondents using their cell phones
for still photos and video.

The sweep of the bookstore and coffee shop took
twenty minutes. The bomb squad found no evidence of
any explosive devices.

The debriefing of the bank manager ended up with a description of the robbery suspect—a young woman in leather and latex with a dystopian duster out of some futuristic western. The robber also had described Thorson's command vehicle, some of his pedestrian watchers and his snipers.

At Thorson's request, Commander Willis had secured a camera shop for the federal agents to hole up. But by that time, at least two images of the imbroglio—showing CIA agents—had been posted on New York media Web sites.

Thorson's head reeled as the enormity of the disaster struck him. He stood inside the camera shop, fists clenched at his side, looking at a news Web site and the photo of one of his own men.

Another agent surged into the shop, spotted Thorson, and crossed to him. He held a beat-up leather satchel with a bowed handle.

"What's this?"

The agent yanked open the mouth of the satchel, revealing a silenced handgun and two extra clips. Another agent joined them and withdrew a manila envelope. He opened it, fanned out a sheaf of legal-size sheets. Some were scrawled in Arabic. Others showed meticulous diagrams, etched by a steady hand holding a hard-nibbed pen.

"I read Arabic," the agent holding the satchel said. "We found this where Belhadj had been standing. He must have dropped it and run."

Thorson studied the sheets. "Is it about the president?"

"Yes, sir."

"Emory University?"

"No, sir. These are aerial and topographic maps. Look!"

Owen Cain Thorson blinked. Several times. "Oh hell."

"Yes, sir. No doubt about it. This is Camp David!"

Another CIA agent burst into the room, eyes wild.

Thorson turned to him. Something in the man's demeanor set off his alarms. Fortunately, Thorson thought, the situation likely couldn't get any worse.

"What?"

"The, ah, our command vehicle, sir."

"Right. I saw someone move it out of the bomb radius? That was good thinking."

"That's just it, sir. That wasn't us. Hill caught sight of it, a block from here, heading east."

"Wait . . . what?"

"He said there was a woman at the wheel, sir. Slicked-back hair, leather coat. It, ah . . . it may have been the Gibron woman, sir."

In the Shark Tank at Langley, Nanette Sylvestri spun to look at the guy manning the primary communication array. "Say again?"

"Field team says the target isn't the president's speech tomorrow in Atlanta! It's Camp David!"

Sylvestri was at the room's bank of secure phones before the word *David* was out of the man's mouth. She had just begun to enter a number when, with a blink, all the feeds from Manhattan died. The audio, the screens, Thorson's team comms, the computer monitor links. Everything.

Eight

The Tunnel Rat of Rafah had grown from malnourished to lean and strong. The Bedouin cousins who employed him grew rich and—as is the way everywhere in the world—the authorities on both the Egyptian side and the Gaza Strip side got a taste of the profits.

The cousins' second tunnel was twice as wide and much better lit. The third through fifth tunnels had tracks, cables, and hydraulic pulleys on either side to move the goods and the profits. The flatbed, small-gauge rail car in the fifth tunnel could move the component parts of a car. Or a cow.

The Tunnel Rat of Rafah was now ten years old—although he couldn't have told you his birth date or exact age—and supervised the distribution of goods in the alleys and back parlors of the Gaza side.

The Bedouin cousins still didn't know the boy's provenance or name. They brought in Iraqi tunnel diggers—those guys knew how to dig!—and the Iraqis called the boy "Kahlet." It meant "filthy beggar." The Tunnel Rat of Rafah was far too keen an entrepreneur to deserve the epithet. But he also didn't complain.

Increasingly, he was given control of the most vital cargos. It took him some time to realize they were guns and explosives.

New York City

Daria disconnected the power for all the communications equipment in the CIA command vehicle. She ducked under the steering wheel and dug around for the inevitable GPS transmitter. She tossed it out the window and pulled back into Manhattan traffic.

She had driven massive, three-axle dinosaurs during her stint in the Israeli army. Those standard-transmission beasts had been hell to drive. In comparison, the command vehicle purred like a Lexus coupe.

Her trainers drilled into their young charge's head: *It's called "intelligence" for a reason. Before you act, learn all that you can.*

The operational command vehicle had been Daria's true target since she identified it back on Forty-second Street. If "intelligence" was the brass ring, this rig seemed ideal.

The Grand Cherokee wound its way to the Queens Midtown Tunnel. Nobody minded the traffic. They had nowhere to be and no one was looking for them. Everyone knew the basic tenet of the operation—to perpetuate a massive distraction for the American intelligence community—had been a rousing success.

However, none of the four in the SUV cheered.

Eli Schullman turned his thick bulk as far as the passenger-side seat belt would allow and turned to Asher Sahar in the back. "That was interesting."

Asher smiled. "Wasn't it?"

The Cypriot driver looked perplexed. "The targets? Gibron and Belhadj. I don't understand. I thought we had them. What happened? One second, we were in control. The next . . . police."

The Croat mercenary in the other back seat grunted. "Lots of police. Waves of police."

Asher squeezed his eyes shut and listened to the traffic. He played back the scene of chaos in his head. The whole thing: it had Daria Gibron's signature. Only that woman could take his well-crafted scenario and turn it into comedia del'arte. Asher admired her so much. Now she was free and would soon get involved in Asher's plans. Plus, the Syrian butcher, who had been digging into his operation, was free as well. It was a tactical nightmare.

"We accomplished our primary goal. Will Halliday will be heading our way soon. Get us to the rally point, please."

His phone vibrated. He checked the incoming message and spoke to the others in the car. "We accomplished our primary goal. Will Halliday will be heading our way soon."

He scrolled through his message. "Drop me off, next corner, please."

Schullman started to speak but Asher smiled at him. "I have unfinished business. I'll catch up."

The Cherokee pulled over. "Damn," the Cypriot groused. "Losing the Syrian fucker was bad enough. But Gibron never even arrived!"

Eli Schullman stayed twisted in his seat. His eyes locked on Asher Sahar. The old friends stared at each other for a few silence-sodden seconds.

"No," Schullman eventually agreed. "She never even arrived."

Los Angeles

FBI agent Ray Calabrese didn't bother going to his West Hollywood condo to pack. He kept a gym bag at work with underwear, undershirts, socks, and a toiletry kit. Plus extra ammunition clips. Within minutes of reading the CIA report on Daria and the plot to kill the president, Ray was in a cab to LAX.

Ray was in line for the United check-in desk when his BlackBerry chirped. It was L.A. Station Chief Henry Deits.

"Heads-up. Spookville is going nutso over this thing with Daria. I don't know what happened, but the alerts just upgraded from a number one priority."

Ray willed the line ahead of him to move faster. "What the hell's the upgrade from a number one priority?"

"Though I walk through the valley. . . ."

"Got it." Ray rubbed his face with one beefy, open hand. He liked to think he had a good grasp on Daria Gibron's ability to create havoc. Once again, he had underestimated her.

"She's still listed as a threat?"

"Al-Qaida, Daria Gibron, North Korea. In that order."

The line moved forward almost seven inches. "Okay. Thanks. Try to run interference for me, boss. Let them know the bureau isn't sitting this one out. She is one of ours."

Henry said, "Done," and disconnected.

The line moved forward another two inches. Ray held his temper rather than shoot everyone in front of him. He checked his phone and scrolled through the buffer of intelligence circulars, looking for Daria's name.

A routine notification had gone out to all law enforcement personnel. A river levee had been breached in Colorado. A motel had been swept away. No word yet on a cause or casualties.

Langley, Virginia

The same routine notification also popped up on John Broom's tablet computer in the Shark Tank at Langley. The Genevieve River had roared over a broken levee and had wiped out several businesses and homes. Out of idle curiosity, John surfed over to a weather Web site. It had snowed three days earlier in Colorado. Other than that, the weather had been mild.

Odd timing for a levee failure, John thought, his attention returning to Operation Pegasus in Manhattan.

Upstate New Jersey

Daria found a construction site in New Jersey and pulled in. The site appeared to be vacant and had a couple weeks' worth of trash and debris to show for it. It included a rusty, corrugated covering, perfect for hiding electrical equipment during rain and snowstorms. She parked beneath it.

She had to find a secure way to contact Collin Bennett-Smith and explain her no-show at Grand Central. She just had to hope he hadn't been swept up in all of this—whatever *this* was.

She rested her forehead on the steering wheel a moment, feeling the adrenaline drain away. She had orchestrated the fake bank robbery and the bomb scare to gain access to the command vehicle. She was positive an intelligence agency was behind her surveillance and the obvious trap in Manhattan.

Dee Jean D'Arc . . .

Daria . . . you are burned.

Then there was the question of the dark-skinned man she had seen crossing the street back in Manhattan. She was furious at herself for not attaching a name to the face, but she was sure she had seen him before.

Daria got busy searching the truck. It took her all of two minutes to confirm the rig belonged to the Central Intelligence Agency. *When did I make an enemy of them?* she wondered. Among the first things she found was a thermos of coffee. She also found a baggie with a roast beef sandwich and a bag of salt-and-pepper Kettle Chips. Such good hosts, the CIA. Her next big find was a folder with a file on the operation. She was a little surprised that a CIA hit-team would bring paper documents, but perhaps the op had come together too fast to brief everyone beforehand.

She noted the name of the takedown operation: *Pegasus?* Her Greek was rusty. Wasn't that some kind of horse?

A horse? Bastards. Why not go all in and call her a fat cow?

She doffed the capelike coat, sat at a command desk, massive boots up on the table, ankles crossed, drank coffee, ate the sandwich and chips, and began studying the file. There was no word on her old friend, Colin Bennett-Smith. But the first name she saw floored her.

Khalid Belhadj.

Syrian assassin, soldier, and spy.

That's the man she'd seen crossing the street.

Belhadj!

She swore in a half-dozen tongues.

Belhadj?

When she recovered from the shock, she read on. According to the CIA, Daria wasn't meeting Bennett-Smith. She was meeting Belhadj. And (or so said the file) she would be selling him a sniper rifle. Their target: the president of the United States. The CIA mission had been to capture or kill both Daria and Belhadj.

The wording was crystal clear. There were no colloquialisms, like *terminate* or *remove*. The file said *capture* or *kill*. Both outcomes were sanctioned.

She read the file, front to back. She scrounged around for a pen and discovered a hidden cache; a Ziploc baggie of three chocolate chip cookies. It was maybe her best discovery yet.

She nibbled the cookies and read the file again, front to back, this time jotting notes.

The situation was very bad. Much worse than she'd imagined.

She and Khalid Belhadj? If the CIA believed all this, who was spoon-feeding it to them? Who had sent her the fake e-mail from her old friend, which lured her into the killing field?

And who had dredged up the ancient code from her childhood, warning her at JFK that she was walking into a trap. *Dee Jean D'Arc.* . . . That code predated Colin Bennett-Smith and Shin Bet and her service in the Israeli Army. For Daria, that code predated puberty.

It was the code of a long-dead woman.

Meanwhile, there was the Belhadj problem. Was this his operation? The man wasn't known as brilliant but he was famous for his dogged determination. What he lacked in imagination he more than made up in guts. Yes, she thought, Belhadj had the balls to carry out a mission on U.S. soil.

But why her? Why drag Daria into this? They had never met. To the best of her knowledge, the Syrian bastard didn't even know she existed. To her, his was just a face studied in scores of PowerPoint presentations, dozens of computer searches.

Finished with the file, Daria searched the command vehicle again. She found a locked steel cabinet. She recognized it as a weapons cache. She retrieved one of the truck's fire extinguishers, pleased that Americans are so thorough in their safety protocols. She turned the tank upside down and used the nitrogen propellant to freeze the lock on the steel cabinet. She reversed the extinguisher, right-side up, and brought it down heavily on the lock.

The cabinet revealed an elegant and opulent array of CIA weapons. She smiled. Handguns, shotguns, stun guns, sniper rifles with sights, Tasers, machine guns. Even a Browning Automatic Rifle. "These are a few of my favourite things . . ." she sang softly.

She dug around some more and found a gym bag with a change of clothes. The owner must have been around five-eight: his clothes could be altered to fit her and she felt foolish in the clubbing outfit.

She took the thermos of coffee and a couple of energy bars and shoved them into a tote. She found a personal cell phone. She almost dialed Ray Calabrese's mobile from memory but paused. It would be better if Ray stayed well clear of this mess for the time being. She would fill him in later, if necessary. She pried the back off the mobile and scanned it for CIA tracking chips. She found one, ripped it out, ground it under her heel, and jammed the mobile into the tote.

Daria prepared a carryall with a change of clothing, all the money she could find from the agents' bags, and enough weaponry to start—and finish—a decent firefight. She moved forward to the cabin of the truck and checked the front and side windows. She'd drawn no police and, as near as they could tell, no CIA.

She took the Project Pegasus (*a fucking horse?*) file, jammed it into the bag, threw open the rear door of the truck and hopped out.

Khalid Belhadj stood behind the command vehicle and pointed a Springfield Auto at her clavicle.

Colorado

Two time zones to the West, Will Halliday finished his breakfast—a frosted Pop-Tart and instant coffee—and stepped out of the mountain cabin he and Asher Sahar's two mercenaries were using as a base.

The mercenaries both asked about the logic of staying in Colorado after ripping off and killing the Secret Service team and blowing up a river levee. Better to put as much space between them and their crimes as possible, no? But Halliday had insisted on holing up in the isolated cabin.

The mercenaries were named Sacchs and Veigel, so of course the big, blond American insisted on calling them "Sex" and "Violence," which he accompanied with a horselaugh and a slap on the shoulder every time he said it. Neither Sacchs nor Veigel thought the joke was very funny.

The coffee was vile and Will Halliday stepped outside the cabin to toss the last half-cup into the grass. He took a deep intake of breath, marveling in the pine-forest aromas of the place. He had grown up in rural areas not unlike this hunting cabin. He didn't miss not being city-bound.

"Yo! Sacchs!" He called back into the three-room, two-story cabin.

Moments later, the taciturn mercenary emerged with his jacket and shades.

Halliday slapped him on the back. "Gimme a hand."

Together, the big American and the dour Israeli managed to get the titanium metal canister and its cooling unit out of the panel truck and hauled it about twenty yards to a two-engine Piper Cheyenne II, which sat on a long field of grass behind the cabin. The devices were heavy as they lifted them up into the fuselage, which stood high on its tricycle landing gear. The canister and the cooling unit were sophisticated, state-of-the-art technology, and while Sacchs was a good soldier, he was no rocket scientist. He didn't know why, once the devices were stored in the fuselage, Halliday made him hold the canister stable as the ex–Secret Service agent tapped an eight-digit string of numbers onto the device's keypad.

Halliday checked his watch, counted to ten seconds, then tapped five more keys.

"Good. It's stable," he said.

Sacchs grunted and backed his torso out of the fuselage. He turned, wordless, and began walking toward the cabin.

Halliday inhaled the fresh air and watched the Israeli walk away. He leaned into the cockpit. From beneath the pilot's left-hand seat, he retrieved one of the many disposable, prepaid cell phones that Asher Sahar preferred. He hit speed dial 1.

The connection clicked. Halliday said, "I picked Sacchs."

Asher Sahar's voice came back soft, calm, and slightly sibilant. "He is infected?"

"Sure is."

"Veigel?"

"Twenty yards away and inside the cabin. No way he's infected. Not from the canister."

Halliday listened to the hiss of long-distance static. "Thank you, Will. Now . . . I suppose we'll see what happens."

"We sure as shit will! See you *mañana*."

Halliday hung up, then disassembled the cell phone and spread its parts around the grassy field.

Nine

A satchel full of guns is of little value against a .45 automatic pointed at your chest.

Khalid Belhadj was a tightly wound, compact man, not quite five feet ten inches, with longish hair and a five-day stubble of beard. His nose had been broken and ill-repaired. His eyes were the same blue-gray color as the marble cutting board one of Daria's lovers used for making bread.

Daria dropped the carryall on the asphalt. "You're Belhadj."

"Climb back into the truck, please." Like many Syrians, Belhadj spoke English with a British accent.

Daria turned and climbed up onto the truck's steel bumper, then into the truck. She walked halfway to the cab before feeling the floor move as Belhadj joined her. She turned to face him.

He studied the busted-open weapons cache. He

spied several sets of handcuffs and keys. He grabbed a set with his left hand and lobbed them to Daria.

She caught them and considered hurling them straight back into his face, but she could tell by his body language he had anticipated that.

Daria cuffed her wrists behind her back. She recognized his Springfield auto as an XD-45, which meant it held a clip of ten rounds, plus a bullet likely already chambered.

Belhadj made a spinning symbol with one upraised finger. Daria turned her back to him. She felt his hand play along both cuffs but could tell he did so by leaning forward, his shins and balls beyond kicking distance.

"Sit."

Daria slid into one of the chairs fixed to the steel floor.

Belhadj kept the .45 trained on her chest. But his eyes glanced around the interior of the truck.

"Stealing a CIA command vehicle. My God."

Daria crossed her knees, knowing it would cause the latex skirt to ride up her tanned thighs. Perhaps she could draw him a little closer. "Pulling a mission on American soil? That's some rare combination of brave and stupid, yes?"

Belhadj shrugged, the barrel of the auto not moving a millimeter. If he had noticed her very short skirt, he gave no indication. "What are you doing here?"

"You're saying you didn't lure me here?"

She could tell by his slate-gray eyes that Belhadj was calculating that last bit of data.

"No," he said. "I did not lure you here. But now I know who did."

He started looking around the inside of the truck, paying attention to the forced-open weapons cabinet. "This will be difficult for your Zionist-trained mind to understand, but I am not the bad guy." He shrugged. "Not today, anyway."

"No?"

"No. You and I were supposed to stumble into each other so those CIA bastards could capture or kill us. Probably the latter."

"And why would they do that? You and I have never met."

Belhadj paused, studied her. A mannequin could not have shown less emotion. "Never met," he repeated, as if tasting the words. He stepped away from the weapons cabinet. "Are the cuffs too tight?"

Daria shrugged, noncommittal.

"Turn around."

She swiveled slowly in the seat, causing the skirt to rise up even further on her taut thighs. Belhadj was human (she assumed). Surely he would notice and be distracted. She braced her punk boots under her center of gravity. When he reached for the cuffs, Daria braced herself and—

Belhadj jammed a disposable hypodermic needle into Daria's shoulder, then quickly stepped back.

"What?"

He shrugged. "It was in the weapons locker."

She turned to him in fury and could feel the trailer start to spin.

"Knowing the CIA, there's a one-in-three chance this is a narcotic designed to incapacitate us for quiet extraction."

Daria's vision blurred. "That means there's a two-in-three chance it's a lethal dose. Not for extraction at all."

Belhadj shrugged again. "Well, that's the CIA for you."

Daria blacked out and slid to the floor.

Washington, D.C.

The longtime executive assistant to Stanley Cohen knew when to pull her boss out of a meeting on Capitol Hill, which normally was verboten.

Cohen took the message in the office of a senior Republican House member and stepped out to the stuffy, high-ceilinged corridor of the House Office Building. He waited until congressional staffers—they all looked like teenagers—were out of hearing distance and called his assistant back.

"Did Pegasus obtain its objectives?"

"No," she said simply.

"They lost the suspects?"

"Oh, they lost a little more than that."

In the Shark Tank, Nanette Sylvestri realized that Pegasus wasn't going to be a quick-and-clean, home-by-dinner kind of operation. She sent her people home, a third of them at a time, with orders to eat and sleep, to be ready for a marathon day to come.

Six hours later, John Brooms's wristwatch beeped once, softly. He was instantly awake. John extricated

himself from the mad maypole of twisted sheets and
soft legs and strawberry blond hair in his Georgetown
apartment. He kissed the girl in his bed softly, so as not
to wake her. He showered and shaved and threw on
Hugo Boss. He lingered over his choice of tie for almost four minutes.

He kissed the sleepy girl again, packed his Vuitton
overnight kit, and dashed.

The second the front wheels of the 747 touched down at
Reagan National, Ray Calabrese whipped out his cell
phone and a small notebook bound with a black elastic
strap. He looked up numbers for FBI agents with whom
he had worked in the past. The jet hadn't yet sloughed
off all its momentum when a flight attendant caught
Ray's eye. He badged her and she remained seated.

Ray called the D.C. headquarters to make sure the
brass there was up to speed with the CIA investigation.
He got a friend he'd known since Quantico, and began
filling her in.

"Whoa, whoa. Ray? This thing you're talking about.
This was in Manhattan?"

"Yeah." The 747 veered off the runway and headed
toward the domestic terminal.

Ray's friend laughed into the phone. "Normally,
the CIA doesn't share so good, and you know that. But
Manhattan . . . Hey, Ray. Want the ultimate get-out-of-
jail-free card?"

Ray grinned. "Hit me."

She told him the latest rumor about a stolen CIA
command vehicle.

* * *

By the time passengers began getting off the 747, Ray had made similar calls to FBI agents in New York City and back home in Los Angeles. He'd scribbled three pages of notes. Information is power, and Ray Calabrese felt armed to the teeth.

A bearded man in a dark suit waited for him inside the terminal. He recognized Ray and flashed him a laminated business card. Most passersby wouldn't have recognized it for what it was: the man's CIA bona fides.

"Agent Calabrese?"

Ray shifted his gym bag to his left hand and shook.

"Burke Evans, CIA. We got the call that you were en route. You're here about the Daria Gibron situation."

Ray nodded tersely.

"Did you check in any luggage?"

"No. I came quick and packed light because it's Daria. Trust me: when she puts her mind to it, she can get into trouble faster than anyone I ever met."

"So we understand." The CIA liaison had a soft Southern accent; Virginia, maybe, Ray thought. "She's on the run, Agent Calabrese. If you can help bring her in . . . ?"

"She's not your enemy."

"And we are not assuming anything at this time. But we need to know what she knows. Come on. I'm parked this way."

They began walking quickly in the direction of ground transportation. Ray reached into the front pocket of his flight-rumpled trousers and pulled out his cell phone.

The CIA agent spoke just loudly enough for Ray alone to hear. "Do you know a Khalid Belhadj?"

"Who?"

"Belhadj. Syrian intelligence. We believe Ms. Gibron is running with him."

When some people fly, they feel brisk and refreshed upon landing. Ray wasn't one of those people. He'd been involved in a crash a few years earlier, which had left him with—if not a fear of flying—an intense anxiousness. He felt slow of foot and a little foggy as he dodged people with rolling baggage. "You think she's running with a Syrian spy?"

"You don't think it's possible?"

Ray didn't answer. Daria had been many things to him. A friend, a fellow fighter, an FBI resource. Possibly, maybe more. But mostly she was an enigma. Could she be running with a Syrian agent? Sure. She'd run with a cadre of Ulster Irish terrorists one time, just to keep tabs on them.

But Ray kept mum.

The smaller man led Ray out of the airport, into the short-term parking lot. They marched the length of the lot, hooked a right at the last row of cars, and kept marching.

Ray frowned at his cell phone. He had no waiting messages. Where was she? "Look, I'm here in an advisory capacity only. But I speak for the highest echelon of the bureau when I tell you, Daria's on our side. If she's running with some Syrian, it's his bad luck. Are we clear on this?"

The agent smiled without mirth. "Advisory capacity?"

"That's right."

They rounded a gaggle of pilots and flight attendants with matching luggage. "Then advise, Agent Calabrese. Please. We'll use every resource the FBI and the CIA have to find her."

They walked into the parking garage. They had marched the width of the short-term lot and were as far from the terminal as they could get. "Can you get a hold of her?"

"No," Ray admitted. "I've tried her cell. She has a Web site and I've left messages there. Nothing."

"Any theories about contacting her?"

Ray said. "Yes: hang with me. She'll get in touch with me. Guaranteed."

Agent Evans turned left at the last row of cars. "You're absolutely—I mean, *absolutely*—sure she'll get in touch with you?"

"Absolutely."

They angled toward the last car in the lot. The overhead lights were out back here. Ray said, "This one?" and was half a step ahead of Agent Evans, who had stopped walking. Ray heard the distinctive sound of an auto leaving a leather holster. He tried to react, but searing pain enveloped him. He stumbled forward, bag falling. Ray slid between the last car and a cement retaining wall.

Ray tried to stop his fall but his body refused to react. He knew he'd been shot. Shot in the back. But his brain was refusing the information being sent to it, and Ray struggled to get his feet under him.

The smallish man with the sparse beard knelt. Ray tried to raise his fists and couldn't tell if he had. He noticed the fake CIA agent had a crescent-shaped scar on his throat. He also looked calm and capable, as if he back-shot federal agents all the time.

He watched the man lower himself to one knee and holster a sound-suppressed auto. The man's soft brown eyes scanned the parking lot. Ray tried to shout. He tried to fight. He felt his vision blur.

"For what it's worth, I tried to shoot you four years ago," the bearded man spoke softly. "Daria stepped in the way. I don't tell you this to make you feel better. I just thought you should know. I wish other options had presented themselves. Then and now."

He retrieved Ray's wallet and shield, plus the gym bag.

Stay awake! Ray screamed inside his head. *Hit this bastard!*

From his angle, Ray saw the door of another car open three parking spaces away. A man in a crisp airline uniform struggled to undo his seat belt to stand. The stranger shouted, "Hey!"

The false CIA agent with the calm brown eyes stood, drew his gun again. Ray heard the *phutt* and saw the man in the airline uniform slump back into his sedan. He slumped forward, landing on his car horn, which began blaring.

The false agent gathered Ray's wallet and bag, and disappeared from sight.

Ray tried to get his hands under him to push up. He tried to remember which pocket had his phone. He thought, *Daria. Damn it. Hang on. I'll be okay. Stay. . . .*

He passed out.

Langley, Virginia
The Next Morning

John Broom got to Langley and went directly to his cubicle, only to find a wicker basket wrapped in green cellophane, with an array of dried meats, cheeses, condiments, and crackers. In it was a card from his soon-to-be-boss, the chief of staff to Senator Singer Cavanaugh, which read:

> *Welcome to the Jungle*
>   *—Axl Rose*

John set his leather bag under his desk and booted up his computer. After it ran through its security sweep, he checked his overnights.

Ever since 9/11, the U.S. intelligence community had done a marginally better job of sharing information. Any analyst could use the joint database as a sophisticated search engine. Plug in key words and, overnight, any news flash or intelligence collected on that topic would be downloaded to a buffer.

John had tagged more than three hundred key words.

He synced his computer tablet, then grabbed a cup of coffee and headed to the elevators and the subterranean Ops Room. Head down, scrolling through the overnights on the tablet held in the crook of his forearm,

John was within a few steps of the Shark Tank when he noticed the din.

The room had been fifteen people deep the day before, as Pegasus had turned itself into *The Muppets Take Manhattan*. This morning, the number ranged closer to fifty. People shouted over one another. Everyone wore the CIA's mandatory photo ID on lanyards. Technicians shoehorned in temporary workstations were ripping up false floors to run high-speed wire. A U.S. Marine guarded the door with a sidearm and a ferocious scowl.

Nanette Sylvestri stepped up next to John, winter coat over her forearm. Standing side by side, she was three inches taller in flat riding boots.

John said, "What the hell?"

"The threat nexus has changed."

"The aerials of Camp David?"

"This is a huge security breach, and in the worst hands imaginable. Time we sat at the grown-up table."

John marveled at the chaos. "Are you still running the room?"

Sylvestri said simply, "Sort of."

John didn't pry. The older woman pointed to the overnights scrolling across his tablet computer. "Anything of interest?"

"Not much. A high-ranking Saudi royal prince is in D.C. He's voiced support for Hezbollah, or at least a thawing of relations."

Sylvestri pondered but only for a half second. "Could be something."

"Yeah. You know that flood in Colorado yesterday? Secret Service lost a convoy team."

She shook her head, distracted as she checked e-mails on her BlackBerry. "Doesn't sound connected to our thing."

John agreed. He checked his voice mails. They had stacked up, as they do every night he actually went home. One caught his eye.

"Hey! Hold on a sec."

John pressed the phone to his ear, listened to the message. He began to smile.

Nanette said, "What?"

"Remember the FBI agent from Los Angeles? Daria Gibron's handler? His name's Ray Calabrese. He called me. He's flying in to help."

Nanette thought about that. "Okay. Soon as he makes contact, you want to be his liaison?"

"Thought you'd never ask."

She lay a hand on his shoulder. "Liaison only, John. You are to help Calabrese help us to reel her in."

John nodded.

"I know you vetted her. But do you honestly believe that she's on the side of the angels? That, somehow, single-handedly, she fell into a CIA trap, then outwitted eighteen agents on the ground, and walked away with our command vehicle?"

John had to admit that the scenario was hard to swallow.

"This is much bigger than we thought. She probably has a full team on the ground. She and Belhadj. We thought they were marching into our trap. We marched into theirs."

"You think?"

Sylvestri nodded, emphatic. "Got to be. Question is: what brings the Mukhabarat to Manhattan?"

John smiled up at her. "What are you, Stephen Sondheim?"

Six floors straight up, Stanley Cohen stood at the side table in his office and fixed himself an Alka-Seltzer. He hoped the speakerphone didn't pick up the fizz. He'd been laying the groundwork for Operation Pegasus to move up the food chain. It had been designated as the number one priority operation for the U.S. intelligence community. Cohen also had ironed out the power-sharing agreement with domestic intelligence and law enforcement. Everyone agreed that the CIA should stay in command, although the agency had suffered one of the most blisteringly humiliating losses in memory. Keeping the CIA in command had cost a lot of markers.

Cohen heard a tight, vaguely military rap-rap on his door and knew who it was. "Come!"

Owen Cain Thorson entered and silently slid the door closed behind him. He had doffed his suit coat but his shirt was neatly pressed, tie firmly knotted under his chin, cuffs rolled down and linked. He was holding his emotions as tightly pressed as his trousers.

Stanley Cohen was not a big man, barely coming up to Thorson's shoulders. But he was a three-decade vet of the agency and everyone knew that didn't happen by accident. His finger hovered over the disconnect button on his phone. "Folks? Get back to you."

He hit the button and gulped the fizzy drink.

Thorson stood at parade rest.

Cohen swiped hands through his thinning ginger hair. "What the hell, Owen? I'm asking, here: what the holy hell happened?"

Thorson, whom no one would call jovial, seethed with anger. His blush reached from his face all the way down and into the collar of his tailored shirt.

"We got ambushed, sir. They saw us coming."

Cohen dug Tums out of his pocket, feeling pretty confident the seltzer wasn't going to cut the acid currently gnawing through his stomach. "And by *they* you mean an ex-spook who doesn't weigh one-twenty soaking wet, and a Syrian who you had eyes on and was well covered?"

After a beat, Thorson nodded. "Yes, sir."

"Tell me about the command vehicle."

"One or both of the targets staged a bank robbery. They told the cops about the truck, my spotters, and even the sniper team. They called in police to screw with us, get us out of the command vehicle. Then they called in a bomb scare. I . . ."

Thorson steeled himself, fists locked behind his back, shoulders straight. The last few hours had been as lousy a time as he had ever experienced since joining the agency.

"I saw the truck, sir. I saw it pulling away, after the NYPD team had cleared us out. I figured one of my men was moving it away from the bomb blast zone."

Stanley Cohen wanted a smoke so bad. Instead, he chewed another antacid. "Thank you, Agent Thorson. A few minor questions. Was the command vehicle armed?"

The muscles in Thorson's jaw clenched. "Yes, sir. Small arms and assault weapons."

"Okay. Good. Thank you. Second question: were you carrying the classified case file of Operation Pegasus?"

Thorson's nostrils flared. For a second, the deputy director was sure the big man was going to deck him.

"Yes, sir. There was no time to debrief the team here and—"

"I see. So they know everything we know about their operation. We shared every scrap of intel we had. And, as an added bonus, we armed them."

The glaring, brick-red agent nodded. Behind his back, his knuckles were white. Stanley let the moment linger a couple of seconds.

"Did they swipe your lunch money, Owen?"

Thorson remained frozen at parade rest, almost shaking with barely contained anger.

The ADAT chewed his chalky tablets. Silence reigned for almost a minute. Finally, Cohen crossed to his desk and picked up a remote control. He aimed it at the small television mounted on the wall across from the windows. It popped on. The scroll at the bottom read *FOX NEWS.* The frozen image showed people milling about on the streets of New York. The image had been shot from a great distance, with impressive depth of field. Four of the clearly identifiable people were CIA agents.

CIA agents who are forbidden to operate on American soil.

Cohen said, "You are relieved of operational command. I am reassigning you to head up a tactical team, to be deployed whenever the targets resurface. That'll be all. Report to the Ops Room."

Thorson stood his ground.

"Owen?"

"None of my guys saw this coming. No one—"

"I've reviewed the goddamn transcripts. The Shark Tank called it in. John fucking Broom called it in. The only *field* that man's ever been in had croquet hoops! But he saw through the con. You ignored your analysts and got your ass handed to you!" Cohen almost never raised his voice. This was the exception. "You didn't just get a beat-down from a tactical perspective. You got embarrassed. You got embarrassed on television and in three local newspapers! Not to mention *The Daily Show* and *The Colbert Report*! And you embarrassed me for assigning you the case. This has political ramifications. Or didn't you know the CIA is a political entity? Jesus, Owen!"

"Sir, they—"

"Look." Cohen reached for his desk and whisked up an old-fashioned, square, pink while-you-were-out memo. "I got a call from the office of the legal counsel of the Congressional Joint Intelligence Oversight Committee. This message came, oh, let's say twenty minutes after *The Today Show* ran a still photo showing CIA agents standing on the streets of Manhattan with their thumbs up their asses. You tell me, Owen: coincidence? Or does the fucking office of the legal counsel of the fucking congressional Joint Intelligence fucking Oversight Committee want to chat about that?"

Thorson vibrated with anger. He tried to respond but the glint of steel in Cohen's eyes shut up the younger man.

"Gibron and Belhadj are threats to the president. For that reason we hunt them down. But they fucking embarrassed the Central Intelligence Agency. They made us—not you, Owen, *us*!—look like baboons. I don't want them just *hunted* down. I want them *put* down. Am I clear, Agent Thorson?"

"Yes, sir!"

"Dismissed. Get your ass down to the Shark Tank."

Will Halliday piloted the Cheyenne II as it crossed out of Colorado airspace and into Nebraska. Veigel sat in the right-hand seat. Sacchs sat in back with the titanium canister and cooling unit.

Halliday whistled as he flew. Thanks to everyone's headsets and microphones, the two Israelis had no choice but to listen to his off-key repertoire of mid-eighties rock classics.

In the left-side rear seat, Sacchs played poker on his cell phone. He wished the big American would stop whistling but he didn't know how to maintain his Hollywood Action Star Cool while bitching about the tunes.

Sacchs tasted something warm and coppery. He lifted his fingers to his upper lip. He realized he had a small nosebleed. He held a wad of Kleenex under it and, sixty seconds later, it stopped. He didn't bother to mention it to the others. Being injured in the heat of battle is cool. Nosebleeds are not.

Halliday asked Veigel to take the stick while he reported in to Asher.

Upstate New York

Asher Sahar, Eli Schullman, and their band of soldiers boarded a Hercules at a small airfield. A flight plan had been filed but it was fictitious. Schullman oversaw the loading of the personnel and their gear. Asher took a call and moved away from everyone else for some privacy.

As the men boarded the plane, Asher rejoined them. Schullman nodded him aside.

"You didn't have to take the FBI bugger yourself," he grumbled. "Dirty deeds are my job."

Asher smiled up at his friend. "I needed to hear the man. Since Daria . . . since the incident, he's known her better than anyone."

"And what exactly did you need to hear from this man?"

Asher studied him. "I don't know. That she is well, I suppose. Or at least well thought of."

Schullman shook his bullet-shaped head. He thought about pointing out how ludicrous that was, but bit it back. "And Halliday?"

"That was him on the phone, just now. Everything is going according to plan. Sacchs is infected."

Schullman kept a poker face, but with difficulty. "God in Heaven. Veigel?"

"Not yet. But by the time we land . . . ?" Asher shrugged.

"And Halliday?"

Asher watched the last of the men climb into the bulky cargo plane.

"He'll be fine."

"He's exposed."

Asher nodded. "Sacchs has contracted it. Veigel will soon. And Halliday is immune."

Schullman clapped him on the shoulder. The big man sounded even more funereal than usual. "God willing. God, and Hannah Herself."

Asher winced. "Hannah, yes. But not all of our plans are sanctioned by God."

Ten

The girl didn't know where she was.

She knew that the place was big. It smelled like boiled cabbage, which partially hid fetid human smells she didn't recognize. The walls had been white once, a long time ago. The children were frightened. The grown-ups were more frightened.

The sound of jet engines made everyone wince. Bombs landed in the neighborhood at all hours. Someone swept the floors, almost daily, but the shelling outside just resettled the dust. The shelling had gone on a long time, the girl thought. But then again, she was about six. And a long time is a relative term.

She knew she was *about six* because she heard the staff say so.

Each child had an olive-colored canvas cot and a pillow with no pillowcase. There were blankets, but not enough, and every night the older, stronger children took what blankets they wanted.

There were two meals per day and both meals included bread, or oatmeal, or koshary, a combination of lentils, pasta, chickpeas, and a tomato sauce. The food was terrible but would get them through to the next meal.

Every third or fourth day, a Swellat Bedouin from Lebanon would come to the big building with the children. He wore a slick Western suit and a shiny black shirt open to the middle of his chest, and shiny shoes. He wore a ring on his little finger and his hair was long and greased back. He would speak to the administrator, and between them they would pick out one or two of the girls, one or two of the boys. The Swellat would hand the administrator an envelope, then the selected children would leave with him.

After one such visit, the girl climbed onto a radiator, raised up on her toes, and peered out through the iron bars over the window to watch. The chosen children climbed into an aged Volvo with the slick-haired man with the pinky ring.

A few days would pass. And the man would return.

One day, the man saw the girl sitting on her cot. Her legs dangled, her sneakers grimy and dull.

He pointed to her.

The administrator beckoned her over.

The girl climbed down off her cot and walked over. She wore a baby blue smock. She had had a matching barrette but an older girl had taken it the first night.

The man picked two more children. All three were ushered out. The girl and the others climbed into the back of the Volvo. It smelled of sweat and something animalish and mean that the girl remembered and associated with soldiers. And pain.

It was the last time she would ever see the big building with the once-white walls.

It was cold in the car. Very cold. And the wall was cement. Only it wasn't a wall. It was a floor.

She lay not in a car but on the floor. Under a bed. Under a—

Daria Gibron's eyes snapped open.

The cement floor under the cot was ice cold. It was the cold that woke her. Then the pain. Her head was a burlap bag of barbed wire.

She lay under a simple bed frame with a simple mattress, in a bare, cinder block room with harsh phosphorescent lights. Daria lay in a tight fetal position, her body a parenthesis of terror. Again.

The nightmares had been her constant companion for as far back as she could remember. Daria thought they might have had the decency to give her the night off. No such luck.

She peered out. The ceiling, the color of bad mayonnaise, was fifteen feet high. She groaned, slowly rolling over. She sat up and hugged her knees, her bum and the balls of her bare feet on the poured cement floor. She wore her matching black panties and camisole.

She looked around. The room was a perfect cement square. The floor, stained with years of accrued residue, sloped slightly downward at the center to a rusty iron drain. There were two identical doors, both the kind that hang off heavy iron castors and roll open sideways. She checked the upper corners of the room for cameras but saw none. It was maybe fifty degrees in the room.

She climbed up onto the bed, off the frigid floor. She remembered New York. The CIA. The trap. The Syrian, Belhadj.

The room felt old. The smell of the air was slightly off, but she wasn't sure why.

She set her feet back down on the cement floor and stood, wobbly. She braced herself by gripping the bed until the nausea passed. Her head swam. She wasn't dead. And so far she hadn't thrown up.

She stumbled over to the door to her right, gripped the vertical iron handle with both hands and hauled on it. It was locked.

She limped to the other door, the floor painfully cold under her feet. She pulled it open. Beyond she found a cheaply hacked-together shower over a simple floor drain, a sink, a lidless toilet, and an aged mirror showing more silver than reflection. A coarse towel lay on the floor, neatly folded, with a single bar of soap.

She stood before the mirror. Being doped and left on a cot with a head full of styling gel made her look like the Bride of Frankenstein. Perfect. Captured by a Syrian spy, called a "horse" by the Central Intelligence Fucking Agency, and a legendarily bad hair day to boot. Simply perfect.

She showered. The hot water helped raise her body temperature and the headache evaporated. She slid back into her panties and camisole. The panties con-

sisted of a few square centimeters of black lace and
silk. They had been prohibitively expensive, made for
her bespoke by a designer in Rio de Janeiro. She sort of
wished she'd chosen something a tad less racy.

She padded back out past the bed to the second
door, which now was cracked open. Peering through
the door, she discovered she was in a warehouse, wide
and vast, with sparrows darting through the rafters and
chirping for freedom. She noted a garage-style exit
door bolted with a padlock the size of a small ham. The
iron-grated windows were grimy and ten feet off the
rough cement floor. Crates were stacked fourteen feet
high. The furniture consisted of one long, chipped For-
mica table and a few folding chairs.

Khalid Belhadj sat in one of the chairs, an empty
holster under his left arm, the Springfield .45 auto resting near his hand. He ate from a greasy takeout box of
panfried noodles, using a cheap plastic fork. A file folder
lay open before him. It was the CIA Operation Pegasus
file.

"Sit, please," he said in English.

The Syrian had set up a sturdy metal chair, away
from the folding table where he ate. Handcuffs dangled
from the slatted back of the chair. Daria sat—the chair
was freezing!—and noticed that the chair legs had been
bolted to the cement floor.

Her eyes on Belhadj, she fixed her wrists in the cuffs,
behind her back.

Belhadj shoveled the food into his mouth in the
manner of soldiers throughout the world: eat when you
get a chance to eat.

The food smelled wonderful.

After a minute, he used an unbleached, brown paper napkin to dab his lips then stood, leaving the noodles but picking up the Springfield. He circled wide around her, approached her chair from the rear and checked Daria's cuffs. Satisfied, he returned to the folding table, set down the handgun and picked up the takeout box. He turned a page in the CIA file. He had hardly glanced at her.

Daria chose to go with Arabic. "I'm surprised you recognize me. I've been out of the game a while. And we've never met, the two of us."

Belhadj kept his eyes on his food.

"What time is it?"

"Almost noon. Friday." He switched to Arabic. He ate voraciously but his left hand never strayed far from the handgun.

Friday? "I've been out two days?"

He didn't reply. Daria stuck out her lower lip and blew damp hair off her forehead. "You could have killed me."

Belhadj devoured the noodles, studied the files.

"Why take me? Why keep me alive?"

"According to the Americans, we are partners in crime. Yes?"

She snorted. "Pegasus."

"A noble beast. A mythical, winged horse."

"I suppose the hippos in tutus from *Fantasia* had already been taken."

The Syrian frowned, getting neither the reference nor her pique. He set down his plastic fork and reached down to retrieve a black messenger bag from behind his chair. "I need your help."

"You should feel free to go fuck yourself."

Belhadj nodded, as if agreeing. He opened the flap of the waterproof bag and withdrew a folder. From that, he withdrew a photo, eight-and-a-half-by-eleven. He held it up, facing her.

She leaned forward, squinting at the photo. Her dark eyes grew wide. They rose from the photo to the sullen face of Belhadj.

"You lie."

The Syrian nodded. "No. Asher Sahar. Former Mossad agent. Convicted in a star chamber of high crimes. Locked away in a secret prison we weren't supposed to know about, but of course we do. And the man who shot you."

He propped up the photo against the greasy bag from the takeout food. Daria studied the photo. It showed Sahar from the waist up, wearing an olive tunic with epaulettes and many pockets. Under the military jacket he wore a wilted white shirt and a cardigan. His hair was both thinner and shorter than Daria remembered and he wore a short beard and mustache. His small, round glasses made him look academic.

"That's not possible."

Belhadj wiped his lips. He shrugged, eyes on his food. "He has reassembled many members of his old covert unit. Plus mercenaries. We do not know why. But then again, this is the same Asher Sahar who planned to kill a member of the Israeli Parliament and start a war. Before you intervened, that is."

Daria sat leaning forward in the unmoving chair. The last time she had seen Asher, he had indeed attempted to kill her. The wound had been near fatal.

"How is he out of prison?"

"He didn't dig out, if that's what you're asking. Someone opened the door and handed him his hat. Someone powerful. We don't know who. As soon as we learned he was out, we had a surveillance team on him. They discovered he came to America to steal something. They also found a code name: the Viking."

"Fredrik?"

That got his attention. "You know him?"

"Fredrik Olsson. The Viking. Specializes in transporting stolen goods overseas. The Atlantic and the Mediterranean, mostly."

Belhadj scraped out the remains of his takeout, then threw it away with the fork and the napkin. He made eye contact with Daria for the first time. "Now. What would Asher Sahar be transporting from America?"

"How would I know? I thought the fuckwit was in prison."

Belhadj sighed as if disappointed. "You're alive to the degree you can help me find him and stop him. Fail to do so . . . ?" he shrugged.

Daria leaned back and crossed her legs at the knees. The Brazilian-designed thong offered him an interesting diorama. "Then best to shoot me now. I was enjoying the company of a rather delicious first officer in El Salvador when this comic opera began. I know nothing of the CIA and Asher. Or of you."

She sat back, half-smiling, looking calm. But her

brain was working at Mach 3, processing data, trying to figure out what was so wrong with the scene. Something just felt ... off. The warehouse was old—nineteenth-century old, although that wasn't unusual for sections of New York. The crates she could see bore stenciled labels in English, French, and German. Again, not too unusual.

Still, something was amiss. It was in the walls, in the stale smells of the warehouse. Even the metal chair to which she was cuffed seemed oddly wrong (and Daria had been cuffed to chairs before; she could compare and contrast).

Somewhere in the back of her mind, she still wondered how she would get out of this jam and help Colin Bennett-Smith with his life and death problem. But, of course, Colin wasn't anywhere near this situation. He never had been.

Once she'd played that bit out, she also remembered that the message had used the Hebrew word for *cat*, *chatoulah*. Colin Bennett-Smith might have known that old nickname. But Asher would have known it for sure. He'd been the one to give it to her.

Belhadj studied her long, lean form, leaning back, looking calm. "You've no idea why Sahar would stage an operation in the United States?"

"The man is capable of anything." Daria willed herself not to shiver from the cold. She was trying to look seductive. "He's a brilliant strategist. He's a chess player; always sees ten moves ahead of everyone else."

Belhadj rubbed his eyes. He didn't look stimulated by the barely clothed woman before him. He looked fatigued. "Unlike you. I never pictured you as the chess player."

Daria remained surprised that the Syrian had even heard of her, let alone had an opinion of her skill sets.

She shrugged as well as she could with her arms cuffed behind her back. "I never had the patience to learn chess. I never saw the point in thinking that far in advance."

"Stealing the CIA command vehicle? That wasn't preplanned?"

"I didn't even know I was under surveillance until my plane landed a few hours earlier." She didn't tell him about the mysterious warning at JFK. *Dee Jean d'Arc* . . . "It just seemed like a good idea at the time."

Belhadj absently played with the Springfield, which lay on the cheap table before him. He spun it slowly, like the second hand of a clock. "You say this Viking, Olsson, specializes in overseas transportation."

"He has access to a fleet of cargo planes and boats. If it really is Friday, I haven't eaten in two days. I'm starving."

"Palestinians are starving," the Syrian replied without rancor. "You're hungry. There's a difference. Tell me more about this Viking."

It was the smell of the warehouse, Daria decided. That's what was wrong. It didn't smell bad. It just didn't smell right.

"He's a middleman. His services are expensive."

"Very?"

"Yes. But he's paid off every field tower and harbormaster from Alexandria to Edinburgh. If you need something to cross the Atlantic or the Mediterranean, he's worth the price."

"So Sahar wouldn't have hired him on a whim."

"Asher Sahar wouldn't take a piss on a whim. But beyond that, the Viking's services are often booked far in advance. Now, you answer some of my questions."

This seemed to amuse the Syrian, who allowed a lop-sided smile to appear on his unshaven face. The bags under his eyes were slightly blue. He kept spinning the .45 slowly on the tabletop. "Oh, really? I am not the one chained to a chair."

Daria smiled meaningfully. "Not today, you're not. No."

He paused, then smiled back and shrugged. "Very well."

"How long has Asher been out of prison?"

"Who knows? I first heard he was out almost six weeks ago."

"Impossible. I would have heard."

This earned her a slow, noncommittal blink.

"How is Israeli intelligence reacting?"

This time Belhadj paused, thinking it over, trying to decide how much to tell her.

"Let us say, they are being very quiet. The Knesset has not been informed. We don't know for sure but we don't believe the prime minister knows."

"How did you get onto Asher's operation?"

"Luck. He hired a Croatian mercenary we were watching. The Croatian led us to Sahar, and Sahar led us to the States. I decided to take command of the surveillance team but, two days ago, they missed a scheduled communiqué. No word since. I assume my people are dead. Okay, my turn: I need you to try to be the chess player for a moment. Say you had money and power enough to get Asher Sahar out of prison. Quietly. Why would you?"

"So I could kill him myself."

"It's a serious question."

She was hungry and freezing and tired of playing by the Syrian's rules. But if Asher Sahar was truly free and had assembled his old squad? The thought was frightening.

"Not for an intelligence mission," she said. "You don't free Asher to bug an embassy or to photograph a deputy minister buggering choirboys. I can think of a dozen crews good enough to do that. I'm not talking about just inside Israeli intelligence, either. Spies, thieves, and mercenaries: take your pick."

"You should know. You've been all three." It wasn't an insult, just a brief recitation of Daria's CV. But it again suggested he knew more about her than seemed likely.

Daria unfolded her legs and sat forward, her back away from the chair, coal-dark eyes locked on Belhadj. "You free an Asher Sahar for destruction," she said. "You free him for something big and awful. The man may be brilliant but he also is a sociopath. You free Asher if you plan to make horrifying headlines."

Belhadj stopped spinning the gun.

"Yes." He seemed to mull the information. Again, he looked as tired as Daria felt. "Thank you. That was my assessment as well. But you know him better than I."

He stood. The sturdy black auto fit snugly in his right hand. Like many natural-born soldiers, Belhadj's hands looked more at ease holding a weapon than not.

Daria had answered his questions. If he had no more to ask, she couldn't think of a logical reason he would keep her alive.

Back in the CIA command vehicle, she'd tried using skin and sex appeal to lure him close enough for a strike and it hadn't worked. She sat here now, in her tarty underthings, bound to this bolted-down chair, and he'd barely made eye contact with her. That left her precious few options.

Belhadj circled around her, keeping his distance. One shot to the back of the skull had been a favorite method of assassination for decades. Do it right and the bullet ricochets around inside the victim's skull, turning the brain into porridge. A shot at the base of the skull tends to lessen blood splatter, too. Neat and efficient.

Daria heard a rustling, as if something made of cloth was being removed from a paper bag. No need for a blindfold, obviously.

She willed herself to sit still. When it comes, it comes—if you play the game long enough. She knew that before she had even reached her teens.

She felt a vibration behind her and it took a moment to realize he had uncuffed her left wrist.

Daria brought her arms around forward, the tension in her shoulders lessening. She dragged the handcuff with her, still pinioned to her right wrist.

She stood and pivoted on the balls of her bare feet.

Belhadj threw something at her and she caught it.

She held it up in both hands. It was a pilled Royal Air Force sweater, midnight blue and woolen, well-worn cloth patches on the shoulders and elbows, and epaulettes.

The Syrian stood ten meters away, gun held by his thigh. His weary eyes didn't blink. From the way he stood, Daria wondered when he'd slept last.

She pulled the RAF sweater over her head, freed her hair from the collar, and threaded her arms through the sleeves, holding the free end of the handcuff in her right fist as she did. It was a tight fit and she tugged it over her breasts and down her torso. It covered most of her bum. But it was deliciously warm compared to the cami and panties.

"In front," Belhadj said.

She understood. She encircled her wrist with the free cuff and clicked it closed.

"Come."

He began walking toward the warehouse's garage-style door. As he did, he dug a set of keys out of the pocket of his thick canvas trousers. Daria padded behind him, suddenly aware of her tactical advantage in his blind spot. Israeli military and intelligence officers train in a form of martial arts known as Krav Maga. It addresses exactly this sort of scenario: taking advantage of blind spots. Taking the offensive.

"Sahar is freed by someone powerful to do a terrible thing, yes?" He turned his head slightly but Daria remained outside his field of vision. "He is brave or confident enough to conduct his operation on American soil. His mission is to steal something. Did I tell you that part?"

"I believe you mentioned it." Daria was only five meters behind him now. With the sturdy metal links between her wrists, if she could get her arms over his head and her hands to either side of his neck, she could then put one foot on the small of his back and launch herself in the air. Her fifty-two kilos would throw him off balance, toppling him backward. The fall likely would break some of Daria's ribs, and there was a better-than-even chance of snapping her sternum, but at least she would have crushed his larynx.

Sacrifice my queen to topple your king? How is that for fucking chess?

But she hesitated as Belhadj did the unthinkable: he stuffed the Springfield into his shoulder holster.

What the hell?

Belhadj used both hands to undo the massive padlock that held the garage door closed.

"Sahar is a weapon of mass destruction," he said, slamming aside the bolt that held the door down. He bent at the knees and used both hands to shove upward on the door. The metal shrieked and rust flecks rained down off the tracks.

Daria hesitated.

Belhadj lifted the door just higher than his own head. He wiped soot off his palms and stepped out of the warehouse.

Daria followed.

They stood in an alley. The building across the way

was redbrick and equally aged. The alley beneath her bare feet was well-worn cobblestone. A lazy, light snow drifted down from a gunmetal gray sky.

Belhadj turned and pointed to his left. "So why, knowing all that, does a man like Sahar come here?"

Daria followed the line of the Syrian's left arm, past his fist and his one pointing finger.

She stood barefoot on the freezing cobblestones, her breath misting around her head, eyes snapping wide.

"Holy hell . . ."

Belhadj pointed at the Eiffel Tower.

Eleven

"Everyone?"

Stanley Cohen hardly raised his voice but the fifty-plus people in the subterranean operations room at CIA headquarters quieted down and turned in his direction. There was no available seating so John Broom leaned against the far wall, coffee cup in hand. Nanette Sylvestri stood by his side. She wore a braided cloth friendship bracelet her granddaughter had made for her. John knew it was her good-luck totem during operations.

Nanette wasn't just the person in charge of the Shark Tank; yesterday, she had been promoted to run Pegasus, taking Owen Cain Thorson's spot. John was pleased. She was the perfect person to call the plays for so large an operation.

"Folks? Thank you." Cohen coughed into his fist. He looked pasty and drawn, but then again, he always did. "We had a pretty good setback in New York on Wednesday. The good news: we know the target of these players and we know they have aerial photos of Camp David, something that we believed didn't exist. The bad news: it's forty-eight hours later and we have no idea where they are. Up to now we have confined our search to the eastern seaboard but we're expanding the net to cover the rest of the U.S., Canada, and Mexico. Nanette?"

She moved away from John and stepped to the front of the room. "While yesterday's search turned up nothing, it did give our own John Broom time to dream up a new scenario. I've often said there is nothing more frightening than John Broom with time to kill."

A wave of good-natured heckling rippled through the room.

"We have two competing theories right now, which I'm going to call Pegasus A and Pegasus B. We all know Pegasus A backward and forward but I think it's helpful to go back to square one from time to time. I've asked Agent Thorson to lay it out for us. Owen?"

It was a touch of class, her asking the former operation leader to make the presentation.

Thorson took two steps down the auditorium-style room to stand by Nanette's side. He nodded to a techie who sat at the controls of the audiovisual table. Images of Daria Gibron and Khalid Belhadj appeared on two of the eight flat-screen TVs in the Shark Tank.

"The president is attempting to broker a deal between Democrats and Republicans on the Hill to sell the next generation of attack drones to Israel, as soon as they come off the assembly line and get beta-tested. We believe this man"—Thorson nodded to the screen—"Major Khalid Belhadj, came to the United States to kill the president. Since he couldn't easily sneak weapons into the U.S., he planned to meet this woman, Daria Gibron, who would supply him with a sniper rifle with silencer and scope."

Thorson nodded to the techie and a third TV screen sprang to life, showing a side view of an olive-colored sniper rifle with a bipod stand, which ended with something that looked like mini snow skis.

"According to the documents we recovered from a satchel in New York, the gun she was selling him was a PSG-90. Swedish, similar to the Brits' L96 series. She also was selling him a case of sabot rounds."

That caught John's attention. Sabot bullets can penetrate most armored shielding, including that used by some portions of the presidential motorcade.

"Four-point-eight-one mike-mike, tungsten carbide bullets. There's a degradation of accuracy for most shooters but the slugs exit the barrel at better than forty-four-hundred feet per second. For a shooter of Belhadj's skill, the slight reduction in accuracy is more than made up for by the fact that he can put bullets on target twice as fast as he could with most NATO rounds."

He pointed to Belhadj's photo again. "We originally thought the assassination was scheduled for Wednesday at Emory University in Atlanta. It's snowing in Georgia, and the PSG-90 is ideal for arctic conditions. But the discovery of the Camp David aerials has changed all that."

He nodded again and a fourth image appeared. It was an eagle-eye view of Washington, D.C., ranging from the White House to the Hill. "The presidential security detail is avoiding Camp David, obviously. And if they have photos of Camp David, they could have Andrews Air Force Base, too. So the president is staying in the White House, completely secure, until we find Belhadj and Gibron. Now, he is scheduled to attend the Group of Eight summit in Avignon but we are negotiating with the president's chief of staff to cancel the visit. I can tell you now, the White House does not want to cancel.

"All domestic intelligence agencies have been alerted, as have all law enforcement agencies. We cannot assume the bad guys have just given up and gone home. They are, as of now, *the* most hunted humans on Earth."

Done, he nodded to Nanette Sylvestri.

"Right." She crossed her arms. "I've asked John Broom to offer up Pegasus B. John?"

John joined them down front. He slid between the techie and the master controls for the flat-screens. "Can I . . . do you mind?" He fiddled with the controls for a second, and a map of the eastern United States appeared on one of the monitors.

"Okay. Here's the competing theory: I can't tell you where Belhadj and Gibron are, but I can tell you where they *aren't*. They aren't in D.C., and they aren't in Atlanta, and they aren't near Camp David. This whole thing has nothing to do with the president, who was never in any danger from either of them."

Thorson said, "The satchel—"

"The satchel was conveniently dropped right where your field agents could find it. It's a ruse. The real action was here."

John played with a computer mouse. The map slid sideways, westward.

"Colorado. And the levee break of the Genevieve River, which resulted in the deaths of at least nineteen people and the destruction of forty-four homes and businesses. Among the dead and missing, as of Thursday evening, were three Secret Service agents on a transport mission. They're the real story. Everything else is sleight of hand."

Thorson rolled his eyes. "So now you think Belhadj and Gibron blew up a river in Colorado? When we have them sighted in New York City at the same time?"

"No. Daria Gibron and Major Belhadj had nothing to do with this. I don't know why they were meeting in New York, but they were a distraction. For us. The real investigation, the real threat, is out there in Colorado."

Nanette said simply, "Explain, please."

"High-ranking Israeli sources informed us that the president is the target of a foreign assassin. Protocol says the president's security detail gets tripled-up."

He turned to Owen Thorson. "Whatever the Secret Service was transporting through Colorado, the minute we got the heads-up from Tel Aviv, the Secret Service convoy went from six agents to three. And within an hour of that, a levee breaks, a motel is washed away, and all three agents are missing."

"They'll be found. I still don't know what—"

"One of them has been found. It was in the overnights," John said. Thorson flushed; he hadn't had the time to study the nightly download of intelligence and journalism reviews. "The agent's name is Boyd Renfro.

His body washed into a ravine about a mile and a quarter from the motel where the convoy had stopped."

Thorson shrugged. "It was a huge flood. I'm sure the other two who drowned will show up eventually. I don't—"

"Agent Renfro didn't drown. He died of a gunshot wound to the head."

That caught the attention of everyone in the room. Stanley Cohen, who leaned on the wall in the back, his lower spine killing him this morning, had been studying the whorls in the conference-room carpet. His sad, hound dog eyes rose now, his attention fully on the briefing.

"With one dead agent, we now are looking at two missing, as well as the package. But I'm betting we only find one more dead agent. The third guy killed his fellow agents and stole the package. That Marx Brothers routine in Manhattan? The threat to the president? That was all to run interference for this."

Not a particularly tall man, John hopped a few inches off the ground and stabbed the TV screen with one finger, hitting Colorado.

Nanette Sylvestri asked the obvious question. "What were they transporting? This *package*?"

"I don't know yet. I put in a request. The Secret Service is stonewalling me."

The room was quiet for a moment. Nanette Sylvestri nodded firmly, coming to a decision. She turned and looked him straight in the eye. "It's a hell of a theory, John, and it's solid analysis. But, honestly? We have an assassin and a potential sleeper agent, a spectacular heist of sensitive CIA property and intel, and photos of the presidential compound, the holiest of holies. This thing in Colorado is intriguing, and worth pursuing. But in my opinion, we stick to Pegasus A. Director Cohen?"

Stanley Cohen pushed himself away from the wall, feeling his spine protest. "I concur."

John turned to him. "Permission to—"

"Yes," Cohen said. "John, you look into Pegasus B. Everyone else: we stay on Belhadj and Gibron."

Paris

Belhadj rolled down the garage-style door but did not relock it. He brushed his palms on the front of his canvas trousers. "Why would Sahar come to Paris?"

Daria shrugged, the midnight blue sweater rising. "What did his people steal in America?"

"I don't know." He walked to a cheaply made steamer trunk, opened it and pulled out Daria's clunky, chain-studded boots and latex miniskirt. He dug the handcuff keys out of his pocket and tossed them underhand. Daria caught them and undid both cuffs. "You expect me to put on those stupid clothes?"

Belhadj looked surprised. "These are your clothes."

"Idiot. I bought them as a disguise. You don't think I dress like that all the time?"

Belhadj let a little exasperation show in his face. "Wear them or not. I could not care less."

Daria accepted the little skirt, stepped into it and wiggled it up her legs. It was so short that only two inches remained visible beneath the RAF sweater. There was no sign of her duster coat in the trunk. She closed the lid, sat, and accepted the punk boots from him.

"We need to find another place to stay and we need to find Sahar."

Daria concentrated on the boots. "If Asher is operating in France, there's a man who might know how to find him."

"Who?"

"Why can't we stay here? I assumed this was a Syrian safe house." It would explain why Belhadj had keys for the place. The lack of first-floor windows also made the building ideal as a safe house.

"You ask too many questions."

Daria stood. She thought the massive boots made her look like a Japanese anime character. "Do you have another place for us to go?"

"I'm working on it. Who is this man who might be able to find Sahar?"

Daria batted her black eyelashes at him. "I wouldn't be of much use to you if I just told you. I'll take you to him."

Belhadj pondered that. Daria tucked the handcuffs into her sweater sleeve.

"I also can find us a place to stay."

"How?"

Daria brushed her spread fingers through her damp hair. "I was stationed in Paris for nearly a year. I know the city well. Plus, while I was here, I was seeing an archeologist. He's probably at a dig in South Africa, this time of year. Give me my mobile."

"It's in the trunk."

Daria bent at the waist, opened the trunk, and rooted around. She found her smartphone. She also found the small, spade-shaped blade that turned on a single hinge inside a leather sandwich. She picked up the phone and the blade in one hand, the blade tucked behind the phone.

When she stood, Belhadj had moved closer to her. He drew his Springfield and gently placed the barrel against her forehead. He didn't press it in, just held it there so she could feel the cold metal two inches above her eyes.

"Speakerphone."

"There's no need for—"

The warehouse echoed with the clattering of empty tin cans. It was a good distance off; not in the cavernous room where they stood. She recognized the sound for what it was: a warning. Belhadj had been expecting trouble and had set up some noisy trap.

Daria saw it in the Syrian's eyes—they no longer were safe in his safe house.

As Belhadj's eyes slid toward the noise, Daria tucked the little folding knife into her skirt waistband. She doubted the tin can warning could be Ray Calabrese coming to rescue her. But if it was, Daria would need a way to even the odds. The folding knife just might do it.

"Come. Now."

Belhadj grabbed an olive sapper jacket and his oilskin messenger bag off one of the folding chairs. He shrugged into the jacket en route to the garage door. He used both hands to open it, rust pellets again raining down on his head.

The cobblestone alley no longer was empty.

Two men in dark clothes and long coats awaited them. They stood with their combat boots shoulder-width apart, their hands clasped before them. Daria noted the telltale ridges of shoulder holsters under their coats.

The men appeared to be Middle Eastern.

One man wore a navy watch cap pulled low over his ears. "Major. Back inside, please." He made no effort to keep the threatening tone out of his voice.

The second man wore black plastic-framed glasses. His eyes raked Daria from head to toe. "Who is this?"

Belhadj said, "She is our best hope for finding Asher Sahar. You know this. Get out of my way." His voice took on the flinty edge of every military officer Daria had ever served with.

"Damascus says this is no longer your concern, Major."

Daria's brain began running the numbers for the calculus of crisis: Belhadj wanted to find Asher. These men did not want to find Asher. Daria didn't know if Asher was behind any of this or if she was being lied to. But if he was, then she wanted to—needed to—find Asher.

She glanced down the long, snow-flecked alley. No car or van awaited them. This wasn't a transport operation. *Major, back inside, please.*

She heard the squeak of a floorboard over her head. One of the two men in the alley smiled and shook his head. The other reached for his gun.

Daria rotated her arm behind her hip and let the handcuffs slide out of her right sleeve. She caught one cuff, the other undone and hanging free. The effect was to extend her reach by eight inches and to give her, for want of a better term, a jagged-toothed, prosthetic hook.

"Please!" She stepped toward the men and wailed in Arabic. "This man is mad! Help me! He—" She turned as if to point at Belhadj. The handcuff arced through the cold air and sliced into the cheekbone of the man in the eyeglasses. His glasses flew. Blood arced. He snapped to his right and stumbled into his partner.

Belhadj stepped forward, right arm a blur, and the heel of his hand smashed up and into the nose of the man in the watch cap. Blood shot upward from his shattered nose as he fell straight back. His spine snapped like fresh asparagus when he hit the alley cobbles.

Daria was on the first man, driving a knee into his balls and a forearm into his ear. He fell like a stone. Daria went down with him, adding her weight to his own. She aimed to incapacitate, not kill.

Daria flipped open the coat of the man she'd decked and reached in to thumb off the safety strap of his holster.

Belhadj grabbed her by the sweater collar and lifted her easily to her feet before she could reach the downed man's handgun.

"Go!"

He hustled her down the alley toward the street.

Langley

The assistant director for antiterrorism called a meeting of the team leaders for the Pegasus Group at 12:30 P.M.

Friday. That included, naturally, Nanette Sylvestri and Owen Cain Thorson. John Broom had not been invited.

John sat a couple miles away, at an Internet café that featured Turkish coffee and baklava. He had bypassed protocol to go directly to a longtime friend at the Secret Service, Constance de Castro. This sort of back-channel communication wasn't usually conducted on one's office phone.

"John, I'd love to help you," de Castro said, flashing that high-octane smile of hers over the Skype connection, "but D.C. police are about to tow our command vehicle!"

John was fairly sure this would be the source of yucks in the intelligence community for weeks to come. He waited for her to stop laughing and wipe tears from her cheeks. "I wish this was a lighthearted call. It isn't. It's about the Colorado thing."

De Castro's grin froze then faded. "John? Are you telling me the CIA had—"

"Not to the best of my knowledge." John tried never to overpromise. "It's just, you losing three agents in Colorado to a levee break coincides too nicely with that cluster we had in Manhattan. I think they're connected."

"How?"

John outlined the theory that now, inside the halls of Langley, was being called Pegasus B.

Constance de Castro didn't sneer at it. "The news that POTUS was the target did chop the transport mission in half. You're not wrong there. And the timing sucks."

"What do you know about the transport?"

He waited. De Castro paused. He could tell she was calculating. John Broom worked hard to maintain his reputation as a guy who offered intelligence, pro bono, and who wasn't quick to collect on favors owed. He was counting on all of that working in his favor.

"Colorado State Police found another of our agents," De Castro said. "He was lodged under a car. He'd been shot in the head, too."

John winced. "God, I'm sorry. So what were they transporting?"

She hesitated, her image flickering a little. "We don't know."

John blinked. "A blind transport? You do that?"

"Not usually. We will, if it's on behalf of another agency. And if the request comes from high enough up the food chain."

"Who asked for the favor?"

"The Department of the Army."

John began nibbling around the edges of the scenario. "Okay. So, the army needs something transported. It's obviously a weapon of mass destruction, because the law is clear that you guys are the only agency tasked with moving something like that across U.S. soil. But there's a handshake agreement at the top of both agencies, and the Secret Service agrees not to look inside the box."

De Castro nodded.

"Search-and-rescue hasn't stumbled on a dirty bomb or a thermos of sarin or whatever, so the package was stolen. Plus, you've got at least two Secret Service personnel dead with gunshot wounds."

She kept nodding.

"Who do I talk to at the Pentagon to figure out what was being transported?"

"Johnny boy, you didn't hear this from me."

" 'Course."

She gave him a name.

"Okay. I got the go-ahead to look into this. I find anything worth sharing, you know I will."

"Thanks," de Castro said, licked her lips. "Hey, John?"

He nodded.

"You didn't state the obvious. The discretion is appreciated."

The obvious was this: three Secret Service agents were ambushed, and two ended up with bullets in their brainpans. The first, most obvious suspect was agent number three. Who remained missing.

John said, "Thanks. I'll keep in touch." And rang off.

He paid his tab and stepped out of the café, buttoning his coat, as his cell phone chirped. He checked the message. It was Nanette Sylvestri.

"Hey." His eyes checked the pewter sky and the bustling people, heads down, shoulders hunched. They were predicting snow or sleety rain.

"John? The FBI liaison, Ray Calabrese . . ."

John glanced at his watch. "Is he in? I'll head over to National. He should—"

"He's been shot," Nanette cut in. "They found him

at the airport. Two to the back. Nine caliber. He's alive, but John?"

John already was racing for the subway.

"It doesn't look good."

Twelve

Paris

Daria and Belhadj took two quick rights through narrow streets filled with more middle-class businessmen and nannies with prams than clusters of tourists. They climbed a short, high canal bridge and Daria tried to gain her bearings. She was used to seeing the skyline of Paris but the point-of-view was unfamiliar, until she realized they were in the western peninsula of the Right Bank, created by the curve of the Seine. It was Paris's Sixteenth arrondissement—9 o'clock, if the arrondissements, or neighborhoods, had been laid out as a clock face.

Daria said, "This way," and led them over the narrow pedestrian bridge toward a commercial district.

Belhadj said not a word.

They caught the metro at Michel-Ange-Auteuil. They found two seats together in a car near the back of the train. Belhadj discreetly kept his sapper jacket closed to hide his shoulder holster.

Daria felt better knowing she had the spade-shaped knife in her waistband. It was, unfortunately, a weapon best suited for hand-to-hand combat. If and when she made her move against Belhadj, she would prefer to fight from a distance.

He leaned toward her and whispered. "Give me the handcuffs."

"Why?"

"Because it never dawned on me they could be used as a weapon."

She sighed and handed them over. "You lack imagination."

"I imagine you're right."

She blinked back in surprise. Had Khalid Belhadj just cracked a joke?

"So"—she leaned against his shoulder to whisper—"that was . . . most interesting. Those men were Syrian."

"Were they? I hadn't noticed."

Daria smiled. "They were agents of the Mukhabarat. They were staking out a Syrian safe house looking for you."

He did not reply.

"This is not a sanctioned operation. Your superiors don't want you going after Asher Sahar."

"Don't speculate about things you don't understand."

"That's assuming Asher is even involved. He could still be in prison. You could be lying about everything."

Belhadj gave her a withering glance. "He isn't. I haven't. Which stop do we want?"

"La Motte-Picquet Grenelle."

Belhadj looked at her doubtfully.

"I told you I was stationed in Paris."

He did not reply.

"Let's say I believe you. Why are you running from your own agency? And why wouldn't your superiors want to stop Asher?"

"This would be a most excellent time for you to stop talking."

Daria didn't take the hint. "Something's not adding up. There is a part of this you're not telling me."

He sighed. "I haven't decided when or if to kill you yet. But the more you prattle, the closer I get to a decision."

Daria figured she had needled him enough for now. They rode in silence.

John Broom strode down the halls of George Washington University Hospital, looking not for room numbers but for dark blue suits and conservative haircuts. When he found a nest of them, he was sure he was close to Ray Calabrese.

"Excuse me." He walked up to the first of five people whose wardrobe, hair, and palpable anger-plus-anxiousness screamed FBI. He presented his photo ID; not the lanyard one with CIA in bright-red letters, three inches tall, but the one designed not to draw attention in public. "John Broom, CIA. I'm the guy Calabrese was coming to see. Who's in charge here?"

A stocky man with a bristly military haircut said, "Special Agent Kitsen." He stepped forward and offered a beefy hand. One shake, up and down.

"How is he?"

No one looked very happy. "Still on the operating table. One collapsed lung. He lost a lot of blood. They have him in intensive care now. It's fifty-fifty."

"And the shooter?"

Kitsen shrugged. "Witnesses have a smallish man with a beard. Someone working for Gibron, probably."

John said, "You have her down for this?"

"CIA says she's running with a known assassin and they have plans for the president. You tell me, Mr. Broom: who's the one guy who could fuck with Gibron's plans the fastest? Her FBI case handler, that's who."

John pulled out his iPhone and started tapping buttons.

Kitsen said, "Her record's been spotty since immigrating here. She did a stint with a cowboy ATF element in Mexico that was way past illegal. Seems Calabrese and the L.A. office have been covering for her since . . ." John kept fiddling with his phone. Kitsen turned to the other FBI agents in the corridor and gave them a "can you believe this asshole?" look. "Excuse me. Mr. Broom? Am I boring you here?"

John put his phone on speaker.

"Hi. Broom? It's Ray Calabrese. I'm at LAX, heading to Reagan National. Look, I don't know what the hell's going on, but I can assure you, Daria Gibron's on our side. If I had a way to stake my life on it, I would. That's 'cause I still have a life to stake, and I have her to thank for that. Got it? Keep the dogs at bay 'til I get there. Broom? I'm counting on you, man."

Click.

John looked straight into Kitsen's eyes. "You're not boring me, Kitsen. How'm I doing?"

The archeologist with whom Daria had had an affair kept a flat on rue Saint-Dominique in the Seventh arrondissement in Paris, less than three blocks from the long, green park that separated the Eiffel Tower from L'Ecole Militaire. They approached the building on foot, Belhadj with his hands jammed into the pockets of the olive jacket, looking doubtful and dour.

The building's door was ten feet tall and wooden, painted a chipped green, embedded in a wall that looked like it had been constructed at least a hundred years earlier. Daria pushed a door button. They waited, eyes on the brass speaker built into the wall.

"Do you carry lock picks?" she asked.

Belhadj produced two picks from his messenger bag.

Daria pushed the bell again. Nothing. She used the picks to manipulate the lock.

Belhadj looked incredulous. "You intend for us to hide here? This is your idea of *inconspicuous*?"

"Look around," she said. "What do you see?"

Belhadj glanced at the street of stores and apartments, the meat shop and fruit shop and florist. Gay bunting wafted from streetlamps; celebrating some-such holiday, though Belhadj couldn't tell which. "What?"

"Tourists." The big door clacked open. "Americans, Asians, Germans. This is a tourism district. No one would think to look for us here."

Inside, they found mailboxes for eight apartments, two each in the four-story building. The archeologist's name was still etched into its brass plate but no other name had been added to it. It was unlikely the professor was cohabitating.

The foyer was poorly lit, the floor covered in clean but cracked white tile. The lift was ancient and minuscule, accessible through an aluminum accordion-style door. A tight helix of stairs wound around the elevator shaft, a long ancient rug with a faded flower design tacked down on the middle of the stairs.

"We'll take the lift," Belhadj said.

They both fit in, barely, facing the side wall, their shoulders touched. Belhadj tensed up and Daria wondered if he had a bit of claustrophobia.

The rickety elevator rumbled to a stop on the fourth floor and Daria shoved open the iron gate. The archeologist's door was to their left. Daria picked the lock quickly. Belhadj entered first, drawing his handgun and turning to keep an eye on her as he did so.

The apartment was large by Parisian standards, clean but cluttered, with a living room, a bedroom, and a small but efficient kitchen. The ceilings were ten feet high and painted pristine white with filigree bas-relief designs in the corners. The walls were peach. The hardwood floors were blond, the furniture masculine and minimalistic. Books were everywhere. Some neatly on their shelves, others strewn about. Daria remembered the old bookstore smell of the place. The living room was exactly as she remembered it. She saw no signs of a woman's touch.

Belhadj snapped his fingers. "Give me my picks. And your phone."

She handed them over. Then she threw open the celery green curtains on one of two windows in the living room. The windows opened inward with black wrought-iron barriers up to belt height close in on the outside; large enough to slip a potted plant out there, but not much else.

The top third of the Eiffel Tower loomed over the building across the busy street.

"You and . . . this man?"

Daria turned from the window. Belhadj held up a framed photo that had rested on the white fireplace mantel. It showed a lean, taut-skinned man with a wheat-colored beard, his arms around two people who clearly were his parents. Daria crossed to Belhadj, cocked her head to the smile. "Thierry, yes. For about two months."

Two months was probably Daria's personal best, but she didn't share that with the Syrian.

"He's old enough to be your father."

"He's kind. And funny. And brilliant."

She moved into the tiny kitchen. Belhadj returned the photo and followed.

"Ah-ha!"

He entered to find her withdrawing a bottle of champagne from a small, waist-high refrigerator. "That's more like it."

She found two champagne flutes, peeled back the foil and popped the cork.

"You haven't eaten in forty-eight hours," he noted.

"My friend will have a well-stocked pantry. I'll find something."

She poured and pointed to the other flute.

"I don't drink alcohol."

"One of the many mysteries of Islam." She sipped the amber drink, sighed theatrically. "Very nice. Dry. You're sure . . . ?"

"Find something to eat. Then take me to the man who can lead us to Sahar."

Daria sipped the champagne. "Why is your own agency trying to stop you?"

Belhadj studied her with tired eyes.

"Okay, fine." Daria let it go. "Use my mobile. I don't know if you can get an Internet connection here, but if so, use it to look up Rue du Terrage. Find out what subway route we'll need."

He studied her. They stood only two meters apart, she in the tiny kitchen with its pristine pearl white tile floor, he with his boot heels still in the short, dark corridor. Daria sipped champagne, reached for the bottle.

Belhadj shrugged his right hand into his trouser pocket, momentarily throwing off his balance, if just the slightest, to withdraw her telephone.

Daria splashed champagne at his eyes. She let the glass go, so that it, too, flew toward Belhadj's face. She grabbed the bottle in her other hand.

It's not like in cowboy movies, where whiskey bottles instantly shatter upon hitting a cupboard, and shatter exactly how you want them to. Especially heavier, more substantial champagne bottles, which are designed to take the internal pressure of the bubbles. But who needs a serrated weapon when a heavy club would do?

Daria's rubber-soled boots gave her an advantage amid all the wine she was spilling.

Daria surged forward, Krav Maga–style. Belhadj stepped back, into the corridor. She kicked out, aiming for his balls. She didn't have room for a proper spin, instead kicking straight out. The tight quarters weakened the strength of her attack.

She reached backward for the spade-shaped knife in her skirt waistband.

Belhadj took the kick on his hip, not his balls. His arm shot out, hand around her throat, and drew her forward. He spun, hip-checked Daria, kept turning away from the kitchen, and she flew over his back, the length of the short corridor, her boots higher than her head. She slammed into the closet door hard enough to crack the wood. She slumped to the floor, stunned.

The little leather sheath slipped from her fingers and came to rest under her thigh.

The Syrian was on her in a second, one knee planted between her breasts, the barrel of the .45 jammed under her chin.

Daria saw stars and she had the wind knocked out of her, even before he knelt on her rib cage. Her eyes fluttered.

Belhadj cocked the gun, thrust it harder under her jaw.

"If you truly believe that Asher Sahar is a lesser threat to the world than I am, you are as insane as he!"

"How many?" Daria croaked, not moving her jaw. They were both splashed by wine. "How many missions in Israel? How many good men and women butchered by you and the Mukhabarat?"

Khalid Belhadj's eyes did not shift and his voice did not change. "Many. You spent years in Beirut and on the West Bank. How many Muslims did you betray or kill? It is what our kind does. We spy, we lie, and, eventually, we die. The body count is between us and our God."

"Go to hell, you fucking piece of shit!"

Belhadj had her dead to rights. He stared into her eyes. He paused, seemed to be considering his options.

He pulled back a bit and surprised her by using his free hand to untuck his shirt. He lifted it. In the corridor's dim light, Daria could see a nasty, puckered scar, left of center, four inches below his pectoral muscle. It was an entrance wound.

"You say we've never met," Belhadj growled.

Daria's brain tried to catch up to him. Of course they hadn't met before Manhattan. What did—

"Damascus. Six years ago," he said, still holding up his shirttail, still showing the cratered scar. "That bridge near Al A'ref School."

It took her a few seconds to recollect, her head still ringing from the collision with the closet door and the pressure of his knee on her sternum. Al A'ref . . . a bridge near a school . . .

Daria said, "What? That . . . journalist? Ahmed?"

"The fat bastard wanted to defect, to tell the Jews about North Korean missile platforms secreted in the Golan Heights."

Belhadj pulled the gun away from Daria's throat but did not ease up the pressure of his knee on her chest.

"I . . . remember," she gasped. "I was covering the meeting from a bridge. I saw a sniper. I fired."

"Yes. From a kilometer away. Not a bad shot."

Belhadj let his shirt fall, hiding the bullet wound. He climbed off her and slid home the hammer of his .45. Daria lay on the well-waxed wooden floor, catching her breath.

He glared down at her, jammed his weapon into its holster. Daria reached for the small leather sheath and tucked it into her fist. Belhadj knelt and twisted her arms, cuffed her wrists behind her back. She kept her fist tightly clenched.

He stood again. Belhadj's fingers subconsciously traced the entrance wound on his flank. "Never met? Go fuck *yourself*, Miss Gibron. Then help me stop Asher Sahar."

He stalked away.

John Broom went directly from meeting the FBI brass at Ray Calabrese's hospital room to a 2 P.M. meeting at the Pentagon, which took place in a conference room that could easily seat two hundred and fifty. It was an odd setting, in that only two people were present.

John removed his winter coat and scarf, and took a seat on one side of a long conference room table. General Neal Glenn sat opposite him in full dress uniform. He was a two-star, a balding man with thick jowls and soft hands. He didn't look like he had ever held a gun or performed a push-up. John wondered how a guy like that came to be a two-star general.

John sat and glanced around the immense auditorium. His voice echoed a little in the vast space. "I'm sorry if you mistook me for the London Philharmonic. I get that a lot."

The general waved off the issue. "This was the only room available for—"

"This room is swept for listening devices," John cut in, smiling politely. "There are metal detectors built into the doors. I bet there are electronic baffles in the walls to make transmission impossible. Nothing said in this room can be recorded."

Glenn's eyes narrowed. He cleared his throat, broke eye contact.

"Anyway, sir, I appreciate your time. By now, you know and we know that whatever the Secret Service was transporting for you through Colorado has been stolen. We need to know what it was, if we have any hope of figuring out who stole it and why."

The general folded his puffy, pink hands on the enormous table.

John withdrew his notepad and uncapped his pen. He paused, the pen over his notepad.

The general said, "Well, first, I need to assure you: It isn't as bad as it sounds."

John paused, smiling. He capped his pen, closed his notepad and rubbed both temples. "Oh, shit."

Glenn's jowly face reddened. "No, no!"

"General, in the history of the Republic, every

conversation that ever started with 'it isn't as bad as it sounds' always ended with congressional hearings."

"Honestly! It's fine." Sweat formed on the general's upper lip. "It's been a communications problem, mostly. Everything's under control."

John let his face betray his utter disbelief.

"You see, it started when the Philippine military raided a terrorist compound about three weeks ago."

"Abu Sayaf." John had read about the raid in the overnights. "Sword of the Father. They're unofficially linked to al-Qaida."

The general clearly hadn't known that. "Um . . . yes. Anyway, following the raid, the Philippine army found a lab. They interrogated some of the prisoners and discovered this . . . Abu Sayaf, as you say, had hired a biologist from Tajikistan. The biologist was experimenting with zoonoses. Zoonoses are—"

"Viruses." John pointedly glanced at his watch. "Viruses that jump from species to species, like swine flu or bird flu. This Tajik biologist was working on something like that?"

"Yes. He was trying to manipulate a strain of a simian flu virus, turn it into a human flu, and release it. Probably in Manila, or to sell it to other terrorist affiliates. Anyway, the raid foiled that plot." He smiled proudly, as if he, himself, had led the raid.

"Was the biologist successful? Did he create a human flu?"

Glenn rearranged his pudgy hands. "Yes and no. He was successful in manipulating an influenza strain but it's completely unstable. I could expose you to it right now and the flu would break down in your system long before you became symptomatic. It's harmless."

"But you brought it to the United States anyway," John added.

"Yes. The boys at USAMRIID wanted to study it and create an antivirus. Just in case. That's—"

Again, John jumped in. "The U.S. Army Medical Research Institute for Infectious Diseases."

The general nodded, as if John were his prize student. "Very good. Yes. The Secret Service was transporting the virus in a supercooled container to keep it alive. They were taking it to a chemical weapons depot, where it could be safely studied."

"And if it got into the hands of terrorists?"

"Harmless. That's why we didn't immediately contact the intelligence community. The pathogen just breaks down too fast to be infectious."

John asked for the name of the Tajik biologist working in the Philippines. Glenn squinted, bringing up the name. "Ah . . . Farrukh Tuychiev, I believe."

John asked a couple more questions but they didn't get him far. He had interviewed top military personnel before and, like a lot of people, he had come to understand there often was an inverse relationship between how high their rank and how much useful knowledge they possessed.

When the potentially useful questions petered out, the men stood and shook hands. Glenn's palm was cool and moist.

As he gathered his coat and scarf, John was left scrambling with the sure knowledge that he'd failed to connect some of the dots. "How did the Philippine military determine the recombinant flu was no risk?"

General Glenn shook his head. "They broke one of two canisters trying to move it. Several men were exposed to the virus but not a single one of them got sick."

John thought about this for a moment. Something was still off. "What did the Tajik biologist do wrong? Why didn't his virus work?"

General Glenn shrugged. The many medals pinned to his chest bobbed. "I don't know. The Philippine military was willing to part with the virus but not with the man. He's apparently accused of other crimes there. He—"

John said, "You have a doctoral degree, General. I'm guessing medicine or biology. Biochemistry, maybe. Am I right?"

Glenn's eyes darted. "Why, yes. Biology. How did—"

"What did the Tajik do wrong? Why didn't the altered flu work as a weapon?"

"I told you. It's unstable."

"What would make it stable?"

Glenn laughed. "A better biologist!"

John continued to smile politely but kept his eyes locked on the other man. John didn't move. Few people can tolerate silence in a conversation.

"Ah. We were lucky. The biologist just wasn't very good," Glenn said. "That's all."

"See? That's the problem?" John made a show of scratching his hair. "The crew we're liking for this heist? They are top-notch. And I gotta tell you, General, they staged a diversion in Manhattan that was a thing of beauty. They did it to cover the theft in Colorado."

Glenn's ears turned pink now.

"So my question is: who goes to that much effort to steal a useless weapon?"

Thirteen

Paris

Daria replayed the so-called fight in her mind. She rewound and did it again.

Shit, she thought. Belhadj had studied Krav Maga, the Israeli martial art.

At least that explained how he managed to kick her ass so competently.

When she could, Daria levered herself up onto one knee, tried to stand. She fell on her butt, tried again, and made it up. Bound and bruised, even inhaling hurt. Her hair was disheveled. Her blue sweater was sour with spilled champagne. Still, the fight had been more humiliating than painful. She'd taken worse beatings at her kickboxing gym in Los Angeles.

This is why she hadn't wanted to confront Belhadj in hand-to-hand combat. He didn't have a reputation as a keen strategist. He had a reputation as a street fighter.

Daria tucked the spade-blade back into her waistband.

She steadied herself, blew stray hair out of her eyes, made sure her breathing was even, and walked straight-backed into the living room. Belhadj sat on one of the two windowsills, thumbing through Internet pages on Daria's smartphone.

"Looking for pornography?"

The Syrian didn't respond. He didn't even look up.

"Tsk. Don't pout. You wouldn't have respected me if I hadn't at least tried."

His eyes flicked up to her. The living room featured a small, oval table for taking meals, and two matched, wooden chairs circa 1950. His wine-soaked jacket hung over the back of one of the chairs.

Belhadj spun the phone in his palm and held it toward her, elbow locked. Daria squinted to see the page he'd brought up.

The page included their photos. They were part of a law-enforcement circular, with a French intelligence header at the top of the page. They were wanted by every agency in the West, the Middle East and northern Africa, regarding a conspiracy to kill the President of the United States of America.

"Ah. That will complicate getting around Paris."

"Yes," he conceded, pulling the phone back and tapping keys. "Do you really know someone who can track Sahar?"

"Maybe. There's no end to the European intelligence agencies. France alone must have seven or eight. They trip over each other. There's a freelance hacker in Paris who keeps up-to-date with all their telephone and computer surveillance protocols. He's completely apolitical and will work with anyone who pays. We used him when I was Shin Bet. Iran did, too."

"That address. Rue de Terrage. Did you make that up?"

"No. He has an electronics shop there. The shop is a front for his hacking job."

Belhadj stood. He examined his jacket, decided it wasn't too stained. He shrugged into it. Daria brought her wrists around to the left of her hips and clinked the links meaningfully.

Belhadj went to the hall closet and found a man's raincoat. He draped it over her shoulders, hiding her arms.

"Let's go."

Both Daria and Belhadj realized using the metro now was too risky, due to the law-enforcement circular with their photos. Outside the apartment, Belhadj led her by the elbow until they found a line of cars blocked from the busier streets by sour-smelling food crates that had been left for pickup. Belhadj drew his lock picks. Daria was impressed that he chose so bland a vehicle: a late 1980s Citroën, painted pale pumpkin and missing its rear bumper. But she didn't want him to know that.

"Really?" she said, climbing in after he held the door open for her. "You couldn't steal something with a little style?"

He hot-wired the ignition, ignoring her. She noted that he carefully repositioned the side and rearview mirrors before pulling out.

She had to sit forward so the cuffs didn't bite into the small of her back.

Belhadj used a map on her smartphone to get them to rue de Terrage. The street was a small cluster of ramshackle retail fronts tucked between the Gare de L'Est train depot and a line of tall, mushroom-gray apartment buildings. As with most of Paris, the neighborhood showed no clear separation between commercial and residential zones.

"This is the place," she said, nodding toward a down-on-its-luck electronics store. They passed by without slowing down. It was heading toward dusk and light, dry snow swirled in the air. Daria couldn't tell if it was snowing or if old snow on the street was being whipped up by the wind.

"What should I know?" Belhadj asked.

"He's . . . colorful. Algerian. He works alone. I've been in his shop a couple of times and never saw any security cameras. I suspect he doesn't trust them because they can be hacked."

"Will he be armed?"

"No."

The Syrian circled the block and parked directly across the street. He sat and watched the door. There was no way of knowing if the shop had customers. According to a sign in the window, they were within ten minutes of closing for the evening.

"How is your French?" he asked.

"Excellent."

"Mine is bad. I sound like an immigrant."

Daria laughed. "You won't stand out. Not in this town."

Belhadj contemplated the scene for a while. His messenger bag rested on the floor of the Citroën, which was rusted out enough to show bits of street beneath them. He reached into the waterproof bag and pulled out a silver .32 Smith & Wesson revolver. He popped open the cylinder and held it butt-first toward Daria's eyes. She could see there were no bullets.

He set it on her lap, leaned toward his window to retrieve the key to the cuffs from his pants pocket. Daria pushed her arms to her left and he unclipped both wrists, took the cuffs with him.

"I don't see any customers." She rubbed her chafed wrists. "He might have seen the circulars with our pictures. We should move quickly once we're inside."

Belhadj nodded, opened his door. Daria stood and shrugged properly into the too-long raincoat, rolled back the sleeves to reveal her hands. She shoved the Smith & Wesson into the coat pocket and walked shoulder to shoulder with the Syrian into the shop.

She thought they looked like extras in a Guy Ritchie movie but kept the observation to herself.

Rene LeClerc wanted in the worst way to be a badass rapper. And that career path would have been fine if Rene LeClerc had any musical skills. Or if he could write. Or if he hadn't had stage fright.

Worse yet, Rene LeClerc wanted to be a rapper circa 1990. He owned enormous gold-painted tchotchki, like American dollar signs, that hung on long gold chains around his neck. He wore them over a New Orleans Saints jersey four times too large, even though he had never actually watched an American football game. He wore droopy pants, enormous knockoff Nike sneakers, and a long, steel key chain that dangled out of his pants pocket and down to his knees. The Algerian immigrant assumed that being black alone made him cool.

In this, he was mistaken.

Daria and Belhadj entered his shop and found no customers. The would-be rapper stood behind his counter, two turntables before him, Mickey Mouse headphones around his neck. He was rummaging through a box of pre-2000 record albums, looking for a hook to riff.

He smiled and spread his arms. He spoke in thickly accented French. "Welcome, friends. Yo yo yo." He attempted but failed to create a gang symbol with his fingers. He didn't appear to recognize either of them but then, he likely was paying more attention to how he looked than how his customers looked. "What is it I am doing for you?"

Daria drew the unloaded Smith from the raincoat and pointed it at the Algerian. Belhadj drew his fully loaded .45. Daria's gun felt light to her experienced hand but the faux rapper wouldn't know the difference.

"Ah, God!" he shouted. "This is three times this month! Come on! I am making the honest living! Why can't you—"

Belhadj circled the front counter from the right, Daria from the left. The Syrian agent reached for the collar of the Saints jersey but Daria slammed the sole of her bulky boot into the side of Rene LeClerc's right knee. He dropped so fast, his chin hit the glass counter, then he fell like damp laundry.

Belhadj took a step back, surprised by the ferocity of her attack.

Daria knelt, scanned the thigh-high shelf behind the counter. She noted a large bottle of cleaning alcohol. Needing both hands, she tossed her revolver to Belhadj. The throw was a little high, and he took a pivot step back, eyes tracking the spiraling gun, to catch it one-handed.

Daria unscrewed the bottle and toppled it.

The acidic liquid spilled onto the Algerian's face and he hacked a panicky cough, spitting out alcohol.

Belhadj took another step back to avoid the bubbling alcohol from hitting his boots.

Daria looked up. "Give me your lighter, please." She spoke in Arabic.

LeClerc reverted to high-pitched Arabic. "Please, no! For the sake of God, no! Please!"

The alcohol bubbled onto his face.

Daria looked up. "Your lighter. Now."

The man on the floor coughed and sobbed.

Daria shook him. "There's an Israeli team in Paris. They are working with the Viking. Have they contacted you?"

"Please stop!"

Daria snapped her fingers. "Lighter!"

"Yes! The Viking is flying them in! Using his airplanes! They arrive tonight! Stop, please!"

Daria looked up at Belhadj, whose eyebrows rose.

"Who is running the Israelis?"

"I don't know! The thin man! The scholar! Glasses!"

Daria felt her chest tighten.

"Did you hook them up?" She referred to the Algerian's famed countersurveillance equipment, which was a must-have for covert intelligence operations in France.

"Yes! But I don't know what they are doing! They tell me nothing! I swear!"

Daria's smile held a predatory glow. "I believe you. I do. But French intelligence upgrades their surveillance protocols regularly. You have to be able to warn the Israelis if that were to happen. Yes?"

Twenty minutes later, LeClerc sat in a chair in the back of his shop, rocking slightly, holding a cool cloth against his eyes, bloodshot from the cleanser, those same eyes never straying far from Daria's legs. He refused to look up or to make eye contact with her. He made no show of recognizing her from her previous visits to his shop.

Daria found a minifridge with a walnut-sized knot of indeterminate cheese and a Spanish apple. She began devouring the food.

"Will the Israelis contact you?" Belhadj went to his haunches and asked softly in Arabic.

"No. I told them I could provide a patch, if the DCRI changes their cyberprotocols." That sentence didn't translate well, so LeClerc reverted to French.

Belhadj glanced up at Daria.

"*Direction Centrale du Renseignement Intérieur.*
French interior intelligence."

The Syrian nodded. He turned back to LeClerc. "So
you can contact them, but they are unlikely to contact
you?"

LeClerc wiped snot off his nose with his sleeve. He
nodded.

Belhadj scrounged around the cash register desk and
came up with a well-chewed pen and the final few pages
of a notepad, a half-inch wall of gummy substance
marking the top of the sheets. "The number?"

LeClerc told him.

Daria said, "Their frequencies?"

LeClerc glanced at her long brown legs, still not
making eye contact. He nodded, then recited numbers.
Belhadj wrote those down as well.

Daria, starving, gobbled the Spanish apple. "And
their emergency backup freq—"

"Yes! All right!" LeClerc gave up that frequency, too.
Belhadj jotted it down.

Daria sighed with the contentment of a cat and
licked apple juice off her fingers.

The Algerian dabbed at his red eyes. He spoke to the
floor. "Whatever you are doing, this is not my business.
Yes? You come, you go. The Israelis, the president, the
Viking, I am not caring. I just want to earn the living."

Belhadj, kneeling, became very still. Daria maintained a serene face while cursing the stupid Algerian
and all of his bloodline.

Belhadj drew his handgun, but did so in a way that did not appear threatening. Daria had no idea how anyone did that. "I appreciate what you said," he told LeClerc. "Discretion is important."

"Of course. Discretion is my business. I don't speak to—"

Daria swiveled, weight on one leg.

Belhadj reacted like lightning, putting distance between them, his gun rising.

Daria's boot connected with the spot directly beneath the left ear of the hapless Algerian. His body seemed to shudder, then collapse in on itself. He fell straight back off the stool, arms outspread as if in supplication to his god, his lower legs propped up on the stool.

Belhadj aimed the Springfield at Daria's sternum. Daria finished the apple, just staring emotionlessly at the Syrian.

The Algerian made a choking noise. His muscles quivered and became still.

Daria studied Belhadj's slate eyes. His right eye was lined up perfectly with the barrel sites of the Springfield. She said, "If my goal had been to kick you . . ."

Belhadj released a few ounces of pressure off the trigger. "The idiot knew about the president, about the circulars."

"There was no need to kill him."

"He'll remember we were here."

"That kick? He won't remember his mother." She turned slowly and tossed the apple core in a rubbish bin

under the counter. She held her back provocatively un-
protected against the unwavering barrel of the auto.
Now it was a waiting game.

But not a long one. Daria heard the shush of the gun
gliding into its holster. She let loose the breath she'd
been holding, but slowly so he wouldn't notice.

Belhadj knelt over the Algerian, rooted through his
pockets, and withdrew a cell phone. He stood.

"That was insanely stupid," he told her. He hit ten
buttons, waited, then spoke into the phone. "Hallo? It's
me. . . . Yes. . . . No names, thank you. I need you to track
down a cell tower for me. No, I mean right now. This
second."

He listened a moment, then read out the telephone
number LeClerc had given them.

"You have it? I will place a call to that number in
sixty seconds. Tell me where it goes. Call me back."

He rang off, still glaring at Daria.

She donned the headphones that LeClerc had been
fiddling with. She recognized the music as French rap.
She knew little of the genre and turned off the music,
tossed aside the headphones. She flipped through the
mildewed record albums. "That wasn't Syrian intelligence, on the phone. Your communications protocols
aren't that loose."

Belhadj leaned his butt against the counter, his long
brown hair falling forward toward his razor-straight
eyebrows. He tossed a gesture toward the bear rug of a
man now decorating the dirty cement floor. "You believe the world is better off because that fool isn't
dead?"

Daria flipped through the albums and pretended to read a couple of the liner notes. She knew that saving LeClerc's life would make her look weak. Good.

"There are tactical reasons to kill," she said. "There are strategic reasons to kill. There are emotional reasons to kill. I admit to you, occasionally, there are fashion reasons to kill. Culottes come to mind."

"What in God's name are you—"

"Not important. My point is: killing a Rene LeClerc? Please. His death would only cause further problems down the road."

He studied her, clearly disappointed. A minute elapsed. He dialed the number the Algerian had given them. He put the phone on speaker.

A phone, somewhere, rang three times.

They both heard a hoarse whisper.

"Hallo?"

Daria felt the air rush from her body. She felt a flood of emotions and no emotions whatsoever. She felt serene and psychotic, assured and adrift. She felt it all simultaneously

That whisper. That voice.

Belhadj disconnected the line. He studied the phone in his calloused hand a moment, then turned blue-gray eyes on Daria. He watched her face.

"I assume I don't have to ask . . . ?"

The phone in his hand rang again. Belhadj checked the incoming number, then answered. He listened. He found LeClerc's pen and the old notepad again.

"Yes . . . yes. Somewhere within that block?"

He placed a palm over the phone and turned to

Daria. "They're in Paris already." He returned to the phone. "And you're sure . . . I understand. Get back to work. We have not spoken."

He disconnected, tossed the mobile phone on to the stomach of the prostrate Algerian on the floor. "Well. We—"

And that's when Belhadj noticed it.

When the Algerian had fallen backward, his baggy trousers had risen up, revealing a fat, plastic holster strapped to his left leg.

A holster. But not a weapon.

Belhadj spun toward Daria just as she pointed an electroshock weapon at his chest. She had stolen it from LeClerc at the beginning—when she had tossed her empty gun to Belhadj, a little high, forcing him to step back and take his eyes off them.

Daria pulled the plastic trigger but Belhadj managed to twist his torso. The tines of the electroshock weapon caught his shoulder and his jacket, not the thin shirt over his chest.

He grunted, stutter-stepped back, right arm constricting in pain, right knee giving out a little.

The Algerian's weapon wasn't a Taser but a cheap, generic knockoff. Not only had the shock been insufficient to knock Belhadj out, but that single shock was all the shabby weapon could muster.

Belhadj, wobbly but still standing, braced himself for her follow-up attack.

Daria tensed, then turned and bolted, her clunky boots a blur. She brushed up lightly against the counter, rounded it, hit the door of the electronics store and pivoted, digging deep and running all-out, arms churning.

Belhadj drew his auto but his hand balked, the muscles clenching, and the draw was slow and shaky. He started running, his muscle coordination a little off, his hip pinging off a display of guitar amplifiers that clattered resonantly to the floor.

Two seconds later, Belhadj burst out of the store, gun down and hidden by his jacket.

Daria was nowhere to be seen.

"Damn it!" he muttered to himself. He checked the streets, both directions. No passersby seemed to notice anything amiss.

Livid, he returned to the shop. He stopped to study the haphazard pyramid of cheap plywood amplifiers he'd toppled. He almost kicked them, but then didn't, because he was a professional and professionals don't—

Belhadj kicked the amps. They broke apart and skidded on the cement.

He waited for that to feel good. When it didn't, he checked the floor behind the counter. LeClerc lay like the crucified, arms straight out, the phone resting on his concave chest.

Belhadj looked at the cash register.

The notepad was gone.

Airspace, Atlantic Ocean

Will Halliday, formerly of the Secret Service, and the two mercenaries he had dubbed "Sex" and "Violence" rode in a Beechcraft King, equipped with an extra fuel tank for the cross-Atlantic route. The plane had been provided by some Swede or Finn or whatever, whom Halliday had never heard of. He had to admit that the dude knew his business: the engine purred, the fake flight plan would pass the white-glove test, and the false registry numbers painted on the tail would have fooled anyone.

They were three hours away from arriving at a private airfield in France and almost five and a half hours behind Asher Sahar and his primary teams.

Before taking off, Will had insisted the Israelis store their handguns in a lockbox. He said it was standard aviation security.

Now, Will sat alone in the cockpit, whistling pop tunes off-key.

Sacchs lay in back on a foldout bench turned into a bed. Curled up in the fetal position, his skin glistened with sweat, he was holding his gut, while his elbows and knees and wrists and ankles all cramping horrendously. A thin white towel rested by his head, most of it saturated in the blood that ran in a steady stream from his nose and ears and mouth and even from his tear ducts. He twitched uncontrollably, partly from the pain and partly from the breakdown of his nervous system.

His fellow mercenary, Veigel, could do nothing to help. He sat at a padded bench across from his friend, holding another white towel over his own mouth, as his own nosebleed began.

Sacchs hacked a wet, bloody cough, droplets spraying Veigel's pant legs and boots.

Veigel rose, unsteadily, hands shaking, and limped to the cabin door.

Will Halliday doffed his Mickey Mouse ears as the mercenary stepped onto the flight deck.

"How's our guy?"

"Dying," Veigel said, and spat blood into the towel he held. "The fuck is happening? I've got it, too."

Halliday shrugged. "Damned if I know. Don't worry, amigo. We're heading to Asher. He'll get us help."

"Are you ill?"

"Me? Picture of health."

"What did we steal from the Secret Service?"

"Printing plates and special paint, used for American currency."

Veigel studied the big blond man for a while. Halliday kept his attention on the yoke and avionics displays.

After a moment, Veigel returned to his friend.

As soon as he was gone, Will Halliday adjusted the radio to a preestablished frequency. "Alpha Sierra, this is Whiskey Hotel. Over."

A pause, and Asher Sahar's cultured voice came back, very strong. "Whiskey Hotel: go."

Halliday said simply, "Veigel is sick."

Halliday waited as that news was absorbed.

"And he was never exposed to the canister?"

"Confirmed. He was exposed to Sacchs."

"So it is airborne. You remain asymptomatic?"

Halliday grinned to himself. "I feel like a million bucks."

Outside the cockpit window, he saw the first smudge of Ireland on the horizon.

"So it works."

"Oh, hell yeah!" the American crowed. "You got yourself a flu you can aim like a gun."

Fourteen

Paris

It took Daria no time to blend into the crowds coming and going in the eastward-facing railway station, Gare de l'Est. She ditched the long raincoat and the spent electroshock weapon. The crowds were hectic, the first hint of holiday throngs. She wended between clusters of tourists and businesspeople until she spotted a pickpocket and began following him from a discreet but close distance. The boy was good; deft, dexterous, and decent-looking. She liked the spit-shine cowlick; a nice, nerdy, endearing touch. Daria herself had been a better-than-average pickpocket when she had been much younger than this lad. She knew talent when she spotted it.

Daria needed, in the following order, a change of clothes, transportation, a decent meal, and a weapon. The young pickpocket would get her started. She bided her time, checking her sight lines for Belhadj.

The youth edged near a cluster of Dutch tourists in

their mid-twenties, wearing the *Clockwork Orange* scarves and caps of the Netherlands Football Club. They were poring over maps of France, the girls giggling, the guys ribbing one another. Daria waited until her pickpocket was sliding past the Dutch, his hand drawing forth a wallet.

"Thief!" Daria shouted in French and shoved the pickpocket from behind.

The boy stumbled and fell, the wallet bouncing off the filthy tile floor. The kid made eye contact with the wallet, as did one of the Dutch, and a melee broke out. One of the Dutchmen let loose with a volley of kicks. The kid scrambled for safety. People shrieked and backed away. Others surged in to watch.

A gendarme heard the commotion and headed into the fray. He bumped into Daria, who dragged one of the wheeled suitcases she'd just stolen from one of the Dutch women.

"The train stations aren't safe!" Daria wailed in French, free hand flailing. "It's these immigrants!"

"Yes, madam," the officer agreed, dodging around her and wading into the fray.

Moments later, Daria rolled her new bag out into the dusk. It took her two blocks to find a cab driver leaning against a dilapidated Toyota Auris, holding up the sports section of a newspaper but watching Daria's legs beneath the brief skirt. He looked to be from Eastern Europe or the former Soviet Union, she guessed.

She rolled the luggage to a stop, standing a little too close to the driver, looking up into his eyes. Daria took a gamble on English heavily tainted with a German accent. "I need a lift but I don't have any money."

Badly accented English means you're a tourist, an outsider. It makes you vulnerable.

The driver grinned, revealing gray teeth. His English was carried aloft with a Ukrainian accent. "You want a ride, I want a blow job. Deal?"

She let her lips tremble. "All right. Find us a quiet spot."

She tossed the bag in the backseat and sat up front with the driver. He wedged his belly beneath the steering wheel and drove. He'd done this before obviously. He quickly found a secluded space in an alley behind a bank. He leered at her and pushed back his seat just as Daria's elbow connected with his temple. The driver was unconscious before his forehead hit the steering wheel.

She dug through his pockets and found a mobile phone; she set it on the dashboard.

She climbed over the seat back of the hatchback and used the driver's keys to pry open the stolen luggage. It was freezing in the alley. Kneeling on the ripped vinyl seat, she quickly stripped. The first thing she found were panties. She checked the label. Extraordinarily cheap. *God*, she thought. *The things a girl does for world peace.*

She found a sleeveless T-shirt known to Americans as a wifebeater. Daria had trouble dealing with American colloquialisms. *Wifebeater?* Is there a part of that term that is funny? She tugged on the T-shirt and freed her hair. Once, in Jerusalem, she had had a master sergeant who was, in fact, a wife beater. Daria had taken his wife to a public hospital and sat up with her through the night, listening to her excuses, why it had been *her* fault, why she had failed as a good spouse. In the morning, Daria walked into the motor pool, picked up a crescent wrench, and told the master sergeant, "I have a message from your wife." She then proceeded to break every bone in both of his wrists.

He never pressed charges.

In the alleyway, she dug through the luggage, found a short denim skirt that would fit. Also black tights. She found a white, ribbed, long-sleeved undershirt. The Dutch woman's feet were enormous, so Daria stuck with her chain-laden punk boots from New York.

She climbed out, opened the driver's side door, and rolled the unconscious man out onto the grimy pavement. She took his wallet and climbed into the car, slid the seat forward, and cranked the key.

As the hatchback's engine turned over and heater began pumping air through the vents, Daria snagged the driver's mobile off the dashboard. She dialed the international code for the United States, then the number for Ray Calabrese's mobile.

In the subbasement Shark Tank at Langley, one tech analyst had been assigned to monitor Ray Calabrese's home, work, and cell phones, as well as his work and personal e-mail accounts. Ray was not on Facebook or any other social media site, making the tech's job a little easier. The tech glanced up at his monitors as Ray's cell phone line went hot.

"Hi, it's Ray. I'm on another line. Please leave me a message." Beep.

"It's Daria. I'm in trouble. And I'm in Paris . . ."

The surveillance tech jumped out of his seat, snapping his fingers at a fellow analyst. "Are you getting this?"

"Don't use my phone, it's in enemy hands. I cannot hold on to this one either, because the CIA is monitoring your phone. Sorry. I'm in trouble with them. I'm in trouble with the Syrians. It's possible I'm in trouble with the Israelis. It's been one of those weeks. Look up this name: Asher Sahar. I will contact you again soon. Ciao, love."

The other tech leaned forward, blowing kinky hair away from her eyebrows, fingers moving so fast over her keyboard they were a blur. One of the eight flat-screen monitors switched to a map of the world. Then a map of Europe. Then France. Then the Tenth arrondissement. Then the Gare de l'Est train station.

"Got her! Near the train station, northeast Paris!"

The cheese and apple Daria had eaten at the Algerian's electronics shop had been sufficient to hold her temporarily. Now she was famished. She spent some of the taxi driver's money on a cheese-and-butter baguette sandwich and a large coffee from a street kiosk, a block from where she'd given the taxi driver his "blow" job. *Perhaps you should make your request more specific next time,* she thought, smiling to herself. She reached under the kiosk counter and wedged the stolen mobile into a hollow triangle made by the counter and its wooden brace.

* * *

Khalid Belhadj parked the stolen car away from onlookers, only two blocks from the electronics shop. He
cursed himself. He checked for observation points,
then stripped to the waist and studied the two nasty red
welts on the concave spot between his shoulder and his
chest, courtesy of Daria Gibron.

The madwoman must have palmed the damned Taser
when she attacked the Algerian, but Belhadj hadn't seen
a thing. He was impressed despite himself.

Belhadj didn't underestimate people very often. In
some perverse way, he always admired enemies who
proved better than anticipated. Being better than one's
reputation was one of the things that had kept Belhadj
alive all these years.

He allowed himself a shallow smile. She was not the
easiest of assets. But his decision to bring her along still
had merit. Belhadj was a soldier, not a general. Against
Asher Sahar? He needed more than brute strength.

He sat in the car and flexed his right arm. The muscles twitched, his hand shaking. He could go after Gibron, but to what end? He had hoped her hatred of Sahar
would be enough to encourage her assistance. He had
misjudged her hatred. Pity.

He would have to deal with Sahar himself, until such
time as his superiors in Damascus could be . . . reasoned
with.

In the Shark Tank, a communication techie doffed her
headset and stood. "Nanette?"

The lanky show runner—a term Nanette Sylvestri's

most admiring staffers had borrowed from Hollywood to describe her—had been hovering over another monitor. She turned.

"DCRI, ma'am."

Nanette nodded and stepped to the middle of the room, where the tech experts had told her to stand when using the room's teleconference system. Someone had even put an adhesive tape X on the carpet. One of the flat screens popped to life. She recognized the man on the screen as Henri-Luc Deschamps, a high-ranking official of the Direction Centrale du Renseignement Intérieur, or Central Directorate of Interior Intelligence.

The French equivalent of the FBI.

"Nanette," he said, nodding slightly. The man was in his late sixties and wore a bristle-cut flattop and a coarse mustache.

"Henri-Luc. Thank you for that cell phone trace. We appreciate your quick response."

"Not quick enough, apparently." He spoke English for the sake of Sylvestri's crew. "Two of my people found the phone. It was at a baguette kiosk. No sign of your Jewish gunrunner. However, the mobile and your fugitive were only a few blocks from a surveillance operation of our own. An operation that, as you say, heated up today."

Sylvestri mistrusted coincidence. He had her attention.

"We have been monitoring an Algerian cyberterrorist for some weeks. A Rene LeClerc," Deschamps said. "This evening, we intercepted three mobile calls, to and from this man's base of operations. One of my people is a linguist and identified at least one of the callers as a Syrian."

Sylvestri shushed a few talkative people in the Shark Tank. "Sorry, Henri-Luc. Go ahead."

"Based on your circular regarding *la bête Syrienne*, we sent an assault team to the site about four minutes ago. We found the cyberterrorist."

"Is he speaking?"

"No, and not for a while. He has suffered a trauma to the brain. He might be unconscious for days."

"The cell calls . . . ?" Sylvestri allowed herself to wish, and she was rewarded by a brief smile from the gaunt Frenchman.

"We recorded them, of course. And translated them. In short: I believe we know where *la Syrienne* and your *trafiquant d'armes* are headed. Tonight."

Daria reviewed her needs: money, a cell phone, transportation, and food—the taxi driver had kindly provided those things. A change of clothes—the Dutch tourist helped with that. Next on her list: a weapon.

It didn't take long for Daria to find drug runners in an inner, northeast suburb of Paris. She cruised through an economically downtrodden neighborhood in the stolen taxi for about fifteen minutes before spotting two teenage boys, dashing out of an alley that faced a street in which eight of ten shops were abandoned. One boy would step up to an idling car, lean in the window, and take a handful of something—euros, of course— then would head back down the alley. A second boy then strolled out of the alley, leaned into the same car window, and handed something over.

They were very efficient. Daria cruised the block twice and watched four transactions take place.

She rounded the block and parallel parked the taxi in the first slot. She walked around the corner, halfway down the block, and into the alley. She shivered in the white undershirt.

"Hallo, boys."

The boys appeared to be twelve or thirteen years old and Asian. Vietnamese, she thought. They looked at each other, then back at her.

"No walk," one of them said in halting French. "Car only."

Daria stood close and smiled. "It's okay. I'm not here to buy drugs."

The two boys frowned, trying to make out her game. One of the boys glanced nervously over Daria's shoulder. The other studied her breasts under the clingy T-shirt. She thought his was the psychologically healthier reaction of the two. "I just want to stand here and talk a bit. See, I recently did some freelance work for a group called the DEA. Do you know them?"

The boy ogling her breasts shook his head. The other said, "No school today. Is day off."

"Yes, I had several of those while in school. I was assured by the DEA that young, street-level runners, such as yourselves, would never face prison time due to your age."

"You go now," the older boy said.

"But you also wouldn't carry firearms, because to

do so would increase your chances of being treated as an adult in court. Was my associate correct in this?"

Daria felt the presence of a fourth person in the alley before she heard him. She saw it in the eyes of the boy not eyeing her breasts. "Which means you would need an enforcer. Correct?"

A hand grabbed the thin cotton strap over Daria's left shoulder, pulling upward, hard. The newcomer began to turn her.

Daria turned with his motion, going in the direction she was being pulled, her elbow slashing diagonally. The newcomer fell to the filthy asphalt of the alleyway, both hands rising to cover a split lip. Daria knelt and drove her left elbow into the enforcer's temple.

She heard the two teens sprinting past her and out of the alley.

The now-unconscious enforcer wore a sleeveless, black hoodie over a woolen plaid shirt. As the hood fell back, she realized it was a girl, also Asian, all of sixteen, if that.

Daria patted her down and found a Glock G17, the fourth-generation model. She smiled. It was among the most dutiful automatics in the world. She had fired literally thousands of target practice rounds with such a handgun and had never seen one jam.

She took the enforcer girl's wallet, fat with folded euros.

With a little difficulty, she lifted the girl's torso to free the hooded sweatshirt. It was sleeveless and midnight-black. It went with Daria's dark denim miniskirt and black tights. Daria shrugged into the hoodie.

The enforcer also wore black lambskin gloves, which covered the first two joints of each finger but not her finger pads or nails. The gloves were very short with tiny gold zippers that ran half the length of each palm. Daria removed them and slipped her hands in. They fit, truncated just short of her wrist bones. She flexed her fingers, picked up the Glock. Daria was impressed. The gloves were warm but thin enough not to hamper her draw. She tucked the Glock into the waistband of the miniskirt and slid the sweatshirt over it.

It took John Broom four phone calls to the army infectious disease research facility in Frederick, Maryland, just to get the name of the person he should have asked for in the first place.

"Research," he told yet another person. "Recombinant influenza. . . . No, just research. . . . Yeah, I'm trying to figure what I don't know. . . . Hang on." He grabbed a pen.

John thought, *I'm CIA. You'd think I could get through a bureaucracy faster than this.*

"James? Major Theo James. Can you connec— No? Okay. Thanks."

He hung up and began looking up more numbers to call. It was rule number one for research: there were always more numbers to call.

He heard a rap on his cubicle wall. One of his fellow analysts rounded the corner. "Dude. Where are you?"

John shrugged, thinking, *Um . . . here?* He checked the time on his computer monitor. It was just a little past four on a Friday. "Why? What's up?"

The analyst rolled his eyes. "Your going-away party, dumbass."

Owen Cain Thorson would not be attending John's going-away party. He and a team of sixteen battle-hardened soldiers were boarding a modified Boeing 757 SP, fueled up and teed up on the runway at Andrews. No flight plan had been filed on any official document, but everyone knew they were heading for France aboard the fastest thing with wings that was large enough to carry that many men.

The operations computer had spat out a random code for Thorson's strike team: Swing Band.

These were not traditional CIA spooks. Outside of Thorson, none of them had ever bugged a boardroom or swiped a classified document. They were former SEALS, Green Berets, and Army Rangers. This was not an espionage mission.

This was a hunting party.

Henri-Luc Deschamps, DCRI, was on call as station chief for Paris. As such, he had at his disposal two independent strike teams courtesy of the French military.

From his subterranean command center beneath the Ministry of the Interior—at Place Beauvau, only blocks north of the Champs-Elysées—the station chief made the calls to bring in both strike teams. That gave him access to an estimated thirty soldiers, complete with air support and mechanized armor. In short, he mobilized the majority of the city's military-intelligence assets.

Overkill? Maybe. But Henri-Luc Deschamps had

just received a file indicating the woman was participating in a conspiracy to kill the president of the United States.

As for Khalid Belhadj? He, too, was implicated in the conspiracy. But French intelligence also had had its share of contretemps with that cold-blooded butcher. Belhadj and his fellow bastards of the Mukhabarat, the Syrian Military Intelligence Directorate, had operated on French soil on at least three known occasions.

It was an account that Henri-Luc Deschamps intended to pay. With interest.

They got John Broom a Costco cake with white icing and the words *So Long Suckers!* scrolled across it in dollar-green cursive. Someone had crafted a black felt bag, a cord tying it closed at the top. One side featured a decal of the Capitol Building. The other showed a dollar sign and the word *Loot!* The oversized Hallmark card featured Scrooge McDuck diving into a pool of gold bullion.

John's immediate supervisor said a few words, as did her supervisor. A retired director of Central Intelligence sent a handwritten note of thanks; an almost-unheard-of gesture for the analysis side of the building. Stanley Cohen and Nanette Sylvestri both emerged, he from the rarified loft of administration, she from the dungeon.

As people queued for cake and coffee or punch, John took Sylvestri aside. "Pegasus?" he whispered.

"We have 'em."

John barely maintained his poker face. "Alive?"

She shrugged. "*Have* is too strong a word. Gibron and Belhadj are in France. DCRI has their location. They're putting together a strike force. It's all over but the shouting."

People in the third-floor cafeteria hooted at John and called him over to the cake table to make a speech.

"Why France?"

Sylvestri sipped her punch. "G-8?"

The Group of Eight, the world's eight most industrialized nations, were gathering in Avignon in less than a week. The president planned to attend as always, this year to discuss the debt crisis.

Nanette Sylvestri threw an arm over John's shoulder and bussed him on the top of his head. "You got yourself a world-class brain, Mister Broom. Go make us proud."

As she hustled back to the Shark Tank, John made a "come here" gesture to a young man with a mop of curly hair and Buddy Holly frames. He was a postdoc from the University of Kansas, doing a practicum at Langley.

"Do me a favor?" John asked, and scribbled a note on a festive paper napkin. "Go look this up."

The postdoc glanced at it. "Are you kidding?"

"No. Go."

Amid more calls of "Speech! Speech!" John Broom returned to the half-devoured Costco cake and addressed his soon-to-be-former coworkers.

Fifteen minutes later, the party was going strong when John's cell phone vibrated. He checked the incoming message, then excused himself and stepped into the hall.

"Mr. Broom? I'm Theo James. Understand you're looking for me?"

"Would you prefer Major James or Doctor James?"

The man on the other end chuckled. "I'd prefer Theo but the darned brass gets hacked off when we say that. I hear you were lighting up the switchboard at USAM-RIID looking for me."

John glanced around to make sure he was alone in the corridor. "You're one of the army's experts in recombinant influenza."

"Yup." The voice sounded jovial. "Nobody's experter than me!"

"Listen. Do you have some time? We're working on a situation and it involves influenza, and I have this feeling I'm being led down the path, if you know what I mean."

"Sure. We could grab a coffee or something. My daughter's playing basketball Saturday morning but I'm free after—"

"What are you doing this evening?"

After a beat, the voice on the line came back a little less jovial. "Do we have a zoonotic incident?"

"I don't know what the hell we have. I could really use your expert advice, and I could really use it to-night."

"Where and when?"

They agreed on a time and place, then John thanked him and hung up.

As he did, a member of the building security detail entered the hallways. "John. Wow, we're going to miss you, man."

John shook the security agent's hand. "Thanks, Phil."

"Look, I need to get your ID and keys, and your—"

"Sunday," John said.

The man's smile faltered a bit. "N-no. I really need to get them now."

"I just had someone look up the employment protocols. I'm on the job until midnight, Sunday. And last I checked, I was officially assigned to Pegasus. If Pegasus is still running, I'm still working. I'll hand in my credentials on Sunday."

Fifteen

Outside Paris

It was almost 11:00 P.M. by the time Daria found the
square block in which, according to Belhadj's source,
Asher Sahar's mobile phone awaited. She sat, Toyota
taxi idling, in a heavily industrial but down-on-its-luck
sector of outer Paris, a few miles east of the city. It
wasn't difficult to figure out which building on the block
to search: an enormous, hulking factory took up the
entire block. Most of the windows on the ground floor
had been smashed and boarded over. Signs and spray-
paint stencils warned *DANGER!* and *NO TRESPASSING!*
Most of those had been covered over with gang graffiti,
Americano-style, which Daria couldn't translate and
didn't bother trying.

The factory sat on a railroad spur. It had stood unused and quite uninhabitable. It had thrived for decades,
used to mass-produce everything from steamer trunks
to canned goods, shipping them by sea to the Americas
and by train to Central Europe and Asia. It was a brick

affair, grimy, built around the nineteenth to twentieth century fin de siècle. A blocklong and a blockwide, with no lights showing at night, it took Daria a good ten minutes to spot the sweep of a sentry's penlight from a third-floor window. If she hadn't been looking for it, there was no way she would have spotted it.

Thankful for the full moon and cloudless sky, she finally spotted the change-of-shift on the roof, as one sniper replaced another.

How classically Asher. He'd found himself an impenetrable fortress.

You can't, mulled Asher Sahar, tell an abandoned factory by its graffiti.

The outer walls of the suburban Paris factory were grimy and decrepit. But Asher Sahar's people had had six weeks to work on the fixer-upper.

The northeast corner of the ground floor had been modified substantially. But only the northeast corner, since the floors for the rest of the building were rotting through and treacherous.

Asher's people had established a grid of aluminum poles directly inside the front door of the factory, sixty meters by sixty meters, then strung sturdy polyvinyl sheets from the poles, creating a room within the room, one foot away from the north and east walls, three feet from the ceiling. They had boarded over all of the first- and second-story windows and had added creosote to the cracks to keep the light inside. Tall banks of halogen lights had been set up at the four corners of the new, plastic cube of a room they had created.

A complicated pyramid of oxygen tanks and compressors was installed, as well as external air vents added to the exterior of the building, then grimed over to avoid being noticed by the daytime neighbors. By the third day, the air pressure inside the white plastic cube room was slightly lower than the air pressure in Paris: In the event of a tear in the sealed fabric walls of the room, air would rush in, not rush out.

Next, a complicated, military tent, also with an aluminum frame, was set up and sealed within the cube but farther back from the factory door. It created a room within a room within a room.

Outside of the white plastic cube, the factory remained dark and dank. Asher did a walk-through that evening, shortly after eleven, to make sure everything was in place. A few electric lanterns had been set on the floor at strategic places, reflecting light up onto his emotionless face and sparse beard as he passed silently through the remainder of the ground floor, picking his footing carefully. The light glinted on his wire-frame eyeglasses. The lanterns had been turned to their lowest setting with photographers' black umbrellas perched over them to keep their light low and focused on the wooden floor, away from the windows.

Much of the ground floor was unstable. Rats squeaked and skittered under the boards, and the stink of sewer water permeated portions of the warehouse. During their first day at the factory, one of the mercenaries had fallen through a termite-infested floor and broken both his ankles. Eli Schullman eventually found a safe route to the roof, mostly using rickety catwalks and a makeshift ladder of horizontal, C-shaped rebar bolted to the brick wall. They used red bandannas to mark the safe passage, so each shift of sniper-watchers could gain access without falling.

Since then, they had maintained twenty-four-hour surveillance of the building for six straight weeks.

Asher returned to the brightly lit cube room and sat in a folding iron chair, a gray winter coat pulled tight around his thin body, long legs out, crossed at the ankles. He felt a slim volume in his coat pocket and remembered that he had picked up a copy of *Night Flight* by the doomed aviator Antoine de Saint-Exupéry. Asher always tried to read literature from the country he operated in.

He looked around. Of the eight men with him, three were former Mossad, four were mercenaries from around the globe. The eighth, the newest arrival, was Will Halliday, recently of the Secret Service. It had been Will who had contacted Asher's benefactors and offered to help any way he could. Halliday had lost too many good men to terrorist attacks. He was a committed anti-Islamist. Now he was fully part of the mission. A true believer. Being paid a king's ransom, yes, but a believer nonetheless.

Asher's eyes roamed the oddly futuristic white cube room. It was such an odd contrast to the dilapidated factory around it. It made the perfect rendezvous point. They just had to wait for the pathologist.

Across the street and half a block down from Asher's factory-turned-fortress stood an old, dilapidated, and badly rusting grain elevator. No grain had been stored there for more than a dozen years.

Throwing a large, oilskin carrying case over his left shoulder, Belhadj climbed the exterior ladder to a narrow iron-mesh balcony, about a hundred meters up, ignoring the lingering pain from the electroshock weapon. He reached the balcony and found a vertical curtain of rust-red iron, dangling by twisted wires from the handrail. It was barely big enough to lie down on but would shield his body from the warehouse. He lay on his stomach. Among the items Belhadj had stolen from the CIA command vehicle—technically Daria had stolen it first and he had stolen it from her— was a pair of powerful Bushnell 10X42 ARC Rangefinder binoculars. He raised the binoculars to scan the vicinity, forcing himself not to flinch when he rotated his right shoulder. He noted one man leaning in the shadows of the front door, smoking. It took him almost no time to spot the sniper-surveillance man on the roof of the oddly disproportional factory, almost two blocks away. The man had camouflaged himself with cardboard boxes. He lay on a roof that appeared to be undulated like a skateboard park. He wondered how the man made it up there without breaking his neck.

Belhadj dutifully and slowly scanned the perimeter; every street, every alley, every rooftop. His diligence paid off when he spotted two men in an aged panel truck, sitting and smoking. Both had military haircuts and bulging biceps. Asher Sahar's external line of security, doubtless.

Although it seemed odd that the guards were looking toward the factory, not away from it.

More patience led to the discovery of movement on an adjacent roof. His binoculars picked up a blur of a human leg in fatigues, ducking behind a ventilation shaft. He also caught sight of a Renault delivery truck, which passed within a block of the factory not twice, but three times inside a forty-minute window.

That's when it dawned on him: this wasn't Asher Sahar's outer line of defense.

This was French military surveillance.

Daria watched as a car pulled up to the factory and flashed its lights: one-two. A pause, then once more.

Two men emerged from the car and walked to the front door of the warehouse. It opened from inside. The brute of a man who opened the door stood aside to let the newcomers in. Even without binoculars, Daria could identify him. He was the size of a bear, six foot six, with a shaven head and a skull oddly shaped like a bullet, protruding upward in the back, making him look half-alien.

Eli Schullman. Former Mossad agent. He had been Asher's most trusted confidant and friend for years. She had known the truth since hearing Asher's voice over the cell phone in the Algerian's shop. But seeing Schullman confirmed everything.

Belhadj, that Syrian son of a whore, hadn't been lying. Asher Sahar truly was behind everything that had happened.

* * *

Eli Schullman stood aside and let two people in through the factory door. He nodded to one of his men, the Bosnian Croat who had been on the scene in Manhattan. "Stay here. Watch the street."

Schullman led the two men inside. One was a bodyguard from the Ivory Coast.

The second man was smallish and wore a nice suit under a calf-length cashmere coat, with gloves, a scarf, and a Russian-style woolen hat. He skin was smooth and a little bit pink, with a bulbous nose that dominated all other features.

The Ivorian bodyguard was the opposite, a man so thin and grisly he looked like a suit of wet clothes hanging from a wire hanger. His eye sockets and cheekbones were deeply concave and his skin so black as to be nearly purple in the low light.

Inside the factory door, they brushed aside long, vertical strips of heavy plastic that hung from a curtain rod. Beyond that, Schullman opened a seam in the white cube room, held together with magnets. He and the newcomers entered the clean room. The newcomers squinted at the bright lights, set up strategically to eliminate almost all shadows.

Asher rose from his chair in one easy move, sliding the yellowed aviation novel back into his coat pocket, gracefully crossing the rickety wooden floor to the newcomer. He held out a hand and the small man shook without removing his kid leather gloves. Between them, they looked like academics greeting each other at a symposium.

"Dr. Rabadeau. A pleasure."

Dr. Georges Rabadeau smiled politely and nodded. "Good evening." They both spoke in French, Rabadeau's a gentile and lyrical blend that suggested a wealthy upbringing and the best schools. He studied the clean room, nodded his approval.

"I trust you were not inconvenienced overmuch, being awakened at this hour?" The question was purely polite conversation. Asher knew any inconvenience had been quickly subsumed by the very large increase in the Frenchman's offshore bank account.

"Think no more of it," the man almost purred. "I am here to serve."

"Splendid." Asher waved an arm theatrically around his sparse, clean, dust-free cube. Plastic sheeting had been stapled down over the aged floorboards, made of the same white plastic material as the walls and ceiling of the room. "Will this do?"

"It is sufficient." the Frenchman nodded.

"And here, your work space?"

Asher's gesture revealed the tent, painted in camouflage colors of greens and golds and grays. It looked like the kind of sturdy tent a hunting party might use, with aluminum pipes creating a frame and the painted canvas pulled taught against them. It was the room within the room within the room. Dr. Rabadeau recognized it for what it was.

The tent featured no open seams. The entry wasn't a flap, but a vertical tube, six feet high, with a flat panel that rotated on its vertical axis like a revolving door. By standing against the panel and pushing, you could enter the tent with just the air that surrounded you. Negative air pressure and powerful fans on the other side of the canvas would assure everyone that precious little air—or anything else—could escape the tent.

Georges Rabadeau had worked in tents like these before. It had been during his stint with the World Health Organization, at a field station in the northern Democratic Republic of Congo. When he had served as a pathologist on the banks of the Ebola River.

As the French pathologist examined his airtight work environment and the full-containment hazardous-materials suit, Asher Sahar stepped next to Eli Schullman and reverted to Hebrew.

"Have the Americans caught Daria and Belhadj?"

The big man reached into his shirt pocket for a packet of smokes and a lighter. "Not yet."

Asher smiled up at the man. "May I ask a favor?"

"Anything."

"Could you not smoke next to the massive tanks of superpressurized oxygen?"

Schullman cast a baleful look at the horizontal pyramid of tanks, eight high, that were stabilizing the air pressure both in the white cube room and in the incubation tent. "It's a sad state of affairs when you can orchestrate an international military strike with global repercussions, but you can't catch a smoke."

Asher nodded. "Life is unfair."

"You said it. Law enforcement, intelligence agencies, everyone's still looking for Daria and the Syrian bastard."

Asher nodded and shrugged as if it were no big deal.

Schullman rolled the unlit cigarette between the pads of his finger and thumb.

Asher's personal cell phone throbbed. He pulled it out of his pocket, entered his security code. A text appeared on the screen.

Schullman held the cigarette under his nose and inhaled the faint smell of stale tobacco. "Trouble?"

"My foster parents." Asher allowed himself a shallow smile and adjusted his bifocals. "They are vacationing in London. Mother wants to see West End plays. Father wants to bomb Parliament."

"For a literature professor, he was always progressive. You have someone watching them?"

"Remember Aguirre? The mercenary from the Dominican Republic?"

"Sure. He's good."

"Hmm." Asher smiled some more and scrolled through the text. His foster parents had visited four bookshops so far: his father's idea of Disneyland.

Asher continued to smile softly, and anyone other than Eli Schullman would have missed the anguish behind his eyes.

"The Knesset plot. The one that got us sentenced to that hellhole prison. Without a public trial . . ." Schullman let his voice drift off.

Asher keyed in a thank-you text to the Dominican. "Without a trial, my foster parents never heard any news about me. Nothing about my arrest, the military tribunal, or prison. They believe I'm dead. Mossad told them I died overseas, in the service of my country."

Schullman kept his counsel, waited.

"My parents sat shiva. Mother had been given a folded Israeli flag at the funeral. No coffin, of course. No body. I'm told she held it on her lap the full seven days. Today, they have a fireplace mantel that they've turned into a shrine. Photos of me in school, in the Air Force. Playing cricket. It's nice."

Schullman contemplated the dimly lit white cube room. "When Hannah Herself found you a foster home, she couldn't have known you'd bond to them as if they were your real parents."

"Hannah knew what she was doing," Asher whispered. "Hannah knew. The Group knew. I'm grateful. Not many people like me have the luxury of parents to worry over."

Schullman seemed to absorb this, nodding silently.

Asher smiled up at his friend. "I wish Daria had played her designated role in New York."

Schullman rolled the cigarette back and forth. He kept an eye on the camouflaged medical tent. "You warned her. Didn't you."

Asher peered around at his men, spread out in the white-walled space.

"That's why you were surprised when she tripped us up in Manhattan. You didn't expect her to even be there. You warned her to stay away."

Asher turned to his friend and the tripod lights

glinted off his flat, round lenses. Schullman waited. He didn't appear judgmental.

"I sent her a message at the New York airport, telling her she was burned. She didn't take the warning. Then again, that one rarely follows a given script."

Asher shook his head, smiling.

"God in Heaven, that was a risk. Why do it? The plan came from Hannah Herself."

"Bringing Daria into this was a mistake. I told Hannah that from the very start. But I couldn't talk the Group out of it. For all that, I couldn't just let Daria walk into the CIA's clutches, either. I owe her too much."

"You spent almost four years in a secret military prison because of her."

"And I shot her. I can't ever forgive myself for that."

Schullman rolled the cigarette between his fingers and kept his face neutral. None of the other soldiers could tell what he was thinking.

"It could have been worse," Schullman said. "Having Daria and that Syrian butcher in CIA custody would have been good. Having them lead the CIA on a romp through America is maybe even better. As long as they stay distracted for another day."

Asher smiled to his friend, thankful that he hadn't been lectured. It never dawned on him to wonder if Schullman would report this news to their superiors. There was no truer friend than Eli Schullman.

And as the big man said, warning Daria did make her more of a roving target for U.S. intelligence, and thus more of a distraction. But Asher couldn't help wondering what mischief she and Belhadj could be up to.

He took comfort in the thought that, at least, they likely hated each other as much or more than they hated Asher himself.

Sixteen

Daria sat in the dilapidated hatchback and watched the darkened factory. From where she sat, she could see the walls had been liberally annotated with *WARNING! DANGER!* and *DO NOT ENTER!* posters.

"Attention psychotic ex-spies," she whispered to herself. "If you lived here, you'd be home by now."

Daria Gibron was not, by nature, a long-range strategist. Her plans tended to stretch out two, maybe three hours into the future. She had found Asher's redoubt, which was as far as her planning had taken her.

She checked the Glock G17 that the young Asian girl had provided. The magazine was full. She slowly jacked the slide a half-inch and spotted the eighteenth round in the pipe. Good. The firearm weighed only about twenty-two ounces with a four-and-a-half-inch barrel.

Now she just needed to come up with a plan.

Being shot in the stomach by Asher Sahar years ago had been bad. But for an adrenaline junkie like Daria, the months it took her to fully recover and return to her fighting strength were worse. The FBI in America gave her unlimited access to physical therapists. They got her up and walking, and eventually jogging, then running.

To increase her upper body strength, Daria took an archery class at a local community college. She could have simply joined a gym and pumped weights, but closing one eye and peering down the range at the straw-filled target and imagining the face of Asher Sahar was oh, so much more fun.

For her lower body strength, she signed up at a gym favored by the Los Angeles FBI agents as well as local police. The joint was owned and operated by retired army sergeants, and was run with all the delicacy of boot camp. There, she took up and excelled at kickboxing. Like archery, it was much more fun than lifting weights and served as a splendid answer to release her pent-up aggression. Kickboxing and archery also had the advantage of being potentially useful in the field; Daria seriously doubted she would ever be called upon to bench-press an opponent to death.

But it was at the master sergeants' gym that Daria picked up another exercise favorite: wall climbing, which supported strength as well as balance and dexterity.

She'd learned wall climbing inside the gym but had quickly graduated to climbing and bouldering around California in places like Williamson Rock, Malibu Creek State Park, and Boney Bluff in Point Mugu State Park—not all that far from where she'd once watched an airliner carrying Ray Calabrese pancake into the desert.

*   *   *

Ten minutes later, Daria stood in the darkened alley between the factory and the next abandoned building, the pitch-black hood over her hair, white sleeves of her undershirt pushed up past her elbows, tugging on the fingerless kid gloves with the tiny gold palm zippers. The alley stank of urine. Around her boots, discarded drug needles glinted in the dull light from the street. A padlocked Dumpster was pressed up against one wall. She studied the old factory with a critical eye. The detailed brickwork of the façade dated back at least a hundred years. It included a pattern of bricks that stood out from the vertical surface in an artistic pattern.

She shrugged, thinking, *The bastards shan't see this coming.*

The clunky boots had good, thick rubber soles that held a grip well. She bent at the waist, rubbed her fingertips over the asphalt of the alley, letting dirt and grit rub away skin oil and sweat. She hiked up the denim skirt and scampered up atop the Dumpster. It rolled a little under her weight and she realized it was empty. She lifted her left boot up atop a long-unused water pipe. Hoisting herself up atop it, she could reach two of the protruding bricks on the warehouse façade, one at shoulder height and the other a few inches over her head. Their surfaces were sooty but dry. The fingerless gloves were perfect for this. Daria brought her right foot up to a protruding brick near her knee. By turning her boot sideways, the ball of her foot took her weight on the brick and her left boot left the water pipe, seeking the next climbing purchase.

Five minutes later, Daria reached the second of three floors and paused to peer into a darkened window. She saw no movement within. She was sweating under the thermal T-shirt and sleeveless black hoodie. She could feel the strain of the climb in her back and shoulder muscles. She grinned like a wolf.

From his vantage point on the iron platform of the grain elevator, Belhadj set down the binoculars and dragged forward the oilskin bag. He unzipped it and pulled out the component parts of a Sako TRG-42 sniper rifle. It wasn't a gun he'd stolen from the CIA command vehicle. Those had consisted mainly of handguns, shotguns, and explosives. A sniper rifle is different. Belhadj had never practiced with the models he'd found in the CIA truck.

This rifle, with its olive-colored stock, was from the Paris safe house. The Sako TRG was a weapon Belhadj knew well. It felt comfortable and familiar in his calloused hands as he unfolded the stock and slid the adjustable aluminum bipod legs into the slot under the barrel. He snapped the monocular night-vision scope into its bayonet mount atop the barrel. He reached back blindly, felt through the duffel bag of weaponry for the five boxes of .338 Lapua rounds. Next came the silencer, bringing the rifle's 124-centimeter—or forty-nine-inch—frame closer to 152 centimeters.

Belhadj's initial plan was simple enough. He was sure that Asher Sahar and his mercenary team were within the warehouse. He had planned to empty all five boxes of subsonic .338 rounds through the boarded-over windows on the ground floor of the warehouse. He'd be firing blind, of course, but the odds of hitting Sahar and/or his teammates were pretty good. They would attempt to hide behind objects, but the sniper bullets would penetrate most materials short of iron or steel. When the boxes of bullets were exhausted, he would quickly climb down the ladder, cross the street, and lob in the stolen CIA hand grenades. Follow that up by entering with the Mossberg shotgun to mop up whoever remained.

Simple. Efficient.

But of course, that was before more and more French surveillance units appeared on the adjacent streets and even on rooftops. Not only could Belhadj not attack Sahar's factory, he doubted he could even climb down from his aerie without getting arrested.

Still, if the French forces did move on Sahar's redoubt, Belhadj might be able to provide them with a little assistance. And if they remained none the wiser, well, all the better.

Belhadj lay on his stomach on the iron-grid balcony of the grain elevator, put the folded-out stock of the rifle against his right shoulder (wincing a little). He spotted the sniper-watcher on the roof with his own eyes before closing his left eye and lining up his right eye with the gun-mounted scope.

He began squeezing the trigger.

But a glimpse of motion, a swirl of brightness in the background behind the watcher, made him pause. Were there two roof snipers? Was it a shift change? If so, he could kill two of the mercenaries before the military rained hell down on the men inside the warehouse.

Belhadj used the green-light scope to check the source of the movement. His eyebrows rose toward the hair that hung over his brow.

A hooded figure flared into view. The figure turned in his direction, facing the moonlight. Belhadj's mouth fell open.

"My God," Belhadj whispered in Arabic.

Daria had never seen a roof like this. The tar paper surface rose and fell like frozen waves of water. In some places it seemed solid enough; in others, she could make out ragged black holes.

She also noted a watcher, one of Sahar's men, lying on a coarse blanket, sixty meters ahead of her, with cardboard boxes leaning this way and that to obscure him from casual passersby. He had binoculars and a sniper rifle, plus a canvas messenger bag. The man wore dark olive clothes. He lay on his stomach, elbows propping him up.

Daria scanned the roof, trying to determine a safe route between them. One false step and he would hear her. Worse yet, her leg could drop through the badly aged roof, leaving her off balance and possibly trapped.

She drew the Glock. She didn't want to engage in a shoot-out up here. Asher's people inside the warehouse would hear it for certain.

She studied the tar paper surface in the moonlight, looking for footprints to define the watcher's path of safety. She spied the roof's trapdoor and saw an array of waffle-soled boot prints running in both directions between the door and the watcher's coarse woolen blanket. The surface was spongy beneath her weight. She stepped gingerly, slowly, until she was at the trap-door. Then she followed the boot prints, the gun in her left fist.

When she reached the edge of the blanket, roughly even with the watcher's knees, she shifted the Glock to her right hand, holding it by the barrel and not by the black polymer grip. She raised her right arm far back and, in one scything motion, swung the gun around and down.

The grip and the metal bottom of the magazine smashed into the watcher's neck. The blow pulverized two of his discs. The man's head flopped forward as his elbows gave out.

Daria knelt and gripped his hair and turned his head. She heard crunching noises coming from his neck. His eyes remained open but unfocused, lifeless glass orbs.

She recognized him as a former Mossad agent, assigned to Asher Sahar's black ops team from before. Yadin? Something like that. She let his head drop to the blanket.

Daria shoved back her black hood and frisked the body.

Belhadj watched it all through his night scope. But he wasn't the only silent observer.

The French military crew of Le Tigre kept a watch on her as well, but from a full two kilometers away.

Le Tigre, an Aérospatiale gunship, hovered at five hundred feet. Even under a full moon, its flat, black paint made it impossible to detect from the factory, and difficult to see had it been hovering straight overhead. Its audio signature had been dampened, as had its radar and infrared signatures.

She hung in the air like a ghost, the 500X forward cameras on night-scope mode, the heads-up display on the cockpit windshield showed Daria rising from a jumble of what looked to be cardboard boxes and other, unidentified detritus at her feet. She slid a messenger bag over one shoulder, the bag resting on her opposite hip.

The gunner, sitting right-flank rear, reached forward to tap the pilot on his well-padded shoulder. "That's her. The American."

The pilot disengaged his ship-to-land radio and said, "She's not American. She's Israeli. And her ass is officially in the crosshairs."

He reactivated the radio. "Ah, base. Daria Gibron sighted. She is on the roof. Requesting permission to shoot. Over."

Five hundred feet straight down and two blocks north, Colonel Céline Trinh stood at attention in the DCRI command vehicle, watching Daria on her own green-hued monitor. The colonel wore silver-and-gray camouflaged fatigues and a black beret. Eurasian and only five-two, some people in the past had mistaken petite for weak. In her two decades in the French Air Force, only a handful of fools had ever made that mistake twice.

"Confirmed," she spoke into her voice wand. "Permission denied. The Syrian?"

"No sign, base."

"Hold position."

Colonel Trinh had complete confidence in the gunship hovering over suburban France. Le Tigre sported a thirty-millimeter turret cannon up front, along with twin twenty-millimeter machine cannons on rotating inner pods, plus fire-and-forget, laser-guided Hellfire missiles on outer pods. Céline Trinh felt sure she could occupy a small city with one Tigre.

In addition, she had two dozen soldiers and airmen on the ground, in a wide array of support vehicles all vectoring toward the factory from the north, south, east, and west.

She knew about the dustup in Manhattan with the Syrian and the Israeli. She knew—didn't everyone in intelligence circles by now!—about their theft of a CIA command vehicle, one much larger but similar in purpose to the one Colonel Trinh stood in now. She knew about their Plan A for Camp David, and she knew about the upcoming G8 summit in Avignon. If the G8 was the new target, then the threat extended not just to the American president, but to the leadership of the entire industrialized world.

Trinh's orders were to wait until both targets had been visually identified, then to remove them both. The Americans had been all too clear. Taking the targets alive was not a priority. Colonel Trinh had permission to take any and all precautions necessary to protect the summit.

* * *

When Daria Gibron had appeared squeamish about killing the idiot Algerian hacker in his shop, Belhadj had interpreted that as the influence of living in America. He thought she had grown weak.

Apparently not, he mused, as she lifted, then dropped, the man's rag doll head. Through the scope, he watched her rifle through the man's messenger bag, then stand and pull the bag's strap over one shoulder.

This woman was not among his favorite people. She had shot him a few years ago, and electrocuted him a few hours earlier. She was about to walk into a firefight between Sahar's forces and the French military. She probably wouldn't survive the onslaught. And, for the most part, Belhadj was okay with that.

Except . . .

If the cavalry waded in and started blasting the factory, there was a better-than-even chance that Sahar, with some clever exit strategy in place, would get away. Gibron, on the other hand, was in a foreign building for the first time. If anyone got caught in the crossfire, it likely would be that hellion.

Good. Great. What did he care?

Except . . .

If Asher Sahar were to skitter free . . .

The reasons why Belhadj needed Daria wouldn't have changed. He'd still need her. He couldn't turn to his own agency. He couldn't and wouldn't expect the Americans or their allies to trust him.

He would be on his own against one of the most agile, if sociopathic, minds on Earth. Daria Gibron matched Asher Sahar, insanity-for-insanity.

"Damn it," he whispered to himself.

He shoved the stock of his sniper rifle hard against his shoulder, peered through the scope, and fired.

On the rooftop, Daria helped herself to a gulp from the dead guard's water bottle, then tucked it into the stolen messenger bag. She glanced around the roof, trying to suss out the next logical move, when a subsonic bullet whistled through the air and snapped off the roof, twenty meters to her left.

Daria threw herself down hard, flat against the dead man's body and amid the bramble of cardboard he had used as camouflage. She began prying his fingers off his rifle when a second, nearly silent bullet tore a rift in the tar paper roof. It hit precisely twenty meters to her left. Again.

When a third bullet landed exactly where the first two had, she quit struggling to pry loose the rifle.

Unless the sniper was monumentally incompetent, someone was trying to get her attention.

Grimacing, Daria righted herself on her knees. There was no question who it could be. She presented the back of one gloved hand into the night, first and second fingers raised and split: the British version of "fuck you!"

A fourth bullet dug another divot inches from the first three.

"Fuck me, indeed," she muttered.

Across the way, on a ghostly grain silo slightly darker than the surrounding night, a penlight flashed twice. Once she had Belhadj's position—it appeared it be a landing halfway up a maintenance ladder—she dimly saw him climb to his feet. He seemed to wave to her. Why? she wondered.

She blinked and watched his arm gesture again. His wave wasn't a wave. It was a signal.

Daria climbed to the edge of her roof. She gripped the cement and peered down.

It took her all of thirty seconds to spot, not one, but two surveillance units lying in wait.

The CIA? French military? Parisian police? An outer ring of Asher's mercenaries? More Syrians? There was no way of telling from the roof.

All Daria knew for sure was that Asher Sahar—her Asher—was in this warehouse.

She wanted his scheme, whatever it was, stopped. She certainly didn't want him dead.

In so many ways, she felt responsible for what he had become.

Daria thought about the bad options before her and, cursing, she chose the least worst. She left the sniper's aerie, turned, and duckwalked back toward the hatch in the roof.

Seventeen

Asher Sahar, Eli Schullman, and the other ex-agents and mercenaries watched as Dr. Rabadeau methodically worked his hips, then his shoulders, into a Tychem biohazard suit that tucked into black rubber boots and black rubber gloves. The Frenchman knelt on his left knee, studying his right leg carefully. He stood, knelt on the other knee, and checked the other leg.

"What's he doing?" Schullman whispered.

Asher cleared his throat and whispered. His old throat wound was bothering him today. "Checking for breaches in his suit."

"Halliday flew that fucking canister across the ocean and he didn't need a space suit."

Asher shrugged. One of the mercenaries helped the pathologist put on the oxygen tank backpack and attach its hoses to the soft helmet.

"Nervous type," Schullman said, rolling a cigarette he couldn't light back and forth across the pads of his index finger and thumb.

Asher smiled up at his large friend. "I like nervous types. You're a nervous type."

Satisfied, Georges Rabadeau stepped up to the revolving door in the tent until his helmet faceplate nearly touched the plastic. He took baby steps forward, rotating the door with him, allowing an absolute minimum of atmosphere to enter, and exit on the nether side of the door.

Asher's men had arranged low-heat lights atop tripods inside the tent, but it nonetheless was stuffy and humid. Rabadeau entered fully, making sure his uncomfortable oxygen tank didn't get stuck in the rotating door. It felt odd, hearing himself breath inside the helmet.

An array of surgical tools had been provided for the doctor. He was told not to bother bringing his own, since Asher intended to have them destroyed once he was done.

On the first of two tables lay a plastic body bag, fully zipped up. The bag was bloated and looked vaguely like a mutant bean pod. Rabadeau reached out with one gloved finger and touched the bag. It undulated the way a bag half-filled with liquid will.

He slowly unzipped the bag a fourth of the way to reveal the head, neck, and shoulders of a cadaver, male, late thirties, early forties, short dark hair, aquiline nose, sturdy jaw. There were brown stains—dried blood— looking like rivulets running from his eye sockets, his nose, his ears, his mouth. His face was pallid, the color of old mushrooms.

"Total exsanguination," Dr. Rabadeau whispered to himself, his voice unnaturally echoic inside the helmet.

In grease pencil, someone had stenciled the name SACCHS on the side of the bag. Below that were two entries of dates and times. Time of Infection and Time of Death.

He picked up a glass slide and a dropper, gathered a bit of the pooled blood in the partially unzipped bag, and dabbed it on the slide. He fit another slide atop it and slid the glass sandwich into a slot in the RNA analyzer Asher had imported from Finland just for this moment.

Rabadeau made a second blood-and-glass sandwich and slid this one into a high-powered microscope. It was impossible to get one's eye close enough to the face shield of the helmet to look through a microscope viewfinder. Fortunately, his hosts had set up a digital camera and monitor, bypassing the oculars. Rabadeau activated the monitor.

He stared at the image.

"Mother of God," he muttered.

"P-pl—"

The RNA analyzer behind him *dinged*.

Rabadeau shuffled his plastic slippers over to the analyzer, as data scrolled across its monitor screen. A series of four letters flashed across the screen: A, C, G, U, over and over again, in a never-ending salad of combinations. Georges Rabadeau couldn't read the nucleic acid alphabet, of course. There wasn't a human soul who could. That's what the analyzer was for.

"Pl-please . . ."

The machine made another sound, and the four-letter novella was replaced by words in English. Rabadeau had studied medicine in England. He had no problem translating it.

He shook his head in wonderment, his helmet not moving. "Good lord."

"Please . . . by . . . God . . . please . . ."

The nuisance from the second gurney was getting to Dr. Rabadeau. He straightened up from the RNA analyzer and turned.

The man strapped to the gurney, already in a body bag but not yet zipped in, looked directly into his eyes. The man was bleeding out from his eyes, ears, nose, and mouth. His skin was ashen. A roadmap of capillaries had burst inside his eyes. Rabadeau noted the petechial hemorrhaging, nodding to himself, unsurprised by the damage. It was consistent with his diagnosis.

Someone had scrawled on the body bag the name *VEIGEL*. Unlike the other one, there was only one time and date below his name: the moment of his infection. The time of death entry was blank.

"M-mercy . . ." the man rasped, and a ruby red bubble popped at the corner of his lips. "Kill . . . me . . ."

Rabadeau turned away, studied the analyzer again, then shuffled over to the tent's revolving door.

Daria climbed down the wooden ladder into the building. She pulled the hood of the sleeveless sweatshirt up, tucking in her hair. She wished the undershirt wasn't white; not ideal for skulking. She shoved the shirt sleeves up to minimize the glint.

At the bottom of the ladder, she paused to let her eyes adjust to the moonless gloom. She knelt and found distinctive boot prints in the thick dust, heading to her left. That was the way to go. She followed the footprints to a square opening sawed into the floor near the exterior wall. Horizontal, C-shaped lengths of rebar had been bolted to the wall to create a makeshift ladder. The centers of the rungs had been wiped clean of dust.

Daria slipped the Glock into her skirt, at the hollow of her spine, then pulled the sweatshirt over it. She took a deep breath, then gripped the rebar and climbed down.

This took her to the second floor, where someone had tied a red kerchief to one of the ladder rungs, probably to mark it as a safe route to and from the roof.

The floorboards at this level were in disastrous shape, with jagged, gaping holes here and there. Again, she knelt to study dusty footprints, letting her enemy do the work for her. She followed a zigzag course toward the far end of the wide-open second floor, toward what appeared to be a set of stairs heading down.

One of Asher's men sprayed down the pathologist's Tychem moon suit with water and chlorine, then helped him remove the oxygen tank and the helmet.

The mercenaries and soldiers stood in a half circle, watching.

Georges Rabadeau stepped out of the biohazard suit and slipped his feet back into his loafers. He shrugged into his suit coat, straightened his tie, shot his cuffs. Only then did he make eye contact with Asher Sahar, who stood, quiet, arms folded so his hands held his biceps, as if hugging himself, light glinting off his round, wireless glasses.

"Yes?" Asher said simply.

"I did not think it possible but . . . yes."

The pathologist wiped his brow with a handkerchief from his breast pocket. "The times written on the body bag. Are they accurate?"

"They are."

Rabadeau's hands trembled. "Incredible. May I wash up?"

Asher made eye contact with the Ivorian bodyguard. "This way," the thin man said, and led the pathologist away from the tent and toward a makeshift bathroom.

The big, blue-eyed American, Will Halliday, lit up the white cube room with his grin. "Told ya."

"By God," Eli Schullman marveled. "We did it."

"Well"—Asher offered a self-deprecating shrug— "we *stole* it. We didn't splice the unholy thing together. And we have Agent Halliday to thank for helping us acquire it. Will."

He shook the American's hand. Will Halliday beamed. "I knew it'd work."

Eli Schullman shook his hand, too. The ex–Secret Service agent grinned like a kid at Christmas. "I'm gonna check the perimeter."

He headed toward the door.

Schullman waited until he was out of earshot. "I don't mind saying it: I had my doubts about him. I was wrong."

Asher nodded. "Mr. Halliday was a gamble. But he

lost many friends in Afghanistan and Iraq. He has learned to hate well."

Schullman said, "Well, we could never have done it without him."

"True."

Schullman looked around the white, plastic room. "We'll leave his body here?"

"With the canisters, yes. As far as the CIA is concerned, the trail ends in Paris."

Schullman nodded.

The pilot of Le Tigre toggled his communications array. "The Israeli has descended into the factory. Still no sign of the Syrian."

Unlike most conventional gunships, in Le Tigre the pilot sits forward and to the left, the gunner in back and to the right. This configuration gives the gunner an unobstructed view out the front windshield.

The pilot turned as far as his five-point seat restraints would allow. "Can I get thermal imaging? Let's see what they're up to."

A heads-up display projected onto the windshield showed the factory, but via infrared. Oval orbs of light moved about.

The gunner's voice came back through the pilot's helmet. "We have . . . I estimate ten, maybe twelve hostiles, on the ground floor. That blob up there is the Israeli now on the second floor."

The pilot relayed the tactical information to the command vehicle.

* * *

Colonel Céline Trinh wasn't happy about losing visual on target number one, particularly when target number two had yet to be located by anyone on the ground or by her eye-in-the-sky.

"Colonel?"

She turned as one of her communications techies doffed a headset. "The Americans are halfway across the pond."

He meant the CIA strike team heading to Paris in their modified 757. Trinh understood the subtext of the message: If the Americans were close enough to Europe before the colonel's team was ready to make its move, the Americans would request a weapons-hold status until they arrived. They also would put pressure on the Defense Ministry and the Interior Ministry and on Parliament and on the damned wife of the president, if necessary, in order to take over operational command.

Colonel Trinh was not having any of that.

She moved her voice wand closer to her lips. "Ground units. Move in."

Belhadj watched the military-intelligence surveillance teams, and from his perch, a hundred meters up the side of a grain silo, the change from hold to go was dramatic. Agents in vehicles and on foot began moving as if directed by an invisible choreographer. His trained ear heard the first sounds of a helicopter drawing closer. It was not a commercial bird. It was a raptor.

On the second floor of the warehouse, Daria slid the Glock out of her skirt waistband. She stepped gingerly forward, her boots falling silently on the fresh boot prints of Asher's team. She was halfway to the stairs when one of the second-story windows, on the north side, shattered.

A high-caliber bullet tore into a floorboard, twenty meters in front of her. What the hell?

She calculated the angle: From high, coming in low. It had to have come from Belhadj.

Translation? *Hurry!*

Then all hell erupted.

Eighteen

Asher lifted a pack on to a sawhorse and unzipped it partway. It was as tightly packed as a parachute. It held two folded, white canvas sheaths: more body bags. Like the first two, there were places for names, infection dates, and death dates. Like the other two, the material had been picked because it would burn well once the interior of the pressurized infection tent was set ablaze.

Will Halliday had just checked the factory perimeter and sauntered back to the group. He saw Asher study the white bundle inside the pack. "What's that?"

Asher studied the name tags, barely visible where the holdall was unzipped. They read *GEORGES RABADEAU* and *WILL HALLIDAY*. He carefully stuffed the white material back into the holdall and zipped it up. He looked up through his lenses at the big American and smiled.

"Stowing our gear. We're moving out soon."

Halliday nodded.

Eli Schullman casually worked his way around behind the blond American and slid a titanium hunting knife from its leather scabbard. He made eye contact with Asher, who nodded slightly.

Somewhere inside the factory, broken glass tinkled.

Schullman, sidling up behind the American, paused.

Asher pretended to brush dust off his palms as he turned 360 degrees.

Halliday had heard the noise. "You got rats, buddy?"

"We do. But they don't generally break glass."

Eli Schullman stepped back and slid his knife into its sheath. He reached for the ArmaLite with banana clip and vanadium barrel.

Halliday palmed a stubby, matte-black .9 mm Ruger and held it taut against his left thigh.

The Ivorian picked up the vibe next and positioned himself slightly ahead of the pathologist, whom he had been tasked to protect.

Dr. Rabadeau had missed the tensing up of the others. He refolded his pocket kerchief. "Remarkable bit of recombinant science, this. If I may?" He offered a clever smile and gestured toward the containment tent. "The Russian? Tuychiev?"

The rest of the solders were on guard now, picking up cues from their cohorts. Asher said, "You know Tuychiev?"

"Yes, yes. We have exchanged compliments from time to time. His recombinant RNA has a certain flair. I recognize his, ah, signature."

"Ah. Fellow artists." Asher listened for more sounds of trouble. "He's an ethnic Tajik, you know. Tuychiev.

Not Russian at all. These distinctions are important. To some of us."

The doctor brushed lint off his shoulder. "Of course. And *fellow artists* may be overstating it. I am not in János Tuychiev's league. He's brilliant. But in my own humble way—"

A groan reached them from the street. It was a heavy vehicle on tractor treads. All of the soldiers came to a stop. They all knew the distinctive rumble. It was an armored war wagon. With the windows boarded over, pitch added between boards, and inside the white cube room, most street sounds were muffled. The fact that they heard this truck approach, then heard it rapidly decelerate, was telling.

Asher turned to Schullman and adjusted his glasses. "Exit, please."

Dr. Rabadeau said, "Is there a prob—"

Just then, one of the boarded-over windows on the ground floor exploded.

Colonel Trinh believed in the strong opening gambit, especially against an adversary as infamous as the Syrian Mukhabarat. If the Americans were correct and this Major Belhadj had allied himself with the Israeli *trafiquant d'armes*, then it was best to assume he was well armed and well protected.

If the Gibron woman was in the factory, Belhadj likely was as well. Plus, one of Trinh's advance teams had reported hearing sound-suppressed rifle fire from the general vicinity of the factory roof. No telling what that meant.

Given an armed and entrenched opponent, the urban assault vehicle was Trinh's gambit of choice. Being smaller than a conventional tank meant it could accelerate and decelerate quickly, and could negotiate narrow urban streets. On her command, the small tank roared up the four blocks from its hiding point, the driver gunning the engine, then slamming on the brakes directly outside the factory with the dozen-or-so heat signatures clustered around the first floor.

Le Tigre flew closer, giving Colonel Trinh in her command vehicle a live feed as a rocket-propelled grenade spat from the turret of the assault tank and smashed through a ground-floor window of the factory.

The building under Daria's feet shuddered under an impact and curtains of dust rained down from the second-story rafters.

Damn it! she thought. *The "good guys" have arrived!*

She abandoned the strategy of tiptoeing on the aged floorboards and sprinted toward the stairs. A saner person might have tried to distance herself from Asher Sahar, the likely target of the assault from outside, but Daria had a tendency not to choose the safe options. The safe options rarely led to clear-cut victories.

A two-meter high, L-shaped wall, which secured the handrail, circled the stairs to the ground floor. The building shuddered under another impact as Daria vaulted over the little wall, both boots landing hard halfway down the stairs, and she was moving, Glock in hand, hitting the first floor and rolling, keeping low, landing on her shoulder then her ass then her boots and she sprang forward, hitting a thick, creosote-soaked timber that supported the ceiling.

The building shuddered again as explosions began chewing through the brick on the north side.

Colonel Céline Trinh spoke into her voice wand. "Gas."

She watched the scene on her monitor. The other ground forces were arriving now, some in civilian vehicles, others in battle-hardened Humvees and some on foot.

The gunner in the urban assault tank stopped firing RPGs and another wider barrel appeared from the turret. Trinh saw the distinctive puff of expanding gases from the barrel as canisters were spewed into the ruined side of the factory.

Her communications technician turned to her. "Colonel? The CIA has contacted the ministry. Asking us to confirm weapons-hold status until their people arrive."

"Please inform the ministry that you are relaying their request to me with all due haste," the petite colonel replied, then turned to the driver of the command vehicle. "Move us up."

The command vehicle—looking more like a UPS truck than the command-and-control nerve center of a military assault unit—began vectoring closer to the battle.

Inside the plastic cube of the white room, Eli Schullman knelt, drew his serrated combat knife and deftly dug two long, straight slices through the white plastic floor covering, coming together at a right angle. He peeled back the plastic to reveal a reinforced trapdoor built into the floorboards.

Asher thought to himself: *The Tunnel Rat of Rafah was not so easily caught off guard.*

Schullman dropped down, feet first, into the hole.

Tear gas canisters flew through the ruined windows of the factory. Almost everyone flinched as the canisters hit the reinforced plastic sheets of the cube room, secured to a matrix of aluminum scaffolding.

But the cube room walls worked like a vertical trampoline. Five gas canisters were hurled into the room; three bounced back out into the street.

One of the mercenaries said, "What the hell was that?"

Asher said, "The law of unintended consequences." He hadn't ordered the construction of the cube room in order to repel a gas attack. But it was a nice side effect.

Two more gas canisters burst through the windows, hit the white wall, but stayed within the factory. Gas began hissing from them. But they were outside the pressurized cube room and of no concern to Asher.

From behind the load-bearing support timber, Daria watched as gas began billowing from behind the weird, alien-looking plastic cube, sixty meters wide and sixty meters high. She had no idea what the hell it was, except that it was modern, sturdy, and the gas seemed to be buffeting around its perimeter.

Daria filled her lungs with air, expelled it in a rush, then filled her lungs again to oxygenate her blood. She rose, shut her eyes tight and, arms churning, sprinted blind into the heart of the mushrooming gas cloud.

As she hit the billowy, pale yellow plumes of gas, Daria slid like a baseball runner, boots first, down on her hip, gliding up against the plastic walls of the cube, her free hand snatching the spade-shaped knife from her boot.

She thumbed out the toughened plastic blade, held it horizontally, and sliced cleanly through the plastic, an inch off the ground, as far as the arc of her arm would reach. She spun on her hip, slipped through the breach headfirst, emerged inside the cube room, opened her eyes a slit, and tucked herself behind a pyramid of heavy iron canisters.

She knew that tear gas is relatively heavy and stays low to the ground in hot climates. But in the cold, it tends to hover a half-meter or so off the ground, trapping a layer of air beneath it. The slit in the white plastic should be too low to allow the gas to enter the cube room.

She heard shouting. Some of it in Hebrew.

Getting this far had not been what one could call a plan, per se. But she nonetheless seemed to be where she needed to be: nearer and nearer to Asher.

Daria grinned, revealing her canines.

Out on the street, three of the gas canisters had bounced back outside and gushed sickly yellow fumes. The heavy gas billowed but staying tightly packed due to the nearness of the buildings, the lack of wind, and the crisp, cold air.

In the doorway, Asher's Croatian soldier panicked. He fired his pistol up at the fast approaching gunship, then eyed the assault vehicle and the quickly spreading gas, and began running away.

By sheer luck, the single bullet from his unaimed handgun hit the bulletproof windshield of Le Tigre. It bounced away, harmless.

"We are taking gunfire!" the pilot shouted into his helmet mic.

Colonel Trinh grasped a looped, leather handhold from the ceiling of the command vehicle. She pivoted to the left as the tall, boxy truck rounded a corner, her up-raised arm taking the strain.

"Tigre. Show them the error of their ways."

The helicopter's machine cannon began pouring heavy shells into the century-old factory at a rate of five hundred per minute.

The thick plastic walls and aluminum scaffolding had repelled some of the gas canisters. But under the helicopter's Gatling-style machine cannon, it turned to Kleenex.

Everyone awaited the all clear from Eli Schullman. The soldiers drew weapons. Not Asher. He stood with his hands folded behind his olive field jacket, wireless bifocals in place, listening and watching as the first hail of heavy shells penetrated brick as if it were cheese, zinging into the factory and burying themselves in the wooden floor, long raggedy sticks of wood erupting under the impact.

Sixty-degree angle, he thought to himself. *Fired from a helicopter . . . military.*

Good. For a moment there, he had feared it was Daria Gibron.

Daria stood and moved toward the Hebrew voices, then dove back behind the horizontal pyramid of massive iron air tanks as heavy shells began turning the brick exterior of the factory into Saint Audrey lace.

A shell panged off one of the six-foot-long tanks and compressed air began hissing free. The impact was enough to rattle the other tanks in the pyramid, which were supported by nailed-together wooden supports and two military-issue, olive-colored web belts. The entire affair probably weighed four tons, and all of it wobbled like gelatin over Daria's body.

Fucking hell! she thought. *Thanks for the help, lads!*

"What is going on!" the French pathologist screamed in Asher's ear. "My God! What is—"

A shell flashed through the brick wall, through the tattered plastic, through the Frenchman's knee, through the floor, into the escape tunnel between the ground floor and the sewer lines, then into the body of one of the first mercenaries to hit the tunnel, through him, and into the sewers below.

The mercenary died instantly.

The pathologist did not, although the shell didn't just break his knee; it blew the lower part of his leg seven meters away.

Asher watched the Frenchman fall.

The helicopter gunner swung his cannon slowly, left to right, then slowly back the way he'd started.

All in all, he fired for fewer than thirty seconds.

The fusillade demolished the northern wall of the factory.

Asher Sahar heard a distinctive *crack!* It came, not from without, but from within his factory. It was organic, not metallic. The floorboards under his feet vibrated.

Support columns were buckling as the northern wall disintegrated. The top two floors and the roof were in danger of collapsing on them.

Asher hadn't assumed the tunnel exit had gone undetected, and he didn't want his team caught in the tunnel where they would have been easily picked off. Eli Schullman had ducked into the tunnel first. Now he reappeared. "Clear! All the way! Come on!"

Asher said, "Yes. Shall we?"

Schullman made room as men began diving for the bolt-hole cut in the floor.

The DCRI command vehicle screeched around a corner and now the combat zone was within view. The driver activated a dashboard camera and one of the monitors in front of Colonel Trinh popped to life, showing a real-time, real-light diorama ahead of them.

Directly above them, the gunship pilot popped on his ultra-powerful searchlight. That, plus the full moon, turned night into day.

Trinh saw billows of dust erupting from the top two floors of the factory. This surprised her, in that all of her crew's firepower had been aimed at the ground floor.

She didn't realize then, but the dust came from upper floors that were beginning to buckle.

The demonic onslaught ended and Daria rose from behind the unstable tower of air tanks. She took four steps to her right, caught sight of the others in the room, raised the Glock and let loose with three shots.

Three of Asher's mercenaries spun and fell.

Daria readjusted her sights. Asher himself was halfway down into the tunnel.

They made eye contact. Held the eye contact. Both froze.

Daria Gibron and Asher Sahar. Siblings, by most measures of the term.

A very thin, very dark black man knelt on the floor, bleeding from his gut. He fired in Daria's direction. His bullet pinged off one of the air tanks and Daria dodged back. She had hit the black man; she was sure of it. She just hadn't killed him.

She dared to glance around again. Asher looked right at her, lights flickering across the flat frames of his glasses. She saw what he saw: his childhood friend, his oldest extant acquaintance in all of the world, standing with a sleeveless hooded sweatshirt and cartoony boots shoulder-length apart, wearing a ridiculous skirt, hair gray with dust and asbestos, firing two-handed and paring his team by a third.

Asher ducked into the crawlway.

Where are you, Sahar! Belhadj chanted silently to himself from his catwalk halfway up the grain silo. His ears still rang from the proximity of the flying gunship's machine cannon. *No way you are cowering under this assault. You have an "out," you mongrel!*

He lifted his binoculars, thumbed off the nightscope status, and began scanning the now-bright streets in every direction.

Because of the tear gas billowing in the streets, the other two dozen soldiers under the baton of Colonel Céline Trinh held back. That left the tank-tread assault vehicle and Trinh's own, boxy command vehicle on point, Le Tigre hovering over them by four stories.

Trinh activated her headset. "Tigre! Bring it down! Disperse the gas! Ground forces: get ready to move in!"

The helicopter dropped straight down until it was even with the roof of the factory. Its propeller wash hit the tear gas, which began to billow and roil, rising and dispersing, clearing the way for Trinh's ground forces.

With Asher's team gone, Daria was the only one still being fired upon.

It was just possible, she realized, that she had not thought this thing through as well as she might have.

Shots were still flying into the ruined factory but from street level, not from the air. They also were coming in twos and threes, not the blinding clip of an airship's rotating cannon.

Still, blind though the shots may be, they were sufficient to keep Daria from making a dash for the trapdoor.

She glanced around the pyramid of oxygen tanks. She had killed two of Asher's men and wounded a third. That man was alive, blood glistening in a spreading stain above his belt. He was struggling to ratchet a new magazine into an automatic weapon.

The French have a damn tank! Daria realized. She could hear its treads grinding up the street, turning it to loose gravel. The assault vehicle was the source of the random firing into the factory, which kept her pinned down. *All I need is for one of their bullets to rupture another air tank, and there goes my cover.*

More heavy shells smashed into the room. A loud, low, resonant groan escaped from the very soul of the factory and three wooden support beams cracked and fell from the ceiling, smashing through the walls of the white plastic cube room and then through the rotting floorboards.

Daria glanced around. A few weapons had been scattered about and abandoned, but nothing to match an urban assault vehicle.

Near the trapdoor, the wounded Ivorian soldier pushed a magazine into his Sten gun and struggled to ratchet the slide. "You . . . will die!" he coughed, blood spewing from his lips. "You bitch! Fuck—"

God, but the man had become annoying! She reached around the tanks and shot him in the head.

First things first. Deal with the tank. Then chase Asher.

She saw tool kits, acetylene torches, sawhorses, a makeshift toilet, tables with canned food, and Sterno heaters. Her eyes lit on a massive iron wrench as long as her leg. It looked more like a cartoon notion of a caveman's club than an actual tool.

Perfect.

She tucked away the Glock and drew the spade-blade from her boot. She sawed through the two web belts that tied down the pyramid of oxygen tanks. The tanks themselves were lined up perpendicular to the ruined north wall. A camouflaged camp tent stood between the tanks and the wall. She had no idea what lay within the tent but didn't much care.

Daria dared to sprint out of the cover of the pyramid. She grabbed the massive wrench and dragged it back. The beast weighed at least a quarter as much as Daria herself. Blowing sooty strands of hair away from her eyes, Daria gripped the wrench with both hands. She huffed, gritted her teeth, and lifted the massive spanner over her head.

Howling, she slammed it down on the release valve of the highest tank in the pyramid.

The valve shattered.

The high-pressure air blasted out of the broken valve exactly the same way that rocket propellant works.

The tank flew. Not straight up, like a rocket. But straight out.

* * *

Colonel Céline Trinh activated the all-call button on her communications unit. "Everyone, move in. LeTourneau, take point. Duvaliere, bring your people—"

A metal missile, six feet long, screamed out of the factory, missing the assault vehicle by inches.

"What was that! What was that!" someone shouted over the comms.

The gunship pilot's voice sounded. "Taking fire! Taking fire! They have missiles!"

Colonel Trinh tried to regain order. "Report! What's happening What's—"

A second metal cylinder erupted from the factory's ruined wall. This one connected to the left front-quarter panel of the assault vehicle. It did no serious damage. But the vehicle pivoted five degrees on its central axis, its treads grinding up the street. Inside, its crew was jarred and shocked, one man falling out of his seat, his head slamming into a console.

Voices rose over each other across the communication arrays. *"Artillery! They have missiles! Fire! Fire!"*

From his vantage point, Belhadj saw a sewer grate pop open in a culvert. Men began racing away. One wore round glasses and had thinning brown hair. Belhadj tried to bring his long gun around by shifting his position on the tight, narrow platform. Not fast enough. Asher Sahar and his crew raced away from the culvert, around the edge of the silo, and were lost from Belhadj's line of sight.

Cursing God, his attention was drawn back to the

street scene. Something exploded from the factory. Belhadj peered through his night scope.

They were oxygen tanks! Oxygen tanks were being fired like missiles! Someone was—

No, he corrected himself. Not *someone*.

Belhadj grinned beneath the binocular grips. He recognized the insanity of it all. She lived. She was giving the French hell. And she remained Belhadj's best hope of reacquiring Asher Sahar.

Belhadj swung the silenced Sako rifle back around and lined up his crosshairs in Le Tigre's rear stabilizer propeller.

The pilot pointed at the factory, his gunner bringing the rotating cannons back online. "Base, lining up for—"

The gunship's stabilizer blade shattered.

Klaxons sounded in the cockpit. The yoke jerked in the pilot's hands, a mind of its own, as the warbird began rotating on its central vertical axis.

"Base! We are hit! We are hit!"

The helicopter's long, heavy tail section—shaped more or less like the striking surface of a hockey stick— had served to stabilize the flying weapons platform. Devoid of its propeller, the tail section's mass threw off the gunship's balance. She began spinning in place.

Until the torque offset the uplift of the main, over-head propellers.

When that happened, Le Tigre began dropping.

The firing from outside stopped after Daria had blasted her fifth oxygen tank. Good thing, too. Her arms felt like linguini and she doubted she could lift the monstrous spanner over her head a sixth time.

More rafters cracked and plummeted from the ceiling, tearing down sections of the white plastic walls. Tear gas began billowing in. The huge support column, behind which she initially had ducked, splintered along its entire vertical length, the roof above it groaning and dropping a meter.

From the corner of her eye, she noted the now-ruined, camouflaged tent fluttering away. Where it had stood she saw overturned medical equipment and two field hospital gurneys, both on their sides. Thick pools of clotted brown liquid spread from them both. She recognized old blood when she saw it. She had caused enough such stains in her years.

Daria had no time to ponder. She had bought herself a few precious seconds. She sprinted toward the bolt-hole.

"W-wait . . ."

A voice reached her. She noticed a man, down on his back, his right leg missing below the knee, a small pool of blood encircling his lower torso. The man wore expensive, well-tailored civilian clothes, even a lavender pocket square, and Daria caught a whiff of expensive cologne.

"Please . . . God . . . please . . . don't leave . . . me," the man begged in French, his eyes bulging in panic.

The well-dressed gentleman was completely out of place, like a crystal chandelier hanging in a latrine.

This man had been of value to Asher.

Daria checked the man's leg. The heavy-caliber

shell had gone straight through his leg, hot enough to partially cauterize the wound. It was the only reason he hadn't bled out. Yet.

She grabbed the man's lapel with her left fist and jumped down into the ripe drainage pipe below, dragging the dapper civilian behind her, leaving a wide blood trail. He landed like a sack of onions.

The ceiling above them continued to collapse, meaning the tunnel was no safer than the floor they had abandoned. Daria began backpedaling as quickly as she could, dragging his ass and one and a half legs behind her across the boards that had been laid down for traction.

Somewhere beneath the soot and dust and grime and sweat-slick hair, Daria Gibron's eyes sparkled.

Nineteen

The gunship didn't plummet; it retained enough lift to retard its descent. It still landed hard on the urban assault vehicle, ruining both.

Nearby, the roof of the factory collapsed into the third floor, and the third floor began its now-inevitable collapse into the second floor.

The destruction was too close to the piled-up ruins of the two attack vehicles for Colonel Céline Trinh's comfort. But she wasn't willing to ask a soldier or airman to do something she, herself, wouldn't do. She strapped on her own sidearm, buckling the belt over her narrow hips. "Captain LeTourneau! Meet me at Le Tigre! Bring Renault and Gilbert!"

She ripped off her headset and threw open the rear door to the UPS-style truck. She leaped down into one of the grooves that the assault tank had left in its wake, concrete turned into rough coffee grounds.

Her two communication techies joined her. Where their colonel went, so did they.

Trinh didn't look three months past fifty-five as she raced toward the devastation, her lace-up boots tearing up the distance, her senior officers arriving from the opposite direction.

The factory shuddered and upper-story windows exploded, creating glittery rainbows of moonlight over their heads. Trinh ducked, arm up over her short-cropped hair, as glass shards rained into the street.

The acrid stink of tear gas permeated the scene and reminded Trinh of spoiled eggs. The rotor wash from Le Tigre had dispersed enough of it, but some of her men donned bandannas across their mouths and noses.

Trinh turned to one of her communications people, who followed her everywhere. "Headlamps!" she bellowed over the roar of everyone and everything else on the street. "Tell everyone: Cars, trucks, get this scene illuminated!"

The strong strobe of Le Tigre lay smashed against the top of the assault vehicle. A bar of five high-power LED lights atop of the command vehicle provided an anemic alternative, and, coming from street level, threw elongated shadows everywhere.

The colonel turned to the ruined factory. Her eyes were watering now.

For a brief time they had had thermal images of the interior, but the insertion of tear gas had degraded that capability—the dense gas tended to mute temperature variations. And besides, like the strobe, the infrared camera lay in a smoldering heap on the street.

She'd come looking for Belhadj and Gibron. Her airship had revealed an estimated ten to twelve hostiles on the ground floor of the building at one point. And she knew Gibron had been in the building. Belhadj? No one had seen him at all.

She had no doubt that the attack had neutralized whatever terrorist war party Belhadj and Gibron had formed inside the factory. But the building looked far too unstable for a follow-up raid. The job now would be to get a mobile camera and transmitter in there, and to start identifying the bodies.

At least the building hadn't caught fire. Trinh counted that as a minor blessing.

She reached the downed gunship just as the pilot kicked open the port-side door. It took three kicks; the door was stuck in the bent airframe. He held his broken left arm pinioned against his flank.

One of her senior officers dashed around the wreckage. He was bleeding from his leg.

"Paul! Get the gunner!" Trinh shouted, hauling the pilot's good arm over her shoulder and half-carrying him away from the disintegrating factory.

Men emerged from the ruined urban assault vehicle, shaken up, banged up, but alive.

Céline Trinh stepped over a six-foot-long metal tube lying in the street. It was one of the "missiles" that had attacked the assault vehicle. She realized now that it was an oxygen tank with a smashed valve. As weapons go, it had been all but useless. But as diversions go . . .

With the big man's arm over her shoulder and his weight against her hip, Colonel Trinh took another look back at the factory.

* * *

Grunting, her muscles screaming, Daria backed out of the drainpipe, moving from pitch-black to night gloom, into the culvert by the railroad tracks. She sucked cold, clean air into her lungs and fell on her butt. The well-dressed man's head and shoulders thumped down on to the winter-hardened ground between her spread legs.

She sat, huffing, and wiped gritty hair away from her face. Her hand came away chalky with sweat, dust, and asbestos. She hawked up a gob of particulate and spat on the ground. Her arm muscles twitched with fatigue.

The civilian—Asher's well-dressed civilian—hadn't bled out yet. He moaned, unconscious.

Daria struggled to her knees and whipped off her stolen black hoodie, leaving on the white undershirt, now a grimy gray. She twisted the sweatshirt into a tourniquet for the man's severed leg. She realized she should have done that inside, but with the building under assault, she'd risked waiting.

A sweep of headlights raked the culvert, dazzling her. Brakes squealed. Her night vision obliterated, Daria twisted on her knees, drawing the Glock, aiming for the headlights. *Now what?* She squinted into the light.

A voice boomed in Arabic. "Get in, idiot!"

She lowered the auto. *By all the sinners in hell. . . .* She groaned. Surrounded by enemies, outmanned, outgunned, and who shows up for the rescue but Khalid Fucking Belhadj!

Belhadj helped her carry the deadweight civilian into the back of the tall, boxy truck. They set him down on a gridded metal floor, none too gingerly. Belhadj raced forward to the cramped driver's seat.

"Asher . . ." Daria gasped, on her knees. "I saw him."

"Escaped. Same route as you." Belhadj jammed the truck into gear and the tires squealed. "Who is this?"

Daria hacked a wet cough and pushed the Frenchman over enough to retrieve his kid leather wallet. She thumbed through it.

"Georges Rabadeau. Doctor."

"What is Sahar doing with a doctor?"

The truck veered around a corner and Daria braced herself. "Don't know. They had a field hospital set up inside an airtight room."

Daria idly pocketed the doctor's eight hundred euros—waste not, want not—and added it to the wad she'd stolen from enforcer girl. She fingered a laminated rectangle from the doctor's wallet. "La Société Européenne de la Pathologie."

"My French is not—"

"Pathologist."

Belhadj's face clouded over. "Foreboding."

"A bit." She rocked as the truck took another corner, and a thought hit her. "Did you bring down that attack helicopter?"

Belhadj shrugged, eyes on the road. "Yes."

"Cobra?"

"No, a Tiger."

"Tiger? They're good."

Belhadj grunted. "Did you hurl oxygen bottles at a fully armored assault vehicle?"

Daria wrinkled her nose. "Well, it seemed like a good idea before you said it out loud."

Catching her breath, she took in her surroundings, the banks of computers, the monitors, the bolted-down chairs, subway-style support straps hanging from the ceiling, the weapons cabinet. Slowly, she smiled.

"Cheeky bastard! You stole a command vehicle!"

Belhadj didn't turn around, but she could see from his shoulders that he was preening a bit.

"Not bad," she conceded.

"Thank you."

"Fast. Armored. A weapons cache. Computers . . ."

The Syrian allowed himself a smile over his right shoulder. "Well, I—"

"Not as impressive as the one I stole. But, you know . . ."

The big man gave her a surly glower and drove.

Twenty

John Broom met up with Major Theo James of the U.S. Army Medical Research Institute for Infectious Diseases, or USAMRIID. They met at a mom-and-pop diner with a décor right out of *Happy Days*. John hadn't known exactly what to expect, but it wasn't the barrel-shaped Irishman in khakis, Notre Dame sweatshirt, and denim jacket. The major's smile brightened a lumpy, slightly square face beneath a receding, red hairline.

"Major. Thank you for meeting me on such short notice."

"Theo will do. You want something?"

John ordered decaf coffee, since it was going on 7:00 P.M. While Theo James ordered regular coffee with cream and sugar, and a slice of apple pie. "Little-known fact: there are no calories in apple pie if my wife doesn't hear about it. You don't have to look it up. I'm a doctor."

When their cups were full, John told the epidemiologist what he knew about the apparently harmless transspecies influenza from the Philippines. John pulled out his notebook and a pen.

Theo James looked perplexed. "Why would anyone ambush the Secret Service for a harmless virus?" He sat forward, leaning over his generous slice of pie. John thought the man looked a little like Spencer Tracy in his fifties.

"See? That's what I keep asking. That's why the army story doesn't scan . . . no offense."

Theo waved him off. "I'm as skeptical of the military as the next man. This General Glenn said a unit of Filipino soldiers was exposed to the virus but nobody got sick?"

"Yeah. Do you know Glenn?"

"No, but I know the name. Stuffed shirt." The major wolfed down his pie. "But the story might be true. Most flu viruses only affect one species. Heck, most viruses only affect one *organ* in one species. Thing is, flus are fickle. They change every season."

John made the T-for-timeout symbol. "You're going over my head, Doc."

"Okay. Every year, flu sweeps through the world, right? You get it. You feel like you want to die. You get better. Winter ends. Flu season is always linked to winter."

John said, "*Influenza del freddo.*"

The major waved his pie fork like a conductor's baton. "There you go. *Influenza del freddo.* Early Italian physicians didn't know what the malady was, but they knew it was *influenced by the cold*. Which's where we get the word *influenza*. So, okay. Winter ends. Cherry blossoms, commencement speeches, big blockbuster superhero movies, skirts get shorter, the Red Sox disappoint me."

John smiled over the rim of his cup.

"Winter rolls around and, what do you know? The flu comes back and some thirty-six thousand Americans die each winter from a standard, run-of-the-mill virus. You get it. Your sainted Aunt Petunia gets it. You're both fine. But some stockbroker down the block gets it and dies. How come?" Theo James leaned in, across the table. "How come everyone didn't develop an immunity the winter before?"

"I honestly don't know."

"Antigen drift. You sure you don't want any pie?"

John nodded, jotting notes.

"The flu virus *summers-over,* if you will, in natural reservoirs. Usually avian. Also pigs and some primates. During its dormant phase, the RNA drifts apart and comes back together, but changed."

"Changed how?"

"A virus is just a packet of information. A chain of nucleotides: sugar; phosphates; the four-letter code, A, C, G, and U."

John looked up from his notebook. "A, C, G, and T?"

"That's DNA. We're talking RNA. They didn't cover this in law school?"

John said, "I was out that day."

Theo sat up straight. "I had perfect attendance in fifth grade. I got a gold star."

"We're CIA. Like we didn't know that."

Theo covered his lips while he laughed. "OK, Mister Secret Agent. When the virus is dormant, it can mutate. Slowly. That's antigen drift. Typically, birds infect birds. Yeah? But every now and then, the virus RNA undergoes a huge change. A big, honkin' whale of a change. That's antigen *shift,* as opposed to antigen *drift.* You follow?"

John nodded.

"You get these massive antigen shifts in, say, a bird flu. All of a sudden, it's not just bird-to-bird transmission. It's bird-to- . . . I don't know, pig, let's say. And once in this new animal reservoir, then the virus can shift again. Now it's not just bird-to-pig, it gets really interesting. It becomes pig-to-pig. You with me? That's fine, but then it mutates again to pig-to-human. And our bodies have no immunization for this brand-new flu. Winter rolls around. *Influenza del freddo.* Yeah?"

John thought this guy's talents were wasted outside the classroom.

"Okay, that's bad. Especially if you work at a hog farm or sell unprocessed meat. But it could be worse. The virus—God forbid—becomes capable of human-to-human transmission. Now, it doesn't matter if you work at a hog farm. If your cousin's cousin works there, the new virus can reach you. You and everyone around you. This is your swine flu, your avian influenza, your 1918 Spanish flu."

John wondered why he couldn't have had this guy for Biology 101 at Columbia. He might have spent more time at parties and less time cramming. "Okay. But the virus from the Philippines: It was professionally mutated by a biologist?"

Theo shrugged. "Why not? The nucleotides of the Spanish flu are in the public domain. You can Google it for cryin' out loud."

"But the Tajik biologist failed."

"Not surprising. I think I could craft a brand-new influenza virus at USAMRIID, using a couple billion dollars of your tax money. But in some hut in the jungle? I'd be lucky if I could grow penicillin. If recombinant RNA were easy, al-Qaida would've done it ages ago."

"So why would someone in Colorado risk attacking a Secret Service convoy to steal a failed science experiment?"

Theo waited until the waitress had refilled their cups. "You're the spy; you tell me."

"Harvard Law, remember? I'm an analyst, not a spy."

"Well, for whatever reason, they . . ." The major's jovial voice drifted away. He stared at the bits of crumbling pastry on his pie plate as if they had just formed a crumb constellation.

"Major?"

"Hmm?" The guy blinked, coming out of where ever.

John repressed a smile. He remembered, a hundred times, his dad doing just that when some passage of the Torah had leaped off the synaptic back burner to snap into clarity.

"You were gone there for a minute."

"I was?"

John nodded.

"Sorry. Did you just say the biologist was a Tajik?"

"Yeah."

"You know his name?"

John started rifling through back pages of his note-book. "Sure. Hold on . . . I've got this . . . ah, right. Farrukh Tuychiev."

Major James drew very still.

"What?"

James set down his coffee cup, reached over and un-zipped a Fighting Irish backpack that rested on his side of the table. He withdrew a laptop, opened it. He waited for the computer to latch onto the diner's Wi-Fi, then typed in a name and password, waited, typed in an-other password. Then a third.

"Major?"

"The USAMRIID mainframe," he said. "Give me a second."

He clacked keys. John waited, sensing it would be worth it.

Theo reached into his denim jacket for cheap, plastic cheaters and peered at the screen.

"Does the name János Tuychiev ring a bell?"

"Just the last name."

"Yeah. We had a János Tuychiev in the archives. From Tajikistan, originally, but mostly from Moscow. Part of a Soviet-era project to weaponize viruses. Working with smallpox and hemorrhagic fevers. They didn't get very far before Gorbachev shut them down. I wouldn't have remembered, except I read the guy's works while I was getting my master's in public health."

"When was this? The 1980s?"

The major nodded.

"Okay. So we have two guys working with RNA, about four decades apart. Both from Tajikistan, same last name. Both working with viruses. Both working to weaponize them."

Theo said, "What are the odds?"

"Longish."

Theo started typing again. John said, "What . . . ?"

"I'm marking this moment in the USAMRIID archives."

"Really? I ask 'cause we have this thing about archives and the Public Information Act and—"

"First steps in the discussion of any new virus," the major said, and didn't stop typing with two fingers. "We may have ourselves a threshold event."

"Is that good?"

"When a new influenza is identified, one that crosses from species to species, it's a threshold event. I'm on an international watch team for the World Health Organization. I'm one of the guys who gets to designate such events. I'd say this qualifies."

John said, "Yeah, but the virus failed."

James shrugged. "Every failed virus can be a successful virus with some knowledgeable tweaking. And we get a little leeway about these things. If we're sure someone knowledgeable is *trying* to create a new virus, that's good enough to make the watch list."

John started thinking of the cold reception his theory had received at Langley. "So once it's on the watch list, you get to bring in some international assistance on this thing?"

"You catch on quick, Harvard. Has the CIA given this beastie a name yet?"

"The virus?"

James nodded.

"No."

"Want to go down in history? John Broom, you get to name your first protovirus."

John gave it all of two seconds of thought. "Pegasus-B."

James winced. "A little Crichtonesque, maybe?"

"Humor me."

"Okey-doke." The biologist typed away, then slapped down the lid of his laptop. "Let's go find out whatever happened to János Tuychiev."

Paris, France

Owen Cain Thorson and his CIA team, now code-named Swing Band, landed their modified 757 amid the heavy airlift transports of Villacoublay Air Base outside Paris. Once they were wheels dry, it took them an additional forty-five minutes to get to the ruined factory outside the city. Swing Band was sixteen people deep and the French Army provided two vans with two drivers. The Americans were kept on a tight leash.

As they approached the factory, soldiers with M-16s waved them toward a staging area. One of Thorson's team, a tightly knit, hyperkinetic, and tech-savvy Los Angelina named Maldonado, tapped him on the shoulder. She pointed out the window. "*Jefe*. Moon suits."

Sure enough, soldiers close to the bombed-out factory wore full biohazard suits, complete with self-contained breathing apparatus.

The CIA team exchanged worried glances.

Soldiers kept the Americans clustered near the vans. A petite Eurasian woman marched over to them. She wore a baggy white suit with a large hood, shoved back and draped across her shoulders. The suit was tucked into white boots. The suit looked comically bulky on her petite frame, and was accentuated by a cinched police-style utility belt and full holster. Water dripped from her suit. Thorson could smell the water-chlorine solution.

"I'm Colonel Céline Trinh. I am ranking officer here."

"Colonel. Owen Cain Thorson, CIA." He stuck out a hand but the colonel was studying a handheld monitor and didn't appear to notice.

Thorson said, "Is this the scene?"

The Eurasian officer looked up and nodded. She appeared wired, like someone on a coffee bender. Short-chopped gray hair adhered to her forehead with sweat. Her English was stilted. "We confronted an estimated ten to twelve combatants in that building, there. Your Daria Gibron was positively ID'd."

"Status?"

Trinh shrugged but the gesture was almost entirely hidden within the bulky suit. "We are not fully inside the building yet."

"Belhadj?"

Again, she shrugged.

Thorson caught a whiff of tear gas in the air. The whole block was loud with chatter and truck noises, and the military vehicles' lights cast long, low shadows everywhere. "Can we talk inside your command vehicle, Colonel?"

Trinh said, "Your initial reports about Belhadj and Gibron didn't say anything about the weapons chemical or the weapons, ah, *biologique*, Mr. Thorson. Is there anything the CIA is not sharing with us?"

"We followed all allied-agency protocols. The DCRI knows what we know."

Trinh looked like she trusted the Direction Centrale du Renseignement Intérieur about as much as she trusted the Central Intelligence Agency. There had always been tension between France's Ministry of the Interior and Ministry of Defense, although Thorson didn't know that.

One of Thorson's senior agents, a wiry-haired Special Forces shooter named Collier, made a show of toeing the ground and clearing his throat. When Thorson looked over, Collier nodded toward a low-riding, six-wheeled Erector Set of a robot inching its way past the stacked ruins of a tank and an attack helo. Two soldiers in white protective suits controlled the robot with a large remote control unit.

Trinh noticed the interplay.

Collier, an Oklahoman and career soldier, said, "Pardon me, ma'am. Those're sniffers?"

He'd noticed the robot's articulated arms and their detectors for hazardous chemicals and radioactive material.

Trinh looked at the slow-rolling robot, then addressed Thorson. "We are seeing what looks like a weapons laboratory, Mr. Thorson. Do either the *Syrienne* or the *Israélienne* have experience with weapons of mass destruction?"

Maldonado said simply, "The G8. Holy crap."

Thorson's heart sank. He knew about the Group of Eight meeting set for Southern France. He also had a flash-image in his head of that arrogant know-it-all John Broom hopping straight up to tap a map of Colorado, like it was a half-court jump ball. Thorson experienced an entirely irrational irritation that Broom's pressed shirt hadn't come untucked when he did that. Thorson had no idea why that, alone, pissed him off.

He ground his teeth. "Can we move this to your command vehicle, Colonel? I'd like to report this to our operational command right away."

Trinh was a gifted poker player. "My vehicle is otherwise engaged, Mr. Thorson. Tell me what you know."

Reluctantly, he began telling the colonel about Broom's so-called Pegasus-B theory.

Dr. Georges Rabadeau's eyes fluttered.

"Doctor? Doctor Rabadeau?"

His vision cleared. A woman's heart-shaped face came into focus. She was beautiful, if bedraggled. Almond eyes, deeply tanned, her hair pulled back in a ponytail.

"Doctor?"

"You . . . didn't leave me . . ."

The woman lifted a lidded plastic bottle to his lips and a tiny amount of water entered his mouth. He swallowed.

"Where . . . am I?"

Daria looked around. Almost two hours had passed since the battle for the factory in Paris. Belhadj had found a farm road off a minor highway, winding itself between scrubby hills and parallel to a national rail line. He'd found a small roadway bridge and a mostly unused road, and had parked the stolen command vehicle under the bridge's cover. The moon was bright enough to cast lunar shadows.

Inside the truck, the doctor with the triaged tourniquet passed out yet again. Daria tapped his cheek softly.

"Doctor Rabadeau? Can you hear me?" She spoke French and gently shook his shoulder as his eyes fluttered. His breathing was shallow, his lips turning blue.

"My . . . leg . . ."

"Yes. I stopped the bleeding." Daria saw no reason to tell the man he was still bleeding internally and that the wound was fatal.

Maybe he knew anyway. A tear trickled through his dust-encrusted cheek. "My God."

"Sir? Asher Sahar. He hired you, yes? I need to know why."

Belhadj had moved back and sat at one of the truck's computer consoles, using a flash drive he had scrounged up to download data on the DCRI's mission.

The doctor wet his lips. "He . . . confirmation."

Daria fed him a little more water and he swallowed. "What did he hire you for? Confirmation of what?"

"He—" The Frenchman's body shuddered, closing down.

Belhadj shook his head. "I'm amazed he lasted this long."

Daria shook the frail man's shoulder. "Doctor?"

". . . flu. . . ."

"Sir?"

"He . . . he has a flu."

Daria and Belhadj exchanged glances. Daria said, "Asher is sick? He has the flu?"

And, surprisingly, the dying man's lips curled and he offered a dry husk of a laugh.

"He has . . . flu . . . from Soviets. It . . ."

"Doctor?"

"Re . . . combinant."

Daria fed him another thimbleful of water. "Flu . . . hemorrhagic but . . . airborne. Targeted. Now . . . bonding . . . HLA surfaces . . . targeted."

Daria cupped his sweaty cheek with her open palm. "What? What does that mean? Doctor?"

Belhadj, in one of the bolted-down swivel chairs, logged on to the Internet. He had severed all of the DCRI protocols so the Google search became just one of a million such searches globewide.

"HLA," Georges Rabadeau gasped. His eyes were dilated.

"What does that mean?"

"Recombinant . . . harmless but to . . . Ash . . . kenazi . . ."

Daria's entire body tightened. "Doctor? Sir, what does that mean? Doctor?"

"The author . . . so beautiful." Tears glistened in the

Frenchman's eyes. "Craftsmanship. The . . . Tajik. Tuy-chiev. Recognized . . . signature . . ."

The man choked and gurgled. And died.

"Doctor? Doctor!" She shook him.

Belhadj said, "He's dead."

Daria turned to him, an insult curling her lip.

"Forget about him." Belhadj stared at his computer console. "I looked up HLA while he was babbling. Human lymphocyte antigens. It's the thing they test for if you donate blood. Or an organ. It's what separates us humans biologically."

Daria swiped grimy hair away from her face. She began burning with an anger that far surpassed her fatigue.

Belhadj peered at his screen. "What did he mean, ash can?"

"No," she seethed. "He said, *Ashkenazi*. The Western Jews. The Jews of Europe."

Belhadj sat up straight. He swiveled his chair, slowly, until they made eye contact. "I'm . . . what? I don't understand. I am not schooled. What are you saying?"

Daria knelt by the dead man, her mind a spinning blender set on white-hot hate. Her vision fractured through tears.

"What? What did he mean?"

"Asher. He has a flu that . . ."

"Gibron?"

"He has a designer flu. A superflu. One designed to . . . it targets Jewish people."

"Is . . ." Belhadj scrambled for a response. "I'm sorry. Is that even possible?"

Daria knelt, fists pressed against her thighs, eyes hot

with tears, a pool of the doctor's blood spreading around her bare right knee.

"It's Asher," she said, her voice tight with rage. "He's the God of Mischief's most ardent acolyte. Fuck his soul. Of course it's possible."

Twenty-one

It was well after 3:00 A.M. French time. Owen Cain Thorson and the CIA strike team code-named Swing Band had reported the information regarding the assault on the French factory, the official identification of Daria Gibron at the scene, and the discovery of a biological weapons program inside the factory.

The consensus at Langley was that the Group of Eight Summit in Avignon was elevated to Likely Target Number One. Heads of state were expected from the United States as well as the United Kingdom, France (this year's host), Spain, Japan, Germany, Russia, and Italy. The European Union would be represented but was prohibited from hosting. The participants represented the world's eight greatest economies—except, of course, they didn't, since neither China nor Brazil was invited. Politics by definition isn't fair.

All summits like this one have preplanned beta sites and gamma sites: Plan B and Plan C.

The call went from Swing Band to Nanette Sylvestri,

and from her to Stanley Cohen, and from him to the White House Chief of Staff, and from her to the United Nations. And within thirty minutes of Thorson's first call, summit organizers began to upstake and move the whole event to Majorca, the third, or gamma, site. The media was not yet informed, and most of the world leaders would hear about the new venue while en route.

Meanwhile, Colonel Céline Trinh's people had maneuvered the arachnoid robot with its long, flexible gooseneck cameras into the factory. They transmitted low-light images of medical equipment, body bags, and a sophisticated metal canister and cooling element. Numbers and letters on the tank were written in Tagalog, one of the primary languages of the Philippines.

The Pegasus-B superflu became the primary focus of every law enforcement, military, and intelligence agency in Europe. And all of it began to vector on the international conference on the Mediterranean island of Majorca.

France, The Countryside

Belhadj drove them to a farmhouse and reconnoitered while Daria knelt in the back of the DCRI van, next to the dead pathologist, hands on her thighs. She fell asleep vertical; a trick she had learned in urban foxholes in Gaza and Beirut.

When Belhadj returned to the van, Daria awoke fully a second before he touched the door; the auto in her fist before the door opened.

She still looked like death on a tough day.

Belhadj studied her, kneeling by the cadaver. He jerked his head. "Come."

The farm was barely visible from the highway and isolated from all other homes. A two-car garage sat empty and there were no lights on. Belhadj led her into the farmhouse, carrying his messenger bag.

"Where are we?"

"South. We passed a cutoff to Dijon twenty minutes ago. I looked around while you slept."

Belhadj had reconnoitered and determined that the family was on vacation, caravanning around North Africa. The house was cluttered but clean. The family had a PC on a side table in the dining room with an ancient, pin-feed printer tucked beneath it. The Syrian plugged in the French intelligence flash drive and began printing out the data from the command vehicle.

Daria stood, still half asleep. Her left leg was tacky with the pathologist's blood. She found the bathroom, turned on the shower, and stared into the mirror until it fogged over. She couldn't remember ever being so tired, not in boot camp, or even during her time undercover. She stripped and stepped into the shower. The pathologist's blood ran pink off her legs, followed by the grit and dust of the factory and the mud of the railroad culvert. She leaned into the stream, letting the hot water pour off her hair.

She lathered up, rinsed off, and repeated the process. She still felt dirty.

Asher Sahar had an influenza virus that targeted the Ashkenazi: Western Jews.

Growing up in Israel, Daria had taken the requisite

"Who Are the Jews" classes. She was no expert, but she roughly remembered that the Ashkenazi of Central Europe were culturally different from other groups, such as the Mizhari Jews of North Africa and the Middle East, or the Sephardic Jews of Spain and Portugal. And, she dimly remembered, each group had differing genetics, too. How much different? This, she couldn't remember. Enough that Asher's flu could pick out one from the other? Maybe.

Daria thought she had plumbed the depths of his mania. She thought she had seen him at his worst. Asher, whom she had once loved as a brother, had new levels of perversity she had yet to discover.

That left her trusting . . . who? Certainly neither the CIA nor French intelligence. The alphabet soup of agencies she had assisted—FBI, DEA, ATF? The Manhattan imbroglio with the CIA clouded all of those relationships, at least for now.

Khalid Belhadj?

At some molecular level, Daria assumed stranger things had happened. Just none she had ever heard of. Belhadj was a Syrian soldier and spy. He was an avowed enemy of Israel and the West. He was the avowed enemy of Daria. Plus, she had shot him. And electrocuted him. Neither of which lends itself as a firm foundation for friendships.

All true.

But he also had bested Daria in unarmed combat—the list of people who had done that was short. And he'd brought down an attack helicopter with nothing but a rifle. Not unimpressive.

He'd fired a tight cluster of shots at the factory roof to warn Daria about the imminent French assault. And he'd stolen a French intelligence command vehicle and had come back to save her.

He hadn't needed to do those latter things.

She stood, watching her own fatigued reflection, mind running in circles.

My enemy, my ally? Nonsense. It didn't work like that in the real world.

She rummaged through drawers and found an old-fashioned straight razor, which scissored into a steel handle. The handle was embossed with a symbol and the word *Sevilla*. Spanish steel, she thought. She tested it on a washrag and the cotton slit easily. It was sharp.

Her collection of stolen clothes was filthy. She dried off and padded naked outside to dump them in a garbage can, the straight razor in her right hand. She stood naked, blade in her hand, and stared up at the stars. The crystalline hoarfrost crunched under her bare feet and the stinging, icy cold air in her lungs revived her.

She reentered the farmhouse. She rummaged about and found a boy's denim shirt. She set down the razor to button it on. Her hands cramped so badly from lifting the spanners and hauling the pathologist that she barely managed one button and gave up.

She returned to the kitchen and dining room. The computer desk was empty but the printer basket beneath it was full. She crouched and thumbed through the pin-fed pages sideways—they were connected top to bottom as one long scroll. She saw the DCRI letterhead over and over, along with the faux stenciled *TOP SECRET*—English had slipped into the French lexicon in such strange ways.

Daria stood and poured the last of the coffee, holding the coffee cup more for the heat on her palms than for the additional caffeine. She tucked the straight razor behind the coffeepot. She padded silently into the living room. It was dark and quiet.

She moved to the master bedroom. Belhadj lay atop the blanket, on his back, in his canvas trousers. His gun rested by his thigh. He woke immediately as she entered and blinked at her, but his fatigued brain registered her as nonhostile and he was asleep again in seconds.

Nonhostile? Daria marveled at the concept. *What's a girl gotta do?*

He'd removed his boots and socks, his sapper jacket and shirt. His upper body was taut, muscled, and well scarred. Her own contributions—an entry wound under his pectoral, two angry red pinpricks near his shoulder—were hardly the only images of violence on the canvas of his torso.

His breathing deepened. He began to snore gently, mouth open. Daria wondered how many days had passed since Belhadj had gotten any decent sleep.

He lay on the right-hand side of the bed. Daria climbed onto the left-hand side and sat on the pillows, knees up, ankles crossed, hands holding the cup that radiated healing heat. She watched him sleep.

His breathing grew even and deep. The farmhouse gave out the kinds of midnight creaks and moans that older houses will. Daria heard the sounds of a train far in the distance.

She whispered in Arabic. "Why did you come back for me?"

His breathing remained deep and sonorous.

She waited.

"Thought I lost you . . ."

Daria blinked in surprise.

Belhadj's breath stopped and his eyes popped open. His fist found the handle of his gun. He rose on one elbow, scanning the dark, confused. He saw Daria sitting on the pillows. "What?"

Daria gathered her thoughts by pretending to blow cool air over the coffee. "You were asleep. I asked: 'Why did you come back for me?' And you said—"

"Sahar. I thought I lost Sahar."

Oh, he remembered all right. He quickly brushed a hand through his already mussed hair. He lay back down, stared up at the ceiling but otherwise didn't move.

"You could have gone after him. I'd cut his team considerably. He was on foot."

"He had too much of a lead."

"You don't give up easily."

"He's smarter than me."

Daria smiled in the dark. "Most foes are smarter than you."

He shrugged, accepting the comment on the face of it.

Daria set the coffee cup on an end table and scrunched herself down the length of the bed. She lay on her back. "I don't—"

"Shut up," she ordered. "Sleep."

Daria's head barely hit the pillow before she felt herself drift off. It was a centuries-old soldier's trick, her body responding to a lifetime's training. Abandoned orphans learn the same.

If you get a chance to sleep, sleep. It may be your last.

Same with food. If you get a chance to eat, eat. It may be your last.

Both of them were asleep in seconds.

Maryland

It was 9:00 P.M. by the time John Broom and Major Theo James got to the major's house. James introduced him to his wife and two of his children—his eldest daughter was enrolled at Brown, majoring in math. James almost levitated when he told John this, showing photos of his daughter adhered to the refrigerator.

"We've no idea where she gets it," James's wife, Ciara, said. She had a lovely Irish accent. Dublin, John thought.

They excused themselves and went to Theo's office. There, the major had a computer pre-cleared for access to the mainframe at the U.S. Army Medical Research Institute for Infectious Diseases.

"Okay." He shoved up the sleeves of his Notre Dame sweatshirt.

Ciara O'Brian-James entered, bringing them both glasses of white wine, plus one for herself. "May I . . . ?"

"Hell, yes!" her husband gestured toward a third chair. He turned to John. "Ciara is the brains of the outfit. I'm the pretty one."

John laughed. The couple kissed, holding the kiss a

moment, then she sat and smoothed her flower print skirt. "You're a spy then, John?"

"I'm an analyst. I have, honest to God, never held a gun in my life. But I am hell on wheels when it comes to deposing people."

Ciara hooted a laugh. "That explains it, then. Theo never brings people back here, unless he likes 'em."

John sipped his wine. "I have a confession. I did a little research before I met your husband. You teach physics. Your husband was board certified in pediatrics before switching to epidemiology. Your daughter's majoring in math isn't really that much of a mystery."

Theo James finished logging on and chuckled. "That's because you weren't there when we found her beer bongs. She was a bit of a hell-raiser in high school. And who do we have to blame for that?"

Ciara smiled but copped to nothing.

Theo slipped on his cheater glasses. "Okay, here we go. . . . We're looking up a Soviet biologist, hon. His name came up in something John is investigating."

John and Ciara moved their chairs so they could see the computer screen. This was a breach in security, but John didn't say anything.

"János Tuychiev. Biologist from Tajikistan. He . . ."

The major's voice faded away.

John said, "What?"

"Hmm. He . . . I don't know. He disappeared after Putin took power. I'm not seeing where he ended up."

The major scrolled down. John pointed at the screen, careful not to actually touch it. He hated when people left fingerprints on his own computer screen. "AISI."

"What's that?"

John sipped his wine. "Agenzia Informazioni e Sicurezza Interna."

Ciara studied him, her green eyes serious. "Sorry?"

"Italian security."

"And you knew that, then, without looking it up?"

John blushed. "Yeah. Sorry. I'm a total nerd."

She turned to her husband. "He's one of your people, love."

Twenty-two

The Middle East
Almost Twenty-four Years Ago

The Swellat Bedouin's Volvo wound through the back streets of the north side of Rafah, past signs of recent aerial bombardment. The girl sat in the back on the torn vinyl seats, straight black hair held back by a rubber band. Her eyes were very dark and very round. She never made a sound.

The Swellat did not speak to her. She did not think to ask him any questions. She did not know him. She did not think he was here to help her.

After a time—she had no idea how long, but maybe hours—the Volvo pulled into a dusty alley. They were well away from the watchful eyes of the Palestinian authorities and the Israeli Defense Forces. No building windows looked out on this particular alley. The only observer was a boy, maybe ten, who sat on a low brick wall and used his fingers to eat koshary out of a cracked bowl.

The Volvo pulled in, nose first. A Renault, also ancient and rusted out, drew into the alley very slowly, moving the opposite direction. The cars drew nose to nose, and then both drivers killed their engines.

The girl sat in the back. She turned her head and watched the ten-year-old boy who watched them. His fingers moved mechanically from his bowl to his mouth.

The driver of the Renault stepped out, a puff of dust—part sand, part concrete from a week's old bomb crater—rose around his boots. He carried a paper bag, the top folded down many times and twisted tightly.

The Swellat in the Volvo stepped out. The men met between the grilles of their cars. The boy watched. The girl watched, but she also watched the boy. He was whip-thin and sinewy, and wore ancient Chuck Taylor sneakers and jeans and a once-white Adidas T-shirt.

His eyes stayed locked on the transaction.

The Swellat took the folded-over bag and unclenched the top, opening it. He peered in, reached in. His fingertip, when it emerged, was white. The girl thought it looked like the dried, bomb-damaged cement at their feet.

The Swellat Bedouin sniffed the white powder off his finger. He reacted as if he'd received a slight shock. He nodded. He carefully scrunched down the paper bag again.

He returned to the car and opened the rear door.

As the black-haired girl stepped down, she heard the crackle of pottery shattering. She glanced around. The boy hadn't moved. But his bowl was missing.

The Bedouin pinched the girl's stick-thin shoulder and directed her forward. The dust puffed under her grubby sneakers. He positioned her in front of the Renault driver.

The Swellat said, "Good material, cousin. Yes?" They were the first words he had spoken in the girl's presence. She understood the Arabic but struggled with his accent.

The Renault man smiled thinly under an even-thinner mustache. His face was pocked with the results of a caustic explosion, his skin as shiny as rubber. "And you wouldn't cheat me? Cousin?"

His accent also was foreign to the girl's ear but different from that of the Bedouin.

He laughed. "I against my brother, yes? My brothers and me against my cousins. Then my cousins and I against strangers. Are you not my brother today?"

Renault man laughed. He nodded.

The Bedouin pinched the girl's shoulder and pushed her forward two steps. She stared up at the new man, who stared down.

The Bedouin Swellat returned to the Volvo, slammed the door as he climbed in. He revved the engine and backed away.

The girl and the new man stood by the Renault. The man with the shiny red skin smiled down at her. She did not smile up.

The boy stepped into her line of sight. He addressed the driver. The driver sneered down at him.

"All praise to God," the boy said, stepping closer, his left hand extended, palm up.

"Fuck off, beggar," the man said. He pulled his arm up as if to backhand the boy.

"Sir, have you—" The boy continued, then jumped forward, whipped his right hand around from behind his back. He jammed a pie-wedge shard of bowl through the man's shiny cheek.

The little girl shrieked.

The driver screamed and stumbled back against the hood of his car. Blood flowed. It was strangely, artificially red against the white dust of the alley. The boy grabbed the girl and ran. The girl weighed nothing and the boy was strong and fleet. He guided her quickly down the alley, hooked a left into another, narrower alley, dashed through a nest of vendors, down yet another alley, to a hiding place behind a tobacconist.

The little girl shuddered. Her eyes were huge and black.

"Are you okay?" the boy tried in Arabic. The girl stared at him.

"Are you okay?" This time in Hebrew.

She nodded.

"My name is"—the boy hesitated—"not important."

"Why did you help me?"

The boy glowered. "I know his kind. I know what they sell children for. Look, there are tunnels to Egypt. I know them. Better than anyone. There's a man on that side. He used to be a librarian. When there were libraries. He can keep you safe."

The boy rose and the six-year-old girl didn't.

"Come on!" the boy hissed.

"Who are you?" the girl whispered in Hebrew.

The boy looked around. The tobacconist had the Hebrew name Asher. It would do for now. "Asher."

"Am I in trouble?"

"You won't be if you follow me."

"Are Mummy and Daddy coming for us?"

The newly named boy didn't have any idea how to answer that one. She could tell from his eyes that he thought about lying, but didn't. "I don't think so."

The girl thought about that for a moment. She turned huge, black eyes on him. "Can you take care of me?"

The boy looked down at the girl. He presented his hand. She took it, and he easily hefted her to her feet. He smiled at her. She smiled back.

Asher Sahar said, "Of course, because Belhadj will—"

"Kill you."

Daria awoke, sweating, her breathing shallow. Always, the damned nightmares. The alley. The Swellat. The driver's bleeding cheek. The . . .

She looked around, eyes wide.

She was in a farmhouse. In the middle of France.

She wasn't under the bed, at least.

And she hadn't awakened Belhadj, who lay on his back, dead to the world.

She got up to use the bathroom. Her mouth felt gummy and coated in dirt. She took a detour to check the straight razor behind the coffeepot. It was still there. She padded to the bathroom looking for toothpaste or mouthwash. She found a box of condoms. She took it down from the shelf behind the mirror and studied the box.

She walked back to the bedroom with it.

Belhadj lay on his back. One wrist behind his head. His eyes were open, watching her move in the low light, inside the boy's shirt, one button done.

"In my sleep earlier," he whispered, "I said, 'I thought I lost you.'"

Daria tossed the box on the bed by his hip. His slate-gray eyes tracked it. Then turned back to her.

Daria lay atop him, unmoving, and he held her.

They made love. And then they slept again, she against his warm, sinewy side, calm.

Old soldiers' tricks: if you get a chance to sleep, sleep. If you get a chance to eat, eat.

Same with finding solace in bed: it may always be your last time.

Twenty-three

Sourthern France

Saturday morning, Daria found Belhadj still looking grungy and fatigued despite a shower. He sat at the French family's aging PC, reading printouts. He had made coffee.

"There's nothing perishable in the refrigerator. Nor piled up mail," he said, peering at the printouts. "I think the family plans to be gone a while."

Daria nodded and let him get on with his research. She showered again. She still smelled dust and asbestos in her hair, though that was likely her imagination. She studied her eyes in the mirror. She felt the glands in her neck. She seemed healthy enough.

She buttoned herself into the boy's denim shirt. She returned to the dining room, poured coffee and sat, one heel up on the seat of the chair, hugging her nut-brown knee. "I don't think I'm infected with Asher's flu."

The Syrian squinted up at her, nodded, his unruly

hair bobbing. He turned back to the dot-matrix printouts and Daria realized he probably needed reading glasses.

"Why did the French hit me so hard? Doesn't knocking down a factory seem excessive?"

"First, they thought they were hitting *us*. They assumed I was with you in the factory. Second, I understand the American president is coming to the Group of Eight summit in Avignon. If we are the so-called villains of this affair, and if we have targeted the president, then the entire G-8 summit would be at risk." Belhadj smiled thinly. "If I were in charge of security there, I'd assume the villains were after the entire free world."

"I'm too tired to attack the *entire* free world." Daria raked wet hair away from her face.

Belhadj rose and poured them both more coffee. "Your one-legged pathologist said something about recognizing the *signature* of the virus. He said, 'The Tajik, Tuychiev.' I thought I recognized the name. A couple of years ago, there was this crazy Soviet scientist, originally from Tajikistan, living in Milan. He contacted Pakistan, the Saudis, us, and offered to sell a flu virus. This was before Assad the younger fucked everything up. Syria was still making overtures to the West, so we declined the offer. I was on a team that investigated the man. If this Tuychiev is still around . . . ?" He shrugged.

"What happened with you and the Mukhabarat?"

Belhadj sat and slid the printouts back into their black plastic shelf. He acted as if he might not have heard her. Daria sat, hugging one knee, and waited him out.

"If I said 'The Group,' would you know who I meant?"

Daria said, "Musical or—"

"Never mind. For a long time now, some of us have been looking for a sort of group. It's probably legend. It's a cluster of Jewish true believers from the 1950s and '60s who decided that no means were too great to protect Israel. This group believed that the Israeli leaders could be trusted only so far, since they were elected by the people. America and Western Europe were great and true allies, but could be trusted only so far. This group, if it existed, believed that once every so often, someone else would need to act. Someone not elected, not beholden to the military or to the United Nations."

Daria watched him. "Do you believe this group exists?"

Belhadj shrugged. "Who knows? Probably not. It might not even be a *group*. More likely it's this person meeting with that person, money exchanges hands, and the family of a nuclear scientist in Riyadh climbs into a car rigged with explosives. Mossad and Shin Bet can honestly say they didn't do it. Parliamentarians can be scandalized and demand hearings. The media waits for the next good story."

He sipped his coffee. "Anyway. For a time now, I have been making it my business to find out if this group exists."

"And did you?"

"Four years ago, Asher Sahar led a conspiracy to

murder an Israeli parliamentarian. He was tried in a
secret court and sent to a secret prison. Why? Why not
a public trial?"

Daria said, "Scandal."

"Okay. I don't understand politics but okay. But then
four years pass and someone drives him away from the
prison. I don't mean he escaped: I mean someone *drove
a vehicle* through checkpoints to free him."

"This *group*?"

"Which you've never heard of."

Daria shrugged.

"I found out Sahar's most-trusted lieutenants had
been freed, too. He had a network, and it had been reconstituted. That requires money and political might. I
followed the trail of foreign mercenaries Sahar had
used in the past. I put together bits and pieces, here and
there, and realized he was running an operation in
New York City. I sent a surveillance team; three men I
trust. I informed my superiors. At first, they were only
too happy to know that Sahar had been found and was
up to something. Then, after my surveillance team disappeared, I was ordered to come home and forget
everything."

"Orders that you ignored. Which is why your own
people tracked you to the safe house in Paris. And
speaking of which, I'm still not sure why you dragged
me there."

Belhadj raked back his unruly hair. "Honestly? I'm
not exactly sure, either. I was told not to go to the United
States. I ignored that order. I tried to rendezvous with
my surveillance team. They were dead. I am perfectly

aware that I am not a match for Asher Sahar. I can play the fiddle, he conducts symphonies, yes?"

Belhadj rubbed his eyes. "Then, I saw you on the street in New York. I knew about you and Sahar. I knew you'd beaten him before. I figured there was a one-in-two chance you were working with him. When I realized you were not, I knew I had an asset he couldn't easily outmaneuver."

"I was never your asset," Daria said.

"One works with the tools God provides."

She considered several retorts but let it slide. "You smuggled me to France."

"Sahar was headed there. And it became evident he knew I was tracking him. Else he wouldn't have involved me in that lunacy in New York. I thought, if I could get ahead of him, if you hated him enough to help, if, if if . . ." He shrugged and finished his coffee.

"But I still don't understand about Damascus," she said. "You'd found Asher. You knew he'd put his old cohorts back together. Why wouldn't Damascus want him stopped?"

"Stopped, or even simply exposed," Belhadj added. "Think about it: just alerting the Americans to Sahar's presence would be enough, yes? It would buy my government a bit of goodwill with the American State Department. We look like reasonable people, and Israel has to answer serious questions, both internally and with allies. But let him continue with whatever he's doing, and . . ."

Belhadj sipped coffee.

Daria worked her way through the story; Belhadj could tell by the way her dusky eyes darted as the threads came together. "Oh, God," she said. "Wait. The Syrians called you off . . . Syria called you off because Asher . . . told them what he was up to? They . . . my God . . . Syria sanctioned him?"

Belhadj said, "Things are insane in Damascus. Who knows who is in charge, one day to the next?" He sounded extremely tired. "But yes. That's my theory."

"But why?"

He smiled a little. "What do you know about the Arab Spring?"

"Democracy breaking out all over. Lots of people on Twitter and Facebook. People with bad fashion sense cramming into squares."

Belhadj rubbed his neck, wincing a bit. "Do you know Israel's secret for success, all these decades?"

"Atomic bombs."

"No. It's . . ." He paused. "Are you confirming that Israel has nuclear weapons?"

Daria rested her chin on her upturned knee. "Yes."

"Can I trust you on this?"

"No."

He winced his version of a laugh. "Fair enough. No, Israel's survival has depended upon being surrounded by radical hard-liners. Arafat, Sadat, Hamas, Hezbollah, Iran. Israel should be a political joke. A bunch of Jews, pressed up against the sea. Before 1967, the country was only nine miles wide. Surrounded on all sides by enemies. But these enemies have looked crazy, especially to the Americans and Western Europe. The West had to trust Israel because, as the Americans say, it's the only game in town."

Daria felt the cobwebs in her brain clear. "Until Arab democracy broke out."

"If you're Israel, in light of the Arab Spring, how do you secure sixty more years of unyielding Western support?"

Daria shrugged.

"You need a new holocaust."

Daria ran her hands through her hair again. She worried her lower lip with her teeth. She tried, as hard as she possibly could, to find a flaw in his logic.

She breathed out a whisper. "A flu."

"A pandemic. That targets Jews. I don't know. It's possible. Then you just have to find the right . . . what's the Americanism? Falling . . . ?"

"Fall guy."

"Thank you, yes. Find a fall guy. Frankly, Damascus has been unhappy with Iranian influence for some years now. The mullahs make good villains."

Daria felt her blood freeze.

"What is the population of Israel today? Seven million? Say Sahar's influenza kills only one percent of them."

"Genocide." Daria's eyes burned.

"With Western powers unilaterally backing Tel Aviv. Let me speculate: say Asher Sahar manages to blame the Iranians. Do you doubt that the West would invade? And now the wells of Iran would be under the control of Texas. Saudi Arabia would sit back and let it happen, happy to be rid of a rival. Israel would see another half century of security."

Belhadj finished his coffee and rose. He looked into the coffee, winced in distaste, and set it back down. "And all it would cost is a few thousand fatalities. Cheap at twice the price."

Asher Sahar and his team crossed the border from France to Italy, riding in style in the back of a truck-and-trailer rig. The truck swayed awkwardly as it took a left onto the A5 to Milan. They sat on crates and on the floor. They ate jerky and drank stale water they had stashed earlier in the escape tunnel under the factory.

No one complained.

The American, Will Halliday, slept on his back on one of the crates, snoring.

Asher sat on the floor. He had nearly finished the Saint-Exupéry book. He reminded himself to pick up another novel in Milan.

Eli Schullman sat on a barrel, legs dangling to the right of Asher. "May I ask you something?"

Asher marked the page by folding down the corner. "Of course."

"How did that benighted bitch find us?"

Asher sighed. He removed his bifocals and breathed on them, then began attempting to clean them with his none-too-clean cardigan. "First, if I've asked you once, I've asked you ten times: please don't call her that."

The massive Schullman tore off a hunk of dried deer meat and attempted to chew it. It would have served better as a boot than a meal. "My apologies. How did that clever duckling find us?"

"Overconfidence."

"Us?"

Asher smiled. "Yes, us. We knew she was alive. We knew she had not been detained by the Americans. We should have anticipated her throwing a spanner in the works."

Schullman continued to chew on the jerky, which seemed not to diminish one iota in his mouth. "I thought we had everything covered."

" 'Optimism,' said Candide, 'is the mania for maintaining that all is well when things are going badly.' "

Schullman thought about that a moment. "Didn't Candide also say, 'Everything is for the best in this best of all possible worlds'?"

Asher slipped his glasses back on and opened his book again. "That was Professor Pangloss. And he was crazy."

Eli Schullman said, "Ah." As if that explained everything.

Langley

It was only 5:30 A.M. on a Saturday when Stanley Cohen, CIA Assistant Director for Anti-Terrorism, took the elevator down to the level of the Shark Tanks. He wanted to check on Pegasus. It was too early for anyone on the administrative floor to have made coffee yet and he was regretting not stopping at Starbucks.

He heard the clack of computer keys being pounded from an analysis room adjacent to the Shark Tank.

Raincoat over one arm, he stepped in to find John Broom, at one of the blue-cloth-walled cubicles, typing madly.

"Broom. I attended your going-away party. I had punch. I remember it like it was yesterday. Wait, it was yesterday."

John smiled blearily over his shoulder. He hadn't gotten much sleep. "My contract goes through Sunday."

"You're kidding."

John retrieved pages from a group printer. "Thorson confirmed that the connection between the stolen flu and the two fugitives is real."

"The virus that hasn't made anybody sick."

John's eyes were red from working through half the night. "That factory shoot-out in Paris: the French found two bodies infected with something. Both had bled out before the attack. They found a cryo-container that fits the description of the canister found in the Philippines and stolen in Colorado."

"Yeah, but the French haven't finished autopsies yet."

"I've been working with this major in the U.S. Army, an epidemiologist. He's USAMRIID. Also World Health. The two of us are working on a theory that whoever's behind this is resurrecting the work of a Tajik biologist who was weaponizing viruses for the Soviet Union back in the day."

Cohen felt the facts spinning away from him. "The Soviets? You're sure the Third Reich isn't behind this?"

But John wouldn't be sidetracked. "The major texted me a couple of minutes ago. WHO is asking him to go to Europe to identify the virus. He's tracked down the original biologist. I'd like to go with him."

Cohen felt the urge to smoke come over him like a migraine. "Okay . . . first, where's the biologist?"

"Milan, Italy. We can be there in four hours."

"And you and this major think this guy's virus is . . . whatever got stolen from the Secret Service in Colorado."

John said, "Yes."

"And you want to track down this lead."

"It's the army's lead. I'll just be advising."

John picked his words with precision. He wasn't asking to be assigned into the field, like a CIA operative. He was asking to advise the U.S. Army. Which was clearly within the CIA's mandate.

Cohen looked like an aneurism was imminent. "You understand, we tend to put our toughest guys in the field. Battle-hardened guys. Macho guys."

John said, "Sure."

"John? What color is your tie?"

"Dusty eggplant?"

"And Jesus wept."

Cohen looked at his watch. He weighed the options. He considered his personnel. John waited. "Milan?"

"Yes, sir."

"Go."

John quickly gathered his things.

"I'll tell Nanette. And Thorson. He'll be so happy to know you're on your way to save the day."

John gathered his attaché case, suit coat, and winter jacket. He was halfway out the door when he stopped.

A stray thought nagged at him. He turned back to the ADAT.

"Sir? In New York, when Daria called her FBI handler, she said a name: Asher Sahar."

"Yeah. Turns out that's the renegade Mossad jackass who shot her before she defected."

John winced, pissed at himself. "That's why I knew the name. Damn it."

"He's doing a life term in a black box lockup somewhere in Israel."

John played it out in his head. "We're sure?"

Cohen studied the younger man. He could tell John's mind was leaping ahead. "It's a black box. We know what the Mossad tells us."

"Okay. Thank you, sir." John shrugged into his coat. "Um, do you think you could . . . ?"

"Go! I'll confirm this Sahar guy is in prison. Just, please, go."

John left.

Twenty-four

Southern France

In the farmhouse kitchen, Daria stood and refilled her coffee cup. "So we find out if this biologist from Tajikistan is still in Milan. If he is, we go find him. He may be our best lead to Asher."

Belhadj finished his coffee. "There's a Syrian intelligence officer working out of a safe house in Lyon."

"Will he help us?"

Belhadj nodded.

"Can you get us there? If you can, I know people in Lyon."

Belhadj returned to the computer and clicked on the Internet provider symbol. "I'll get a map."

Daria leaned against the kitchen counter and crossed her bare ankles, watching him. He sat in the dining-room chair turned into a mini-office, eyes on the aging PC. An hourglass symbol began to rotate, telling them to wait.

He said, without looking up, "Do we need to talk about last night?"

She studied him in profile. "God, I hope not."

"Fine." He studied the unmoving screen.

"But if we did . . . ?"

The Syrian darted a glance at her brown legs, which disappeared up into the chambray shirt. "I'm fine not talking about it."

"Is this a Muslim thing?"

He jettisoned a puff of air, making his cheeks bulge for a split second. It took Daria a moment to realize that's what passed for a laugh from Khalid Belhadj. "Making love to you was not a *Muslim* thing and not talking about it isn't a *Muslim* thing. By God, you were under-cover in Beirut and the West Bank for years. Did you learn nothing about us?"

"Hmm. Less than you'd imagine, really. My cover was a twenty-something political science student, Western-oriented but curious about the Islamist move-ment. I was supposed to like clubbing and MTV. It made me a good target for the extremists."

The PC's hourglass continued to rotate. Belhadj kept his eyes on the screen.

Daria said, "Are you a believer?"

"It's complicated."

"We appear to have some time."

Belhadj turned directly toward her, sitting sideways in his chair, left arm thrown over the back, locking eyes with her. "I believe. I do. But . . . a very long time ago, I made a vow to be a killer. To do things that the

Holy Quran expressly forbids. I believe in Allah and in
Heaven but I also recognize that men like me have no
place there."

Daria studied his slate-gray eyes.

"And what of you? Are you a good Jew?"

"No. I lost my faith early. In my childhood. By the
time I was working in Lebanon, I realized I could have
served the other side easily. I enjoyed being undercover,
and the danger. But I didn't do it because of faith."

He snorted another huff of a laugh. "So. Whoever is
in charge of Heaven has chosen me to defend Islam, and
you to defend Judaism. I'm starting to think the pagans
got it right."

The Internet screen flared to life. Belhadj turned
frontward in his chair. He typed a few keys, waited for
the screen to catch up.

"I hunted you."

Daria said, "Sorry?"

He didn't look in her direction. "I hunted you. After
you shot me. I had a dossier created for you. I retasked
overseas teams who were supposed to be doing other
things to shadow your operations for the Shin Bet. No
matter how pedestrian or business-as-usual they may
be. We bugged you, but only in places Shin Bet would
expect to find Syrian bugs. When they got swept up,
they would be associated with specific operations, not
with you. You were watched, nonstop, for the better
part of a year. I . . . I hunted you."

Belhadj typed orders on the keyboard with his two
forefingers, hunched forward, squinting. His hooded

eyes glanced at the keyboard every time he typed. He made many type-overs.

Daria watched him. He took pains not to look in her direction. She waited.

"I wanted to kill you. I asked permission for a kill order."

She sipped her coffee.

"Eventually, anger and hatred gave way to respect. That night, on the bridge near Al-A'ref School, you made a shot from a kilometer away. Dead of night, no moon, and precious few stars."

He typed, peering at the screen. Daria stood, ankles crossed, damp hair falling forward toward her charcoal eyes.

"When the kill order came?" Belhadj clucked his teeth. "Damnedest thing. I threw it away."

He typed some more.

Daria waited almost a minute. "I'm not sorry I shot you that night in Damascus."

"Nor should you be."

"But I'm glad I didn't kill you."

The Internet screen flared to life. Belhadj turned in his chair. "Ah, good. For a moment there—"

Daria crossed the wooden floor in bare feet and straddled his lap. She held his head tight and kissed him ferociously. Belhadj kissed her back, his hands along her flank, raising the shirt.

She used her leg muscles to rise long enough to reach down and unzip him.

The dial-up Internet screen waited patiently.

* * *

Later, Daria found clothes; a sleeveless white undershirt, the boy's chambray shirt, a girl's matchstick
jeans, a jean jacket, and boots with Spanish heels. She
stole a small backpack with a Hello Kitty decal.

They pushed the DCRI command vehicle into a dry
ditch and set the interior ablaze. They doused the interior with petrol, turning the truck into a furnace. No
reason to leave the pathologist's bloody body around
for the farm family to find.

Belhadj changed, too. They left the pathologist's
eight hundred euros behind as payment, then stole a
sixteen-year-old compact car and drove back roads to
Lyon.

Twenty-five

Lyon, France

Raslan Nadr grumbled the entire way across the de Tattre Bridge toward Lyon's Second arrondissement. The handle of the plastic Monoprix grocery bag dug into his palms. That prick Abdul insisted on adding Coca-Cola and tins of tomato sauce to the shopping list. Of course. When it was Abdul's turn to shop, he never returned with anything heavier than a baguette.

Nadr wore jeans, aging Doc Martens, and his Lyon Villeurbanne rugby jersey with matching scarf. He looked like a couple thousand other shoppers. With white buds in his ears and a Nano stuffed into his hip pocket, he drew no stares, no attention.

He switched the two heavy plastic bags to his right hand and stared glumly at the ligature marks the plastic had left on his left-hand fingers.

Abdul . . . that prick.

Nadr turned right after he cleared the banks of the Saône River. Twenty minutes later, he was at the safe

house. He could barely feel the fingers of either hand.
He thought it would serve Abdul right if he drank two
of the six Coca-Colas before that prick got home from
his shift at the garage. Maybe three.

Let him complain.

Raslan Nadr let himself into the safe house and
hefted both bags up onto the peeled linoleum counter
between the two-burner stove and the shallow aluminum sink.

The sink was filled with dirty dishes from last night's
tin of potato soup and pita with hummus. Nadr yanked
the earbuds free, the music fading.

Prick.

He unwound the scarf, threw it over the twelve-inch
TV in the living room and froze, his right arm still extended from tossing the aqua-and-black scarf.

Abdul, the prick, was facedown on the aged, orange
shag carpet, his arms at his sides. The carpet was only a
little bit stained with his blood. Being orange shag, Raslan
Nadr doubted it would affect the cleaning deposit.

Major Khalid Belhadj sat on the room's radiator,
hugging a sapper jacket around his frame, a mug of
coffee balanced precariously atop the curved, white-
painted radiator.

A bird sat on the raspberry-colored couch. Raslan
had picked up the term *bird* from expatriate English
rugby fans at the Villeurbanne home matches. She was
nicely rounded with good muscle tone, shoulder-length
black hair, very straight, and midnight-black eyes. Wearing tight jeans and boots, she sat with legs crossed. She
was reading a magazine as if she were the only one in

the room, and as if her left boot wasn't resting on the upturned ass of that prick, Abdul.

Nadr had always thought of Belhadj as the ultimate soldier. He never imagined the man with a woman. He never even imagined the man having friends.

The curvy bird ignoring them suggested something different.

Raslan Nadr said, "Is Abdul all right?"

Belhadj plucked the mug off the radiator and sipped. The bird turned a page in her magazine.

"Was he ever?" Belhadj seemed to ask the mug.

Nadr shrugged. "No. He's a prick."

"Well, the prick lives."

With no hint of emotion, Nadr said, "Praise God."

"I know. His uncle is a such-and-such in the party. A big whistle. At least, he is this month."

Raslan Nadr studied the plastic-handle creases in his palms, as blood returned to them. His eyes turned to the upturned soles of Abdul's virgin-white Nikes and realized they were pristine, unscuffed, and American.

"When I was a boy, I had a hermit crab in a little balsa wood cage. The thing hardly ever moved. It would have made a better partner than Abdul."

The dark-haired bird laughed. So she spoke Arabic. Nadr filed that away.

"Of course. It's been like that since . . ." Belhadj didn't finish the sentence, just shrugged. Both men knew he was talking about the civil war in Syria. There were far too many cooks in the kitchen of Syrian intelligence these days. No way of telling whose broth one was tasting.

Belhadj said, "So. What is the official story?"

"You went insane. You attacked our own people. Killed your own crew in America. You're attacking Western forces. You're so enraged by the betrayal of Islam in Libya, in Egypt, in Tunisia, and especially at home, that you snapped."

Belhadj sipped his coffee, nodded. The bird ripped a preperfumed page out of the magazine, sniffed it, set it aside. Nadr had no idea how to describe her eyes. They were—simply—black.

"The story is, your loyalty to the Assad family is such that you are on Jihad. And while that is admirable and speaks well of your family, you are to be stopped."

Belhadj did something very uncharacteristic. He smiled. Then he puffed out his cheeks in a semi-laugh. He made eye contact with Nadr. "And . . . ?"

Raslan Nadr smiled back. "Good to see you, Major. What do you need?"

Nadr drove them to a seedy bar that gave seedy bars a bad name. He peered out through the grimy windows of his Toyota. "Are you sure, Major? Perhaps the young lady would be better off waiting in the car."

In the backseat, Daria said, "Afraid of criminals, Mr. Nadr?"

"Tetanus," he said, studying the tavern. "Mostly just the tetanus."

Daria opened her door and said to Belhadj, "I like this one."

When she had stepped out, Nadr handed the major a cheap drawstring bag, the kind you get when you buy sunglasses. "Contacts for the biochemist in Milan. A mobile. Also some euros and a couple of credit cards that are clean. I can get guns but it would take a day."

Belhadj took the bag. "We have guns." He nodded out the window at Daria. "My friend is fast and quiet. Abdul never saw who hit him."

"Then praise God, the filthy thieves who stole his phone, euros, and credit cards didn't kill him." Nadr shrugged. "Also, they took his new Nikes, I noticed."

Belhadj poked through the bag, nodded his approval.

Nadr said, "I posted a query through Russian intelligence channels. I said one of my sources spotted you in London. A lot of eyes will turn that direction, I think. It might buy you some time."

Belhadj hefted the drawstring bag. "You're a good man."

"Our country—" Raslan Nadr broke off. He peered out the window again and shook his head forlornly.

"I know."

"Go with God, Major."

Daria entered the bar first. Belhadj waited ninety seconds, then walked in. It was dark and dank, ripe with the funk of sweat and old beer. Belhadj ordered a coffee and found a corner table, where he could use the light of a neon Pilsner sign to read his new cell phone.

He kept his head down so as not to be obvious about watching Daria. She was by the pool tables, getting reacquainted with Lyon's smuggling elite. She had told him that she had worked with them often when she'd been stationed in Paris. They seemed to remember her well—a little intimately, Belhadj thought but kept to himself.

Twenty minutes later, Daria slid in beside him, rather than opposite, to keep her eye on the room. She had secured the only glass of good cold champagne the bar likely had ever served. Belhadj had seen the bartender send a boy out to retrieve it shortly after Daria entered.

"I have a pilot with a Skyhawk," she said. "He can get us over the border to an airfield outside Stressa. The price was reasonably unreasonable, given the time constraints."

"Raslan gave me some money. It's not much but—"

Daria said, "It's paid."

He angled the phone her way. He'd found a story on al-Jazeera about the battle at the factory in Paris. "The site's been quarantined. The World Health Organization said they are investigating a pandemic they are calling Pegasus-B."

"Pegasus." The file name for the CIA operation in Manhattan.

"Yes. Come on," he said, pushing the table away so they could both stand.

Daria led him out of the bar and around to a snow-covered pétanque pitch. It gave them privacy. Raslan Nadr had secured both the phone number and the name "Bianchi," under which the biologist had been living.

Daria made the call. The voice that answered was elderly and male. He spoke in Italian but was no native.

"Dottore Bianchi? I am sorry to bother you, but my friend and I wondered if we could talk to you about one of your creations."

She waited through the long-distance hiss, hugging the phone against her shoulder and zipping up the denim jacket.

"Who is this, please?"

"My friend does business with Damascus. You once contacted his organization regarding a product you had created. We wish to drop by and see you, later today if we may."

The elderly voice hacked a dry cough. "I don't know you. I don't know that to which you refer, signora."

"No, but perhaps we could share a cup of tea and discuss it. Hot tea would help for a winter conversation that is influenced by the cold."

She used the Italian idiom: *influenza del freddo*. She thought the word *flu* might be too common to trigger computerized antiterrorism monitors, but she didn't want to chance it.

"You wish to speak to me about this?"

"We do, sir."

The old man sighed. It was difficult to separate the sigh from the static. "I can see you around four? But not in my home. Do you know the Café della Amalfi?"

"No, sir, but I know Milan. I can find it."

"Across from the cathedral."

Daria said, "Then of course I can find it."

"I'll be seated outside, drinking tea. Four o'clock?"

"Four o'clock, Dr. Bianchi."

She hung up and winked at Belhadj. "We're all set."

Milan, Italy

Dr. János Tuychiev's childhood accent from Tajikistan had completely evaporated but he still held a trace of the Moscow accent from his twenties, thirties, and forties. "It was a woman," he said. "Not Italian. I cannot place the accent, but—"

Asher Sahar sat opposite the old man in the cluttered Milanese apartment, in a forest green armchair with an old-fashioned antimacassar thrown over the humped back. He smiled and cleaned his lenses on the tail of his cardigan.

"Your phone line is quite good, Doctor. I could hear her."

The thin, pale Israeli's smile was difficult to categorize, even for someone who'd been around as long as János Tuychiev. Wistful? Intimate? Predatory but patient?

"She is an old friend," he said. His voice was dry and soft, a little reedy, and the old man eyed the comma-shaped scar on his throat and wondered if that wasn't the cause. He also had a somewhat professorial air about him, which Tuychiev liked. He hated working with the peasant types who tended to migrate into the terrorism world.

"She mentioned my influenza strain. And Damascus."

"Yes. She is traveling with a Syrian but is not herself Syrian. She is with American intelligence. They badly want to stop our project."

The old man's pale blue eyes grew as hard as Candoglia marble. He was frail, with a long, thin neck showing blue veins, and long, brushed-back white hair, which made him look like someone's cliché of an orchestra conductor. But he wore an immaculate suit, tie firmly knotted, and had offered good sweet tea to his guests. His apartment was large for Milan and expensive.

"She agreed to meet me at the café."

Asher turned to his companions, the hulking Eli Schullman and the happy-go-lucky psychotic, Will Halliday. If they were surprised to hear that Daria Gibron was alive, they were keeping up their poker faces.

Asher drew an envelope out of his olive tunic and handed it to the elderly biologist. Dr. Tuychiev studied the cashier's check. It was for the amount that they had agreed upon weeks earlier.

Asher crossed his knees and leaned back, teacup and saucer on his lap, his demeanor oddly offset by his fatigue jacket, rumpled trousers, and sturdy working-man's boots. "An antidote, Doctor?"

"Antiviral drugs are not like antibiotics. They do not destroy the targeted pathogens, but lessen their impact. And it would take the West eighteen months or more to culture my chimera and develop a sufficient cache of antiviral injections."

"But you have an answer to this dilemma?"

The old man preened a bit. "The antigen groupings in my virus can be broken down by contact with a second one of my viruses. The second virus disrupts the protein bonds with the host cells. Infect the infected, and my original virus becomes as dangerous as the common cold."

Asher's eyes almost disappeared whenever he laughed. "Oh, sir. There is nothing about you, nor your creations, that one would describe as *common*."

* * *

Asher led the two men outside the apartment, bundling his coat and adjusting his scarf. The sky was the color of wet cement. An array of subcompacts were parked with barely more than three inches between bumpers. Milanese hustled by, walking briskly, heads down.

Asher turned to Will Halliday. "Could you get the car?" They drove an SUV, which was all but impossible to park in Milan's residential neighborhoods. They had left it three blocks from János Tuychiev's place.

As the American ambled away, Schullman lit a Diana Caraterre. Surprisingly, he had come to like the Italian cigarettes in the plain black-and-white packs. "And so Daria lives."

Asher tugged gloves out of his coat. "To be expected."

"Halliday?" Schullman blew smoke straight up.

Asher watched the receding back of the American, who ambled the way Asher had seen in movies and read about in westerns. He'd never actually seen a real person do it. "I have an exquisitely difficult needle, which I would like you to thread."

Schullman shoved the cigarette between his lips and looked at his gorilla-sized hands. "Threading needles. That's in my wheelhouse."

"What I need is—where does that term come from? Wheelhouse?"

Schullman rolled his eyes. "Baseball."

"Really? I would have thought—"

"Asher."

"Yes. Right. Sorry, never mind. Thank you. At the cathedral: Belhadj dies; Will Halliday dies; Dr. Tuychiev gives us access to his second virus, which gives us a virtual off switch for his flu, then he dies. As for Daria . . . ? If there is a way to frame her, even if it requires wounding her, slightly . . ." He shrugged. "I don't mind her being caught by the Americans or the Italians. But I don't want her dead."

"And what does Hannah Herself and the Group want?"

Asher cocked his head, studying his friend. Very few people ever attempted to lecture Asher Sahar.

"That's what this is all about," the soldier grumbled. "The Group only ever had one goal. Survival for Israel. Of making sure our historic allies have just cause to remain true. You know this."

"And you think I forget this?"

Schullman smoked the cigarette to its filter, absorbing the last half of it in one great drag. He shrugged.

Asher said, "I don't want Daria dead."

Schullman tossed the butt to the pavement, ground it under his boot, and looked his friend directly in the eyes. He spoke softly, clearly, and distinctly. "I know."

It wasn't I obey. Just I know.

Both men understood the subtext.

Will Halliday tooted the SUV's horn and pulled up next to the apartment building.

Langley

Nanette Sylvestri had just arrived at the Shark Tank in time to see one of the signal intelligence analysts stand, rising up on the balls of her loafers, arms stretched upward, fists extended.

"Got 'em!"

"Gibron and Belhadj?" Others turned to see Sylvestri, as she doffed her quilted parka. "You know where they are?"

"We know where they're going to be in, ah, just over four hours."

"Highlights, please."

"Last night, the World Health Organization filed a potential threshold event."

Nanette said simply, "John Broom's thing."

The seniormost analyst on the early morning shift raised his hand and angled his monitor toward the still-standing Sylvestri. "Broom's with Major Theo James, U.S. Army, who filed the event. The DCRI found two bodies with signs of a hemorrhagic fever. They declared the entire firefight a biohazard zone."

The audio tech pointed at her screen. "World Health referred to a Soviet-era biologist living in Italy. We set up an audio trap on his phone. Gibron called him. She set up a meet, four P.M. Italian time, in Milan."

Sylvestri hadn't even had time to set down her coat. "Okay, the G8 Summit has been moved to the Beta Location?"

Someone else piped in. "No. They took the precaution to skip ahead to the Gamma Site. Some of the delegates are already wheels-down in Majorca."

The senior analyst caught her attention again. "The French are reporting some pretty sophisticated medical and lab equipment in that factory. Something called an RNA sequencer."

"And who'd have need of that?" Sylvestri asked.

"Somebody working with recombinant flu."

God, Sylvestri thought. John's Pegasus-B theory. "Okay. Get Swing Band to Milan. I want a videoconference with Thorson inside of ten minutes. Get me ÀDAT Cohen. Get me DCRI, Paris station chief, and let him know when Swing Band is clear of French airspace. Get me AISI in Rome, station chief or better. Ask for a weapons-hot status for Swing Band. The Italian premier is going to the G8 Summit, so Italian Security should be accommodating. Find out—"

"Nanette?" The senior analyst suddenly sat forward, peering at his monitor. "Hang on."

"Now what?"

"World Health. They've named the threshold event. They're calling this new virus . . ." He squinted at his screen.

"What?'

"Pegasus-B."

"Honest to God?"

"Ah, yes, ma'am."

Nanette Sylvestri tried really hard not to start laughing. That had John's sardonic touch to it, all right. "Okay, get me everyone I just asked for. But first get me John freakin' Broom."

Twenty-six

John Broom met Major Theo James at Reagan National. The ruddy Irishman lugged mismatched, wheeled luggage and wore a fisherman's vest with a couple dozen pockets. He slapped John on the shoulder. "John! Thanks for coming."

"I'm your official CIA adviser. I'm just along for the ride."

Theo checked his vest for tickets, an itinerary, pens, and extra palm-sized notepads. "I never had an official CIA adviser before. Do you have a cyanide-capsule tooth?"

John said, "Sure." His cell phone hummed. He checked the message and looked shocked. Theo James took a last dash to the men's room.

When he emerged, he thought John Broom might have been crying. The agent wiped his eyes, smiled shyly.

Theo said, "What? Any of my business?"

"Ah. Got a call from a woman I've never met, is all. She just flew in from Chicago because her brother, an FBI agent named Ray Calabrese, got out of surgery an hour ago."

Theo said, "A friend of yours?"

"Not really, but . . ." John rolled his eyes, a little embarrassed. "Ray's sister called me on Ray's cell. She said Ray came out of his surgery pretty all right. Said the docs let her talk to him for a minute."

Theo waited while John composed himself.

"Anyway. This guy gets shot in the back, twice, and undergoes hours of surgery. He comes out of sedation long enough to find his sister in the room. What does he say? He asks if their mom is okay. Then he asks her to call me. Says. 'Tell Broom: Go get our girl.'"

Theo smiled. "Guy said that?"

John toed the carpet, hands on hips, nodded.

"Meaning this Daria Gibron of yours?"

"Yeah."

"So let's go get her."

Two hours later, John and Theo had talked a soldier, rotating back to the Middle East, into exchanging seats so they could sit together. They leaned in toward each other to avoid being overheard. It wasn't one's typical midflight conversation.

John said, "So what's our play?"

"My French counterparts are confirming something that looks a lot like a hemorrhagic flu at an abandoned factory outside Paris. They tracked some terrorists there. You know that big brouhaha that was all over

CNN yesterday? Tanks and helicopters and whatnot? That was this thing.

"The French have started autopsies. They're also excavating the factory—I guess the dang thing actually collapsed during the fight—and anyway found lab equipment you'd need for a recombinant virus."

John lowered his voice even further. "Funny. I always figured the first terrorist attack of this kind I'd have to deal with would be nerve gas."

Theo's craggy Irish features cracked into a thin smile. "Flu versus nerve gas? I'll take the nerve gas, please. And twice on Sunday."

"You're kidding!"

The beverage cart arrived at their row and they waited for a little privacy. John had seltzer water with lime. Theo James had a beer. They both got an insufficient number of pretzels to sustain a squirrel for ten minutes.

The major finished off his pretzels in seconds. "The Spanish flu in 1918 killed thousands of folks in a few weeks. Some people contacted it in the evening and were dead by morning. Horrible beastie."

John dragged out his notebook and pen.

"Don't mistake a superflu with your garden-variety flu. People in 1918 drowned in their own secretions, or convulsed to death with fever. Terrible. Now, compare that to nerve gas. Remember Aum Shinrikyo?"

John said, "Cultists. They planted sarin in the Tokyo subway system. It was back in '95 or '96."

"Righto. These guys wanted regime change in Japan. They released the gas on five subway lines simultaneously. At rush hour. Thousands and thousands of commuters were stuck in the tunnels with it. Know how many people died?"

John shook his head.

"Thirteen. About five thousand were hospitalized but the majority of them were put on oxygen and released without staying overnight. Most nerve agents aren't reliable killers, John."

They flew in silence for a while, John's mind churning. After a few minutes, he nudged his seat partner.

"Okay, here's how little I know about viruses. They're just a packet of information. DNA, right? So what does this packet of information do exactly?"

Theo said, "RNA, not DNA. And you got the thing about a packet of information right. They invade cells. The virus is covered in a shell of proteins, which anchor to the cell. The RNA is injected into the cell and begins to rewrite its own sequences. The cell then becomes a carrier for the new message. When it subdivides into two cells, you get two carriers. Then four, then eight . . . The thing we worry about the most is a combination of factors."

Theo ticked them off on his hand, using his little finger first. "One: does it transmit easily? Two: does it transmit between species? Three: is it lethal but not too lethal? Were you going to eat your pretzels?"

John handed over the packet. " 'Not too lethal'? There's such a thing?"

"Sure. If the virus is too good at its job, the carrier dies, bam, right on the spot and can't spread it around. It has to be lethal but it also has to take a while, in order to jump from host to host."

"And what happens if the virus gets outside a host?"

"They don't stay active in the air or on surfaces. Mostly, they get spread when people aspirate and others breathe in the particulate. We have to assume—"

A flight attendant knelt by them, smiling. John and Theo stopped talking abruptly. "You two doing okay?"

"Sure," John said.

"Your first flight to Europe together?"

It took John a couple of seconds to get there. Theo was faster and touched John's arm. "Yes! Italy. It's going to be very romantic."

She winked at them, rose, and moved on.

Theo finished off the pretzels. "Five bucks says she brings us champagne."

John turned to the major, shaking his head. "Okay, that was hilarious!"

"I know! I'm always telling folks I'm the funny one in the family. Nobody believes me."

Twenty-seven

There was little to remember about the flight from France to Italy except that the rusted-out Skyhawk, which was older than Belhadj, managed not to fall out of the sky. If the smuggler had ever attempted to keep a maintenance schedule, it had fallen to the wayside like the many thousands of bundles of marijuana hurled from the Skyhawk's windows over the years. The doors were bungeed to stay closed. There was no heat. The ill-kept engine conked out twice in mid-flight.

Daria slept through the ride.

The pilot set them down in a sheep pasture. The snow had melted in northern Italy but the ground was as hard as iron. A shepherd was there to collect his portion of the earnings and an extra helping of euros to lend them a Volkswagen bus, white and swimming pool blue, circa 1985, that might get them to Milan or might just explode.

Daria and Belhadj packed their gear in the bus.

Daria gave him a lewd grin. "Want to *talk* about it some more?"

"We'd best hurry. To make the meet in this thing, you might have to get out and push."

"See how you changed subjects there? That was quite clever. You should have been a spy."

Belhadj had been bantering but his face returned to its usual stoic stare. "Daria?"

"Come on, then. I was joking. I won't jump you randomly until we're clear of this farce."

"Daria . . ."

"Now, he wants to talk. Fine then—"

Belhadj pointed at her.

"What?"

"Your nose is bleeding."

Daria wondered if this was his idea of a joke. It was hard to tell with Belhadj. She reached up and touched her upper lip.

Her fingertip came away with a pink smear.

A million thoughts ricocheted off the inside of her skull. She touched her nose again. It seemed to have stopped.

"It's nothing. It's the altitude change."

"Altitude change? How many times have you flown before?"

She shot him a look, her black pupils flashing. "Come on. We're going to have to drive like hell to—"

"How many times? Helicopters, single-engine, multiple-engine. How many?"

"Shut up and drive."

Belhadj slammed his open palm against the side panel of the VW.

Daria snapped, "A thousand! Okay? A thousand-thousand! I piloted gunships during the second intifada!" She swiped hair away from her face. "I never had a license but Israeli intelligence wasn't too picky about—"

"Damn it! How many times did your nose bleed!"

"Never, goddamn you! Okay? My nose bleeds when I get punched! Care to take a swing?"

"You have—"

"Don't you fucking say it!" She raised one finger in warning, took a step closer into his space, boots apart, weight distributed on both legs, ready to fight. "I'm serious. Get in the van, get us to Milan. Now! Do it!"

They stood, toe to toe, four hands transformed into fists, eyes shooting cannon balls at each other.

"Khalid," she whispered, backing up half a step. "We're the only ones who know what's going on and we've been blacklisted by every agency on Earth. There is no one else."

Still he didn't move.

"It's Asher. He can't win. He can't," Daria pleaded, for maybe only the third time in her entire life. "Please."

Belhadj stood with teeth clenched. They faced off for several seconds. Then the Syrian turned, scooped up his messenger bag, and marched around the aging bus, ripping open the door and hurling his bag into the backseat.

Daria flinched, but none of his stolen ordinance blew up or fired off a round. When she was sure the messenger bag wouldn't go nuclear, she opened the passenger door and climbed in.

"We'll deal with it when we're done," she promised.

Belhadj ground gears and the bus jolted into action.

From a hundred yards away, the smuggler and the shepherd shared a reefer and watched the commotion.

The French pilot inhaled, held it, and wheezed, "Lovers."

The Italian took a hit and shrugged. "What else?"

Milan

John Broom awoke during the descent into Malpensa International Airport. He rubbed his face with the heels of his hand, then slipped a breath mint into his mouth.

"How's the honeymoon so far, dear?"

But Theo James wasn't listening. While John slept, Theo had unpacked a legal pad and a pencil. He scribbled madly, some notes in English, some in advanced mathematics. He squinted, his jaw set.

"Doc?"

Theo glanced over. He looked intense.

The 747 touched down gently.

"What?"

"France," Theo said. "You asked about the RNA sequencer in that factory fight? My French counterparts were able to reconstruct it. The last thing it sequenced was a virus that may have a specific target."

The reverse thrusters kicked in and both men lurched forward. "I'm not following."

Theo rifled back and forth through his scribbled

notes. "It's a flu that can target specific people. I don't know who. Say, black people. Or Asians."

John started to smile. "You're kidding. It can't . . . they can't . . . Come on, Doc, seriously. No one can . . ."

But Theo James looked up from his notes and whisked off his cheaters. John saw true terror in the man's eyes.

"I don't know, John," he whispered. "I think, maybe, they can."

Twenty-eight

Asher and his people had set up shop in an abandoned apartment on the west side of Milan.

Asher asked that Will Halliday and Eli Schullman take the remaining mercenaries and reconnoiter Milan's Piazza del Duomo. While Halliday was in the toilet, Asher cleaned the lenses of his glasses and said, "Go over the plan, please."

The massive Schullman scowled down at his academic friend. "The plan is the plan. The plan hasn't changed since the beginning. Renaissance masters could have painted a fucking mural of the plan."

Asher smiled, nodded, and even patted Schullman's shoulder in acknowledgment. All of which—to anyone who knew Asher—meant: Go over the plan, please.

Eli Schullman said, "We kill Halliday in the plaza. We kill the old man in the plaza. We make sure the rogue American agent goes down in history for stealing and selling the virus, and that his perfidy is known to God and CNN alike."

Asher blinked up at the big man. "Perfidy?"

"It's a perfectly good word."

Will Halliday rounded the corner.

Schullman and Halliday took the three surviving mercenaries in an Escalade to conduct the initial reconnaissance of Milan's Piazza del Duomo. They found parking. Schullman deferred to the American, instilling him with confidence. "How do you want to handle this?"

Halliday checked his watch. "We've got two hours. See that café over there? That's the meet. Everybody split up. Walk to the edges of your sight lines. Get some elevation if you can. We meet back here in thirty minutes. Go."

The men trotted off in different directions. Schullman, too.

Will Halliday stuffed his gloved hands into the pockets of his long tan duster and walked to the very center of the expansive plaza. It was the latter part of November and not too cold—maybe thirty-five degrees, he guessed, maybe a bit less—and the plaza was bustling. Businessmen in fitted overcoats and polished shoes strode carefully, watching for patches of ice amid the geometric patterns of the stone pavers. Schoolchildren on group excursions flitted about, laughing or flirting. Milanese young women, flawless and thin, strutted past him in gleaming riding boots, fur hats and collars, gaily colored gloves, and coats that floated behind them like superheroines' capes.

Will grinned. A guy could fall in love with Milanese women.

In the dead center of the plaza, he stood and turned slowly, smiling, drinking it all in. Nannies from the Far East pushed prams. Tourists carted wheeled luggage. He saw a couple dozen bicycles. More than half of the people walking through the plaza paid no attention to the art or history; they were texting.

The cathedral itself was fantastically huge and as spiky as a cactus, with its gothic pointed arches, its marble saints, and hideous gargoyles. It looked like an alien spaceship ready to launch. The monument had taken centuries to build, at a time when a man's life could run forty to fifty years. *Who puts a lifetime of work into something his great-great-grandson won't see completed?* Will wondered. He was from California, where a building from the 1960s can be considered historic.

He turned and took in the façade of the Galleria Vittoria Emanuele, which looked like it could have been government or high church offices, back in the day, but now was a glorified shopping mall. He spun on, slowly, watching the automobile traffic flow along via Torino and via Mazzini to the south, via Orifici to the west, via Meravigli to the north.

Lots of police cars, he noted. Mostly Fiats, some in black, some in white. He couldn't read Italian but could tell that more than one agency handled day-to-day security for the shrine.

He turned, watched the pedestrian patterns. He noted the difference in speed and direction between the tourists and the Milanese.

He looked up at the sky. It was nice, even overcast,

the clouds pearl gray. Good. Snipers prefer a steady overcast to direct sunlight—less change of squinting at a back-lit target or having the target alerted by lens flare from the telescopic sight.

The men regathered at the Escalade.

"Whacha think?" Will asked.

Each man made a report, detailing the best spots to put shooters, the interferences, the wind and weather.

Will leaned against the SUV and winked at Eli Schullman. "You know these badass mofos better than I do. How should we deploy?"

Schullman blew on his ungloved hands. He pointed to his men. "These two are our best snipers. Set them up to the north and west."

Will nodded. "Classic cross fire."

The hulking man with the cranial ridge pointed to the third mercenary, a buzz-cut blond, the battle-hardened Croat he had used in New York. "Tuck this man in close, at another table at the café, behind the bitch. He's an able street fighter, good with knives."

"Cool."

"You and me in the piazza. Close but not too close. Daria's exit strategy will be to run that way"—he pointed north—"to lose us in the Galleria, or into the restaurant, to lose us in the kitchen or upstairs in the businesses."

"So we cut off those exits."

Schullman nodded.

"Solid. And she meets the Commie at one of the out-side tables. He gets here first, so we can determine which way she faces."

Schullman shook his head. "*Commie?* The Russians are better capitalists than you guys, these days."

"Hey, I'm old-school. Will she bring the Syrian fucker?"

"No. She'll hold him in reserve; not sure where. Our snipers will have to find him."

The two gun hands nodded. Everyone had been given photos of Daria and Belhadj.

Will said, "Okay, fellas. No point in freezing to death. Go get warm somewhere. We meet back here in thirty minutes to set up. Smoke 'em if you got 'em. Eat, if you want. Get laid, if that's your pregame ritual. But we meet back here at three sharp."

The men dispersed.

Two blocks north, near Teatro alla Scala, a short, brown bus with tinted windows backed into an alley. Its backing up warning beeper had been disabled.

Standing next to the driver, Owen Cain Thorson held binoculars up to his eyes and scanned the Piazza del Duomo. Collier, the grizzled Oklahoman with a coarse mustache and SEAL tattoos on both shoulders, stepped up next to Thorson.

"Lotta collaterals."

"Yeah." Thorson was none too happy about the glut of pedestrians walking the plaza. "That's the café, there."

Collier leaned forward, following the boss's finger. "Exposed."

"Put your guys in civvies. Have them walk the

perimeter of the plaza. Get some altitude if they can. I want a sit rep in twenty."

Collier stuck a wad of chew in his cheek. "Sure." It came out *shore*.

Thorson turned to Agent Maldonado, who would be handling their communications. "Will we have audio?"

"Out there?" Maldonado rolled her eyes. "No way. Everyone walking and talking. All those cell phones and Bluetooths, spiking the frequencies. Stone pavers to bounce audio off of. It'd be like aiming a shotgun mic in the stands during the Super Bowl."

Thorson absorbed that. "Any word from the Italians?"

Maldonado glanced around to see who on the team was listening in. "They have taken our request for weapons-hot status under advisement and reminded us not to proceed unilaterally."

Thorson smirked.

Collier got his shooters off the bus and began their reconnoiter of the plaza.

Thorson considered his request for the use of lethal force on Italian soil. Gibron had infiltrated U.S. domestic intelligence. She had badly embarrassed Thorson— the kind of embarrassment from which a CIA career does not recover. Indeed, she had turned the CIA itself into a laughingstock. She had conspired first to kill the president, then targeted the leadership of the Western world.

Thorson had not *requested* permission to use lethal force. He had politely informed the Italians that they were going to need body bags.

*   *   *

A communications techie in the Shark Tank doffed his headset and handed it to Nanette Sylvestri. "John Broom."

Sylvestri held one of the two earpieces up against her head, the voice wand near her lips. "John?"

"Hey! We're on the ground, heading into—"

"Do you have my personal cell number?"

"Um, yeah."

"Wait ten minutes, then call me."

She disconnected, turned to the man watching a live satellite feed on one of the flat-screens. "Is that the Pentagon bird?"

He nodded without looking away. "They retasked it from over Fallujah, after plenty of kicking and screaming."

"Okay. You have the room."

She grabbed her coat off the rack, left and took the elevator up to the ground floor. She wound her way through the corridors of Langley until she came to the little-used VIP entrance, with parking large enough for the presidential motorcade. Security signed her out.

Sylvestri stood just outside the reinforced doors and thought about cigarettes until her phone, already in her hand, rang.

"John?"

"Yeah."

"Policy expressly forbids analysts from being deployed into an active, tactical operation."

After a beat, his voice came back, along with a rumbling in the background. "It sure does."

"Which is why, if I were to inform you that Gibron is meeting with your Tajik doctor at four P.M., Italy time, at a café in the Piazza del Duomo, and that Swing Band is on site, it would in no way constitute my permission to get your ass there, fast. Understood?"

Another longish beat. "Nanette?"

"Yes, John?"

"Christmas is four weeks away. What do you want Santa to bring you?"

"A new pair of eyes. Daria Gibron did a couple of big things in New York this week. One of them was to derail Owen Thorson's career. John? I cannot have *this* thing be about *that* thing."

John said, "Got it," and hung up.

The reader board on the Malpensa train read: NEXT STOP: MILAN TRAIN STATION.

John turned to Major James. "There's a complication."

"I'm in the army. There are no complications, just opportunities."

John looked the heavy Irishman dead in the eye. "Daria Gibron is meeting Dr. Tuychiev in a really crowded plaza, in about an hour, and one or both of them likely has access to Pegasus-B. Plus, a CIA hit squad with a chip on its shoulder is setting up to eliminate the threat."

Theo stopped smiling. "Okay, that's a complication."

"I'm going in."

"Well, that sounds sort of dumb."

"A little, yeah."

The train began to slow down. Theo offered a lop-sided smile. "Well, let's get to it then."

Twenty-nine

In two years, the Tunnel Rat of Rafah, who had dubbed himself Asher, turned twelve and the girl he'd rescued turned eight. By that time, the boy was organizing not only black-market goods in Rafah, but other towns as well. It was 1985 and he had become masterful at breaking into the many Jewish settlements that were sprouting like mushrooms throughout the Gaza Strip. He also had learned how to sneak into the Israeli Defense Forces compounds.

The girl had become a most capable pickpocket and thief. She looked so damned innocent! Not to mention quick; quick as a cat. Asher had started calling her that, in fact: Chatoulah. Western aid workers and foreign journalists fawned over her huge black eyes as she all but curtsied and picked their pockets clean.

One day, in an alley near an open-air bazaar on the north side of Rafah, the boy dug into his pocket and held out a bit of leather. The girl has seen Western playing cards and thought the thing looked like one of the suits.

"What is it?" she asked around a mouthful of rice and raisins.

Asher grinned and showed her that it wasn't a single bit of leather but a leather sandwich, with something metal and form-fitting within.

He flicked the metal bit with a ragged thumbnail. The metal slid out on a single hinge.

Asher picked up a discarded bit of corrugated cardboard and cleaved it in two with hardly any effort.

He closed the blade back in its spade-shaped sheath. "It's sharp. Be careful."

He tossed it to the girl.

"What do I need a knife for?"

"Because I won't always be here to protect you, Chatoulah."

She shoved his shoulder, thinking the Hebrew word for *cat* was an insult regarding her lack of size. "Your mother's only dowry was a sailor's cock!"

"Hey!" He nudged her shoulder and grinned. "That's a pretty good one."

He'd been teaching the girl to swear in Arabic. She blushed. She'd been saving it for a special occasion.

He took some of the rice and raisins, and handed her the bowl. "I won't always be here to protect you," he repeated.

"Yes, you will."

"No." There was something definitive in Asher's voice. "The cousins want me to work up north, in Khan

Yunis and Deir al-Baleh. If all goes well, I'll be working Gaza City by this time next year."

The girl ate, handed back the bowl. "So take me with
you."

He switched to French, to test her. "Maybe. We'll
see. But keep the knife. You never know."

"You never know," she acceded in French.

"What is your name this month?"

Since discovering that "Asher" had been a spur-of-
the-moment choice, the girl had shifted her name seven
or eight times a year.

"Daria."

"God, that's awful." He rolled his eyes. "You sound
like a mark. I want to rob you myself."

"It's pretty," she countered, rubbing her tiny thumb
over the leather, spade-shaped sheath.

"I have been studying American cinema. *Back to the
Future* is number one at the box office. It stars a girl
called Lea. That would be a good name."

The girl wrinkled her nose.

"*The Color Purple?* It has an Oprah."

She thought about it. "Is that a common American
name?"

Asher gave her his most worldly scowl. "In America, every fifth girl is an Oprah. Trust me. It's perfect."

They finished the rice bowl.

"Why do I need an American name?"

Asher sucked rice off his fingers, then wiped them
with the hem of his T-shirt. "There's a war on, Chatoulah."

"Where?"

He hesitated. "Here. I think."

"A war between who?"

He shot her a look. "I haven't figured out all of the angles. Even the Bedouin cousins, God grant them huge profits, don't know all the details. I just think a war is coming. And . . ."

The girl was half paying attention, fingers playing with the leather-and-blade sandwich in her small hands. "What?"

"I think," Asher switched to English, to see if she could keep up, "we need to align ourselves."

"With who . . . *whom?*" Her English was stilted.

"With the side that wins."

The girl said, "It's hot."

The boy didn't seem to hear her.

Daria Gibron said, "It's hot!"

Belhadj said, "Wake up. You have a fever."

Daria snapped awake. "Ash—?"

The blue-and-white Volkswagen bus rounded a tight bend, eight kilometers out from Milan. "You were complaining about the heat." Belhadj looked worried. "You're sweating. You have a fever."

Daria's fingers rose to her upper lip. She wasn't bleeding. But her elbows and knees ached.

"You're not well. You—"

"Get us there," she interrupted, her eyes on the traffic.

He drove, jaw set.

"There's something about Asher Sahar you're not telling me."

Daria leaned back in the cracked plastic seat, skin glistening.

"Were you lovers?"

"No."

"You always call him Asher." He drove, his mood deepening. "Are you siblings?"

Daria turned to him. She mopped her forehead with the sleeve of the jean jacket. "Not by blood."

"Don't be so damn cryptic!"

A half-assed smile twitched to life on her lips, then guttered out.

"We were orphans."

Belhadj drove in silence.

"Another battle, another neighborhood destroyed. A . . . group of Israeli loyalists read the tea leaves and realized Israel would never know peace. So . . ." Her voice drifted away.

"Daria?"

"They collected orphans. Street urchins. Pickpockets, beggars, child prostitutes. The unwanted fruit of the tree of war. Asher was one. So was I. He was almost four years older. He protected me."

"How old were you?"

She shrugged. "Six? Eight? Something like that. I don't know my real age. Nor my birthday."

"Why?"

"To train us."

"To train children? I don't understand. Are you saying . . ." Belhadj kept his eyes on the road. "Are you talking about the Group?"

Daria was quiet.

"My God. I thought they . . . you . . . were myth."

"Like the golem."

He didn't know the reference and just shrugged.

"Golems. Protectors turned monsters." She wet her lips with her tongue. "You called them the Group. As good a name as any. Believe it or not, we never had a name for them. They were just . . . the club, I suppose. But only Asher and I called them that. They taught us to fight. To sabotage. To infiltrate. To murder. Then they found us foster homes in Israel and hid us among the farmers and merchants, where no one would look for us. They knew that someday, somewhere down the violent path of statehood, Israel would need its monsters."

They rode a few blocks in silence.

Belhadj thought long and hard before speaking. He knew she would be either crushed or acknowledge the truth of his observation. "Israeli jihadists."

Daria didn't move. After about a block, she reached out to Belhadj and tucked a disheveled lock of graying hair behind his ear. His voice carried such a wide array of emotions, although his face remained passive.

"Killers," she corrected or acknowledged. "Killers who could do the unthinkable, who could do terrible deeds. Deeds that politicians and conscripted soldiers could never be asked to do."

"Like kill a member of the Israeli Parliament and blame the Palestinians, to set up another holy war."

"Yes. Asher was just following his programming. I tried to stop him. You have to believe, I never wanted him dead, never wanted him imprisoned. Just stopped. It wasn't even a bad plan. It could have worked."

"But you did stop him."

She didn't reply.

"Why didn't you become like him?"

She shrugged off the question. "It's not important. What's important is stopping him. Again."

Belhadj gripped the wheel tight. "That might not be possible without killing him."

"Don't."

The rode for a while. The city center of Milan was fast approaching.

"Look. I realize you were raised together. You say he protected you as children. Fine. But when the time comes—"

"Don't kill him."

She wet her lips.

"That's my job."

Thirty

Belhadj parked two blocks from the Piazza del Duomo. Daria checked her Glock, made sure it was fully loaded, and threw three extra clips, seventeen Parabellum rounds each, into the Hello Kitty backpack she had stolen from the French farmhouse.

The Syrian had raided both the American and French command vehicles and had amassed a brilliant array of weapons of destruction. He reached into his sack and pulled out a massive silver handgun, a Desert Eagle, which, like a rifle, uses pressurized gas and not a hammer to propel the heavy .50 caliber bullets. The gun was a chunk of metal that, had it fallen from the heavens, would have killed all the dinosaurs.

"Holy hell." Daria eyed the cannon. "You picked an Israeli handgun?"

He nodded. "Your people are Zionist occupiers and the killers of families, but you make one hell of a good firearm."

"That thing should be bolted to the deck of a navy cutter. Are you sure you can aim it?"

"Fifty caliber rounds? Your aim doesn't have to be perfect to turn your enemy into a graffito."

She ratcheted open her car door. "When you fire, try not to topple the cathedral, will you?" She stepped out. "I'll meet Tuychiev. You find a place to lurk."

"Don't be stupid. You're in no—"

Daria said, "Our *army* is exactly two guns deep. I'm sick and you're not. Which of us should play the hare and which of us should lie in wait?"

He ground his back teeth, annoyed that a woman so devoid of military strategy always seemed to grasp the obvious tactical approach.

He crossed to her side of the van. Daria was swiveling at the hip, raising one heel, then the other, of her Spanish boots.

"Are you in pain?"

She was looking at the VW's side mirror. "I'm trying to decide if these jeans make my ass look fat."

When she glanced up, she thought Belhadj was wincing in pain. But no, it was his strange translation of a silent laugh.

"What?"

"You . . ." He composed himself. "You're serious."

She made a look-around gesture. "This is Milan."

"Spare me, God. Is there a plan?"

"I always think everything is a trap. Let's assume I'm right. We're east of the Duomo. You cut south, into the plaza. I'll cut north. The café is at the opposite end of the plaza. Tuychiev said he'd be seated outside. I'll meet him, find out what he knows about this flu. See if there's an antidote."

Belhadj's slate gray eyes flickered. "Fine."

"What?"

"Nothing. I said *fine*. I'll circle around, come up to the café from the south side. Don't bother looking for me. I'll be there."

Daria removed the denim jacket, tossed it in the van, then slung the backpack over one shoulder, the heavy gun and clips against her lower back. She was sweating. It was maybe thirty-five degrees out.

"What is it?" she asked.

"What do you mean?"

"You flinched when I said 'antidote.'"

Belhadj bristled. "The last time I flinched, I also was teething."

"Is there something you're not telling me?"

Belhadj threw the strap of his bag over his shoulder, cross-chest. "Yes, there is. I forgot to tell you this plan is stupid and you are pigheaded and you should be in hospital, and your ego is out of control and you are not half as clever as you suppose you are."

Daria ticked off his points on her fingers. "No. No, I believe you said all that in the van."

"Oh. Then, no. Nothing more to tell you. Sorry."

"There is no antidote for influenza, is there?"

Belhadj studied the pearl sky. When he looked back, Daria had the illusion that his eyes had been dyed to match the day.

"No. There are antivirals."

"Oh. Good to know. Then after stopping Asher, we get this flu to World Health or the Centers for Disease Control or whomever, and have them concoct the anti-virals."

Belhadj didn't respond.

Daria said, "How long does it take to make them?"

"About a year."

Daria paused a beat. The pain in her elbows had increased. "Oh."

They stood. A lot of information passed, but silently.

"Okay," she said. "Well. See you."

Belhadj walk-jogged the length of the cruciate cathedral.

Daria waited until Belhadj disappeared around the south side of the gothic cathedral, then bent over a corrugated tin garbage can and puked. She was surprised by the amount of blood in her vomit.

She sat on her haunches and gathered her wits. Once her vision refocused, she wiped her lips and blew her nose—more blood—and stood, loping down Corso Vittorio Emanuele II toward the piazza.

She studied the massive, ornate wall of the cathedral to her left. Part of it had been cleaned and glistened white. Part of it still held a centuries-old patina of soot and mold. Some was covered in scaffolding and the scaffolding itself covered in billboard-sized ads for shoes and women's clothing.

She reached the plaza and the noise level rose. Tourists and Milanese roamed, children chased each other, African hucksters offered bright, cheap tchotchkes, a

German camera crew staged a live broadcast of a travelogue show, a large cluster of Asians circled a tour guide who used a raised but closed parasol as her sigil. Pickpockets earned an honest day's fare.

Inside of ninety seconds, Daria clocked a black Fiat with the uniformed carabinieri—state police—and a white Fiat marked Istituto di Vigilanza. Private, city-paid security.

Daria pulled a Kleenex from the tight thigh pocket of her girl's skinny jeans and held it under her nose. No blood.

She was the only person in the plaza sweating by the time she crossed the geometrically designed pavers and approached the farthest café. Very few of the outdoor tables were occupied, and those that were served couples or families wrapping mittens or gloves around grand tasse coffees.

A lone man sat at one round, wrought-iron table, in a long silvery woolen coat with a black silk collar and short-brimmed Borsalino hat, black leather gloves and a woolen scarf. He had a long, thin neck and swept-back white hair. Daria, an insomniac, had recently watched a 1970s Hammer Films monster flick at 3:00 A.M. and thought this man looked remarkably like the mad scientist. *Talk about typecasting*, she castigated herself.

She approached his table. "János Tuychiev?"

The old man beamed up at her. "That name is a suit I have not worn for years. Please, sit."

She did, feeling her left knee buckle a little so that she fell, rather than glided, into the iron chair.

* * *

"It's Daria."

Eli Schullman spoke into his comms. He stood behind a spinner rack of postcards, two doors down from the café. Thirty feet to his left, Will Halliday studied a wall of Serie A football jerseys and scarves. "No sign of the Syrian. Shooters?"

The first sniper, in the men's room on the third floor of a fashion warehouse, came back quickly through Will's earjack. "No. Nothing."

The second sniper, on the roof of a second restaurant and café, spoke up. "I have him. He's on foot, coming from the south. He's walking with a bunch of tourists."

Schullman adjusted his position. He caught sight of a travel guide, walking backward, amid a gaggle of tourists with maps, guidebooks, and cameras. It took him a moment to spot Belhadj among them.

"I have him."

One of the snipers said, "Shall I kill him?"

"Yes," Schullman said. "On my mark. Ready?"

With Daria and Belhadj now on the scene and under the eye of his snipers, Schullman moved into position to knife Will Halliday, then kill Dr. Tuychiev. It was working out better than he could have hoped.

Schullman sidled behind Will Halliday. He reached for his knife.

His earpiece crackled.

Asher Sahar whispered. "Everyone . . . hold position, please."

In the brown bus with the smoked windows, Owen Cain Thorson scoured the rooftops of the plaza with binoculars. He knew where his shooters were; otherwise, he wouldn't have spotted them. Collier's guys were true pros.

The team's communications tech, Maldonado, glanced up from her monitors. "Everyone's in position."

Thorson turned from the window to the two monitors that Maldonado had set up. One showed an elevated view of Gibron and an old guy with long, white hair. The other framed up on Khalid Belhadj, looking inconspicuous as he listened to a tour guide pontificating. The real-time images were being transmitted from the snipers' high-tech scopes.

He would have liked to have audio, but he understood the technical nightmare of long-distance mics in the piazza.

He toggled his radio. "Collier? Get in close. Take two guys. When you're within ten yards, I want both snipers to open up. Put Gibron and Belhadj on the ground. The old guy is positively identified as our biologist, Tuychiev. Take him into custody."

The Oklahoman drawled back, "Confirm."

John Broom and Major Theo James shoved their way up the stairs from the metro stop below the plaza. The stop served both the red and yellow lines, and was jammed with Milanese and tourists. Climbing the stairs felt like swimming upstream.

"Now what?" Theo asked.

"Daria Gibron is five-six, straight black hair, dark skin, early thirties, and a fitness buff. My boss said she's meeting a guy at one of the outside tables." John hopped up on the stand of one of the plaza's light poles, leaning out à la Gene Kelly, and scanned the open area. He saw at least a dozen restaurants with outside seating; most of them were empty due to the cold but a couple dozen brave souls were fortifying themselves with coffees or hot chocolate.

He hopped back down. "You go counterclockwise, I'll go this way. We'll meet at the other end. Give me your cell phone."

John plugged their numbers into each other's phones and handed Theo's back. "Right. Sing out if you spot her."

They separated.

Daria, in the blue shirt and tank, was the only person in the plaza without a coat save for the waiters.

Dr. János Tuychiev said, "Surely you are cold, signora."

She was sweltering. "My name is Daria Gibron. I want to talk to you about your influenza."

The Tajik had ordered a pot of black tea and two cups. A waiter with a long white apron brought them out. Tuychiev poured. "Which one? I have designed a few."

"The one that targets Jews."

"Ah!" His face lit up and he slid a cup in Daria's direction. She almost reached for it, but a sharp pain ran through her elbow, locking the joint for a second. She struggled not to show it on her face. "Yes. That one is a masterpiece."

"A madman has stolen a canister of it. I fear he plans to launch a pandemic."

"Why would he do that?"

"Insanity." She mopped sweat off her forehead. Her eyes were bright with fever. Strands of hair stuck to her forehead.

"And what is your role in all of this, Miss Gibron?"

"I intend to stop him."

She heard a voice from behind her, very close to her ear. "Stop me?"

Daria's heart trip-hammered.

"Remember the last time you stopped me? It ended poorly. For both of us."

The CIA snipers' scopes transmitted to the brown bus, and from there the signal traveled via secure satellite to the Shark Tank. One flat-screen for each of the snipers, plus a high-definition bird's-eye view from the U.S. Army's borrowed eye-in-the-sky satellite.

Nanette Sylvestri and her team watched as a slim man with a beard, thinning hair and spectacles approached the seated subject from behind. He leaned into her chair and spoke to her.

"Why don't we have audio?" Sylvestri spoke into her voice wand.

The voice of Thorson's comms tech, Maldonado, came back over the Shark Tank's speaker system. "Acoustics in the plaza, ma'am. Too much bounce-back from all the stone surfaces."

"Well, who's this?"

The newcomer, in an olive tunic with a striped scarf and rough, brown gloves, stole an iron chair from an adjacent table and sat with Gibron and Dr. Tuychiev.

On the second flat-screen, the Syrian assassin continued to listen to a tour guide. He didn't seem to notice the newcomer at the café.

"Unknown, ma'am."

One of Sylvestri's data-crunchers waved to get her attention. "Running facial-recog software now. He's . . . ah . . ."

"He's Asher Sahar." Nanette Sylvestri turned to see Stanley Cohen march into the Shark Tank.

"Who?"

Cohen said, "Asher Sahar. I just got confirmation from Tel Aviv. He's supposed to be in prison but he's not. And we weren't informed. That's the traitor who shot Gibron before she defected to the States."

Sylvestri turned back to the flat-screens. "That's the name she used on her FBI handler's voice mail." She activated her transmitter. "Swing Band: get ready to bring everyone in for questioning. The old guy in the hat, the new guy in the olive jacket and striped scarf, too. Repeat: all subjects are to be held for questioning."

Everyone in the Shark Tank waited a moment. The drama on the screens played on.

Sylvestri said, "Swing Band: confirm orders, please."

Inside the CIA command vehicle, Owen Cain Thorson approached Maldonado's communications array. He stood, she sat. Thorson made sure they had steady eye contact, then he popped the maintenance hatch off the back of her computer and used a penknife to slide out three of the sheathed wires. A flick of the wrist, and the wires sheared.

Maldonado's externals comms—those linking her to Langley—went dark.

Thorson looked deep into Maldonado's eyes.

She nodded her approval.

Thirty-one

Asher Sahar pulled up a chair and smoothed his tunic and sat. He set a messenger bag gingerly on the stones.

A rush of emotional slush sluiced through Daria's veins. There was anger and hatred and love and longing and silly joy at seeing his face again and an acidic longing to pay him back for all the pain he'd brought her.

She thought about shooting him, calculated the odds, her dark eyes flashing like lighthouses amid sheet lightning. Had he come alone? Would he? No. Would she be covered by snipers? Likely.

Asher said, "May I have your gun, please?"

She slowly withdrew the Glock from the schoolgirl's backpack and handed it to him. He nodded approvingly then slipped it into a tunic pocket. "That's a very good gun."

Daria studied his all-too-familiar face. He smiled shyly, avoiding eye contact, as he adjusted his coat and scarf and removed his rough gloves.

When he finally locked eyes with her, Daria's heart stuttered. His eyes were the same soft brown she had remembered. His smile was gentle.

"I cannot . . ." He stopped, cleared his throat. He picked up his gloves, fumbled with them, and set them back down on the table. "I am so sorry about shooting you. There have been no decisions in my life I regret more than that."

He looked close to tears.

"The American FBI agent, Ray Calabrese. He seemed in charge. I aimed at him. You stepped in. . . ."

She didn't reply.

Asher cleared his throat. "Believe it or not, it's really good to see you again. I've missed you."

"And I, you." She turned to the old man with the white mane. "You two have met."

The old man smiled benignly. "Your friend reintroduced me to one of my creations. The influenza virus of which you spoke. I have not seen it in years."

Daria said, "I'm told the Americans are calling it Pegasus-B. Asher plans to—"

"Pardon me." János Tuychiev's forehead wrinkled. "The Americans? They have . . . *named* my virus? What right have they to—"

Asher cleared his throat. "Perhaps we could get into intellectual property rights later, Professor. Daria, you were saying?"

She locked eyes with the Tajik biologist. "Asher plans to release your virus."

Tuychiev shrugged inside his expensive woolen coat.

Asher edged his chair closer to the table. "Do you know why, Chatoulah?"

She smiled at the childhood nickname. She remembered the original message she'd received, luring her to Manhattan. "To make Israel look like the victim of another holocaust."

Her oldest living friend smiled, nodded, his fingertips playing along the frilled edges of the wrought-iron table as if it were a keyboard. "Yes. You understand."

"Who will you blame? The Iranians?"

"Why not? They are ready-made villains for the West. Both Syria and the House of Saud grow weary of Persian influence in the region. The Americans and the European Union will react predictably."

"How many Israelis will you need to kill for this plan of yours?"

He shrugged apologetically. "Some. A great many. But that would be true if we did nothing. Bombardments from the Golan Heights. Another uprising from Gaza. Al-Qaida suicide squads. A strengthened Muslim Brotherhood. A third intifada. Israelis are going to die, one way or another. My way: their deaths will not be meaningless. They will usher in a new era of peace for—"

"Asher?"

He adjusted his glasses on the bridge of his nose, turned to her, expecting her lecture, preparing his counterarguments.

Daria touched her upper lip. Her fingertips came back pink.

"I have it."

János Tuychiev bit off a brittle little laugh. "Oh, my."

Asher blinked through his round lenses. "I'm sorry?"

"His flu. Pegasus-B. The factory outside Paris. I'm infected."

Asher stared at her, his mouth open, forming silent first syllables that refused to become audible words.

Over their comm links, Will Halliday spoke without moving his lips overmuch. "Is he gonna green-light this bitch or cut bait?"

Eli Schullman had maneuvered around behind the American and gripped the handle of his knife in his fatigue jacket pocket. He, too, wondered what Asher was playing at.

In the brown bus, Maldonado said, "Collier is in position. He wants the go-no go call."

Thorson felt remarkably calm. The French had confirmed the presence of a superflu in the bombed-out factory. They had positive ID on Gibron entering the building. Putting her at a table with the biologist, János Tuychiev, seemed like icing on the cake.

For the sake of their testimony—in a week or a month or whenever—Thorson said, "Have we heard from Langley?"

Maldonado's eyes flickered to the severed wires, breaking her audio link to the Shark Tank. "No, sir."

"Right then. Shooters? On my signal: take them. Collier, your priority will be Tuychiev and the newcomer. Once Gibron and Belhadj are down, I want the other two in custody. Everyone ready?"

Asher blinked again. "I . . . what?"

"I have Tuychiev's flu. I'm infected."

Asher spoke to the old man without taking his eyes off Daria. "Expose her. Give her the other flu."

Daria's black eyes flashed. "I'm sorry? What the fuck . . . ?"

János Tuychiev concurred. "What?"

"The second flu!" Asher spoke, still staring at Daria and the pink smudge of blood on her upper lip. He now noticed she wore no coat and that she was sweating.

"I think one flu is more than enough, thank you!"

He talked through her, reaching out, gripping her forearm. "No, no. The second flu weakens the protein bonds that link the first flu to your cells. It renders the first flu useless." He turned to the biologist. "Infect her."

The old man adjusted his teacup on its saucer and smiled down at it, looking at neither of them.

Daria reached out and cupped the back of Asher's hand on her arm. "Oh, God. What have you done?"

He turned back to her. "Chatoulah?"

"There is no second flu. You don't know any more about *protein bonds* than I do. You're echoing words this old fool told you."

Asher slowly turned back to Dr. Tuychiev.

The elderly man smiled. "She's very clever, this one."

Asher blanched.

"He told you his flu could be turned on and off like a faucet. And you believed him." Daria was incredulous. "It can't. Asher, there is no off switch. If you release this flu in a major Jewish population, it will infect thousands. Hundreds of thousands. Perhaps more."

János Tuychiev looked so proud. "She is your Patient Zero. The virus spreads through her. This woman is a gun. All you have to do is aim her."

Daria turned to the old man. "You will rot in hell."

Dr. Tuychiev smiled. "Save me a seat."

Asher reached into his tunic, drew a SIG-Sauer, and shot János Tuychiev through the heart.

At the first *crack* of gunfire, a couple hundred pigeons—who normally tolerated the noisy tourists well enough—bolted for the sky.

The CIA sniper who was lining up on Belhadj pulled his eye away from the scope, just in time to see one of the targets fall backward, a brimmed hat flying, white hair wafting.

Thorson's voice boomed over the comms. "Shots fired! Snipers: go! Collier: go!"

The shooter put his eye back, flush against the viewfinder. The pack of tourists popped into clear view, people flinching, ducking, heads spinning, following the echoes of the gunshot.

The Syrian was gone.

The second CIA sniper had Daria in his crosshairs. He applied even pressure to the trigger.

Someone stepped into his shot. It was an enormous

man with a shaved head and a bullet-shaped skull. He was moving fast. He was moving toward the targets.

The sniper said, "No shot, no shot. Someone get that palooka out of the field of fire."

As Asher's shot rang out, Daria kicked with both legs, tipping her chair straight back. It hit the pavers hard. She turned the fall into a somersault, tumbling fast. She spun on her knees, skittered under the closest iron table. A .223 bullet, fired from on high, panged off the tabletop and ricocheted toward the patrons in the café.

Daria rolled and skidded under tables, putting distance between herself and Asher until she bumbled into the jeans and boots of a stranger.

A blond man in a buzz cut grabbed her by the shirt collar and lifted her up to her knees. The man was all muscle, no fat. She recognized him from the factory in France, where she saw him duck into the escape tunnel.

He swung a gravity blade, inches from her face.

Daria's thumb flicked free the spade-shaped knife as she was hauled upright. She slid the toughened plastic blade into the newcomer's arm, severing his biceps tendon.

He howled, his hands opening, dropping both his knife and Daria to the pavers.

Daria rose to her feet, bending her knees, using her weight and center of balance to dance the man in a half circle.

Her fist swiped left to right, the spade blade severing the blond man's throat.

Before her killing stroke did its job, a high-caliber bullet from three stories up slammed into the man's back, propelling him forward. He collapsed, taking Daria down with him.

Asher turned back from killing Dr. Tuychiev. Daria was gone, her chair overturned.

Three men were approaching from Asher's ten, twelve, and two o'clock positions. All three had drawn handguns, shouting over one another in Americanized English. Asher made a show of quickly setting down his weapon and raising his open palms.

He watched as the CIA trio closed in but his own people moved up behind them.

Eli Schullman sheathed the knife—intended for Will Halliday's back—and instead drew his auto and fired. Not at Halliday, but at the closest CIA agent to Asher.

Will Halliday dropped another CIA agent. He glanced at Asher and winked.

Asher marveled at the American's luck, then he picked his gun up from the tabletop and heaved over the heavy iron table. It might provide a small modicum of cover.

Bullets began raining down from on high.

One of the CIA snipers saw the shots peppering the plaza from the high ground. He deftly calculated the angle and spun his rifle in that direction. He spotted the opposition in less than a second.

He ratcheted the bolt, fired, ejected the shell, and

ratcheted in another round. "Taking fire from above! They have snipers!"

Blood drenched Daria's shirt as she shoved Asher's man off her. The sniper slug that killed him should have been a through-and-through, killing Daria as well. How it had missed her was a mystery.

The dead man had a blackened .357 Colt Python tucked into his belt. Daria grabbed the revolver left-handed and glanced over the dead man's shoulder to see Asher sprinting across the plaza toward the cathedral.

Assistant Director Cohen and Nanette Sylvestri stood side by side, thunderstruck as two of the flat-screen TVs turned into a live-fire urban battlefield. The bird's-eye view from the military satellite showed tourists and Milanese scrambling for safety, some falling, others trampling them.

There were too many combatants in too small a space to tell friend from foe. Sylvestri spoke into her mic. "Swing Band: break off the firefight! Get to cover! Too many civilians. Confirm!"

Fiats of *carabinieri* and city police screeched to a halt all around the plaza. The Shark Tank's software included a small descriptor for each car in semiopaque lettering.

Sylvestri shouted into her mic. "Swing Band! Law enforcement is on scene! Disengage firefight!"

She turned to her techs. "Are they getting this?"

The technicians had no answer. The Shark Tank was transmitting. They just weren't hearing anything back.

Owen Cain Thorson had always believed in a simple rule of conflict: bring more guns than the other guy. First overwhelm, then sort things out.

Between his snipers and Collier's men in the plaza, Thorson had more than enough firepower to kill Gibron and Belhadj, and to capture the old biologist. Also, by using the transmitted images from his snipers' lenses, Thorson and Maldonado could watch it all unfold as planned.

All that changed in a heartbeat.

Even without everyone's comms, Thorson could hear the crackle of gunfire from the plaza. Men were shouting. Plus, the CIA snipers now were firing back at someone else's snipers, robbing Thorson of their transmitted scope images of the situation on the ground.

He turned from the monitors and ripped open the weapons locker, nearly springing the hinges. He tossed an American-made Ruger MP-9 machine pistol to Maldonado, who was doffing her headset and reaching for a Kevlar vest. Thorson underhanded her a long magazine of 9-millimeter shells, which she shoved home.

He grabbed an identical machine pistol and vest, and leaped out of the bus.

In the Shark Tank, Sylvestri watched the real-time satellite image, which took in the entirety of the Piazza del Duomo as well as half of the gothic cathedral.

Someone said, "Still no audio from Swing Band. We—"

Something caught Sylvestri's eye. "What's that? Who is that?"

The screen showed panicky civilians pouring toward the streets and into surrounding buildings. They danced in every direction. But one figure sprinted, as straight as a laser, toward the cathedral.

Sylvestri adjusted her voice wand. "Swing Band, can we—" She ground her teeth, threw off her headset. "I need comms!"

Stanley Cohen said, "Nan," and pointed at the satellite monitor.

A second figure separated itself from the throng. This one, also, vectored true. Destination: the cathedral.

But even from space, the satellite made the identity of this second runner obvious.

She was the only person in a plaza not wearing a coat.

The spiky, peaked towers of the cathedral seemed to rise higher and at a more oblique angle as Daria sprint-stumbled toward it, each craggy, ivory tower with a saint perched at its apex like medieval Cirque du Soleil acrobats.

Daria wheezed like an old man, her arms and legs pumping, eyes stinging with sweat. Her left leg buckled, only a little. She caromed off a stranger in the plaza, knocking him flat on his ass but using the impact to right herself.

She sprinted on, feeling weaker than she had since Asher had shot her years ago.

Asher opened the distance between them.

John Broom sat in the plaza, legs spread, knees up, one palm bleeding.

He had never heard live gunfire before. It wasn't like in the movies.

He hit the speed dial for Theo James, who answered after one ring.

"John! John! Are you okay?"

John shouted into his phone, "I just got knocked on my ass by Daria Gibron!"

"What the heck? Why?"

"She was . . . I don't know! She's chasing a guy! I tried to get her attention. They're heading toward the cathedral!"

"This is a firefight, son! Get inside!"

John tested his legs. They were shaking from fear but seemed uninjured. His heart was rabbiting. He climbed to his feet.

"Doc, listen! She's bleeding from her nose and at least one ear. She's pale as a ghost and sweating heavy."

"Was she hit?"

"Don't think so! She's sprinting! But she looks sick!"

"Those sound like early stage symptoms of the virus. She could have it."

John tested both knees and winced a little. He'd twisted his right knee in the fall. His hands were shaking and he tasted acid on his tongue.

"Are you safe?"

Theo shouted, "Yeah!"

"Okay, well, I'm really sorry, about this, but I need you at the cathedral! Quick as you can!"

"Why? What—"

John hung up, steeled himself, and limped after Daria.

Thirty-two

The interior of the cathedral—the fourth-largest in the world—was vast and dark, seemingly as tall as it was long. The building was shaped like a giant cross, the long dimension stretching one and a half times the length of an American football field. It was split into several naves, and on that day it was filled with tourists and supplicants, church staff, and a children's choir. The Duomo offered an air of serenity.

Outside the cathedral, two armed soldiers stood guard. Both were twenty-two. Neither had seen combat. When the shooting and shouting began, they glanced at each other, wide-eyed.

The senior of the two was a pimply faced youth from Modena with dreams of a career in computer game animation. He wet his suddenly very dry lips. "Get the doors. Keep everyone out of the cathedral!"

"But . . ." the slightly younger soldier had studied for the priesthood. Guarding the Duomo meant something a bit more to him than a field duty. "It's sanctuary! The shooting. We have to let everyone in! The gunmen—"

Asher Sahar looked like any other tourist or Milano, dashing past the two, right up until he slammed into the senior soldier, catching him between his shoulder blades. The man tumbled into his cohort and both fell badly. Both youths wore right-hand hip holsters. Asher drew a SIG and put a bullet in each man's right wrist. Crippled, the youths howled and writhed.

Asher didn't need them dead and he didn't need them drawing their weapons on him. He needed them making a ruckus and bleeding. Tourists scattered, moving away from the cathedral.

He displayed both of his SIG P-220s, one in each fist, high over his head. "Move!" he bellowed, and shouldered aside the few people who hadn't yet fled. He marched into the grand church.

Inside, it was like stepping into another country: The quiet of it, the darkness of it, and, surprisingly for so vast a space, the warmth of it. It was twenty-five degrees warmer inside than out. A children's choir sang sweetly, at least a hundred voices deep. Pigeons roosted at the upper levels, some flitting about, but most waiting for closing time and the humans to leave their church.

So dense was the pink Candoglia marble walls that the tourists and true believers within weren't aware that they had missed a gun battle without. There were no signs of panic inside the cathedral. That did not suit Asher's needs. A *carabinieri* in a severe tunic with brass buttons, striped trousers, and a Sam Browne belt and sidearm peered at him down a long, aquiline nose.

Asher said, *"Scusi, signore,"* lifted one of the matching SIGs, and shot him through the heart.

Tourists began to scream and back away, ramming into one another, falling, creating a scrum at the entrance to the cathedral. Someone knocked over an iron array of votive candles.

Asher turned three hundred and sixty degrees, letting everyone see his twin handguns. The brazen act drove scores of people deeper into the church and away from the entrance, as he had planned.

Asher hefted his messenger bag, which was so heavy that it had banged against his hip during his mad dash for safety. He pulled open the flap and studied the red iron canister with its pressure gauge and valve.

What had Chatoulah called it? Pegasus-B?

Why not? As good a name as any.

He began striding straight down the left-hand aisle of the long axis of the cruciate complex, making sure people trapped inside could see his twin guns.

Tourists flocked back out of the main entrance, colliding with people who had been outside seeking sanctuary from the still-roiling firefight at the other end of the plaza.

Two-tone police sirens echoed from every direction. *Carabinieri* and *Polizia Locale di Commune* would have been on the combatants already, but the cops were busy not getting trampled.

A large woman in Euro Disney sweats looked at Daria and shrieked a long, sustained, slasher-film sort of shriek. Daria glanced down and realized her shirt was pink with blood and globby bits. Getting arrested or shot by the Italian police wouldn't be helpful. She grabbed the shirtfront in both fists, Clark Kent–style, and yanked. Buttons flew. She shrugged it to the ground. Her white tank top was only mildly bloody but drenched in sweat.

She hefted the .357 magnum Python, heavier and more awkward than her reliable Glock. She waved it, shouting in Italian, "Move! Get out of the way! Go!"

Daria regularly ran five to ten miles in her workout regimen. Dashing across the hard stone plaza left her gasping, lungs spent. Her hair was matted to her skull. She wiped salty sweat away from her eyes and looked at her palm: it was pink with blood.

Her window of opportunity was closing. Quickly.

Back across the plaza, Eli Schullman saw Asher bolt toward the gothic cathedral. He knew what lay within the cathedral. He knew the Tunnel Rat of Rafah had one more trick up his sleeve.

Asher's gambit was winnable but time-consuming. And time was, maybe, the one thing Schullman had left to give his old friend.

His own auto was empty, if he'd counted his shots right. And of course, he had. He made his decision in less than a second. He grinned.

It had been a good run, he thought. Better than most.

He picked an American who was just entering the fray. The tall man wore a Kevlar vest and carried a Ruger MP-9 machine pistol. Schullman bellowed, charging him.

The newcomer—flanked by a woman with a matching

vest and machine pistol—targeted the sound of his bellow. The man raised his weapon and spat three slugs into Eli Schullman's gut.

The big man staggered but didn't fall. He held an arm across his wounds and raised an empty pistol, aiming it true.

The female agent with the Ruger fired and hit him twice, in his shoulder and chest.

Schullman plowed into the man, knocking him over. He swung his now-empty pistol like a club and the woman in the Kevlar vest staggered and fell. She hit another CIA agent moving toward Schullman, and both tumbled to the ground.

Schullman drew his combat knife. He glanced toward the cathedral. His smile blooming as he hacked up blood.

Eli Schullman heard the gunfire from the others, but he never really felt the impact.

Daria vaulted over two wounded guards outside the cathedral. The crowds had dispersed. She ducked inside.

Chaos reigned. Crying civilians huddled in corners. A police officer lay on his back, a chest wound oozing blood. Daria knelt, snapped open his hip holster and drew his sidearm. She put the spade knife back in her boot, and now had a revolver in each fist.

Dizziness and nausea swept through her. Adrenaline was battling the virus for all its worth and the virus was winning. Daria shook sweat from her eyelashes and stood, moving stiffly in the direction of the loudest screams and shouting. She found several people attempting to hide amid the wooden pews. Others had climbed over hip-high safety glass into displays of saints and cubicles dedicated to effigies and catafalques.

Daria got to the intersection, where the longest part of the great church met with two shorter naves, creating the crosslike structure. Directly ahead was the Duomo's Chapel of the Masses. Daria glanced first to her right, both guns extended, and heard the telltale clack of a gun being cocked behind her.

"Chatoulah?"

Both of her hands shook and lightning bolts of pain coursed through her elbows and knees. She had trouble drawing a decent breath.

"Guns." He spoke softly from behind her.

Daria went to one knee, set both guns down amid the ornate, nutmeg-and-black floral marble. She stood again, turning, arms out a little from her torso.

Several of the faithful who watched put their hands together or knelt or made the sign of the cross. Collectively, they prayed.

Asher aimed a SIG at her sweat-drenched T, the other hand gripping a matching automatic. To his right, a bright red canister with a pressure gauge and valve lay on an ancient and illuminated Bible, which itself stood on an ornate wooden choir stand. Asher's shoulder bag sat at his feet.

The trapped tourists had stopped screaming. Daria's voice echoed amid the towering marble support columns. "Still sorry you shot me that night?"

"God, yes! A day never passes that I don't regret that."

"You'll have to again."

Diffused light from stained-glass windows lent a rose-and-gold glow to the room. Their voices echoed off the high ceilings, which looked like the hulls of massive, inverted ships. Close to two hundred and fifty trapped tourists grew quiet. The children's choir hadn't had time to leave their risers. The pigeons hunkered down.

Asher stared into her eyes. "Get free of this. Let the Americans get you to an intensive care unit. The flu is survivable if treated quickly."

Daria felt her knee twitch. She worked up a wry smile and a small shake of her head.

He said, "I have a way out. You need one, too."

"The CIA is on our doorstep."

Asher shook his head in annoyance. "Every contingency is accounted for, Chatoulah. Workers have been excavating an ancient baptistery. They're using tunnels. I'm good with tunnels. You know that. I can be blocks away while the CIA and the Italians are dealing with the panic in here."

"So you can reunite with the Club Sennacherib?"

For the first time, Asher smiled a true smile. Light glinted off his wire-rimmed glasses. The barrel of his SIG didn't deviate a single millimeter from Daria's heart.

"The Group has been reconstituted. Our original mission—the mission for which we were conceived and born and raised—is needed today, now more than ever. Israel needs us to do the things it cannot and must not do to survive. We—"

"Hey. Hi."

An American in a jacket of supple chocolate leather edged through the crowd, empty hands up by his shoulders. "Sorry for interrupting. You're Asher Sahar, aren't you? Hi, Asher. I'm John Broom." The American turned and gave her a little wave. "Hi, Daria."

Daria blinked in befuddlement at the perfect stranger.

Yet another stranger—this one, a strapping, blond man with an incongruous grin—stepped free of the trapped crowd, put a meaty hand on John Broom's shoulder, and plowed his other fist into John's gut.

John folded like a paper kite. He landed on his hands and knees, face going red, hacking great, wet coughs, eyes squeezed shut.

Daria recognized the bigger man from the hellish firefight in the French factory.

Asher said, "Hallo, Will."

The blond American nodded. "Hey, buddy."

Asher bobbed the barrel of his gun toward John. "Friend of yours, Chatoulah?"

The smaller man gasped on his all fours. "I'm . . . CIA . . ."

Will Halliday drew his hand-gun and placed the barrel against the base of John's neck. He patted him down, turned to Asher, and shook his head.

"Hallo, Mr. . . . Bloom, was it? You're interfering."

"Broom." John rose up to his feet, hands on knees. "Yeah, I do that. Look, the guy who hit me sounds American, so I'm gonna go with Will Halliday of the Secret Service."

The scene was getting away from Daria, who recognized neither American.

"I'm an analyst. I wrote the briefings on Daria Gibron." John held his gut gingerly. "I know Agent Halliday here killed some of his fellow agents in Colorado and stole the Pegasus-B virus, which you tested at a factory in France. You're hoping to use it to stir up a war."

Daria didn't interrupt. The stranger was buying her the time to catch her breath. All she needed was some breath to catch.

John stood as straight as he could. "Thing is, your plan only works if nobody knows you're behind it all. And by now, everyone in the CIA knows. Everyone in French intelligence knows. Everyone in Italian intelligence knows. Everyone who's ever been to a Starbucks knows. My mom, in Queens? She's calling Aunt Edna right now, so she knows. No fall guy means no war."

Daria spat a pink glob of blood on the floral floor. "The virus. It targets Jews. Does everyone know that?"

John pivoted slowly in her direction, hand on his gut. He blinked, his brain trying to wrap itself around the concept. Theo James had suggested that a targeted virus was possible. But the idea . . .

John reached for a gold chain around his neck, yanked a Star of David pennant out of his shirt and flashed it to both Daria and Asher Sahar. Daria could practically see gears churn in the man's brain. "The Filipino Army broke open one of the canisters but nobody got sick."

"Surprisingly few Jews in the Filipino military,"

Asher deadpanned. "Make me a promise, Mr. Broom, and you're free to go. Get Daria to an American medical facility, fast. Have her treated for a hemorrhagic fever. Will you do that, Mr. Broom?"

John hesitated.

"Well, sir?"

John inwardly chanted, *Stupid! Stupid! Stupid!* "Are you going to release the gas in here?"

"After the two of you leave. And myself, of course. Will?"

Halliday reached out and Asher handed him the red canister. Halliday already had proven himself immune to Pegasus-B.

On a second-story walkway of rose-colored wood and fleur-de-lis filigree, three pigeons took wing, cooing in annoyance, and swooped over the tableau below. Will Halliday flinched, nerves raw. Asher and Daria kept their eyes on the canister in the American's massive hand.

Daria's heart raced. She took a stiff step to her left, knee twitching.

John held his aching gut. An image of the going-away Costco cake flashed through his mind. *So Long Suckers!* "I'm not sure I can do what you ask, Mr. Sahar. I can't let you release the gas. I'm really, really sorry."

Halliday said, "You're sure as shit gonna be."

Daria collapsed to her knees, palms to the floor, long, limp strands of sweat-wet hair obscuring her face.

"Take her out of here!" Asher's voice rose as high as it could, taking on a reedy, strained quality, and John heard real emotion behind it. "If we have to carry her, I'll help. We have to move now, Mr. Broom!"

Asher aimed his gun at him.

"Please, Mr. Broom."

Daria got one boot under her. She looked up through a sheet of hair like a confessional's curtain. Her voice rose. "Take . . . the shot!"

From the rosewood walkway above, Khalid Belhadj heard Daria's command. He raised his Desert Eagle and fired once.

The velocity of the .50-caliber shell was so great that it sliced cleanly through Will Halliday. The bullet was too massive to break up and so fast that his muscle, bone, and skin put up as much resistance as a Japanese paper lantern. The exit wound was only marginally larger than the entrance wound.

But the water that makes up so much of the human body fared less well. The hydrostatic shock of the impact made Halliday bolt backward, chest concave, arms and neck snapping forward, his whole body shoved backward three inches. It looked like a modern jazz dance move.

The baptistry floor took the impact of the .50 caliber bullet. Well-trod for centuries by sinners, saints, and supplicants alike, it erupted as if hit by a small mortar round. The hostages reacted with panic to the gunman's strange, almost acrobatic spasm and the eruption that appeared to come from *beneath* the floor. Screaming, they stampeded toward the exit and the other naves.

The impact snapped Halliday's arms up and out. The red canister flew.

The size of an American football, it arced through the air, end over end. The dull red paint reflected the stained glass light of the cathedral.

Asher Sahar reacted first. He let both guns fall to the floor and charged forward, arms extended, his eyes on the canister.

Daria pushed up on her one good leg, flashing forward, slamming into Asher from behind. She palmed the spade-blade from her boot, flicked it open with her thumb, and shoved it into Asher's back with all her waning strength. It slid in less than an inch.

Asher caught the canister and cradled it to his chest with both hands.

Daria leaped onto his back, her weight and trajectory adding to his forward momentum. She rode him down, her body weight driving the serrated knife through Asher's spine.

The blade snapped off its hinge.

Daria lay atop Asher, and Asher atop the canister. She turned bloodshot eyes away to see Will Halliday fall amid the mini mushroom cloud of floor debris, on his back, arms wide, his handgun clattering away.

She saw a dim flurry of shoes and trouser legs. The crazy CIA analyst who seemed to know her knelt and gingerly slid the red canister out from beneath their pileup.

Daria slid off Asher's back onto the cold floor.

Asher's eyes were wide in pain and shock. His lips moved but no sound escaped.

Neither his arms nor legs were moving.

His eyes slid to her bloody hands, cradled now against her chest as if in prayer. He looked at the well-worn spade sheath, clutched in her hands.

His eyes closed slowly. His breathing slowed.

Daria's own vision grayed out.

Thirty-three

Belhadj had dislodged the pigeons to let Daria know where he was. He shot the big, blond American and turned his massive gun toward Asher Sahar, just in time to see Daria's suicide dive.

The Syrian watched the stranger in the brown jacket kneel and hide the red canister in Asher Sahar's messenger bag.

Belhadj ducked back out of sight as the throng of trapped tourists scattered and five people with American accents shoved against the tide. A wide array of weapons broke through.

"Freeze! . . . Nobody move! . . . Do it!"

The thunder of boots and barked commands seemed to revive Daria, who stirred, rising off the floor to kneel beside Asher, her head spinning.

Owen Cain Thorson boomed, "Do not move!"

Daria, on her knees, realized opponents were in close proximity. She couldn't focus enough to see them and their voices were tinny and muddled, as if over a walkie-talkie on a stormy night.

"Stop!" Thorson ratcheted the slide on his machine pistol. "Don't move!"

Daria felt a hard, cold shape by her knee. One of Asher's SIG autos. She wrapped her fingers around the handle.

Five CIA weapons locked on her.

Major Theo James pushed his way through the crowd, panting, his face red.

John Broom, also on his knees, skittered across the floor and into the line of sight of the CIA weapons. *"Wait, wait, wait!"*

He raised open palms toward Swing Band.

Thorson's jaw dropped. "Broom? How the hell—"

John pointed behind the CIA assault squad. He had never spoken so quickly in all his life, and was appalled to hear his voice rise an octave. "This is Major Theo James! U.S. Army! He's USAMRIID! Also World Health! Major? Identify yourself!"

Theo gulped. "Ah, yeah. Me. That's me. Hi. I'm him." His instructors in officer training school had never covered this scenario.

John, freaking out, saw the steely glint in Thorson's eye and the seething anger in his jaw. He figured the odds of Thorson shooting through him to kill Daria to be about fifty-fifty.

"Owen! The major has primary responsibility for the virus! Do you hear me? Whatever else happens, containing the virus is his job! Major?"

Theo couldn't figure John's angle but played along. "Ah, yeah. Yes! Absolutely!"

Thorson held his machine pistol in both hands, aimed at John Broom's chest and, through him, at Daria's chest.

Daria gripped Asher's fallen weapon and tried to push through the dizziness. *What was happening?*

"B-Broom?" she tried.

Agent Maldonado squinted through blood from her badly cut eyebrow. Two other agents bled on the floor.

"Owen, protocol!" John barked. "The major takes control of the virus. Right?"

The ex-SEAL, Collier, squinted over the sights of his .45. His bristly gray mustache twitched. "That is protocol."

Up on the rosewood balcony, Belhadj didn't move.

Thorson didn't move.

John didn't move.

Theo James said, "Fellas?"

The moment passed, and everyone could see it in the subtle shift of Thorson's stiff shoulders. He nodded, once. "Yes. Army takes the virus. Do it."

But the barrel of his weapon didn't budge.

John exhaled. "Good. Okay. We good, everyone?"

This wasn't Collier's first firefight. He watched his boss, then his eyes flickered to the dead and the dying on the floor. He looked at the unarmed civilian on his knees. Behind him, the Israeli target looked barely conscious.

Collier said, "Stand down, people. We good."

When Thorson didn't move, Collier's mustache twitched again. "Boss? We are good."

Thorson lowered his barrel about three inches.

John tried really, really hard not to pee his pants. "The major gets the virus?"

Thorson rolled his eyes. "Yes, Broom. Step clear of the prisoner."

"Major?" John gulped. "This is my friend Daria Gibron. She *is* the virus culture. Take her, please."

Thorson's eyes almost shot out of his skull. "What?"

But Theo was quick on the uptake. He had pegged Collier as the most regular military man in the bunch. "You. I'm Major Theo James, U.S. Army. This woman is Patient Zero for a biohazard threshold event. Help me secure her for transport."

Collier holstered his weapon. "Yes, sir."

Thorson went apoplectic. "What? No! She's—*no!*"

But the other agents had already lowered their weapons and were securing the onlookers, calming the crowd.

Daria, on her knees, lay one sweaty palm on John's shoulder. "What . . . what . . ."

And she passed out.

On the balcony, Belhadj waited a few beats. He lowered his handgun, then melted into the gloom of the Catedral de Milano.

Thirty-four

"There's a war on, Chatoulah."

The Tunnel Rat of Rafah gave the girl a spade-shaped knife in a leather sheath. The girl had grown taller and stronger. The children did not know their ages or birth dates, but estimated that she was eight.

"Where?" she asked.

"Here. I think."

"A war between who?"

"I haven't figured out all of the angles. Even the Bedouin cousins, God grant them huge profits, don't know all the details. I just think a war is coming. And . . ." He paused. "I think we need to align ourselves."

"With who . . . *whom?*"

"With the side that wins."

"And that's which side?"

"The Jews. And the West. I think."

A woman's voice broke in. "That is a very astute observation, young sir."

Both children leaped to their feet. The woman stood confidently at the mouth of the alley. Tall, beautiful. Dressed in Western desert kit: khakis, fine boots.

Israeli, the girl thought. But here? In Rafah? That's when she noticed the other two men with her, both blonds. Both armed.

"You are a gifted political scientist." The woman had a strange, foreign accent. "You have a keen understanding of the Gaza Strip. If you wish to align yourself, I can help you. Both of you. A war *is* coming. And lucky me: I know which side wins."

The girl's first thought was to flee. She felt Asher tense, ready to bolt. He reached back blindly for her hand. She switched the spade knife to her left and took his dry palm.

"Which side wins?" Asher asked the tall woman.

"My side. My name is Hannah Goldman. You are . . . Asher? And?"

The girl took a shy step behind her brother.

"Daria, I believe you said." The tall woman smiled. "Daria, it is. Such a lovely name."

"Daria? Daria?"

Daria Gibron dragged herself up from the grasp of anesthesia. She blinked in the too-bright light. The first face she saw was familiar. She tried speaking, despite being intubated.

She mouthed the name, *Asher*?

"John." The swimming, half-formed face before her smiled. "John Broom."

Thirty-five

Germany

Daria recovered.

Interestingly, it was at the best and closest medical facility Major Theo James could whistle up: Ramstein Air Base in Germany. Interestingly because that's where the FBI had taken her the first time she'd been injured while fighting with Asher Sahar.

Her treatment, such as it was, consisted of keeping her on oxygen for five days, balancing her fluids, pushing the electrolytes, and keeping an eye out for secondary infections. After that, the medical regimen relied on prayer and dumb luck.

On the sixth day, she was informed that CIA analyst John Broom had been infected with Pegasus-B. By her. His treatment lasted half as long because he was asymptomatic when the treatment began. He was up and walking about before Daria was fully awake. He visited her every day. They didn't tell her right away that the World

Health Organization had coordinated responses to two outbreaks of a novel influenza. The French Ministry of Health handled three cases in Lyon, France, while the Italian Ministry of Health reacted to seven cases in Milan, Italy.

The cases ended after that and the health ministries relaxed. It would be months before anyone realized that all of the victims had the genetic markers of Ashkenazim, or the Jews of Central Europe.

On the seventh day in the hospital, she was well enough to realize he was keeping other secrets from her.

"Best tell me. You know I'll find out anyway."

John sat on the edge of her bed, one foot on the floor and one knee up by her side. "Asher Sahar shot FBI Agent Ray Calabrese."

Daria stared at him, blinking rapidly but otherwise appearing unemotional.

"He's alive. He's facing, I don't know, six or seven months of physical therapy. I'll set up a Skype call for you this afternoon. He really wants to talk to you. If that's okay."

It explained why Ray hadn't been part of the rescue in Milan. And hadn't been in touch.

"Thank you. And Asher?"

"Medics on the scene said you probably severed his spine when you jumped him. There was no way to tell at the cathedral how bad the spinal injuries were."

Daria absorbed this, the skin around her eyes shrunken and mottled darkly.

"Here's the thing, though: an Israeli Army medical

team arrived and took him into custody. But when we tried to follow up, guess what: the Israelis don't have any record of a medical team being dispatched to Milan. The CIA hasn't been able to locate him."

A soft smile skittered over her pale, cracked lips. "And you shan't."

"Oh, I'm not CIA anymore. Didn't I tell you?"

Daria reached up and touched his arm. "Oh. They gave you the sack?"

"No. I took a job with a senator. Well, I will. As soon as they let me leave the base, anyway. But hey, I got this back for you . . ."

John held out a spade-shaped sandwich of leather, with an eighth of an inch of air showing between the identical pieces. They connected at a broken hinge.

"Oh." Daria took the empty sheath in both hands and turned it over. It had fit into her palm so many times, for so many years. It had almost been part of her.

"My dad knows a guy who sharpens knives. I could get it fixed for you."

Daria smiled her thanks, then tossed the sheath into the bedside rubbish bin. "Thank you. No."

"I understand." John had been there and knew where the broken blade had ended up. "There's this, too." He handed her an antique straight razor. Its handle was steel and was embossed with a symbol from Spain and the word *Sevilla*. Daria took it, pressed her thumb against the tang. The six-inch blade *snikked* free of the handle.

John said, "It looks old."

"World War I, I imagine. Thank you."

She used her other palm to slide the blade back into its handle. She slid it under her pillow. John pretended not to notice. Daria touched his knee gently. "I never thanked you properly for keeping me alive."

"You know how you can thank me? At the cathedral, you mentioned an organization. The Club Sennacherib. CIA tells me they've scoured intelligence databases throughout the West. Nobody's ever heard of them."

Daria smiled and let her tongue venture around her parched, pale lips. "I was delirious."

He smiled. "I looked it up. Sennacherib was an Assyrian king. Tried to lay siege to Jerusalem. Around 600 B.C. or so. His army was wiped out, overnight, without the Jews lifting a weapon. Lord Byron wrote about it. 'And the might of the gentile, unsmote by the sword . . .'"

" 'Hath melted like snow in the glance of the Lord.' "

She smiled through the fog of fatigue and nodded up at him. "You're a nice man, Mr. Broom."

"Who sprung Sahar from prison? Who bankrolled him? Who evaced him from the cathedral?"

She let her eyes flutter. "I'm feeling tired. I think I'll sleep a little."

John stood. "Okay. We should maybe talk later."

She was asleep before he made it to the door.

John was as much a fan of physical comedy as the next guy. But he still was embarrassed to leave Daria's room, stop by the commissary for a cup of coffee, walk to his private hospital room, step inside, see Khalid

Belhadj standing there, and perform a textbook spit take.

Belhadj wore a shapeless olive jacket and thick trousers and sturdy boots. He was unshaven and an end parenthesis of hair, traced with gray, hung near his straight eyebrows. He leaned against the institutionally painted wall and folded his arms.

"Mr. Broom."

They were on one of the largest U.S. military bases on Earth. John had seen dozens of closed circuit cameras and scores of army guards. Yet here stood the Syrian, looking just a little bored.

"Major Belhadj."

They stood a moment. John used the back of his left hand to wipe coffee off his chin and his too-large, army-issue T-shirt.

"Tell me about golems, Mr. Broom."

"I'm sorry?"

"Golems. Please."

Thoughts pinballed off the inside of John's skull as he nimbly cobbled together a rough understanding. "Ah . . . sure. Golems. In the Torah, they're mythical beings made of clay. Brought to life by rabbis to protect the faithful. They appear in lots of literature, too. Frankenstein's monster was a golem. You wanna, maybe, sit? Some coffee? There's a vending machine?"

Belhadj's blue-gray eyes hid all emotion. He waited, arms crossed.

"Golems were unalive, and, as such, unstoppable. But also uncontrollable. Eventually, their creators had to stop them. In one story, a rabbi wrote the Hebrew letters *Alef, Mem,* and *Tev* on the creature's forehead."

Belhadj said, "*Alef, mem, tev.* The Hebrew word *emet:* truth."

"Yeah. To kill the creature, you erase the letter *alef.*"

Belhadj smiled. "Giving you *met:* death."

"Yeah."

Belhadj seemed to consider it.

John said, "There's another legend among analysts in the CIA. The people on Operations side never bought into it. The legend is about a Group."

Belhadj's cheeks puffed out in a silent laugh. John wasn't sure what to make of that.

"Tell me about this legend."

John said, "Bunch of folks formed in the 1960s and '70s. Industrialists throughout the world. Guys who wanted Israel to have a fighting chance. These guys knew conventional war wouldn't be enough. Even conventionally unconventional war wouldn't be enough. They needed to think outside the crazy."

Belhadj studied him without moving.

"This Group? If there was a Group? They created really, really, *really* good spooks. Who could do what Israeli intelligence wouldn't or couldn't."

John could taste fear flooding his nervous system. He willed the hand holding the coffee cup not to shake.

"The Group created golems?"

John said, "Well, like I say . . . it's a legend."

Belhadj said, "*Emet* and *met*. Truth . . ."

John said, "And death."

Belhadj nodded. He unfolded his arms and stepped away from the wall. John felt his heart rate spiral up.

"Thank you, Mr. Broom."

"Sure."

Belhadj stepped past him and opened the room's door.

"If they come," the quiet man said, peering out into the empty hall, "and they will come, it's to erase the *Aleph*."

The men stood about ten inches apart, shoulder to shoulder, facing opposite directions.

John said, "*Emet* to *met*. Truth to death."

Belhadj nodded.

"Can we stop them?"

Belhadj stepped out into the corridor. He held the doorknob, the door almost closed. "Should we?"

John didn't hesitate. "Hell, yeah."

Belhadj eased the door closed. "Good answer, Mr. Broom."

It took the U.S., French, and Italian authorities some time to realize that there were any number of charges that could be brought against Daria Gibron, but to prosecute her would require the various intelligence agencies to look like perfect idiots. Ultimately, none of the agencies wanted to risk it.

When she could, Daria toured the secure medical building that served Ramstein, the sprawling home of

the United States Air Forces in Europe and a major
NATO installation. The place had a drab, dank 1950s
institutional feel to it. She found the perfect spot to get
away from the doctors and the nurses and the Western
intelligence agencies who wanted to question her in-
cessantly. It was an indoor swimming pool dedicated
to physical therapy. Daria memorized the daily schedule on the door to figure out the quiet times to sneak
away and hide.

It took two more days for her visitors to arrive.

Daria was in the physical therapy pool room. She sat
in a wheelchair, equipped with thick, gripping rubber
wheels for use around the pool. She wore a hospital
gown that tied in the back, with a long, coarse blanket
over her legs. She had watched the last twenty minutes
of a water polo match played by U.S. Marines injured
in Afghanistan, laughing as they splashed her and
flirted madly with her. Once they had been helped back
to their wing of the hospital, the acoustics changed, the
echoes grew louder.

Daria arranged her wheelchair at the far end of the
room, near the deep end of the pool, where she could
catch the late-afternoon sunshine, feeling the warm,
humid air cling to her bones and frame, nurturing her
like a sauna. The blue cement floor was covered in
half-inch-deep puddles of chlorinated water.

Daria never heard the pool room door open. "Daria.
Darling."

A thin woman in a conservative pearl-gray suit and

elegant heels had entered. Behind her stood two men, both wearing Gortex winter coats that forgave a multitude of sins, including concealed weapons. Both men wore lanyards and United Nations ID cards.

Daria said, "Hannah. My God."

Hannah Goldman smiled warmly. She wore a simple gold chain around her neck and no rings. She had to be seventy, Daria calculated. At least. Her hair was cut short and had turned a shiny silver.

The two blond men made sure the door to the indoor pool was locked, as Hannah stepped close, gingerly avoiding the larger puddles where she could.

Daria said, "Dee Jean d'Arc . . . ?"

The older woman shook her head. "Daria, you are burned. It was a warning. At the New York airport, I think?"

Daria nodded.

"That Asher. Never one for obeying orders."

"Asher warned me off?"

"He tried to, yes." After all these decades, she retained a hint of her childhood Austrian accent. "He had argued for leaving you out of the whole plot. When that failed, he resorted to melodrama. We were furious!"

"Was he punished?"

Hannah Goldman laughed. "No. He acted out of kindness. And love. You are like my own children. I find it hard to stay angry with either of you."

Hannah stepped within two meters of Daria's wheelchair. The blond men stepped closer, too.

Their voices took on a hollow tone, affected by the

body of water and the thick concrete walls. "We need to talk about the future."

Daria said, "The first time you came for me . . . for me and Asher, in that alley in Rafah. Do you remember? You pretended then to know the future."

Hannah Goldman said, "I did know the future, that day in Rafah. And I know it today. For our nation to have a future, it needs strategists like Asher and soldiers like you."

Daria locked the brakes on her wheelchair. Inches to her left, the surface of the chlorinated pool gently bobbed, splintering sunlight. "The Group was a dreadful idea. Raising children, radicalizing us, weaponizing us. It was sociopathic."

Hannah studied her sadly. One of the blond soldiers squatted and reached his hand into the pool, down to his first knuckles. He stirred the water.

"The CIA has declared you persona non grata, darling. You embarrassed them. That's simply not done. You won't be allowed back into the States. Not ever."

Daria nodded solemnly. She expected as much.

"Israeli intelligence will leave you out in the cold. They know better than to defy us. France and Italy have their own reasons for wanting distance between you and themselves. The other Western powers will do as the CIA instructs. That leaves . . . who?"

Daria pondered the question. She adjusted the blanket over her legs. "I honestly don't know."

"Then come back to us. Israel's darkest days lay ahead of her. Our purpose is to provide—"

"Golems."

Hannah bristled. "Golems! Certainly not. Never. We—"

"Unstoppable monsters. Who, having performed their mission, run amok, and must be put down."

Hannah looked resigned. And saddened. The kneeling soldier touched the pool water with his fingertips. His eyes darted to the wheelchair. The standing soldier gripped his holstered auto.

Hannah said, "I beg you to reconsider."

Daria sighed. "It's a bit late for that."

She whisked away the blanket on her lap to reveal a coil of electrical wire. One end snaked around Daria's waist behind the wheelchair and was plugged into the wall. The other end hung between her legs. She peeled back the insulation, revealing copper wire that dangled an inch above the standing water.

Daria let it drop into the puddle.

The crouching soldier with his hand in the water convulsed without a sound. His muscles rigid, he fell, splashing into the pool.

The blond standing amid the swimmers' puddles shuddered, frozen in place, keening a high-pitched scream muffled by his locked jaw. His knees buckled. Even down, he continued to spasm.

Hannah Goldman simply dropped like a stone.

Daria lifted the power cord out of the puddle, reached back and yanked the plug out of the wall socket. She rose from the rubber-wheeled chair, sneakers in the splashed water.

She knelt by Hannah and checked the woman's pulse. It was weak but steady. There had been a better-than-even chance the brief electrocution would stop the older woman's heart.

Daria moved to the soldier by Hannah's side. She removed his Glock, lifted his head out of the puddle, and yanked free his lanyard and faux-UN identification. Before standing, she shoved him into the pool to drown with his friend.

She paused a moment to touch Hannah's cheek. The woman's skin was dry and powdery. She breathed, her eyes darting beneath their thin, veined lids.

Daria stood and crossed to the pool room door. She tucked the Glock up under her T-shirt, by her spine. She hurried through the halls to an exit she had identified days earlier.

She found a BMW X5 suburban utility vehicle with good, German snow tires and United Nations plates, parked in a little-used alley behind the base laundry.

Khalid Belhadj met her halfway down the alley. He, too, wore a fake UN security lanyard. He looked fatigued.

He looked at his watch and sighed. "Be honest. You were making a speech."

Daria held her forefinger and thumb a few millimeters apart: *a little one*.

She said, "I got your message. Through John Broom."

"He's not bad, that one." That was one hell of a begrudging compliment for the Syrian to give a CIA analyst.

"The Group sent two soldiers inside for me. Only two. I'm insulted."

"I took care of two more." Belhadj nodded toward a Dumpster. Daria didn't need to ask for details.

Belhadj tossed her keys. Daria peered down the alley at the BMW and noted paperwork on the dashboard that would get her through security.

Belhadj said, "What now?"

Daria tucked hair behind her ears. "The Group has blackballed me with every Western intelligence agency. I am, as they say, out in the cold. You?"

He shrugged. "Syria is in trouble. I head back to Damascus, make amends."

"They'll either promote you or shoot you."

Belhadj nodded. "Or both."

She said, "You know about the others now. What you called the Group."

"Do I?" Belhadj gave his soundless laugh. "What do I know? What do I tell Syrian intelligence, when I don't know who *is* Syrian intelligence from day to day? And what evidence would I have to give them."

He paused a moment. His gray eyes raked the industrial buildings. He turned back to her. "You?"

Daria rested a palm on his chest.

They stood a moment. The rest of the army base was bustling but Belhadj had chosen this alley with care. They had the space to themselves. But that wouldn't last forever.

Khalid Belhadj thought about it long and hard, then stepped in and kissed her. She kissed him back.

He studied her a moment and allowed himself a quick, wistful smile.

"Well then . . . good-bye."

Daria nodded.

They pivoted, Belhadj nearer the alley entrance,

Daria nearer the car. They stepped away from each other, both walking backward.

They smiled. Then they turned after ten paces. Just like duelists.

Read on for an excerpt from the next book by

DANA HAYNES

GUNMETAL HEART

Coming soon in hardcover from Minotaur Books

Caladri, the coast of Italy

The quiet man stood in the entrance to the taverna. The regulars didn't remember seeing him enter. They hadn't noticed the flash of too-harsh, too-white sunlight when the door opened. They hadn't smelled the tang of salt and seaweed invading the tobacco and hashish funk of the bar.

But there he stood.

He wore an American cowboy hat, a denim shirt, jeans, and boots. The shirt had pearl snaps, and the sleeves were rolled up past tattoos and well-defined biceps. It was unbuttoned to reveal an off-white sleeveless undershirt.

One by one, the patrons of the taverna noticed the quiet man, then went back to their beer and their boredom.

The quiet man seemed to rouse himself from a half-sleep. He walked to the bar. He removed the cowboy hat—old and badly sweat-stained—and set it on the bar. His hair was black and almost shoulder-length and swept back. His face was leathery, tight and deeply pocked. He had a thin, lipless mouth and exceedingly flat planes along his cheeks and forehead and a nose that had been badly broken and poorly mended.

The old bartender, a drain pipe cleaner of a man, rubbed a filthy rag on the filthy bar and took his time looking up. When he did, he flinched at the sight of the customer's face.

"Birra, signore?"

The quiet man nodded.

The manager limped on spindly legs over to the proper handle, poured, and returned with a pint. The quiet man had neither expected nor received a clean glass. He reached into his shirt pocket and withdrew a much-bent photo. He set it on the sticky bar and slid it across.

It was a photo of Daria Gibron.

The old man peered at it, squinted, made a point of scratching his thin patch of hair. He looked up at the quiet man and shrugged.

"Seen her?" He spoke English.

"No."

"Sure?"

"Si."

The quiet man reached into the back pocket of his jeans and withdrew a folding knife, the handle carved of bone. He kept the knife closed.

The bartender peered at the knife, then up into the flat, reflectionless eyes, then back at the knife, then up into the quiet man's eyes. He shrugged, making a calculation; what a businessman would call a cost-benefit analysis.

"Signorina Randagia?"

The quiet man looked skeptical. As if the name were unfamiliar.

"Gatta Randagia. It is what she calls herself, *signore*. Yes. I know her."

"She's here?"

The old man shrugged. "She's out."

The quiet man nodded solemnly and picked up his dirty stein with his left hand and sipped. "Out where?"

"*Cimintaro.*"

"Graveyard?"

"*Si*. For, ah, old things, not people. Pieces . . . ?"

"Junkyard?"

"*Si!*"

The manager grabbed a beer mat, turned it over to the blank side, and drew a map. He'd begun to sweat now. It wasn't just the unspoken threat of the closed knife. It was something intractable and menacing on the man's scarred face.

That, plus the signorina. The old man had feared her from Day One. She was radiant, whereas this man radiated nothing. And yet somehow she carried that exact same menacing air.

The quiet man studied the beer mat. "Junkyard?"

"*Si*. For aircraft."

The flat-planed face turned to him.

"Old aeroplanes, *signore*."

"Why?"

The old man wet his lips. "Running."

"From what?"

The bartender shrugged. "Who can say? The devil, I think."

The quiet man drained his beer. He seemed to contemplate that.

"The devil."

"*Si.*"

He pocketed the bone knife, shook his head. "Can't be two of us."

The bartender wasted no time in alerting the people about the presence of the quiet man in Caladri. The residents of Caladri detested strangers, as they had for well over seven decades. In a town in which the two main industries were the importation of illegal immigrants from Africa and illegal drugs from South America, a snooping foreigner was no friend.

Within minutes, the grapevine spread the word that the stranger was looking for Signora Gatta Randagia.

Nobody could remember if the town had named her or if she'd coined the nickname for herself. *Gatto randagio* meant *stray cat.*

She crouched in the shadows, fingertips on the ground, slightly forward of her hunched shoulders, the heels of both sneakers up off the dirt, and surveyed the battlefield.

It was getting on noon and only mid-July but already the weather had turned nasty on the Mediterranean coast. Where much of the region was sun-swept and touristy, Daria Gibron had picked a spit of land shoved uncomfortably between a barren strip of rocky coast and the Trenitalia railroad tracks, wedged crooked like a broken rib up against the rest of northeastern Italy. The villages to the west were rich fishing waters, and the villages to the east catered to a trendy, moneyed set. But on the rocky gouge of land that Daria had made home, almost nobody had made an honest living in decades.

It suited her to a T.

The temperature was in the 90s and the humidity matched it. Yellow-white clouds filled the sky and turned the sea a mottled green. They were the kind of clouds that promised rain, just to taunt you with what they denied you.

Daria was hunched like a sprinter in the starting blocks. She squinted against the white glare and the painfully glinting metal all around her. Everywhere she looked, Daria saw bits of things that once had been aircraft but were now permanently confined to the ground. Warped wings here, rusted fuselages there. Piles of treadbare tires, desiccated cockpits strewn about like the shells of mutated beetles. The debris dated from the 1950s to the 1990s. Some military aircraft, some civilian. The only things in eyesight that weren't ex-airplane were the bits of hard-packed earth and waxy yellow weeds.

Daria's dark skin glowed with sweat. She wore ratty cutoffs and a short Violent Femmes T-shirt, sleeves ripped off and neckline badly and unevenly stretched out. Some boy, some year, had left it in her bed, but for the life of her, she couldn't remember his face. Her sneakers were new. She'd pulled her straight black hair into a ponytail. She wore fingerless black gloves with golden zippers that ran halfway up each palm. Her only other "accessories" were bandages here and there, stretch tape wrapped around both wrists, and a yellow swoosh of a lovely new bruise on her flank, under her left arm.

The junkyard had been built in the remnants of a

mercury mine tucked into a geographic wound of a
valley between scrubby hills. Almost no plants beyond
weeds grew in the narrow valley. The stunted earth
was a remnant of Caladri's pre-World War II past. A
sadly faded Italian flag fluttered for a second in a gut-
tering breeze. A flicker of a smile ghosted across Daria's parched lips. *What's a nice Jewish girl like you
doing running in a place like this?*

She heard the squeak of shoe tread on aluminum
and knew that the Kavlek brothers were on the move.

Daria bolted.

She pushed off with her right foot from beneath the
truncated wing of a Phantom F-4F fighter. Her goal was
the stubby, roof-gutted Tornado dead ahead. Its cockpit
had been blown out, avionics rusting in the thin haze and
sun. The Tornado would offer scarce cover—a whacking
great hole had been torn out of the top of the fuselage,
likely from a mid-air collision or a missile rather than a
crash landing. (Daria Gibron had some passing knowledge of aircraft disasters. Some she'd witnessed. Some
she'd caused.)

The goal wasn't the snub-nosed Tornado but the huge,
mothballed Airbus A-320, just beyond. The narrow-body
airliner was about one hundred and twenty feet long, she
guessed, providing plenty of running room. It sat flat on
the rocky ground, sans landing gear. If she could get inside that beast, she could buy herself some advantages.

An Israeli Army drill sergeant had once ragged her,
"In an open-field flight, your advantages are eyesight,
space, and liberty! Rob the enemy of them, and it's advantage you!"

Daria leaped from her cover, sneakers hitting the hardpan earth, legs and arms pumping.

A flash of skin to her left and above her. Mehmet Kavlek, the sturdier of the Turkish brothers, diving off the fuselage of the Phantom. He'd been above her all along.

Daria guessed that the husky Turk couldn't leap from atop the Phantom to the wing of the Tornado. He'd either land on the ground between . . . or atop Daria.

She threw herself forward in midair, ending with a tumble, shoulders first, then her back, her ass, her sneakers. Once her shoes hit the packed soil, she used her momentum and her bunched legs to leap.

Mehmet Kavlek thumped to the ground a meter behind her.

Where was the other brother?

Still running, Daria caught hold of the wing of the grounded fighter craft and swung her body up and to the left, one knee clearing the airlift surface of the wing. She grunted and used her momentum to roll along the surface, completing the roll on one knee and one foot.

She glanced back. Mehmet's meaty hands appeared before her eyes as he leaped for the wing.

Daria turned and ran, springing for the front half of the fuselage.

Ismael Kavlek made his appearance. Lighter than his brother, he sprang like a gazelle onto the horizontal elevator of the Tornado's tail section. A normal human would have smacked into the vertical stabilizer and rudder, but the whip-thin man raised one foot, kicked at the stabilizer, re-routed his momentum ninety degrees, and deftly surfaced atop the fuselage with Daria.

The roof was holed—too great a distance for even Ismael to reach her directly—but the bigger Turk had hauled himself up onto the port wing behind her, so there was nowhere for Daria to go but forward, toward the starboard wing.

She landed, knees bent, and hauled ass down the length of the wing, which sprang under her weight like a pirate ship's plank.

Behind her, Ismael Kavlek did the impossible. He leaped—not *over* the hole in the fuselage, but *through* it, head first, into the aircraft, landing in a somersault, springing to his feet, shoulder slamming open the flight deck door. He was running perpendicular to Daria now.

The windshield was long gone. Ismael hit the pilot's seat with one boot, threw himself forward, out through the missing windshield, his right hand snapping onto a still-firm support post. His grip, plus his momentum, spun him clockwise. He let go in midair and landed deftly outside the aircraft, on the starboard wing.

Damn it! Daria gritted her teeth.

She dove off the end of the wing, using it like a springboard, and hit the ground. Ahead of her lay an aged, gray barrel of an obstacle: the remains of a Rolls-Royce Deutschland turbofan engine, sitting in the dust, cocked at an odd angle.

She could sprint around it, but that would take time. Daria sprang forward in a headfirst dive, hitting the top of the hot metal with both gloved hands, tucking her bent legs tight against her abdomen, and leap-frogged over it.

The Airbus now was five meters away.

Daria caught blurs of movement from the dumping ground's flag, from the squat, African palm trees, from the sagebrush hillsides. Her mind shut out the irrelevant, reached for the stunted forward landing gear of the A-320 and climbed like a monkey, through sharp, rusty holes up into the underbelly storage section of the airliner.

It was filthy inside and rats scampered away from this strange, sweat-drenched alley cat.

Daria duck-walked as fast as she could, forward to a service hatch. She used her legs for strength, shoulder to the hatch, and heaved it open.

Ismael Kavlek appeared behind her, through the landing gear opening.

Daria hauled herself up into the single-aisle fuselage of the airliner, near the nose cone. The passenger section gave her almost one hundred and fifty meters of straight running space and she dashed aft, leaping over debris where she could. She had spotted a blown-out starboard window, back near the bathrooms.

She heard Ismael's boots behind her and, simultaneously, Mahmet's boots thumped against the roof of the fuselage, over her head.

Daria dove headfirst through the smashed-open window.

Beneath her lay long weeds and rusty, razor-sharp bits of iron. She twisted in mid-air, landed on one shoulder, the banged-up rib punishing her. She rolled and was up again, as the bigger Turk jumped from atop the plane onto the tail and from there to the ground.

He landed badly, skidding on his side in the weeds.

Daria caught sight of a Bell helicopter, a bubble-domed dragonfly, Korean War–era. She angled for it. She heard Ismael mimic her mad dive through the starboard window and land right where she had. Had he missed the ragged bits of metal as well?

Yes.

Mehmet was on his feet, but huffing, and now it was a straightaway foot chase. The prehistoric dragonfly rested on its twin skids. Beyond lay even more debris, more densely packed. The better for scampering and sliding. The longer she could draw this out, the better.

The tail of the Bell was an open-air scaffolding affair, and Daria reached for it like it was a playground monkey bar, swinging beneath it, letting go, arcing five meters in the air and landing on her feet, running, gasping for air.

The big Mehmet ducked and ran under the tail.

The lighter Ismael grabbed it with one hand and catapulted over it.

She hadn't gained a half second on them.

Daria reached a corridor between two gutted fuselages so damaged she didn't recognize their provenance. She attempted a difficult, full-speed, right-angle turn, caroming off one of the aluminum frames, running full tilt, until her left leg simply gave out, her knee buckling in the turn.

She landed clumsily. No grace, face-first in the dirt, her chest taking the brunt of the impact, air expelled, a mouth full of caked dirt. She tried to stop her momentum but that only resulted in a tumbling roll that landed her, crumpled, against the gutted fuselage.

Ismael Kavlek rounded the corner but, unlike Daria, didn't try the right-angle turn. He leaped like a dancer, hit the fuselage with his boots, and ran two steps along the wall, literally running sideways parallel with the earth, his momentum defying gravity, until he pivoted in mid-air and landed, knees bent, in front of her.

Daria sat up against the curved aluminum, unable to catch her breath, chest on fire, now bleeding from her right cheek.

Mehmet Kavlek rounded the corner and, unlike either of them, simply let himself hit the fuselage with his shoulder, bleeding off his momentum. He was moving at only a jog as he reached his brother's side.

Daria squinted up into the white haze at the two men who loomed above her. She realized her hand rested next to a rusted spanner.

Ismael Kavlek grinned down at her. "Did you think—"

The three of them were so intent on each other, that the man in the cowboy hat and dusty boots appeared as if by a conjurer's trick. One second they were a threesome, then a quartet. One second only Daria was down, then the butt of a sturdy Colt Python thudded into Mehmet Kavlek's ear and he dropped as if through a trap door.

The quiet man turned the gun on Ismael, whose eyes bulged.

Daria grabbed the spanner and grunted, throwing it with her waning strength. It slammed into the raised arm of the newcomer, his aim shifting ten degrees, and the .45 boomed, the bullet missing Ismael by inches, the sound deafening, echoing, and re-echoing back at them through the jungle of metal skeletons.

"MercifulGodWhatInHell . . ." Ismael yelped in Turkish.

Daria sprang to her feet, hoping to fake any remaining strength. Once up, she peered up into the ragged face of the newcomer.

"What th—you!"

The quiet man looked at her. If his arm hurt from being hit by a wrench, he didn't show it.

"Diego?"

Mehmet, on the ground, groaned. Ismael toyed with a cardiac arrest.

The flat-planed face took in the three people. He turned back to Daria and nodded.

Daria huffed for air. One hand stole to the badly bruised rib under her left arm. "What . . . the hell . . . are you doing?!"

"Saving you."

She began to see red. *"Saving me? Sav—"* She ground her teeth. "Diego, you idiot! You almost killed this man!"

The deeply pocked face didn't change, but the quiet man mulled that for a second. He still hadn't lowered his Colt. "Yeah."

Daria wiped sweat from her eyes, tried to calm her beating heart. "Put away the gun. Do it now."

He did.

"I'm going to ask you once again: What are you doing here?"

The man called Diego said, "Here to hire you."